REAVE

C.MILLER

Text Copyright © 2012 C. Miller

First Paperback Edition: December 2013
Second Paperback Edition: February 2023

Cover Art: C. Miller

ISBN: 9798355845766

THE
REAVE SERIES

REAVE

ELUDE

ASCEND

TO FALL

PROLOGUE

THE RULES

THERE ARE NOT MANY RULES when you live outside the confines of the cities. *Keep your head down* and *never, ever, draw attention to yourself* in some ways are all that matter. If you fail to abide by those rules, the Reavers—or worse—are the consequence.

It was such a long time ago for me, but I remembered. I remembered those rules, and the consequences of failure never allowed me to forget. I was far too young then to comprehend that, sometimes, following rules doesn't matter.

Sometimes, there is absolutely nothing you can do.

Sometimes the circumstances of the world can render everything else—your efforts, your knowledge—useless. Circumstances can twist your entire existence until your life is nothing more than a distorted memory, placed away with those other memories that are all too painful to be thought over. Circumstances can change your existence so very much, until all your happiest moments in life must be tucked away, never to be heard from again.

The world, with wretched cities filled with evil people, was not made for happiness.

I always heard stories about the cities when young. Once, before my father was gone, he took me close enough to see one of them, but only just. I remembered the feel of my back against him where he had me hidden inside his jacket; I was so big that I could hardly fit. I remembered the feel of the stubble on his chin as it tugged at my long, blond hair. I remembered his voice in my ear, quietly telling me it would be the one and only time my eyes would ever look upon that hell.

That glorious hell, with its high walls, rested on two sides against things my father told me were called *mountains*. Those mountains appeared as though they were touching the highest part of the sky. Despite the atrocity I'd been told lay behind those walls, I could not deny the beauty of it.

My father had been so wrong when he told me I would not ever see one again. Different walls could be the same walls.

I wondered now, if he had not gone, whether I would've been spared of everything that followed. Would my father and I have lived together forever in that small house he built for us in the wilderness? Would our lives have been filled with our love? Or perhaps it was all inevitable. Perhaps there was nothing anyone could've done to have changed the outcome.

I'd waited for him, just like he always told me to. I'd waited and stayed inside until all our food ran out. He'd left to get us more of it, traveling farther into the wilderness. I waited for him what felt like an entire lifetime. Then I had to make a decision—listen to my father as I always had and starve, or defy him and survive. I was young then, but I was old enough to make such a decision when faced with it.

I'd gone to the only person I could trust—my father's friend Ben. I might've been old enough to make a decision on survival, but I was too young to comprehend the way the world worked. I was too young to understand that there was no such thing as friendship.

Ben and his wife kept me for a month, but with one extra mouth to feed for that long . . . it was only a matter of time before their decision was made for them. It was only a matter of time before they had no choice.

I remembered the night the Reaver came for me. I'd heard such tales of them—those human monsters. They were to be feared for what they did and for what they'd done in the past. They were to be feared for what they were capable of and for what their presence meant. It had been so difficult for me to continue believing the stories upon finally seeing one for myself. The lady was so pretty—so clean—that I could not stop staring at her. She was not a monster in appearance.

I even still sometimes thought on her face, the look I'd been unable to comprehend when she'd asked, "Where did you find her?"

"She is ours," my father's friend lied.

She smiled before stepping over to me.

I remembered nothing else until I was already inside the walls of the city. Everything between was a hazy darkness that did not feel real and hadn't even then.

When there was light again, a man stared down at me, frowning deeply. His face blurred in and out of my vision as I wobbled and swayed on my feet in front of him.

"She is pretty but not pretty enough," he'd said as he stared down his hooked nose at me. For the briefest moment, that nose crinkled in distaste before he turned away. "Take her to Agatha. I believe this one will make a fine servant."

I was dragged down hallways and stairs—the hands holding and shoving me were so unbelievably strong—until eventually a door was opened and I was thrown inside a room. The stone was terribly cold on my body as I lay on the floor, clutching a knee that had been skinned as I'd fallen. I had only enough time to let out one small sob before someone else spoke.

"Another one," a woman said from the other side of the room, which sent me skidding myself across the floor, trying to locate safety in a corner.

I felt a hand on my exposed back where I'd curled myself up in a tight ball, surprisingly gentle for such a place.

"It's all right," the same voice said from directly above me.

I'd not heard those words since my father disappeared, so I slowly turned my face up to the woman.

She had tears in her large brown eyes as she leaned over my shaking body. "What's your name?"

"A . . . Aster," I stuttered.

"Like the flower," she said quietly with a small smile.

I nodded. My father told me once that my mother had named me after a flower. It was the only thing he'd ever mentioned of her to me.

"How old are you?"

"Eight," I answered.

She frowned for a moment before forcing a tight smile back onto her face and pushing away a strand of her dark hair that had fallen from a bun.

"I'm Agatha," she told me. "I'm going to take care of you."

At the time, I couldn't have known she was not telling me the truth. There was such sincerity in her voice and on her face that I could not possibly have known the truth when looking at her with my childish eyes. But I found out very quickly that, no matter how badly Agatha wanted to protect me . . . she could not do it.

No. Our world would not allow happiness or security. After some time, I stopped expecting it. After more time, I stopped wishing for it. One day, I stopped believing it truly existed. And I eventually realized the world could take nothing from me, if I did not have it in the first place.

CHAPTER ONE

THE LEADER OF NEW BETHEL

LMOST TEN YEARS HAD PASSED since I was brought into the city. Almost ten years of endless cleaning, walking, and carrying. The man who'd sentenced me to a life of servitude was no longer here. The leaders of the city—New Bethel— were never here for very long. They disappeared sometimes. Occasionally, one of the servants would find them. I stumbled upon one myself once when I was eleven, lying dead on the floor, his lips blue.

Poison, I'd heard whispered under the breath of the other servants in the days that followed.

No matter how many I watched pass through the doors, there were always more powerful people waiting to take over. The Valdour House—with its endless stone halls and spare rooms filled with useless, pretty things—was never empty long. New leaders would come in, try to make their changes to the city, and then . . . they would die so another could take their position. In a place that changed constantly, we were the one thing that remained the same. Nobody paid any attention to the servants, so long as they did their jobs and caused no trouble.

I quickly learned there were many more than two rules, although keeping your head down and not drawing attention to yourself were still the most important.

Do not go into any room unless you are working inside it. Do not touch anything unless you are cleaning it or using it for job-related purposes.

I was quite good at following rules, most of the time.

You learn things when you're invisible. It took me a while to realize the Reavers were harmless if you'd already been taken. They were not the worst monsters of our world, as I'd been led to believe. They were never spoken of by anyone, in fact. Had I not seen one with my own two eyes, I likely would've stored them away with all the other bedtime stories from a past life that were of no use to me now.

The Reavers searched the world for children and beautiful people to bring into the cities. Some would be used as servants, wives for wealthy men, or children for couples who could have none themselves. But what they searched for most of all was special children—abnormally strong or exceptionally bright. They wanted them young so they could be trained.

The Reavers were nothing more than glorified thieves of people. It was the special ones brought in that I quickly learned to fear. The true monsters were those trained to be thieves of life—Reapers. They were assassins, spending their entire lives stealing the lives of others.

As a servant I was invisible to everyone, apart from the Reapers.

They watched everything. They overlooked nothing—no minuscule detail, no minuscule person. They did not have to look directly at you, but when you spend most your life being invisible, you know when someone is aware of your presence. The Reapers were always aware of everything.

No leader, no Reaver, could ever be more frightening.

Agatha's voice from behind me pulled me from my thoughts. "You're distracted this morning, my flower."

I smiled at her over my shoulder, and then I winced at the sharp pain brought on by the slight movement.

"Still hurting?" She reached a hand out, touching my back gingerly.

As I watched her, I wondered when she'd developed those new wrinkles on her hands.

I contemplated lying to her and telling her I was feeling fine, but I would not do that. Instead, I turned back to my work without responding.

"Was it worth it?"

I didn't have to look at her again to know she was frowning at the back of my head. Agatha was quite predictable.

"Yes," I answered quietly.

"I told you that you'd get caught again eventually." She sounded disappointed, but her tone was not condescending.

"Yes," I said. "You did."

"Do we have to go over this every time someone new takes up position here?" She huffed quite loudly in an unsatisfied manner, heard easily from where I stood.

I smiled a little and, although she could not see it from her position behind me, I was sure she knew I was doing it. I was rather predictable to her as well. Agatha knew almost everything about me.

Almost.

"Aster, when are you going to learn that—"

"Did you know people used to be happy in cities?" I rarely interrupted her, and she rarely called me by name.

"What?"

I turned around to face her and smiled again when I saw that her eyebrows were scrunched together. It made the wrinkles on her face even more pronounced, which I found endearing despite knowing the weakness of age was setting into her body. I wondered how much longer they would consider her useful.

The confusion gave way to something else on her face. "Is that what you were looking at this time?"

"They were smiling in the drawings." I shook my head slowly, thinking of the unbelievable images I'd seen. "So many of them walking around together and smiling."

Her face drooped. I couldn't tell if she was unhappy with me or just sad. "Honey, why do you risk your safety to look at things that aren't real?"

"It was real before." I breathed out quietly then added, "I don't expect it to happen again."

"That's good."

I nodded my head and proceeded to wash the dirty laundry in front of me. Agatha could not understand my need to look at the pictures I'd found in the library books. She thought I believed we could have it again in our lifetime—that beauty.

I did not believe that.

True beauty was gone from our world. We had destroyed it. They had destroyed it.

Most of the time, I just contemplated over the images—of splendidly rolling fields, trees, happy people that were safe—and felt joy that someone, at some point in time, had been able to experience it. Occasionally, I allowed myself to imagine that I was standing next to one of those trees or talking with those safe people. I always wondered what they would say if they could see the state of our world now. Would they be sad, or disappointed, or angry?

Would they be thankful they were not here now?

I never told Agatha about those ridiculous fantasies. She certainly would not have approved.

Agatha could never have understood even the simplest of explanations for my misbehaviors.

"He wants to see her."

I turned too quickly at the sound of the male voice behind me, and I winced again from the movement, finding a Guard member standing at a distance. They mostly liked to keep it—distance.

"She's busy doing her work, Sir." Agatha was clearly making her displeasure known by glaring at him where he stood waiting, his hand resting loosely on the hilt of the standard-issue sword sheathed at his hip.

They liked to do that as well—draw attention to it whether there was intent or hope for use or not.

"You can finish it for her," he replied, uncaring.

Agatha's jaw clenched and I could almost hear the silent screaming in her head. I turned around so I could ensure my mouth stayed firmly shut.

No one—not even the Guard, who were servants in their own right, although somewhat glorified ones—could understand that every person had their own list of things to do for the day and that any one person being called away did not mean another would have the time to get everything done. Distractions caused sleepless nights for many, so it was good they were a rare occurrence here.

Agatha took a deep breath and spoke in a calm tone. "I need to replace the bandage on her back, Sir. She's bleeding through it." She refrained from telling him that was due to being startled over his unexpected arrival. I knew she would not make me look weak in front of him.

"Possibly," the Guard began, "if she were intelligent enough to follow rules, she would not need to be punished for breaking them."

My own jaw clenched.

Agatha's voice went stern. "Will you allow me to replace them so she isn't bleeding all over the House, or not, Sir?"

There was a very brief moment of silence before he responded with, "If you are capable of doing so quickly."

A gentle hand touched my shoulder before I heard words I'd heard many times in my life. "Come along, my flower. I'll take care of you."

I did not look at the Guard as I was being led away, but I could hear his footsteps following close behind.

Agatha suddenly stopped moving, turning on her heel to face him. "I'll not have you looking at her body."

I sucked in a breath and warily turned myself around to see how he would react. I was not expecting to see him grinning. We were not allowed to tell anyone what to do, and we were always required to say *Sir*.

"What is a body, if it does not belong to the person occupying it?" Snideness was clear in his tone. "Do not allow yourself to be confused. You are property. The girl is property."

"But not yours," Agatha told him firmly.

He shook his head before raising a brow and saying, "You should watch who you speak to in that way." He smiled before turning his back to us.

I waited until Agatha had retrieved the new bandages, staring at the back of the leather armor all Guards wore while on duty, before removing my shirt. I tried to remain still as she pulled the old away from my skin, but I could not stop myself from twitching as the pieces that had dried to it were ripped away. The cool sensation of water being dabbed on was only halfway satisfying—a strange yet horribly familiar mixture of pain and relief.

"You're lucky this hasn't become infected," Agatha said under her breath as she secured the new bandage to me.

I said nothing as I waited patiently, not mentioning the ones that had become infected in the past. Although neither of us said anything, I knew she and I were both anxious for the moment that I could put my shirt back on.

The moment eventually came.

When my plain, off-white shirt was once again in its proper place above my brown trousers, I turned to face Agatha.

She gave me a look I understood perfectly, if only because I knew what was to be done in this situation. She wanted me to be careful in my actions and words.

I offered her a stiff smile in response, which she understood perfectly as well. I would do what I was supposed to do, the same as I did almost all the time. I said nothing, but I touched her arm briefly as I passed and followed the Guard away.

He and I walked in silence for a time—with me following a step or so behind—and I was not expecting him to break it. No one bothered speaking to us directly unless they needed something. When we passed by the doors to the library, where two Guards had been stationed as of four nights previously, he spoke.

"Why do you insist on breaking rules?"

I held my head up, but my gaze was directed at the cold, stone floor. I took in a small breath and then released it, remembering the silent promise I had made to Agatha.

When he presumably realized that I was not going to respond to him, he pressed on. "Are you truly that unintelligent?"

I fought against the urge to react to his provocation outwardly. I'd had quite a lot of practice throughout the years, so the smile stayed off my face.

"You could never understand." I paused before adding, "Sir."

He grabbed hold of my arm, yanking me to a quick halt.

He narrowed his eyes at me in a clear mixture of disbelief and hardly contained rage. "Are you implying your brain is capable of understanding something mine is not?"

"I would never, Sir."

He did not release my arm, so I believed it necessary to continue. I wanted his disgusting hand off me.

"Given that my body is nothing more than a piece of property, it would be a shame for you to damage it to the point where it could not function correctly enough to serve its purpose."

"You do a decent enough job of that on your own, don't you?"

"Yes, Sir," I replied.

He released his hold on my arm then and gestured for me to continue forward. I assumed my response was satisfactory because he did not speak to me again.

When we arrived at our destination, one of the Guards left his post to inform the occupant of the room that I was here for him, as requested.

Several long seconds passed before the Guard returned.

I was surprised when he held the door open for me, but not surprised enough to look at him. I would not look at a man in that way, nor would I allow the person past the ornate wooden door to witness it if I did.

He was sitting at his desk—the current leader of New Bethel. He'd only been in his position for a month or so, which was just long enough to have gotten adequately accustomed to the place and finally begin taking some sort of notice to the servants and their habits. Although he knew I was there, he did not look up at me.

"You wanted to see me, Sir?"

Only then did his eyes meet mine.

"Ah, yes," he said, feigning surprise at my presence. "I'm curious to know if your back is healed."

Rather than tell him how aware I was of the fact that he could not care less about my well-being past the point of it being a hindrance to my job, I said, "As healed as it can be after a few days, Sir."

"I forget you're not given medicine," he said almost distantly.

I remained standing there, waiting for him to inform me of whatever it was he needed from me. It did not take him long.

"I've been going through some notes written by my predecessors." Indeed, he was looking down at papers littered across his desk, but I could not fathom what any of those papers had to do with me. "It seems you make a habit of going to the library when new leadership is instated."

He looked up at me again, expectantly this time, but I said nothing.

His eyebrows rose minutely. "Are you going to deny it?"

"No, Sir."

He smiled a little, glancing back down at the scribbles on the paper. "At least you're honest," he said, sounding distant again. His gaze once more met mine. "I know you were looking at pictures there. Are you thinking of running away?"

"No, Sir," I repeated. I was somewhat startled he would draw that conclusion from my excursions to the library. They never asked me that sort of question.

He studied me for what felt an extremely long while, and I stood there, entirely still, waiting and thinking.

"I'm failing to understand what this is about," he said. The feeling was mutual. "I've read the notes. I've seen the old scars on your back. *Why?*"

"Forgive me for saying so, Sir, but I learned a very long time ago there is no point trying to explain why about anything pertaining to my life. I am insignificant, Sir."

Again, he watched me, and I knew that he did not care about the why.

These leaders were all the same. The only thing they cared about was power. Eventually, *power* came to include every aspect of invisible people. Eventually, they came to realize that people—no matter how insignificant—have eyes and ears.

He watched me analytically before saying, "I brought you here to discuss two matters with you. The first of which is your Branding."

For the first time in such a long time, I was not able to mask my true feelings. My face contorted—my skin feeling like it was pulling itself too tight across my cheeks and near my closed mouth—before I was capable of making it even again.

"I will ignore your reaction in this one instance."

"Thank you, Sir." I clenched my jaw, though the skin on my face still felt much too tight.

"I'm sure you're aware that the time for it was coming," he said almost lazily. "You've been here for ten years. You're already past your eighteenth birthday, are you not? I honestly don't know how you've gotten away with it for as long as you have. Perhaps my predecessors have become perplexed as to where to put it. It would blend in quite nicely on you, wouldn't it?" He paused for a moment to purse his lips before adding, "I'm also sure you know that, given the House you serve, you could not be bought off by anyone else. Though, if one were judging by appearances, I sincerely doubt the opportunity would ever present itself for you."

I could not be bought off, so long as I had a tongue to speak of the things my eyes and ears had picked up on over the last ten years. And if anyone ever caught a glance at my back . . . they would not have me. I belonged to this House, and I would remain here for the entirety of my life. The Branding would be proof of it.

"Yes, Sir." I looked down at the floor and fought against the tears that were threatening to well in my eyes at the thought of it.

"I was thinking we could put it off for a time."

My gaze darted to his as I sucked in a breath. "Put it . . . I don't understand, Sir."

He waved a hand in the air dismissively but said nothing more on the matter. "Since you seem to be remarkably honest, I'm going to ask you a question. You will not be punished for answering it truthfully." He again paused for a moment. "When I am no longer in power here, will you continue to do as you've always done? Will you continue making trips into forbidden rooms and touching things that should not be touched?"

"Yes, Sir," I admitted.

He looked again to the papers on his desk, and he shook his head slowly. "The others couldn't understand, could they? They could not understand that your spirit won't be broken with physical punishment. I suppose it must be something in your blood." He seemed to be waiting for some sort of response, but I knew he did not truly want one.

I did not give him one, even if he might.

"I will have to try a different tactic."

I stood there in silence as he pretended to be studying the notes in front of him. For a moment, he absentmindedly messed with one of the long sleeves of his pure-white tunic as though it were somehow bothersome despite the chill in the air. It wasn't long he spent doing that before shuffling more of the loose papers across his desk, like one of them would hold some sort of key. I knew he was simply demonstrating his authority over me by forcing me to wait for him. It was unnecessary.

Eventually, he said, "We have a . . . *special guest* arriving today."

I sucked in another breath, knowing what—if not who—he was talking about. Every *special guest* was a Reaper returning home from a death mission. If he was making it known to me . . .

"What would you like for me to do, Sir?"

"I would like for you to make yourself presentable," he said. I watched a tiny grin appear on his face, which was still cast downward at his desk.

"I don't understand, Sir."

I heard him let out a breath as he stood up, and I fought against the urge to cringe away from him as he stepped in front of me.

"Are you afraid of them?" As he asked the question, he was analyzing my face with a level of intensity that sent a creeping feeling across the skin of my back, nullifying my discomfort at his proximity.

"Yes, Sir," I admitted.

"You need to understand that I am in control here. If I tell you to move, you will move. If I tell you to stay out of a room, you will stay out of it. If I tell you to stand next to a Reaper, you will stand next to one. Are you hearing what I'm saying to you?"

"Yes, Sir." I pursed my lips together, clenched my jaw, and struggled not to respond nor react in any other way.

"I can see it's difficult dealing with a servant who has a spirit. I'm wondering if it would be better to encourage it than try, and fail, to destroy it."

I blinked hard a few times in confusion, not understanding what he was saying. If I couldn't discern that, I could get nowhere near the potential purpose in it.

He moved quickly, walking toward his desk and returning with something in his hands. "This is what you were looking at, wasn't it?"

I nodded, and it took me a moment to answer him appropriately. "Yes, Sir." My eyes were on the book in his hands, the exact same one he had caught me looking at four nights previously.

"If I find you satisfactory tonight, I will allow you to have it."

My gaze shot to his once more, and I could not stop myself from saying, "You wouldn't." I instantaneously covered my mouth with my hand and said, "I apologize, Sir."

He ignored another of my reactions by smiling in what appeared to be a genuine way and saying, "I would."

I blinked tears out of my eyes and realized I had never really looked at him—this current leader of New Bethel. I rarely wasted my time. There was rarely reason to, all things considered, not the smallest of which being their survival rate. There simply was little if any point in looking at any faces here, typically only reasons to not, but I was too curious to stop myself from examining this one now.

He was much younger than I would've thought, with absolutely no hard lines on his face, and brightness in his wide, green eyes. There was something very strange and unsettling about him, even beyond the variances from the norm.

"We are not all bad," he said, almost like he was somehow following my thoughts.

"You had me beaten like all the rest, Sir," I stated blankly.

I watched as the smile began disappearing from his face, the corners of his mouth moving down and his lips tightening into a straight, hard line.

"You'll forgive me if I'm incapable of finding any good at all in this world."

"Would you not agree that you bring the punishment upon yourself?" he asked, his voice taking on an inquisitive tone.

"Do you believe the punishment is befitting of the crime, Sir?" If Agatha had heard me ask him that question, I would never hear the end of it.

"These materials are forbidden," he reminded me, dangling the book in front of me.

"And yet you're willing to let me have it, Sir."

He shrugged. "I'm going to assume you cannot read."

I kept my face impassive as I stared at him.

"And as you've informed me you have no desire to run away, I see no harm in allowing you to have it for my term."

I refrained from staring longingly at the book—not wanting him to know just how badly I coveted the contents held in his hands—and continued looking at his face to ensure I would not be tempted.

"As long as you are satisfactory tonight, as I said."

"Why are you making me do this, Sir?" I asked, both on guard and curious.

"I've already told you," he said. "I believe I should try a different tactic. One way or another, you will come to understand that I am in control here. You're like an animal. You have continued your bad behavior, and your punishment has not been a sufficient enough teaching method. I will try for positive reinforcement instead. In order to receive what you want, you will have to do something you desperately do not wish to do."

"I understand, Sir." I could not understand why he wanted to continue to punish me and yet reward me at the same time, nor could I fathom the true purpose behind this, but I did at the very least understand that I must do what I'd been told to. "How am I . . ." I paused to clear my throat. "How am I supposed to *make myself presentable*, Sir?"

He stepped away from me once more then returned with a bag and a piece of paper in his hands. "Supplies to do so are in here. If you're stopped by a Guard for having these things, show them this note and they'll leave you alone."

He handed the bag and note over to me, and I winced as the weight of the bag pulled at the healing wounds on my back.

He frowned and then sort of coughed before saying, "You have five hours. I'll expect you to continue your work until you have sufficient enough time to prepare yourself. When you are presentable, go to the kitchen. They will have further instruction for you. You're dismissed."

"Yes, Sir." I inclined my head slightly in his direction before making my way out of the room.

CHAPTER TWO

EQUALITY AND ADVANTAGE

I SHOULD NOT HAVE TAKEN Agatha away from her work only to inform her of what had transpired with our leader. If it had been anything else that happened, I would not have done it. Life here was nothing if not predictable. Life here never changed. Something out of the ordinary taking place needed to be discussed. I needed an outside perspective. I was hoping it would help me understand, or at the very least locate some shred of sense in it all.

The first thing she did was nothing short of scream at me for having the bag in my hands, which was only to be expected. It didn't take long to explain the items had been given to me and that, once I'd used them for their intended purposes, I would ensure everything was returned to him. Satisfied he'd given it to me himself—she could not read to know what the note said, but she took my word—I relayed everything that had happened.

Save one or two things that she did not need to know.

Not surprisingly, she brought up the most important part first. Her voice was both disbelieving and baffled when she said, "He said you could put off your Branding?"

"Yes." I felt new tears welling in my eyes again at the thought. "I cannot understand why he would allow that. There are rules."

"Yes." Agatha's expression was distant as she fiddled with the bottom of her shirt. "There are rules."

I knew she was playing with the fabric in her hands, either refraining from the urge to touch her back or thinking of when she'd gone through her own Branding. I had seen the scar—thick between her shoulder blades, of a large circle enclosing a V, its three points touching the inside of the circle. She had shown it to me when I was twelve, when she thought I was old enough to learn what my own fate would be. What it was *and* what it meant.

"It makes no sense," I said after a long moment of picturing that scar and a younger Agatha who was not so troubled. I'd not been such a burden on her when I was younger. "Why would he put off the Branding and allow me to keep the book? Why would he tell me that not everyone is bad here?"

Her voice went firm to say, "Don't you let that young man fool you, Aster."

"No, Aggie, it's not that." I stared down at the floor and shook my head. "I'm not important enough for someone to waste their energy in effort of trickery. I'm inclined to believe this is all due to my trips to the library, but if he believes me unable to read . . . I cannot see why it would matter." I looked up at her again to ask, "Can you?"

She let out a deep breath as something near to a sigh before responding with, "No, my flower, I cannot." She stood and walked over to the bag I'd brought in with me.

Rather than accompanying her, I remained in the wobbly, wooden chair, attempting to work everything out inside my head.

Nearly a minute had passed before I heard a very confused, yet firm, "Aster."

I focused in on Agatha's back. "Yes?"

"He's given you medicine."

"You're mistaken," I told her assuredly as I stood and began stepping over. "He said he'd forgotten we weren't given medicine. He wouldn't have said he'd forgotten if he hadn't, and he wouldn't waste it on me, even if he had remembered."

She turned somewhat and held in her hands a small, rounded container that was opened, revealing a pale-green salve. It had a strong yet not entirely unpleasant smell to it. Upon realizing that it was in fact what she'd said it was, I began sightlessly sorting through the remaining contents of the bag in order to have something more to do than think on it. I did not like the feeling that small container being in my possession brought on inside me.

I could feel her gaze on me, but it took her a long while to say anything. "Why would he give you this?"

Rather than mention the possibility of remorse for ordering and watching my beating four days previously, I said, "I would imagine he simply doesn't want me bleeding through this contraption in front of our special guest." I held up a plain black dress, showing it to her.

"I would imagine you're right." She sounded distant and looked the same, her attention momentarily on the slinky material held in my hands before she directed that attention to my face. "Sharks in the water, Reapers."

THE NEXT SEVERAL HOURS were spent doing the work I had done every day for most my life, but when I attempted to go inside the grand ballroom to do my dusting, I was turned away by Guards.

"You're not to go in there today, Miss," one of them said in a startlingly polite tone. I couldn't recall ever having been acknowledged with a title. Property had no title.

Deciding to disregard what must've been a slip of tongue from what must've been someone riddled with confusion, I said, "I have work to do in there, Sir."

"Not today," another told me. "Go about the rest of the things on that little list of yours."

I did not tell him how far from little my list actually was, and I certainly didn't ask how he knew about our lists. Instead, I turned and walked away.

I could not waste time dallying in front of a door I was not permitted entrance through when so many other things needed doing. I wondered if, after I had done what was required of me for our leader, I would have to stay up for a full two days to finish everything else. The cost and weight of the book weighed heavy on my mind, as did all the rest.

I did more laundry, I made beds, and when I was in the process of assisting with the dishes that had been brought in after dinner, I was interrupted.

"Excuse me, Miss." There was that same startlingly polite tone I'd heard before.

I turned quickly and nearly flinched, expecting to experience the painful aftereffects of moving too hastily with an injured back, but I felt nothing. I'd seen a few times how efficient medicines were at healing the body, but I had never experienced it for myself.

Just a little scraped kn—

I pushed it from me, staring at the Guard.

"I was sent to ensure you stopped your work, so you could be ready for this evening."

I felt a moment of panic that overpowered all else, wondering how I had allowed the time to slip away from me. Did time pass more quickly when something dreaded was standing in your way, even with all there was to think on?

My panic must've been apparent because the Guard smiled and said, "Don't worry, Miss. You still have an hour and a half before you're required to be in the kitchen."

"Why do you keep calling me that?" I blurted out. I mentally scolded myself, but I could not understand his behavior. I quickly added, "Sir."

The pale skin of his cheeks flushed a little before he answered with, "Because you are a lady."

"I am property, Sir," I corrected him.

"You are a *lady*." He said it more obstinately then.

I felt some sort of hotness on my face that I was not accustomed to, and then another surge of panic rose at the realization that I was alone inside a room with a young man who seemed insistent on the fact that I was a lady. Agatha had warned me to stay away from the men here and of situations that could result from being alone with any of them. It was simply another reason to despise them.

"I need to find Agatha," I said under my breath, my gaze down at the smooth stone floor beneath my feet. I needed to get out of this room and far away from him.

"What was that?"

"Oh, I'm sorry, Sir." I slowly took a few steps back, watching his eyebrows furrowing downward in confusion beneath his light brown hair. "I was just telling myself that I need to find someone. I'm afraid I don't have the vaguest idea how to make my own person presentable."

"I can accompany you, if you'd like."

"No, Sir." I took several more steps away that would make it easier to get around him, holding my right hand slightly in the air. "I've been here most my life. I'm quite certain I can find my own way around this House." I left him standing there as I hurriedly vacated the room.

I found Agatha shortly after, polishing silverware in one of the rooms adjacent to the kitchen.

"My flower, what's wrong?" She stood and walked over to me with a concerned expression on her face.

I must've been doing a poorer job at containing the whirlwind of emotions and worries swirling around inside my head than I realized.

"N-nothing," I lied, not knowing why I didn't want to divulge my experience with the Guard. I should've wanted to tell her everything.

She knew I was being untruthful, but she let it go. "Our leader informed me that I'm to help you prepare for this evening."

I released a very large breath of relief at the words, and the change of subject. I would've felt incredibly guilty for pulling her away from her duties to assist me without permission, knowing that every minute she spent dawdling was another minute she would spend sleepless tonight.

She took my hand and led me away to the servants' quarters, walking down the stone stairs that brought us below ground. She drew me a bath in the communal wash space, and after a long while of scrubbing my own body, I decided I was clean enough to pass. It was while she was doing unknown things to my face and hair in our shared room that she ended the silence.

"What had you all out of sorts when you came to me earlier?"

"This is very strange," I told her in an attempt to divert the matter once more. "Having this done to me, rather than doing it to someone else, I mean."

She frowned. "Don't you do that."

I sighed and unhappily admitted, "It was a young man in the Guard. That's all."

"Did he do something to you?" Her hands stopped their busy-work and came to rest on either side of my face, as if she could tell whether he had by examining me in such a way.

"No," I said quietly and then looked down. "He was being polite, and it made me uncomfortable. That's all that happened."

"Polite in what way?" She moved her hands back to her person, resting them at her sides.

I cleared my throat before saying, "He called me a lady." Then, I forced a laugh, though it came out sounding nearly as uneasy as I currently felt. "Isn't that ridiculous?"

Agatha laughed a little as well, but it did not sound forced in the way mine had. "Did he, now?"

"Yes." I focused in on her face. "Why would he do that?"

She shook her head shortly and got back to doing whatever it was she was doing to my hair. "I fear I may have done wrong by you all these years." Her voice sounded somewhat distant.

"Don't be ridiculous, Agatha. You're the only mother I've ever had, and you've been more wonderful to me than I deserve."

She sighed quietly. She would not tell me I was the only daughter she'd ever had, because I was not. "I'm talking about the things I've told you about men."

"You've told me enough to understand." I clenched my jaw for a moment. I had to let it go to say, "I simply cannot fathom why he would waste his breath with pleasantries for me. With what you've told me, there's no need for them to do such things to get what they're after where women are concerned."

Men did not waste their breath with pleasantries where anything was concerned, not when there were so many other options.

She sighed again. "Yes, I believe I've done you a great injustice."

I did not know what to say to that, so I waited for her to continue.

"Our leader was right when he told you that not all people are bad, my flower. Sometimes people say and do good things for the same reason people do bad things—because they want to."

"That's not what you've told me," I stated. It also had not been my experience, past Agatha.

"I know what I've told you, dear, and I don't want you to forget any of those things. I've been warning you for years now that, given the changes in your body, you need to be especially careful around them, which you have. But sometimes . . . sometimes people are able to see past what we are."

"That's not what you've told me," I repeated.

"This boy, was he attractive?"

"What?" I asked, confounded.

She stopped her busywork again and investigated my face, but she didn't repeat herself.

I thought hard on how she might've meant it. *Why* she might've meant it.

"I don't know." I shook my head, still lost. "Why does it matter?" I had never looked hard or long enough to discover whether I found any of them attractive. Attractiveness was irrelevant.

"Sometimes, things matter," she said cryptically with a small smile. Then, her lips pursed tightly together for an instant. "Still, don't be alone with him. Especially if you believe he's taken an interest in you."

"I don't believe he's taken an interest in me, Agatha." I chuckled, not needing to tell her that her warning was unnecessary. "I don't see how he could."

She stepped several paces away before coming back with a small mirror in her hands. I'd seen myself in mirrors before, briefly when I was cleaning, but we had none in our quarters. We were expected to be presentable, but only to the point of not being sloppy in appearance. Reflections were not necessary to ensure such a thing.

She smiled as she handed the mirror to me, but I frowned as I took in the image of myself.

My lips were covered in that red paste the circulating wives so often expected us to apply to them, and they looked much fuller than usual. My eyes when rimmed with the dark stick looked wider than they normally did, and it made the green of them stand out vividly. My light hair, which was no longer in the tight bun that always choked my head, hung down past my shoulders in a way I'd not ever seen it before. I hastily looked away from the unfamiliar girl staring back at me.

I could not return Agatha's smile. Given the fright I'd experienced due to the Guard member earlier, I could not be happy when I didn't look the way I should have. Knowing I would be in such close proximity to a Reaper, I wanted to be invisible. How could I manage invisibility when I was not myself?

My stomach plummeted to the floor as I finally understood the purpose of what our leader was forcing me to do.

ALL SERVANTS WERE NOT CREATED EQUAL. One would think there would be no differences, considering we were all property. There were those who did the dirty work, and then there were servants who were well-groomed, better taken care of, and did no hard labor. They served food or beverages to our special guests. They pretended to clean the rooms that were occupied, making the guests think all things in the House looked a certain way. They pretended while the guests were in, and then we came when the rooms were vacated to do the real work.

I should've known instantly when I saw the plain black dress the female servers wore. I should've known, but I'd joked about it instead.

I understood perfectly as I walked down the hallways, when no one was near tugging at the hem of the dress in an attempt to pull it down to a passably acceptable length, listening to the annoying clicks the uncomfortable shoes made on the stone floors.

The outfits were far too revealing, even for the few male servers. They were covered in all the places that were necessary, but there was something about the way their clothing fit that was slightly inappropriate. The servers never seemed to have a problem with any of it. They never seemed to mind interacting with Reapers and citizens, smiling at them, leaning on them, touching them.

In my opinion, they were all mad.

I was not confused about my place, despite all the confusions of the day. My place was the least confusing thing in my life. I believed it safe to assume that my requirement for the night would not be required again, so long as I learned my lesson.

Our leader wanted to show me that he had every right to make me as uncomfortable as possible. He was not kind, and he did not care about the injury on my back. The joke I'd told Agatha was spot-on. He simply didn't want me to bleed on the ridiculous dress. He felt no remorse for the beating. This was proof.

Had I needed proof?

The Guard members stepped aside as I came upon the oversized wooden doors of the kitchen. I did not like the way their eyes roved over my exposed legs. I did not like how much they could see of me in the exposure, even beyond the thought of skin. I did not like being looked at or noticed at all. I fought against a wave of panic as a chill ran down my spine when I stepped past them into the room.

It was one of very few instances where more people being near was a good thing and cause for relief, and yet the feeling lingered in its way.

I made my way over to Francine, the main chef, being as inconspicuous as I could manage in my distress. My slight unsteadiness in the shoes did not help. I was glad for the hustle and bustle of the space—all the pans banging while the cooks rushed to get everything done, servers moving, and cooks shouting things at one another.

"What am I supposed to do?" I almost whispered. I was not accustomed to being unaware of what to do. I did not like that, either.

Another relief was that she was at least in the room, which meant I would in no way—likely—have to speak to anyone else.

Francine looked over her shoulder at me and jumped a little, in a way recoiling almost as if the sight of me had slapped her awake and into a stupor at once. "Aster?"

I stared down at the floor in shame, my cheeks burning. It felt for a moment that even she hadn't recognized me, and she was one of very few people I believed knew I existed.

That somehow almost made it worse.

"Please just tell me what to do," I begged, looking up from the floor to her face and hoping she would not say anything about my appearance. That, also, would make it so much worse than it already was.

She did not answer me. Instead, she looked then stared at something past my shoulder.

"Precisely on time," our leader said from behind me.

Slowly, I turned around to face him.

"Well, don't you look lovely?" He smiled. "I can't say I'm entirely surprised."

Lovely.

I knew the appropriate response was, "Thank you, Sir." I said it to the floor and not his face, fighting against tears of humiliation and fear.

He reached out to touch my elbow, and I felt my body cringing away no matter how I told myself internally to not move nor react.

He withdrew his hand. "Will you talk with me for a moment?"

"Of course, Sir." I spoke as politely as I could manage.

I followed him to an unoccupied space in the room, next to a wooden table near the right wall, where the kitchen staff ate after they finished preparing food for everyone else. The servants also ate there, most of the time.

When we were properly out of earshot, he spoke quietly. "I'm sensing your fear is not only of our guest."

"Our guest has been out of my mind, Sir," I admitted, frowning as I thought again on what was really happening tonight. With so many things that had been more pressing, it had been easier to put Reapers out of my thoughts than I ever could've imagined.

"I would like for you to tell me what you're afraid of."

"I very much wish you would not make me, but I will tell you if you require it, Sir," I said, my gaze on the long, wooden table rather than him. I could see the bright red fabric of his tunic in my peripherals, the darkness of the belt he wore seeming to cut it in half.

"I require it."

I had not expected anything less from him. Or anything more.

I took in a deep breath and forced myself to look at his face when I answered. My voice was void of emotion when I admitted the truth to him. "I am afraid of what will happen to me after, Sir."

His eyes narrowed in confusion, and I fought the urge to tell him that his dirty-blond hair was looking particularly unkempt this evening, far more than it had this morning. I assumed he had done it on purpose, and he was young enough that it only looked partially ridiculous and not entirely so.

"After?" he echoed. "You will have to be more specific for me. I'm failing to understand what you're getting at."

"After," I repeated, trying so very hard to remain impassive. I was not entirely successful in my attempt. "When our guest is gone and all attention is away from the staff once more. No one notices what happens to the servants, Sir, and if they do . . . they don't care."

"Has someone taken advantage of you?"

I was surprised to find that he seemed concerned—if not for me then possibly for the entire staff. Surely, though, there was reason for it beyond what would be thought.

"No, Sir." I held my head high and forced my jaw to stop quivering. "Though I fear you've doomed me to it now. Please tell me what to do so I can work. I would rather not stand around and give myself time to think." I sniffed quietly before adding, "Sir."

CHAPTER THREE

THE REAPER

I WAS NOT SURPRISED to discover that our leader thought me incapable of working and thinking at the same time, and I was happy to find I could deceive him, even if only in such a minuscule way. Most things I did or said in my life, I asked myself whether Agatha would approve of them. She would never approve of me being deceitful, unless required for safety, but this was not one of those instances where I concerned myself over her approval.

At the end of the day, I could go to sleep knowing he was wrong. Our leader, and all the rest of them, would still be far more ignorant than they believed us to be.

After being told our special guest tonight was somehow more special than the rest of them but not how or why, I was sent off to serve tiny bites of food to our guests.

Posture and smile, the head server told me, his hands making a short, vertical slashing motion in front of him as if to reinforce the unparalleled importance of the instruction. *Posture and smile*. I didn't typically concern myself with such things, and I wondered what purpose a fake smile might serve—not one out of forced respect but simply fake, with absolutely no internal motivation pushing the action. Surely they could be seen through.

But perhaps not.

Given the Reapers' occupation, one could think they'd need to remain anonymous and hidden, that they would not be flaunted inside our city in front of the highest members of our broken society.

Their anonymity didn't matter because they far more often than not did not work here. When they did, there was rarely need to conceal themselves. Mostly, they were sent to other cities to take out influential people who caused problems for whatever leader was in power. And then they would return to their home city to be paraded in front of us all like deities we should fall to our knees and worship without thought.

I'd never been allowed inside one of functions *welcoming their return*, but I had heard a great many stories from the kitchen staff. One could hardly believe some of the things they overheard from the servers when they would come back to get more food and drink.

The younger Reapers enjoyed the attention, from what I had gathered. Some, but not all the older ones—there weren't many of them, given their survival rates over extended periods of time—did as well.

I would've liked to imagine that even the most heartless person would feel remorse for their actions, particularly those leading to the harm or detriment of others, especially if coming close to the end of their own life. But from what I knew of the Reapers, I did not think it was possible for them to feel anything at all, let alone so great a feeling as remorse.

Despite my discomfort, I smiled as I'd been instructed while I served the small bites of food to people. At first the expression was forced, but when I noticed they did not look at me often, it became in part genuine. Relief pushed it onto my face, not making it sincere, simply easier.

It felt far less like a grimace on my face when the relief existed at all. The realness of it or not also gave me a great deal to think on.

Once my first tray had been emptied, I spared a short moment at the top of the staircase, observing the scene, before leaving to retrieve another. I watched the servers as they interacted with guests, and I realized they were only noticed if they desired it.

I could still be invisible, even in a room filled with hundreds of people. I just had to pay mind to myself.

"I almost didn't recognize you, Miss."

I turned and found the Guard who had spoken to me earlier standing relatively close by. He was still on duty—wearing the leather armor with the mark of our Branding over the heart—which was not surprising. Nearly all the Guards were required to attend these functions to keep the citizens safe and in order along with protecting our leader from those with whom he kept company.

There was a strange feeling inside me, down deep, at him again speaking to me—almost a turning in my stomach. Along with that, though, there was also a rising frustration.

Why could he not just leave me be?

I forced a smile at him as I pulled myself away from the banister and began the long trek down the hallway toward the kitchen. The clicking of the horrible shoes became accompanied by the distinct sound of boots on stone. I wasn't accustomed to all the sound and, for a moment, felt it was making me insane. When it reached the point of the sound being unbearable added onto his presence causing the same, I stopped and turned to face him.

"May I ask you what you're doing, Sir?"

I watched his cheeks turn slightly pink, as they had done earlier. "I just wanted to tell you . . ." He said nothing else.

I watched his gaze settle on a painting hanging on the wall behind me. *Sunset*, I knew without looking. I narrowed my eyes slightly in confusion.

Why would a person follow another with intent to speak and then say nothing at all, instead staring at a painting they likely had no interest in? How pointless.

He brought his full attention back to me, his wide brown eyes settling in, and he finally said, "You look nice."

"I look ridiculous, Sir," I corrected.

My words seemed to puzzle him, for some reason.

I found it—*all* of it—infuriating. "I wouldn't presume to tell you what to do with your time, but I would very much appreciate if you would refrain from wasting it by lying to me. If you'll excuse me now, Sir . . . I have work to do."

I didn't wait for any form of acknowledgement as I resumed my journey down the hallway, but I was very satisfied that I did not hear an extra pair of feet beside or behind me. I kept listening, though I didn't look back, not allowing relief to set in until I reached the kitchen.

There, surprisingly, I found Agatha. I'd hardly stepped inside before she came barreling over to me.

"How is it down there? Has anyone been inappropriate with you?"

"It's fine." I sighed. "And the only person who's even noticed my presence in the world is that young man." At least who'd not forgotten about it immediately after, if noticed at all.

"That boy in the Guard?"

"Yes." I grabbed my next tray from the table. I added quietly under my breath, "He told me I *look nice*."

I quickly turned to face her, due to the sound she'd made in response.

"Why are you laughing at me?"

"Oh, my flower." She chuckled as she shook her head at me. "What did you say to him?"

"Nothing important."

The smile instantaneously dropped away from her face. "Were you rude to him?"

"I was perfectly polite, I believe."

"So that's a yes, then." She nodded, sounding certain.

I knew Agatha well enough to know she was amused by me but did not want me to be aware of it. And I knew well enough why that was.

I had been perfectly polite, as I always was, in my opinion.

"I have to get back to work." I smiled wanly. "I'll see you later tonight and will tell you all about the rest of this nonsense."

She touched my face briefly.

On my way to the door, I stopped and turn to add, "I love you, Aggie."

I barely heard her say, "I love you too, my flower."

I did check when out, to ensure the Guard wasn't there.

Nowhere to be seen, so I began walking.

I was distracted by the annoying clicks on the floor as I made my way. I was accustomed to nearly complete silence in the Valdour House, so it took me a long moment to realize it was silent when it was not supposed to be. Unfortunately, I was already halfway down the staircase, clicking away, when it finally registered and I stopped in my tracks. Only one person's gaze was directed at me, while everyone else stared only at him.

The Reaper had arrived, dressed in the standard all-black clothing they wore, adorned with straps. The silver of knives stood out vividly over the black, almost reflecting in the light.

I thought, for just a moment, that he was laughing at me.

THE MOMENT OF SILENCE when Reapers return home is said to be in respect to or for the dead they leave in their wake.

I didn't believe that to be accurate.

I was almost entirely certain that everyone took their moment of silence to acclimate to the Reaper's arrival, like jumping into a bath of freezing cold water. If anyone truly cared for the dead, they would not celebrate the ones who caused it. If respect was involved to any degree in the practice, it was respecting the knowledge that the ones you celebrated could end your life as easily as they'd done with the last person.

I watched from the staircase as our leader walked over to the Reaper and spoke to him—likely introducing himself—and all at once, the cacophony that had previously occupied the space resumed.

I carried on about my way.

Hours passed as I handed out food—not enough of it to sustain any one person for longer than five minutes—to people who did not notice me. I would walk past and they would grab at my tray with their grubby hands, but they far more often than not would not look at me directly. They would speak to their company, and I would move on.

I kept a wary eye on the Reaper, noticing that he was consistent in holding his back to the walls. He would move, though, I noticed. No matter how hard I attempted to keep him on the opposite side of the room from me, he was always right there again when I turned my head. Not necessarily close, but still far too close for comfort. Their sheer existence in the world was discomforting, but being in the same room as one was indescribably worse. All the people between in no way lessened it.

Eventually, our leader came over to me with an easy smile on his face and a glass in his hand. "Are you okay?"

"I, um . . ." I paused for a moment, frustrated at myself for becoming so perplexed by such a simple question. That it was asked was one matter and the answer another. "Yes, Sir. I'm all right."

"Have you offered food to our guest?" His tone almost made it sound as though he were telling me a joke.

"No, Sir," I admitted. *He* was what had me so perplexed.

"You understand that each server offers something different." His eyebrows rose minutely, but the tone was light. "It would be incredibly rude, don't you think, not to give him everything we have to offer?" Though the tone was light, I knew what he was saying.

You're to go over there.

I took a breath and held it briefly before saying, "Of course, Sir. Horribly rude."

"Good girl."

I clenched my jaw because those two words had felt like a smack in the face. I assumed he did not notice my reaction when shooing me on with his free hand.

"Go on."

I did not have to search for the Reaper. All I had to do was follow the gaze of the crowd. Some people stared at him outright, while others stole glances. My heart was beating so quickly in my chest that it was almost painful as I walked to where he stood. The sound of it pounding in my ears nearly cancelled out all other noise in the room.

Or perhaps it was just fear.

I had never been close to a Reaper before. I'd always stayed as far away from them as I could manage, glad that my position required it.

I found myself standing face to face with one. Ten feet away was still too close.

It took the man speaking to him five full sentences to realize he did not have the Reaper's undivided attention any longer, if he'd ever actually had it in the first place. The man speaking and the three others with him all turned in my direction, nearly as one.

I stood there for far too long, attempting to think of something appropriate to say. I could not tell the Reaper that I wanted to offer him food, because I did not want to offer him anything. Rather than say anything, what I did was far worse.

I stepped closer, holding out the tray and staring at the nearest wall.

Several seconds passed before . . .

"Is it poisoned?"

My gaze darted to the Reaper's eyes. For a brief instant, I found myself startled to see such humanly blue eyes on the face of a monster. He appeared to be on the verge of laughing, but the strangeness of it all could not hold my attention long.

His hand was outstretched, steady over the tray of food I was currently holding. For a moment, I let myself wonder how many people he'd murdered with that hand which was so incredibly close to me.

How long it took to clean the blood off each time.

As he pulled it back to himself, almost like he knew what I was thinking, I heard myself say, "Unless you've seen people dropping dead behind me, I would not imagine so, Sir."

My free hand darted to my mouth as I realized how my words had sounded—far less reassuring, likely, than accusatory.

I did not expect him to laugh. I'd expected a broken neck, once it struck me.

His reaction was startling but not as astonishing as how joyful he sounded.

How could a murderer feel joy?

"I apologize if that sounded rude, Sir," I told him once I'd recovered enough from the shock to do so. I would never hear the end of this if Agatha found out.

"Are you sorry?"

I focused back in on his face. "Excuse me, Sir?"

"Are you truly sorry if that sounded rude?" he clarified.

I opened my mouth to speak and then closed it again, finding no appropriate response to his question. "Would you like some food, Sir?" I moved my gaze away from him, again looking to the wall.

I wanted to throw the tray at his face when I heard his laughter following my question. It certainly was not the brightest errant thought or urge I'd ever had.

"No thanks," he said through his chuckling. "I don't eat or drink anything at these ridiculous parties."

I was amused that he found all this to be a load of nonsense as well, just a little. Amused. Confused. Other things that I wasn't yet sure on.

"Enjoy the rest of your evening, Sir." When I spared one last glance at the Reaper, I saw him smiling at me in what appeared to be a genuine sort of way. I believed his expression was the most incomprehensible and astounding part of the entire interaction, but I did not want to think about it. I'd done what was required of me.

I turned away, breathing a sigh of relief over the fact that a horrible situation had turned out to be quite harmless—bafflingly harmless. I had interacted with the Reaper and emerged shaken, yes, but unscathed. I'd insulted him, I was sure, and he had not killed me for it.

He'd *laughed*.

Smiled. Not the typical smile that occurred on the rare occasion I spoke.

I'd made it four steps away from them when I heard, "I'd like to show that one an enjoyable evening."

I stopped for a moment, easily recognizing the voice of the man who'd been speaking with the Reaper upon my arrival. I felt the muscles in my back twinge at his implication. Then I took a deep breath and continued walking away.

I heard the Reaper start to say, "If you believe . . ." His voice was soon drowned out by the cacophony in the room around me. I was glad for it because I did not want to find out what a Reaper could or would say in response to such a statement.

I KNEW HOW LONG THESE FESTIVITIES LASTED. They continued long into the night and occasionally well into the next morning. We'd had one leader who'd kept one going for three days.

He'd not lasted long.

I was relatively certain that the practice as a whole was just an excuse for the well-to-do to gather together and get intoxicated. Excuse being needed could give one a great deal to think on.

I was accustomed to being on my feet for hours on end, so continuing shouldn't have been an issue in that regard, but I was not accustomed to wearing insensible shoes. My feet had felt as though they were enduring an unrelenting stream of torture almost immediately upon putting them on, but after several hours they had simply gone numb. Painfully numb. That pain could both exist and be numbing could at times be a great deal to think on as well.

I did not think about my feet, beyond a stray thought here or there wondering if I might be leaving a trail of blood behind me as I made my way.

Instead, I wondered why the Reaper had extended his hand to grab the food from my tray, even though he claimed he didn't eat or drink at these parties. Although it wasn't important, the strangeness of it also gave me something to ponder over to pass the time. It was a nice distraction from reality.

Slowly but surely, the occasionally sensible talk of our city turned into slurred words and raucous laughter. I watched a lot of the servers begin paying special attention to the guests in ways they hadn't quite at the start, and I was confused as they studied them in the way predators watched their prey before making a conscious decision to attack.

For the first time, I wondered if they actually got something out of this, if they somehow enjoyed the things they did. They were more dissimilar from the rest of us than I'd ever realized before, if that were true. I couldn't fathom why the kitchen staff had never told us as much. Surely if anyone knew how the servers truly were beyond themselves, it would be those in the kitchen. Though it didn't matter, it was interesting, as was wondering just how much was different inside this House than I'd gathered.

I tried as best as I could to remain invisible. I kept my body away from the men, as they seemed to be growing less interested in food and ever more interested in flesh. The sight of it all sent a creeping, heavy feeling over me, as if I were bathing in a pool of mud.

I would've preferred mud.

No matter how many times I contemplated sneaking away and slipping back to my quarters, I kept on. I would occasionally catch the eye of our leader and, when I did, it almost seemed as though he were searching me out to ensure I was still doing as I'd been told.

Knowing I could not get away without being caught and enduring punishment for it, I persisted. And still, I kept an eye on the Reaper when I could, ensuring I remained as far away from him as was possible.

It was never anywhere near as far as I would've liked.

IT HAPPENED WHILE I WAS ON MY WAY to retrieve another tray, weaving my way through the crowd several hours after interacting with the Reaper. A sloppy hand grabbed at my rear.

I startled, making some sort of noise not unlike that of a dying animal, and I turned.

The man who'd made the remark about showing me an enjoyable evening smiled drunkenly at me, a somewhat lopsided thing.

I backed away, shaking my head and attempting to drown out the whirlwind of nearly incomprehensible thoughts and feelings swirling around inside me.

"Now, little girl, you're going to have to let me—"

I was distracted enough by the people moving around him that I did not hear the rest of what he said.

I watched as the Reaper stepped through the crowd of people, and I allowed myself the briefest of moments to wonder why he'd finally taken his back away from its place against the wall before I turned to make a hasty departure in the opportunity his movement created.

All were so focused on him, the talking and laughter had become a quiet murmur. It was close enough to silence that I was able to hear the strange crack that preceded a very loud scream.

I halted.

Slowly, I turned back to what I'd been attempting to leave behind.

It was not difficult to find the drunken man standing there with his hand bent the wrong way at the wrist.

Everyone was staring at the Reaper—the grin on his face could be considered nothing but *satisfied*—while the drunk shrieked obscenities, his eyes wide and filled with sober horror as he stared at his hand.

I could not discern whether the Reaper appeared to be amused or serene, though I somehow realized through the hysteria inside my head that it could've possibly been some horrible combination of both.

After an unmistakably satisfied moment of staring at his work, the Reaper looked in my direction.

I watched the grin slip away from his face, almost as if he'd not wanted or expected me to see what he'd done.

Everyone near followed his gaze to me.

For the first time since coming to the Valdour House . . . I was not invisible to anyone.

Slowly—so very slowly—I stepped backward, until I was far enough away for it to be in *any* way acceptable to turn and run.

CHAPTER FOUR

MONSTERS AND GRATITUDE

ERVANTS ARE PROPERTY. Property has no feelings, no emotions. Property is incapable of any sort of reaction.

We had no right to any of those things. You only had to be reminded of that so many times before you began to harden yourself to it. We felt, of course, but only in places where no one who would tell us otherwise could see it happen. It was more difficult for some than others.

There was a certain stone balcony overlooking the gardens on property. It was attached to a room that no one entered for any reason, apart from cleaning. There was nothing wrong with it, of course. It simply was considered *lesser* than the other rooms of its same type, no matter the view. Elsewhere held *better*, in what seemed to be a consensus.

It was the only place in the Valdour House where I did not feel like what everyone saw me as and told me I was. In all other rooms—even the library—it was only a matter of time until someone might or would step inside and look at you whether they saw you or not.

Sometimes I was able to look out at the garden and ignore the sight of the broken city. On rarer occasion, I was able to nearly disregard its existence entirely. Only the tips of a few buildings were visible beyond the walls that enclosed the House as a last line of defense if the city were to be invaded. Only a small section of the city's taller defensive wall could be seen from this location in the House.

There was not a single position in the Valdour House that granted sight at what lay beyond the second wall—New Bethel's security from the rest of the world. The garden was all I had.

Sometimes it reminded me of the pictures I would see in the forbidden books that told the hidden secrets of our past. Most of the time, I looked out and saw it for what it truly was.

The grounds were nothing more than props resting on the stage of a play. It was something to look at and be fooled by, nothing more.

I would've expected to find myself staring out tonight and hoping upon all hope that I could think of it as real—that there could be true beauty somewhere in a world of darkness, that beauty wasn't some illusion. Trickery. Instead, my eyes were closed as I stood bent over against the smooth, carved stone railing of the balcony, my forehead resting on my arm. The frigid winter air bit at my exposed skin, reminding me it was all too real.

I gave myself permission to sob quietly enough that no one would hear me if they were passing below. I was allowed that much, I thought. Property or not, I was still human, and I had been violated. No one could tell me otherwise if they did not know.

I had never been inappropriately touched. Not even any of the leaders had ever paid me the slightest bit of attention past beatings. I preferred being invisible. If you were invisible, you could not be hurt by anything or anyone. I was a phantom that cleaned and did the laundry. I enjoyed existing outside the limits of other people's sight. It had kept me safe enough all these years.

Our current leader had taken my ability to be nonexistent away from me, almost as though he'd known something of this nature would occur tonight. The beatings wouldn't work, so he'd find something that would. And the Reaper . . .

The Reaper had put me on display for the world to see.

There she is.

Why had he done what he had? Was it simply because I'd been violated? Why would that in any way cause him to move? Was it possible that a monster could have a heart?

They could not have hearts, and I was not valuable enough for a heart to be wasted on.

Would I be punished for this? Did I have any right to my own body?

I was sure if anyone else had done what the Reaper had, there would be hell to pay—and I would be the one required to pay it. But Reapers could do whatever they wanted.

The door leading back inside opened audibly, which caused me to straighten myself back up, horror coursing through me, knowing . . .

The room had been compromised.

The room was gone.

I got myself straightened only a few seconds before . . .

"Miss?"

Resisting the urge to scream, I forced away the tears and then turned around to face the Guard who would not leave me alone. "Have you come here to tell me more lies, Sir?"

"I've come to make sure you're all right, Miss."

Emotions I had never felt before whirled around inside me, each of them seeming to find lesser, comprehensible versions of the same feelings—fear, frustration, anger—and rip them apart. I found myself unable to refrain from laughing.

"Yes, Sir," I said with more sarcasm than I'd ever used in my life. "I'm perfectly fine, as you can very well see."

He stared at me, in shock surely brought on by what he would consider *my insolence*. Only a moment of it passed before the door opened behind him, pulling his gaze away from mine.

The Reaper stepped onto the balcony with us, the silver of his blades somehow appearing more sinister in the moonlight than they had before in all the light of the House. The sight of it—and of him—deflated all my hostile feelings, leaving only fear and an almost morbid sort of amusement. I would've laughed again at the downright absurdity and horribleness of it, had he spared a single glance at me, and if I'd not seen the expression on his face.

"Do you realize how this looks?" The Reaper nearly shouted at the young man in the Guard. "Following her out here while she's alone? Do you realize?"

The Guard had straightened to his full height by that point, only having to look up two inches or so to be eyelevel with the Reaper. "Somewhat similar to the spectacle you put on back there, I would think." He sounded irritated, angry, and not at all polite as he'd sounded before.

Imbecile. Even men, in all their pride, should have a much better sense of self-preservation than to provoke a Reaper intentionally.

I held my breath for what felt like an eternity as I waited for the Reaper's reaction.

For a time, nothing happened at all, apart from a slow-spreading smile making its way across his face.

I had only enough time, really, to wonder what would follow it before it came.

"I suggest you go back inside," was what the Reaper said, his voice startlingly composed and yet undeniably firm. How far could he be pushed?

"And leave her alone with you, Sir?" the Guard retorted.

"Her lady is just there." The Reaper nodded his head toward the door, though his eyes didn't leave the person in front of him.

The boy in the Guard looked toward the door, then at me, almost as if he'd forgotten I was here during their entire exchange despite having just spoken of me. He appeared embarrassed for an instant before he said, "I apologize for the position I've put you in, Miss."

And then he was gone, leaving me alone with the one person I had been trying to stay away from throughout the entire night. I didn't move, nor did I say a word. I stood precisely where I was, looking at his body standing between myself and the door to enter back into the House.

The Reaper waited, staring at that doorway—until the Guard must've been halfway across the House—before he looked at me. He did so for only an instant before making to leave, as if there were nothing at all to say. And I knew.

He'd simply been ensuring the Guard didn't return.

That was all.

When he was almost to the door, I heard my own voice speaking without my wanting it to.

"Why did you act as though you were going to take the food?"

He stopped moving, but several long seconds passed before he turned to me.

I sucked in a breath before saying, "Sir."

"What are you talking about?"

I felt my stomach sinking as I watched his head tilting slowly. Though I'd seen the same body language many times when people

were confused, there was something different about it. It was something about the eyes. His expression didn't quite match the appropriate response. There was something almost . . . *predatory* in the
simple movement, and I found myself wanting to run away. The
only option would be over the balcony to fall as a heap onto the
ground below.

It in some way seemed the right thing to do.

I in no way moved.

Troubled, I cleared my throat before answering his question.
"The food, Sir. You acted as though you were going to take the food,
and then said you never eat or drink at these functions. Why would
you do that?"

I could not explain why I continued talking to him. I should've
just told him it was nothing when he asked, but for some reason . . . I
needed to understand why he'd bothered. Perhaps it would explain
why he had bothered with any of this. A discovery would be worth a
few moments of discomfort and fear.

I fought against another urge to run away from him when he
stepped closer to me. If I moved even a little, it would put me closer
to the edge of the balcony, which would not make me any safer,
regardless of the railings. All it would take was just a little tip
over. . . .

He stopped several feet away from me. "Out of everything, that's
what you're asking me?"

"Yes, Sir," I replied. "I cannot understand why you would do
that. It makes no sense to me, Sir."

He rubbed a hand over the bottom half of his face briefly and I
tried not to cringe at the sight of that hand again. It was even more
threatening now, being alone with him in the dark.

Before I could properly think about the fact that I was alone with
a Reaper in the dark, he said, "Will you please stop calling me Sir?"

"Wh . . . What would you insist I call you?"

"My name," he answered, his voice even.

"I am not permitted to do so, Sir."

"Stop," he said, holding his hands in the air. I was quite certain
my face gave nothing away, but he quickly brought his hands back to
himself and stared down near his feet for a moment. "You don't have
to call me by my name if it makes you uncomfortable, but I insist
that you stop calling me Sir. Is that acceptable?"

When I said nothing, I heard him laugh once—humorlessly, beneath his breath—before turning away from me again and beginning to make his way toward the door.

"Why would you allow me to do that?" I heard myself ask him, nearly whispering.

I almost wished he hadn't heard me. I certainly wished I'd not asked, but I had, and he must have.

He stepped too close to me, and panic seemed to rise all the way from my stomach to my throat, but he walked past, leaning over and resting the weight of his body against the balcony railing. He said nothing.

He was . . . baffling.

"Why are you showing me your back?" I asked him with a mixture of confusion and curiosity.

He looked over at me, grinning, and I felt inclined to continue.

"I fully understand I'm no threat to you, but it goes against your nature, doesn't it? Showing your back to a person."

He looked away from me, out to the garden below us, as he laughed shortly. "You and I aren't so very different."

"You and I are very different, Sir," I insisted.

He sighed loudly, but it was interrupted part of the way through with another short laugh. "You've spent the majority of your life being forced to show respect to people who have no respect for you."

"And you've spent the entirety of yours being shown respect when you deserve none." My hand shot to my mouth and I added, "I apologize for my words, Sir, but I do not appreciate being compared to a monster." When he chuckled, I demanded, "Why do you keep laughing at me?"

It took him a moment to respond, but he eventually straightened himself up. I watched as he took in a deep breath. He then released it and closed the several feet of space separating us.

I forced myself to stare at his face as he approached, but in my peripherals, I saw one of his hands reaching out.

It stopped when it was halfway to me, and then he brought it back to himself.

He was smiling in a closed way, but there was no humor on his face or in his tone when he said, "It was nice to finally hear it." There was nothing but sadness in his expression and sincerity in his voice. "Thank you."

I opened my mouth to speak, but I could not think of anything that would be appropriate to say. He did not give me a chance to say anything at all, had I been able to formulate something. Perhaps there was finally nothing else to be said.

Without another word, he turned and left me standing on the balcony alone, but it was not five seconds before Agatha barreled through the doorway toward me.

"My flower," she said quickly, "what in the world has happened tonight?" She appeared sleepy yet startlingly alert, and seeing her face suddenly drained me of all energy.

I sat down hard, leaning my back against the railing and staring sightlessly at the doorway in front of me. Agatha knelt down close, her face suddenly taking up the entirety of my sight.

"That Reaper," she went on when I said nothing. "He came to get me. He said you'd been touched inappropriately and likely needed me. And that boy—that's the Guard who's been speaking to you, isn't it? What was he thinking, following you out here while you were alone? Is that three times today that he's spoken to you alone?"

Her endless questions always exhausted me, but they could not compare to everything else currently taking up the space inside my head.

It took me a moment to truly meet her gaze. "Did he tell you what he did to the man who touched me?"

"The boy in the Guard?"

"The Reaper," I corrected.

She shook her head slowly, and her voice was hesitant when she asked, "What did he do?"

"He snapped the man's wrist, Aggie," I told her in disbelief.

"He broke a man's wrist because he touched you?" Each word sounded deliberate, as though she hadn't wanted the wrong one to fall from her mouth. The deep lines that appeared on her face when she was confused were so apparent now, even in the darkness.

"Yes," I whispered in response, feeling my own head shaking. That he'd done as much for the reason stated was the only explanation, but it sounded so different when spoken than it did inside my head. "Snapped it like a weak branch in a strong wind. Why would he do that?"

Several extended seconds of silence passed before she reached out and caressed my face. "I don't know, honey."

I was not afraid of her hands.

With my eyes, all I could see were the wrinkles on Agatha's face, but in my mind I saw something else entirely. There was a brief image of the Reaper, smiling at what he'd done to the man who had violated me. Then, the image was replaced by another, and all I could see was the sadness on his remarkably full lips when he'd thanked me for calling him a monster.

"I don't know."

CHAPTER FIVE

THE HEAVY PRICE OF GIFTS

SLEEP DID NOT COME EASY to me that night.

Upon realizing the remainder of my chores had been attended to by someone else, at our leader's insistence, I'd lain down next to Agatha on our shared bed and closed my eyes. For a time, I attempted to distract myself with guilty thoughts of all the extra work that had been done by others on my account, whether assigned or not, but even those thoughts couldn't keep my mind from going where it wanted.

I thought of the Reaper.

I thought of his smile that seemed so easy to put onto the face of a monster.

But he did not have a monster's face, did he?

He did not look like a monster in the slightest. The young man in the Guard kept telling me lies, but everything about the Reaper was a lie. His smiles, his laughter . . . they only hid the evil that lurked inside him.

Could a monster fake sadness? I was certain I hadn't been mistaken about what I'd seen in his eyes.

I understood that he was pure evil. I wholeheartedly knew it to be true. I simply could not fathom why he would waste the efforts of his lies on me.

Ten years of invisibility and, in one day, I was being filled with lies from everyone. Lies from the young man in the Guard, lies from our leader, and lies from the Reaper.

Why?

Eventually sleep came, no matter the distractions. Though when it came and went, I wished it hadn't.

I woke up gasping, having dreamt the Reaper had forced me to watch him break the necks of everyone in the House. He smiled as I looked upon the dead bodies of the people I knew, and he told me again that we were not so very different.

Of course, my stirring woke Agatha.

When she asked me what I'd dreamt, I lied to her, telling her the man who had touched me had plagued my mind. And, in a sense, his action had led to what it had. I let her play with my hair as she assured me that, thanks to the evil Reaper, she was sure the man had gone from our House. His wrist would need tending to, after all.

I did eventually at some point succumb and wake once more. There was no gasping when I woke, though horror came in a different form. I thought hard on the images that had played inside my unconscious mind.

The Reaper again. Though that time, he'd touched my face with his hands of death, but he did not kill me the way he killed everyone else he touched. He touched my face, and he smiled at me in such a way that I'd never seen before.

The horror existed, showing itself not in gasps but tears that fell from my eyes, my gaze on the grey stone wall in front of me. I worked through it as well as I could, realizing Reapers were far more evil than I had ever been told.

I had never dreamt of a boy before. I had never dreamt of being touched in any way I found to be pleasant. If the Reaper was putting those thoughts inside my head . . . he was more of a devil than I ever could've known. Agatha had told me what happened when men touched women. She had told me everything unpleasant about it. It was not something to smile about, not even in a dream.

I laid awake for the short remainder of the night, not wanting my unconscious mind to be invaded once more, worried what other forms of trickery he would put inside my head. I laid there hoping, more than anything in the world, that he would be gone shortly after the sun rose in the sky.

I hoped with everything inside me that I would never have to see him again.

WHEN IT WAS AN ACCEPTABLE HOUR to be out of bed, I snuck out carefully, not wanting to wake Agatha. For a moment before dressing myself, I stared down at her face.

In the peacefulness of her sleep, her wrinkles weren't visible at all. I was ashamed of myself for putting those wrinkles there, for adding stress to her already troubled life, for lying to her repeatedly for no explicable reason. I was so unbelievably ashamed of myself for not being a better daughter.

She deserved so much more.

Agatha had laundered my clothes and set them out for me at some point during last night's festivities. I always loved the feeling of putting on freshly laundered clothing. By the end of the day, soaked with sweat, clothes felt like nothing more than a second, perpetually dirty skin. I despised not feeling clean.

Time passing and altered circumstances could change so many things, but they did not change everything. My dislikes had remained the same from one life to the next, though the list had grown much longer over the years.

What's made you have such distaste for being a small bit dirty? Didn't you say you'd been out in the wilderness with him? Surely you got dirty out there, far more than here. Didn't you?

I spared one last glance for Agatha before going about my day as usual, knowing she would be up as soon as I left the room.

For two hours, I did what I always did. Then I went back to my quarters.

When I opened the door, I noticed Agatha had also gotten the black dress laundered, though I couldn't imagine when she'd had time. Perhaps I'd been far more shaken than I'd realized, as she must've left the room to at the very least hand it off to someone else after I'd taken it off.

I folded the dress neatly and stuck it inside the bag. When I was satisfied that I'd forgotten nothing, I grabbed the bag and note and began making my way to our leader's office.

I enjoyed the lack of clicking as I walked, along with the silence throughout the entire House. Everything was precisely as it was supposed to be or would soon be that way.

Upon my arrival at his office, I informed a Guard that I was there to return the bag and its contents if he was awake to receive them.

He was awake, which was a relief. I wouldn't part with the bag unless I gave it to him directly because I would not allow myself to be beaten for someone else misplacing it.

There was only a small bit of formalities and exchanges—the asking for him, the inquiry inside the room, the return then allowance.

I stepped inside. Once the door was firmly closed behind me, I said, "I've come to return these to you, Sir."

He was sitting at his desk, staring down at more papers and absentmindedly rubbing at his forehead with several of his fingers.

"What?" He almost shook himself, as if waking up when already awake. "Oh, yes."

He stood and walked over to me while I contemplated over him acting surprised yet again at my presence despite having closed the door quite loudly just before and him conversing with the Guard on my presence just before that. Perhaps he tuned out things he didn't wish to hear.

Perhaps he truly was faking nothing on his focus and could direct it so quickly and so thoroughly.

Odd.

Rather than take the bag when he came close enough to do so, he stared hard at my face. "You look as though you've had a sleepless night."

I attempted a warm smile. "I could say the same for you, Sir." I closed my eyes for a moment. "I apologize, Sir. I in no way meant for that to sound rude."

He chuckled a little at me, which made my face burn in embarrassment.

He said, "I haven't slept at all yet, actually. I spent nearly the entire night waiting for that ridiculous party to be over so I could work."

I narrowed my eyes at him, confused.

He smiled, in a very odd way. "Is that difficult for you to believe? That I would rather work, or that I work at all?"

I opened my mouth to speak, but I stopped myself from saying what I would have. I held the bag out and repeated, "I've come to return these to you, Sir."

He snorted. "He told me you have a spectacular way with words."

"I apologize, Sir," I began slowly, "but I'm unaware of whom you're referring to."

"Chase," he said, which made no sense to me.

I shook my head before he clarified.

"The Reaper."

I forced a tight smile at that because it was the only passably acceptable thing that came to mind. When I realized that he wasn't going to take the things in my hands, I brought them back to myself.

"Do you like him?"

My brow furrowed. "Excuse me, Sir?"

"The Reaper," he said again. "Do you like him?"

"No, Sir."

"No?" He grinned at me, but I was unsure of the earnestness in it.

I took a deep breath before repeating, "No, Sir."

He narrowed his eyes slightly. I couldn't tell if he was disappointed, amused, or something else entirely. "He's taken quite an interest in you."

"I am sorry to hear that, Sir."

"You already know that though, don't you?"

Before I could do more than shake my head a few times, he spoke again in a different tone.

"Do not play so ignorant with me. With all the events that transpired last night, I'm sure you know. You are not as unintelligent as you make yourself out to be."

I clenched my jaw for a moment. "Am I going to be punished, Sir?"

"Punished?" he asked, his tone returning to light and airy, yet firm. "Punished for what?"

"For causing a disturbance last night, Sir. I apologize, but I am not aware of how the situation should've been handled. I've never had anything of that nature happen to me, Sir."

His tone was either caring or apologetic—at least in sound—when he said, "I believe the experience itself was punishment enough. Don't you agree?"

I looked away and replied tightly. "Yes, Sir."

"Would you like to sit down?"

"Sit . . . *down*, Sir?" I asked, bemused.

"Yes. I've been on my feet for far—" He stopped speaking immediately when he reached out to touch my arm and I flinched away, dropping the bag to the floor.

"I apologize, Sir," I said quickly. My left hand unwittingly went over my heart, which seemed to be beating out of my chest, and my right shot out in front of me in precaution. I hoped I hadn't broken anything, though if the sound were any indication, I suspected the small mirror had shattered.

He did not move nor say anything for several extremely long seconds.

"Are you that afraid of being touched?" He seemed quite stunned.

I pursed my lips together and said nothing, wrapping my arms across my front and grasping hold of my shirt on either side.

He frowned deeply. "I'm inclined to believe you were dishonest with me when I asked you whether or not you'd been taken advantage of and then again just now."

"I did not lie to you about that, Sir," I told him a little more loudly than I should have. "Last night was the first time a man has ever touched me in that way."

He watched me, likely attempting to figure out whether I truly was lying to him. He leaned down, putting his face too close to mine and I realized my body was shaking, not necessarily in fear but something remarkably close to it.

"Will you tell me?" he asked, his voice near a whisper.

I felt my forehead scrunching in confusion.

"If someone hurts you, will you tell me?"

I looked away from him, urgently wiping away a falling tear as I responded with, "No, Sir." It was only then that I realized the extent of my impropriety. I held my head up and rested my arms at my sides, but I could not force the stiffness from my form.

"If you truly need something, I would like for you to speak with me about it."

"I would not bother you, Sir," I told him, averting my gaze.

What a ridiculous offer.

After a long moment spent with the heavy feeling of him analyzing me, he straightened up and took several large steps away. "I'm reassigning you," he said in a businesslike manner.

"I don't wish to be a server, Sir. I'm afraid I wouldn't be able to do the job properly." After having seen them as the night had worn on, I *knew* I couldn't.

He turned his back to me. "I've asked our special guest to stay with us for a time before being sent on his next mission."

I felt my stomach drop, and I put both my hands over my face, attempting to hide my reaction. Surely this could not . . .

"Since he's taken such an interest in you, I thought it would be appropriate if I assigned you to him."

Hearing the words felt like the weight of the entire world had been dropped on me. He either ignored the strangled sob that barely lived for an instant inside my throat before choking itself, or he simply hadn't heard it.

"You're to ensure he has everything he could possibly want while he is in our House. Is that a problem?" His voice sounded much closer to me than it had a few moments before.

I took a deep breath and removed my hands from my face, wiping more tears that had accidentally fallen from my eyes on the way.

"No, Sir," I said, gritting my teeth. I forced out . . . "No problem at all, Sir."

He nodded. "That's good." He turned away from me again, walking away and briefly fiddling around with something on his desk. Then he returned, holding a book out to me.

When I made no move to take it, he stepped even closer.

"I don't want that, Sir." I said the words then clenched my jaw so tightly that I worried my teeth might break.

He analyzed my face. "You're not lying." A few seconds passed. "That was our deal. I told you if I was satisfied with you, you could have it."

"I don't want it, Sir." My breathing began coming in ragged spurts as I struggled to get a grasp on myself.

Softly, he said, "If you don't want to think of it as payment, think of it as a gift."

"I'm afraid I cannot take it, even then, Sir." I looked straight into his eyes, inadvertently noticing the coloring was not unlike mine. Perhaps I'd not realized what mine looked like until the small mirror had shown me. "Your gifts come with too heavy a price, Sir."

"I am sorry you feel that way." I did not care how sincere his voice sounded. I had already discerned that he was a very skilled liar.

"Is there someplace else you wish for me to put these, Sir?" I gestured at the items I'd dropped on the floor.

"There is fine."

I nodded.

Before I could turn to leave, I heard, "Is your back properly healed?"

"I don't know, Sir."

"I would like for you to keep the medicine."

"I would rather not, Sir," I told him, my voice sounding passably restrained.

He let me turn away then, and he allowed me to get all the way over to the door with my hand outstretched toward it before he spoke again.

"He is in room number four."

I balled my hand into a fist where it hung suspended in the air, staring at the door while my hand shook in the small amount of space between it and the rest of my body. I ignored my fingernails digging into the flesh of my palms. I took in a deep breath and turned back to face him.

"You keep pretending to show me kindness and then condemning me," I began, shocked by both my words and my tone. "I'm simply failing to understand why you would bother."

His eyes widened. I wasn't sure if it was due to my tone, my words, or simply the fact that I hadn't addressed him by title.

I forced a smile and mustered up as much pleasantness as I could find inside myself to say, "I very much hope you're able to sleep well, Sir."

And then I exited the room, not bothering to close the door behind me. The Guard would do that one thing for me, after all. I was not required nor permitted to clean our leader's office. I would not close the damned door.

Chapter Six

Reassignment

F I HAD SPOKEN IN SUCH A WAY to any other leader we'd had in the House before, I would've been punished for it. I likely would've been beaten worse than I was ever beaten for any of my excursions to the library.

As I was walking down the halls, dimly lit by lanterns attached to the mortar between the stone of the walls, I justified my behavior with our leader by telling myself he deserved to be spoken to in that way.

But did bad deserve bad in turn? Was it all right to defend yourself when—to everyone else—your own person was not yours to defend?

I knew what I was, and he had deserved it. He deserved worse.

I would've preferred a beating to the punishment I was receiving. I did not even know why I was being punished. I had already been penalized by him for the library and there seemed to be an understanding that I would not return there so long as he was in power, so I failed to see what, exactly, this was truly about. It was bad enough, being forced to tend to wicked people day in and day out, but to be assigned to a Reaper?

I most certainly would've preferred the beating.

Back at my quarters, I permitted myself to cry without the restraints of forced quietness, though I was quiet enough on my own with or without them. I would allow myself a few short minutes of the freedom of it, to release my frustrations and fear, and then I would do my new job without complaint.

That was how Agatha found me—curled up in a ball on top of our stiff, shared bed with my face buried in the flimsy blanket.

"My flower!" she shrieked.

I straightened myself up quickly, sitting rigid as a board and wiping at my face. She was perched on the edge of the bed by the time I managed to fully regain my composure.

"What's happened?"

"I don't wish to talk about it just yet," I told her, hoping she would not press it. "I need to calm myself. Speaking about it will only make things indefinably worse."

She pursed her lips together into a hard line but nodded her head as though she understood. I watched her stand and walk over to the door. I fully expected her to leave so I could carry out the remainder of my fit in peace. Instead, she looked through the door once she'd opened it and said, "Now is probably not a good time."

"Who are you speaking to?" I asked, baffled and wary.

"Camden."

"Who?" I'd never heard the name.

"The boy in the Guard."

I believed I could scream then, at every person in this wretched House. I stood and came close to stomping my way over to the door. I didn't believe I'd ever stomped before in my life, even as a child.

"What are you doing here, Sir?" I demanded.

He opened his mouth to speak, and I watched his cheeks redden as he turned to Agatha. It looked as if he were pleading with her.

She said, "He came and spoke with me about something."

"Oh?" I asked, hearing a small laugh coming out of my mouth. "Pray tell, what could he possibly speak to you about, given how high and mighty our Guard is in comparison to such lowly property?"

"*Aster!*"

When I said nothing as I waited expectantly for her to answer my question, she sighed loudly.

She said, calmer, "He came to speak with me about you."

My eyes narrowed at her. "What about me?"

He drew my attention back to him with, "I would like to spend time with you."

I could feel myself gaping at the preposterousness of it all.

He added, "Supervised, of course."

"Why?" I paused before adding, "Sir."

He looked at Agatha in a pleading way again, and I heard her say, "Go on. Tell her what you told me."

I wondered then if it were possible for cheeks to turn redder than his currently were. "I find you quite beautiful, Miss."

"Why do you keep *lying* to me, Sir?" I nearly shouted at him.

Agatha put a hand on my shoulder and spoke apologetically. "I am truly sorry for her behavior. I fear she's heard too many stories of the horrors in our world, and she is very mistrusting of men."

"Don't you speak to him as if I'm not here, Aggie," I snapped. "Not you, of all people."

She said nothing to that, though I'd not expected nor wanted her to.

I took several deep breaths, calming myself so I could deal with this situation in the proper way.

"Understand, Sir," I began slowly so he could process my words appropriately as I stared straight into his dark eyes, "that my time is not mine to give and that anything you believe you can get from me will not be given. You should find a way to take back whatever interest you've lost to me, because I can assure you . . . I have nothing to offer. And I have far less that I'm willing to part with."

I for only a few seconds watched him try to process.

I then looked down at the floor for a moment, shaking my head in outright disbelief. "If you'll excuse me." I shrugged off Agatha's hand and maneuvered past the boy, ensuring I in no way touched him, hoping I'd just put an end to the harassment. "I've been reassigned, and I have work to do."

"Reassigned?" Agatha said as I hastily made my way from our room. "Reassigned to do *what*?"

Her voice faded as I walked down the long corridor that held all the servants' rooms, and I did not acknowledge her at all.

I knew she was staring at my back as I walked away. When I reached the set of stone stairs that would take me back aboveground, I found myself trying not to think about a past life.

No matter how unbearable a situation was, it was preferable to chasing phantoms in my head.

I'D NOT EXPECTED TO BE HAPPY while making my way to room number four. Not happy, exactly, but relieved to be escaping the combined madness of the young man in the Guard and Agatha. I wondered briefly if I was going mad myself. The frustration and confusion of it was maddening enough that I worried it was in fact causing some sort of internal harm and alteration to me—something internally detrimental opposed to external.

As I walked, carrying a covered breakfast tray, I told myself that my day simply could not get any worse than it already was. It wasn't asking for worse to try; it was simple fact.

I had come to terms with my assignment to the Reaper for the extent of his stay. I could handle that, and I could hope he would leave quickly. He had his own job to do, after all. He couldn't stay here forever. That meant it would have to be over at some point or another. Knowing as much, reminding myself, was certainly something to be pleased about.

I assumed he would be gone the instant I'd learned whatever lesson it was that our leader was attempting to teach. That was not any belief that I was of such value, only an assuredness that this was both punishment and an endeavor at *teaching*. I would try my hardest to discover what that lesson was in order to learn it and speed up his departure.

To make it easier, I tried to imagine the Reaper was just a young man staying in our House and absolutely nothing more.

He was just a young man, not a murdering monster.

I paused in front of his door with my hand outstretched to knock.

It cannot get any worse, I reminded myself.

I took a deep breath, held it, and I knocked.

I heard him shuffling around with what sounded to be haste inside, and then the door opened.

"I already told—" he began and then stopped immediately.

I felt my jaw drop, and I struggled to keep the tray from falling to the floor and making a mess I would be required to clean, as it felt all at once that my hands along with the rest of me lost ability to simply continue being as they were.

I had never seen a man with no shirt on before, apart from my father once or twice as a child. Not ever. I hardly noticed the strap containing a knife on the inside of his left arm or the numerous, random scars covering what I could see of his partially exposed body. I *did* notice it all, though in an oddly distant sort of way. I was nothing more, or less, than utterly stunned.

It took me far too long to look away. He had already vacated the entryway and then returned before I could force myself to look down at the floor rather than at him, as my gaze had for some reason followed him as he'd gone then returned. I hadn't been able to stop it, as I hadn't been able to fully comprehend it was doing so until after it had already been done.

I wanted to apologize for finding him in such a state, but no sound would come out of my mouth despite how hard I tried to force it.

He said, "I'm sorry."

It drew my gaze back up to his face. My eyes felt like they were ripping apart at the edges and I wished, so desperately, that I could make them return to normalcy. The fact that he was fully clothed did not take the mental image away.

"I didn't know it was you. Your stride is different in those shoes."

"I brought you breakfast, Sir," I said quickly, holding the tray out and staring at it. If he was not going to mention my lapse in composure, I certainly wasn't going to do so either.

"I thought we were done with the *Sir*?"

He was smiling when I looked at him again, and I had an errant thought of wondering if he could hear my heart pounding.

"Come in." He stepped aside, motioning for me to enter.

"I would . . . *rather not*, Sir." My voice sounded much calmer than I was, which sent relief flooding through me. Perhaps I appeared the same—calmer than I was.

His brow furrowed. "I won't hurt you."

I forced a nod and stepped past him into his room.

I fought against the shivers threatening to run down my spine when I passed too close to him.

And then, I fought against the nearly overwhelming panic and fear welling inside my stomach when he closed the door behind us.

Alone with the same Reaper twice in less than a full day. Had I been wrong in thinking it couldn't get any worse? At least it was no longer dark, but that only meant he could kill me more quickly if he decided to. Quicker and surely with more efficiency. I would have to be very careful and just do my job. I wasn't certain that contemplating over which would be better or worse—quick and efficient or not—would in any way aid in that.

I ensured my voice was polite to ask, "Where would you like me to place this?"

I could not do my job properly if I was worrying about him killing me. He either would or would not, and there was absolutely nothing I could do past being careful and respectful. There was no point in thinking of it.

Don't think of it.

"I'll take it." He stepped close.

I held the tray out as far as I could. He didn't touch me at all when he took it from my hands, not even an accidental brushing.

"I watched everyone while it was being prepared," I said as he began to step away.

He stopped moving and turned back to look at me, cocking his head to the side in a similar manner to what he'd done the night before. Slowly, a smile spread across his face, which only furthered the strangeness of the action. "Did you?"

"Yes, Si—"

I stopped speaking when he shook his head quickly.

I cleared my throat and tried again. "Yes, so that I could assure you it was not poisoned."

He smiled widely at me, different in some small way than the smile that had already been there.

I looked toward a wall. "I didn't believe you would eat it otherwise."

"What did you think I was getting ready to do, just now?"

"Pretend," I replied, still speaking to the wall.

"Why would I waste my time?" Amusement was apparent in his voice.

"I've been failing to understand why several people have wasted their time doing certain things, as of late." I brought my gaze back to him, and I discovered that I did not have to make myself smile at him to add, "You pretending to eat the food I've given you would make more sense to me than most other things."

When I realized I was still smiling at him, and that he was still smiling at me, I turned away again and cleared my throat.

I asked, "Would you like to tell me a time when you'll be out, so I can tend to your room?"

"I don't plan on being out very much." He moved and sat down at a desk between two windows against the wall opposite the door. The heavy, embellished drapes were all completely removed from the windows, letting light spill freely into the space of the room. I didn't know where they were, only that they were supposed to be hanging and were not.

I spent a moment glancing around, attempting to find the drapes. "Oh." They were nowhere in the open. "When would you prefer me to do it?"

"Now's as good a time as any."

"Oh," I heard myself say again. "I . . . I'm really not allowed to do that, Si—"

"Don't," he said, cutting me off. "If you have something you need to do in here, you can do it now."

"All right," I said quietly. I moved over to his bed—the blankets were a mess, completely askew—and hesitated.

It was strange, thinking that a monster needed to sleep.

"What are you doing?" His tone did not sound rude at all, only curious.

I found myself wondering how long, exactly, I had spent paused near his bed to have drawn his attention. It hadn't felt long, and yet my head felt quite funny and I was unsure if that would alter my perception of time.

I glanced over at him and answered with, "Thinking."

"About what?" His lips turned up in a slight smile.

I watched him take a forkful of eggs into his mouth and chew, and I did not answer him until I'd watched him swallow it. Then, I found myself smiling again, just a little.

I told him, "I would rather not say."

"Okay."

"*Okay*?" Confused, I shook my head. "You're not going to insist I tell you?"

"No." The small chuckle that followed left me almost as baffled as the singular word.

I took in a deep breath and let it out, finding myself perplexed as I pulled the sheets off his bed.

Perhaps taking care of a monster wouldn't be as bad as I'd anticipated, if he would allow me certain things I was not normally allowed. Not being required to answer a direct question was unheard of.

"That's not necessary," he said, bringing me back from my thoughts.

I ceased, wondering if I'd done something wrong. "What's not necessary?"

"I'm just going to sleep on it and mess it up again. There's no point for you to waste your time."

"Yes, but it will be made fresh for you to mess up again," I told him, laughing lightly. *Wasting time.* . . . What a thing to say. "I must do it. I'm just typically not seen when I do these things."

"Don't the maids normally do it?" he asked through another bite of food.

I stopped and eyed him, puzzled. "The maids?" I shook my head for a moment, lost, until . . . "*Oh*, you mean the servers?" I laughed genuinely before saying, "No. They only pretend to." My body stiffened as soon as I'd finished saying the words. "I shouldn't have said that."

Would he tell our leader I had let the information slip? I should not have been talking to anyone, given the looseness of my tongue as of late, least of all a Reaper. Very least of all this Reaper.

"Do you do everything here?" he asked me seriously.

"Not everything, no," I replied.

"So what do the servers actually do?"

I'd already let the secret of their near-uselessness slip, so I felt my face scrunching in amusement when I replied. "Look pretty."

I did not look at him again for a moment. I stopped moving when I realized that, so long as he was on the other side of the room, he was remarkably easy to speak to. He was the only person to ever insist I drop titles while speaking to him, the only one who had ever spoken to me as though I were . . . not what I was here. Perhaps that was the issue with my tongue, or at least part of it.

"May I ask you a question, Si—" That time, I prevented myself from saying the rest of the word without any sort of encouragement from him.

"Sure." He was so baffling.

"You don't have to answer, of course, I was just curious who you were expecting me to be."

When I saw his expression, I realized he didn't have the vaguest idea what I was talking about.

"When I first arrived, you opened the door already speaking, as if you were expecting me to be someone else. I simply wondered who."

"A group of your servers."

He had answered my invasive question. He hadn't told me I had no right to ask. I was so stunned that it took me a long moment to respond.

"A group of servers?" I involuntarily took a step closer, thinking there was surely some sort of misunderstanding.

"Yes, they were pestering me on and off all night." He shook his head in clear frustration. "I had to turn them away three times."

"They shouldn't be bothering you." My voice went firm, as I couldn't believe anyone had done such a thing. "Did they tell you what they wanted?"

He looked away from me, down at his food. "They made their intentions quite clear."

"What was it they needed so badly that they came to your room multiple times through the night in an attempt to get it?" I was nearly horrified over both the treatment and the idiocy. I could not imagine anything that would be so important to bother a guest for. And what sort of imbecile would pester a Reaper?

I watched his gaze linger on the bed before returning to my face. He responded with, "Something I wasn't willing to give them."

It took a moment, but it came.

My hand shot to my mouth as I realized what he was getting at, and I rubbed it with my fingernail to pretend the action had been intentional instead of the furthest thing from it. Hurriedly, I finished gathering the blankets, and I nearly tripped over them as I walked to the door. Them, or perhaps myself. Perhaps something else.

I rarely tripped over anything.

I stopped when I reached the door. "Have you decided how long you'll be staying with us, Sir?"

"I'm undecided." That time, he didn't tell me not to call him Sir. I didn't know if he could choose when to leave or if he was entirely at our leader's mercy. I wondered if he wanted to go and simply wasn't permitted.

I tried hard not to wonder what might happen to me, should he discover that his being required to stay was in any way tied to me.

I nodded stiffly and forced a smile. "I'll be in and out periodically to do my job. I'll try my best not to be a hindrance to your life here, however long that may be. Just overlook me while I'm in the room and pretend I'm not here."

"If that's what you want."

I looked down at the floor and heard myself release a breath of air. I almost wondered if it was a laugh, but it did not feel like one.

"I prefer being invisible, Sir. It's the only thing I'm allowed to have in my life." My voice was nearly a whisper when I added, "I very much hope you enjoy your stay with us, Sir."

"Thank you."

I blinked hard at the floor and forced another smile onto my face for him. But no matter how hard I tried . . . I could not bring myself to look at him again.

CHAPTER
SEVEN

GIVING TIME

GATHA NEARLY LOST HER MIND that night when I told her about my reassignment. I was not surprised. I'd been expecting and preparing myself for her reaction. Those preparations had been a decent distraction from the reality of my situation.

Reassignments were a rare occurrence here, but when they happened, they were usually not so bad as being singlehandedly responsible for the needs and comfort of a Reaper. It was far more often than not leaders failing to grasp that they surely weren't going to figure out a more efficient way of running the House. When they'd be gone, all would for the most part return to the way it had been. Most didn't care to bother and certainly didn't bother to care. Or were unable, for all the reasons they were.

Agatha's hysteria over my situation and new responsibilities had been quite understandable.

"He was perfectly polite, Aggie," I assured her of the Reaper. "I saw him several times today, bringing him food and the like. He hardly said a word to me."

I did not tell her about the interactions I'd had with him when tending to his room the first time or that his politeness had seemed both genuine and beyond the word *perfectly*.

The other instances I'd gone in there, he seemed to be going along with pretending I didn't exist, as I had asked. Mostly, he simply stared out the window. Once, he was writing what I assumed was a letter, but even then, he seemed distracted by the window and what lay beyond it. He sat there at the desk for a long while with the pen in his hand, bleeding ink onto the paper where it rested. I'd believed at first that it had been to avoid me and my presence. By the end of the day . . .

I did not believe so.

"You were *alone* with him?" she shrieked, aghast.

"He insisted I do whatever work I needed to, when I needed to do it." I sighed, quiet, trying to find some sort of internal fortitude to simply get through the conversation. "He said he didn't plan on being out very often. I must do my job, Aggie, whether he leaves his room or not."

"All the stars in the sky." She sounded distant as she shook her head and stared off at nothing in particular. That she'd said what she had in the way she had gave me a better indication of her feelings on the matter. After several seconds had passed, she appeared to mostly come back to herself. "I was hoping you would never have to see him again."

I stared down at the bed. "As was I."

She drew my attention back to her, sounding disbelieving when saying, "I cannot *believe* you've had to be alone with him." She kept shaking her head.

"He was the one who came and retrieved you last night," I reminded her. "If there's one man in the world I don't worry about touching me, Aggie . . . it's him." I blinked hard several times, stunned by the words that had come out of my mouth, but he thus far had—

"Are you hearing yourself *speak*?" she demanded. "The monster is already getting inside your head. Don't you let him in, Aster. All evil does is destroy, so don't you *dare* let him in."

"I wouldn't allow *any* man inside my head, Agatha. You've made sure that I clearly understood just how evil all of them are, as if I required assistance in comprehending the non-complexities of men."

She recoiled as if I'd slapped her, but I did not feel guilty over my words. They were true, and I had meant no offense.

Slowly, she said, "They're not all evil, my flower."

"Most a lifetime of knowledge cannot be changed with a few contradictory words." I stared unseeingly in the direction of the unstable wooden chair in the corner of the room, only letting the beginning of that knowledge seep through before pushing it away.

I knew I'd had some confusion over the recent interactions. I knew that I was failing to understand certain things.

Understanding would come, I was sure. Men were simple creatures.

I knew they were. Life had shown me as much. No matter their variances . . .

I pulled myself from my thoughts, looking to Agatha. "I'm going to sleep. Love you, Aggie."

"I love you too, my flower." I heard sadness in her voice. I also saw it in her eyes, though whether the sadness was because of or for me . . .

I was unsure.

I faced the wall and cried silently. I simply could not tell Agatha that he was already inside my head. She would throw a fit, and no amount of fit-throwing could change what was.

The only thing that could change it was force of will. If I dreamt of him again, I would not acknowledge that I had. When I saw him, I would try my hardest to pretend he was invisible, too.

It was the only thing I could do to protect myself from him.

THE REAPER AND I fell into a strange sort of routine over the following month or so.

I would not have to knock on his door for him to know I was there. He never answered the door again with a harsh tone meant for someone who was not me, and he was always fully clothed. He would smile at me, and then he would step aside. I would enter his room and place his food on the desk. I did his laundry.

Before I watched the cooks prepare his dinner, I would stop by his room and place some paper and a pen on his desk. It was the only time I went there during the day that he wouldn't be inside.

I did not ask him where he would go daily at the same time.

He did not ask me if his food was poisoned. Eventually, I began preparing it myself. I was sure it didn't taste as good, but one could not have everything, and he never said a word about the difference. Yet I for some reason believed he knew there was one and what it was.

Sometimes, when I would pass by some of the server girls, they would laugh—most often some quiet thing, where they would make the sound and also whisper behind a hand being held in front of their mouths. Not always quiet at all though, and not always intended to be such, as I knew they were capable of speaking without being noticed should they wish. More than once, I overheard them call me a word I did not understand being applied to me. I would've been certain they were speaking of someone else if not for all the other indicators that assured me I was the subject. Their focus on me—or notice of me at all—was strange, but it gave me a great deal of new information to work through. I disregarded them beyond that, and I did my job.

It was remarkably easy to forget what he was, more so with every day that passed.

Every so often I would think I felt him watching me while I was gathering the things in his room, but he was never looking when I would check.

Eventually, I did not have to gather anything. Most mornings after a certain point, he would have the blankets from the bed put in a pile next to it. Some days they were folded, and some days they were not. I knew where he liked to put his dirty clothes—neatly placed next to the bath. Several days in, he'd started putting them next to the blankets, although I knew he did not like them there. It was the way he'd first looked at them. The way he'd first looked at me after having done it.

I could not understand why he did those things. Initially, I'd assumed his intentions were for me to vacate his room as quickly as possible. But as soon as those things that cut my time in his room short had been put into place, he began finding other things for me to do. One day, he informed me that he'd smudged a pane of glass while staring outside. He'd helped me clean all of them, though I tried to stop him—insisting that it was my job—and he'd said nothing else. The next day, it was smudged again. And then again, on the next.

He liked having coffee in the mornings, black with no sweetener and no cream. But on Saturday evenings, he liked having it with both.

He was strangely particular about where things were located in his room.

Once, when he was out, I nudged the desk that he wrote at a couple inches to the left. The next time I came in, it was back where it had been. I found it amusing and, some days, I did it just to see if he would ever voice frustration with me over it.

He never even mentioned it, but he would always move it back to the way he wanted it.

I'd discovered the location of the hidden drapes quite early in. They were folded in a wardrobe, but only during the day. The first Saturday evening, when bringing his coffee as requested, I'd found them hanging in their rightful place. It took me several days to come to the conclusion that the strangeness of it must've had something or other to do with his training. And it *did* make sense, when thinking on the way things were visible in light and dark. The variances.

That gave me a great deal to think on.

Nearly a whole month had passed before he left one of his weapons out—a knife in plain view on his nightstand. I felt his gaze on me heavily when I spotted it, so I looked away quickly and pretended not to have noticed the knife at all.

It was the only time I'd ever seen one of his weapons off his person, and I rarely saw him wear more than one or two easily visible knives. I did not know where he kept them when they were not on him, but I knew from the first time I'd seen him that he had quite a lot.

I assumed they were hidden exceptionally well, though I did not actively seek them out.

I looked at him sometimes, but not for any longer than a few seconds at a time and no more than a couple of instances per visit. I knew he was aware of it, though I tried to convince myself that I was being perfectly inconspicuous. It was sort of a game I played with myself—trying to see how many new details I could discover about him while he wasn't looking.

His hair had been shaved quite close to his head when he'd first arrived, but it had grown out since. It was almost entirely black, like the ravens I would occasionally see through the windows.

He had one freckle on his nose, two on his forehead, and several on his cheeks and arms that I'd not been able to count properly.

There was a scar on his chin, but I did not ask him how he received it, nor did I let myself wonder about it. It was the only scar on his face, although I knew he had many more that could not be seen so easily.

I liked to imagine that, when he looked at me and pretended that he was not, he was doing the same thing I was.

Every night when I went to bed, I would remind myself of what he was. He was a devil with a beautiful face. That was all. I'd stolen enough glances at his face to know that I found it to be . . .

Handsome.

Agatha accused me of being distracted, and I most assuredly was, but not in the ways she assumed. I allowed him inside my head when I was around him, but only to a certain extent. I wanted to understand how he could pretend to be something so far away from what he truly was and why I felt safer in the presence of a monster than I'd ever felt around anyone else in this House. I hadn't felt safe for a single moment since my father had disappeared. Yet, there were moments when inside the room with him . . .

I felt quite safe.

Logic fought itself from opposing sides inside me, neither having more strength than the other and yet the same one most always prevailing. It just couldn't kill its opponent entirely.

I nearly always dreamt of him.

Some nights, I would dream of the devil. I would dream of him going on his death missions. I would dream of him killing everyone in the House. He never killed me.

Some nights, I would dream of the other side of him, of the person he pretended to be around me. I would dream of his smile.

The nights were split down the middle in frequency.

At least once a day, Agatha would ask me if I had apologized to Camden—the boy in the Guard. Every day, I would tell her that, no, I had not.

She relentlessly encouraged me to speak to him and told me there was no harm in giving a person a small amount of my time, under the appropriate circumstances.

She did not understand that I was already doing as much.

I wondered, during my nearly silent interactions with the Reaper, if Agatha actually understood what giving a person your time meant. I wouldn't have, before. I also wondered often on what *appropriate circumstances* meant, whether they could vary from person to person. Her explanation for them made no sense to me, not even when I tried rewording the question in the hope of getting a better answer.

Still, her continual prodding on the matter eventually wore on me. It had taken me a while to see that she was not going to let it go. It had also taken me a while to realize that something could potentially be learned.

So, after a month or so with the Reaper, I sought out Camden. I could spare a few short moments to see if it felt the same. It would please Agatha, but I was mostly doing it to satisfy my own curiosity on the matter.

I found him standing outside the library.

"Have you come here to see if I'll let you inside, Miss?" he asked me flatly.

"No, Sir," I told him, feeling my forehead scrunching in confusion. "I've come here to apologize."

The Guard standing beside Camden sneered. "Apologize? What could she have to apologize to you for?"

I should not have been in any way stunned at or by his behavior.

"Look at her. Being around that Reaper has twisted her mind. Forgetting her place, that one. Perhaps she needs a good reminding."

I forced a smile at the floor and said, "I apologize for wasting your time, Sir."

Camden said nothing, though the other Guard snorted, unwittingly reinforcing what I'd already assumed.

I'd made it down the hall and into the next before I heard Camden's clunky boot steps running up behind me. I despised the sound of it.

I stopped, turning to him.

"I'm sorry for his rudeness, Miss.

"You say you're sorry to me now, yet you said nothing to contradict him, Sir."

"I did once you'd gone." He ran a hand through his slicked-back hair.

"Yet you said nothing in my presence," I stated. "Sir."

"I didn't believe it would be respectful to say the things I said to him in front of a lady."

I was unable to conceal my amusement when I informed him, "I believe you and I have very differing opinions about what is respectful and what is not, Sir." I paused for a moment. "I have to be going now."

The corners of his lips began tugging upward. "To do your job with the Reaper?"

"Yes, Sir."

He chuckled a little beneath his breath before walking away, back in the direction of the library. I watched him go, trying to understand his behavior, but I did not care that I was being laughed at. I'd grown somewhat accustomed to it. I had a job to do, and there was nothing humorous about it.

I carried on about my way.

The Reaper opened the door when I arrived at his room, like he always did. He held it open expectantly, waiting for me to come inside, but I did not. I froze, watching his lips curl up in that slow and easy smile of his.

The same thing, and yet so different.

"What is it?" he asked.

"Do you allow everyone to call you by your name, Sir?"

He laughed shortly. "No."

"And would you still allow it of me?" I asked curiously.

He nodded, and I was going to ask him why he would, but I had expended my allowance of speaking to him for the day. I did not feel as though I'd wasted it.

"Are you going to stand out there for the entire day, or are you going to come inside?" he asked, his voice light. He eyed me curiously—still holding the doorknob—knowing I would enter and waiting for it.

Wordlessly, I stepped into the room, trying to ignore the strange, leaping sensation in my stomach. I did not know when I'd stopped shivering in fear around him, only that it had happened at some point.

It had stopped, and things had changed.

Though nothing had changed.

Had it?

THAT NIGHT, WHILE LYING IN BED with Agatha, I found myself staring at the stone wall and wondering about something.

"Aggie?"

"Yes, my flower?" Her voice sounded strained.

I presumed it was my fault. Despite keeping talk off my reassignment as much as I was able, she worried enough that it had disrupted her ability to sleep in relative peace.

Steeling myself, I asked her the question. "Have you ever felt . . . *feelings* for a man before?"

"What?" She chortled. "You're asking me if I've ever been in love?"

I thought hard on that. I thought on the past, briefly. I thought on the circulating wives. One in particular stuck out inside my head —her looking at her husband and smiling at him in a different way than most seemed to.

I thought again on the past.

Briefly.

Only long enough.

"I suppose so."

"Why are you asking?"

"I'm simply curious."

There was a long pause before . . . "Are you in love?" Wariness was clear in her tone.

"No," I told her in disbelief, hearing a shocked sound escape from my mouth. I didn't even know what it was in that regard, past knowing the word and that it varied from the love one would have with their family. Love in general was such an irrelevant notion in my opinion. What I'd seen of it . . .

It was not a good thing.

Still . . . I was curious.

Agatha said, "I was once before, yes."

"You don't have to answer me, but . . . I'm just wondering if he treated you like what you were, or if he treated you like something else." A strange, unpleasant feeling was taking place in my stomach, like my insides were twisting.

"Something else?"

"Yes. Did he treat you like a servant or like a person?"

"Both," she answered quietly. I had only enough time to wonder how that could possibly be an answer before she cleared her throat and loudly said, "These questions have nothing to do with the Reaper, do they?"

"I spoke to Camden today," I told her. "I wanted to apologize for the way I'd behaved."

"*Did* you?" She instantly sounded both stunned and pleased. "How did it go?"

"Love you, Aggie," I whispered.

I heard her sigh as she patted down my hair. "I love you too, my flower."

I WAS IMPATIENT THE NEXT MORNING as I prepared the Reaper's food for him. The kitchen staff no longer voiced their opinions on the matter. I was glad for that. I was even impatient with walking to his room.

He opened the door just before I got to it. I didn't stop as I walked in, though I did pause to give him his breakfast rather than placing it at his desk. I heard the familiar click as he closed the door behind us, and I realized . . .

Some part of me enjoyed that sound.

I did not want to use up my two-sentence allowance first thing in the morning, but he broke the silence and forced me into it.

"What's wrong with you this morning?"

When I glanced over at him for an instant, I saw that his brow was furrowed and he'd not yet moved away from the doorway.

"Are you okay?"

I stopped as I was reaching down to grab the blankets, and I felt both corners of my mouth trying to tug themselves up. I wanted to ask him how he'd known something was different about me, but I already had my two sentences planned out and I would not waste them.

I turned to him so I could watch for signs of deception on his face. I was sure he could deceive me if he wanted to, but I had faith he would not.

"If I asked you a question, Sir, would you tell me the truth?"

"Yes," he said without hesitation. "Is this about my job?"

I opened my mouth to ask him why he thought I would inquire

about his job, but I quickly shut it again.

"It must be important, if you're not willing to waste your second sentence to ask me whether or not I would actually tell you about my job."

I pursed my lips together in an attempt to mask the reaction I had to his words.

He narrowed his eyes at me, grinning playfully. "It must be very important for you not to accuse me of keeping track of how many times you speak to me per day."

I stood there for what felt like a long while, rearranging my thoughts. I'd planned my second sentence out the night before and had been repeating it inside my head all morning. But now, looking at him, I wasn't certain I wanted the answer.

We watched one another inquisitively for a time before he finally moved from the doorway and set the breakfast tray on his desk. He stopped about ten paces away from me, which was the closest he ever came if he was not taking something from my hands.

"Aster, what's wrong?"

"You called me by my name." My voice shook.

I had never told him my name. I was never called by my name, apart from the other servants on the very rare occasion that I spoke to anyone other than Agatha. I was quite sure many of them didn't even know my name.

I was quite sure many of them didn't even know I existed.

Or hadn't. Until him and my reassignment.

"Yes," he said, and I thought I heard a tinge of amusement in his tone. "I'm sorry for causing you to waste your second sentence. I suppose you'll have to wait and ask me whatever it is you're wanting to know tomorrow." He chuckled before turning his back to me.

"Would you only have me call you by your name in private?" I blurted out. If I had been speaking to anyone else, my hand would've shot to my mouth. It didn't. It hung tightly at my side while I held my breath and stared at his back.

He turned around slowly, tilting his head at me. I'd grown quite used to seeing it. He seemed surprised, but I could not tell whether it was due to the fact that I'd gone past my sentence allotment or simply because of my forwardness. I couldn't understand the feelings churning inside me while I waited for an answer. I had never felt them before to know what they were.

He stepped closer to me than usual—eight paces away. I was not afraid of his proximity in the slightest, I realized, only his response. He smiled at me, although it didn't hold its usual mix of amusement and warmth. The amusement was gone.

"You can call me whatever you like, in front of anyone," he said believably. "I don't care."

"I'd be beaten for it," I reminded him, my voice shaking again.

I watched his jaw clench as he took four small steps closer to me. He shook his head. "Not while I'm here."

This reminded me he was a monster. I wondered if he'd said it strictly to remind me of the fact. But he had stepped closer, and even with the intense expression on his face . . . I was not afraid.

One word. There were so many questions I wanted to ask him, but nearly all of them could be boiled down to a single word. I had never heard such desperation in my voice as I did when it came out.

"*Why?*"

The hardness drained away from his face then. He closed his eyes and breathed in deeply, rubbing his face with his hands. I did not watch his hands in fear, as I had initially. I'd seen them do many things. I'd seen them write, and eat, and clean windows. I'd seen them touch his face and random things throughout his room. I had never seen him kill with those hands. When they dropped away from his face, he smiled at me.

"I think we've gone past our two," he said. His nose crinkled a little, and it made my stomach feel funny in some incomprehensible way. "We'll continue this tomorrow, if you'd like. I don't want you to look back and regret anything about it."

Though I did not understand fully, I understood enough to nod and carry on with what needed doing.

Later, when I felt his eyes on me and I turned to check, he did not pretend that he'd been doing something else. I would look, his expression would soften, and he would not look away. I knew with certainty then . . .

I'd not been imagining or mistaking him looking all those other times.

My heart felt like it was fluttering out of my chest all day, but I didn't know why.

That night, while lying in bed, I had a new question for Agatha.

"Aggie? What does it feel like? To be in love." I stared at the wall as I patiently waited for her answer.

She chuckled a little, I believed to herself, possibly reminiscing. "It feels like every part of you is floating away." There was a short pause before she hesitantly asked, "Why do you ask?"

"I was simply curious." It was not a lie.

I felt a tear slip from my eye as I realized . . . I was in love with the Reaper.

All the stars in the sky.

CHAPTER EIGHT

EMOTIONALLY COMPROMISED

THE NEXT MORNING, I remained in bed after waking, wanting to put off seeing the Reaper for as long as I possibly could. My revelation of the night before terrified me in more ways than I could fully grasp. Still, even if I spent five more minutes in bed, I had a job to do regardless of how I felt about it.

Then again, perhaps there was something I *could* do about it.

I jumped out of bed after being struck with the thought, making myself presentable as quickly as I could manage. I had to prevent myself from running all the way to my destination.

Outside the doors to the leader's office, two Guards stood, eyeing me suspiciously.

"I need to speak with him, Sirs," I told them, desperation and mania mingling together in my tone no matter how I tried to calm myself.

"He is very busy this morning," the one on the left said. "We've been ordered not to bother him for any reason."

"It's urgent, Sir." I spoke with more force than I'd intended, but I did not apologize and my hand did not shoot over my mouth.

"Urgent?" The other sneered. "What urgency could you possibly have?"

I said, "More than you, who stands outside a door doing nothing every day, Sir."

The first snorted, but the one I had directly insulted stepped closer with his hand held up to backhand me.

"What did you just say to me?" he snapped in utter disbelief, his hand still up, not yet having moved to make contact with me. I sincerely doubted that any servant had ever spoken to him in such a way.

Our leader burst through the door.

"What in the world is going on out here?" he demanded.

I looked past the Guard's arm and hand, finding our leader standing there with a stunned expression on his face.

He grabbed the Guard, turning him around quickly. "Were you about to attack her?"

"She insulted me, Sir," he said in justification.

"Did you deserve it?"

"W-What, Sir?"

"He did," the first Guard said.

I blinked hard several times over the lax response.

Our leader turned to me. "Now, what is this about?" He must not have noticed the informality, with the uproar of all else.

I quickly put my thoughts together and said, "I need to speak with you about something urgent, Sir."

"And did you tell them as much?"

I nodded. "I did, Sir."

"You told us not to bother you, Sir," the first stated. He had called him *Sir* that time.

"Yes, I informed you not to bother me with nonsense, but wouldn't you find it odd that she needed to speak to me so desperately she would risk a beating? Clearly, she was causing enough of a scene to draw me out."

"I was just following orders, Sir," the first responded with an inappropriate amount of nonchalance.

Our leader sighed, clearly exasperated. "Yes, well, if something incredibly out-of-place happens, you have my permission to fetch me. And if this one comes to me at any time, you're to let her inside, given her assignment." He paused for a moment. "Are we clear?"

"Yes, Sir," they both said.

I could not fathom why the first almost sounded as if he were mocking our leader, nor could I fathom why our leader would have such a relaxed Guard protecting his door. I supposed he must've typically been good at his job, impropriety aside.

It was not pertinent.

Our leader stepped back into his office, and I ensured I didn't so much as look at either of the Guards as I followed him.

"That was what you were doing, wasn't it?" he asked once I'd closed the door behind us. "Creating a scene to draw my attention?"

"Mostly, Sir," I admitted, trying to hide my discomfort. "And I partially said what I did because it was true."

"Now, what is so important that you risked a beating for?" He leaned against his desk, not at all masking his amusement, staring at me where I stood halfway across the room from him.

I waited a moment, but it seemed he wasn't going to even ask me what I'd said to insult the Guard. If he wasn't . . .

I took several steps forward and attempted to steel myself for whatever would happen next. "I apologize for causing trouble and drawing you away from your work, Sir." For a moment I wondered how he had managed to stay alive to work for another month. They rarely lasted so long. I shook that thought from my head. "You told me once that I could come to you, if I needed to."

His brow furrowed. "I remember telling you that, yes. Has something happened?"

"I . . ." I stared down at the floor for a few seconds, breathing deeply and attempting to summon enough courage to get the words out of my mouth.

The worst he could do was say no.

"I believe I need to return to my old assignment, Sir."

"I should tell you that you are not at liberty to choose your own life, shouldn't I?" he asked. "I must admit, I'm too curious about the why to say that straight off."

Leaders never worried about the why, I knew. Rather than wonder about that, I blurted it out. "I have been emotionally compromised, Sir."

I was not expecting for him to laugh at my words.

He did, though. "*What?*"

"Emotionally compromised, Sir," I repeated, nearly whispering and staring down at the floor.

"Emotionally compromised with a Reaper?" He was still chuckling.

"Yes, Sir," I admitted, still speaking to the floor.

Movement from him drew my gaze.

He straightened and stepped closer to me. "Why should that matter?"

"It shouldn't, Sir."

Several seconds passed before he asked, "So why would you think it would matter to me?" All amusement had gone from his voice, leaving only blankness in its wake.

"I don't, Sir," I said. "I was simply hoping you would have mercy."

There was a long pause, likely spent—by the expression on his face being one of trying to work through something—contemplating the word *mercy* and its relevance to the situation. "Have you told anyone your feelings?"

I looked away to the wall, shaking my head and clenching my jaw hard in an attempt to keep it from quivering.

"Agatha?" he prodded.

I shook my head.

"Have you told him?"

Again, I shook my head.

"Why not?"

When I forced myself to look at him, I saw that he was closer to me than I'd realized—leaning his body down, bringing his face quite near to mine. I stared at him as he blurred through a tear that welled and spilled. I mentally screamed at my quivering jaw and at myself for my inability to control it.

"There is no point in telling anyone, Sir." Despite my attempt to hide my emotions, and the rules against failing to do such things, a tiny sob built up inside me. I couldn't stop it from happening. "Especially not him."

He said nothing; he just stared at me.

It took me too long to say, "I apologize for my reactions, Sir. I'm not accustomed to dealing with such things." I breathed heavily as I strained to get my emotions under control. I stared into his eyes, and I waited.

He stared into mine, and it took him a while to say, "I'm going to give you a special assignment for the day."

"*Special assignment*, Sir?"

"Yes, I want you to spend the day thinking over several things."

The thought of *more* things . . .

I told him, "I already have too much in my head that I don't want, Sir."

"Yes, I would imagine so." He glanced in the direction of the window for a moment, absentmindedly rubbing at his forehead with several of his fingers before bringing both his hands to his sides.

I watched him rub the thumb of his right hand against the outside of his pointer finger a few times before both his hands balled up into loose fists.

I was looking into his eyes when he said, "I want you to think about what makes a person worthy of love from another, in any form of the word. I'm also curious to see if you can discover a way to continue duty, when feelings get in the way of it. I'm wondering if you can figure out the difference between good and evil. I'm mostly curious to see if some time away from him can give you the proper perspective."

I nodded, but that seemed like too much.

How was I supposed to find answers for those questions?

How could *anyone* find those answers?

I had to know, though . . . "Sir? Who will be taking my place for the day?"

"Why does it matter?"

"I need to instruct them to watch his food, Sir."

"Watch . . . his food?"

"To ensure it's not poisoned during preparation, Sir." I unwittingly fidgeted a little.

He seemed to find that funny for some reason, momentarily turning his face away from me in an attempt to conceal a partial grin. "I will allow Agatha to take your place for the day, and you hers. I'm sure you don't want to expose your feelings to her, but at least you can trust her. Is that fair?"

"More than, Sir." I was so relieved. I could deal with Agatha's fury on the matter if she discovered my true feelings. I could trust her, and that was infinitely more important. "May I go now, Sir?"

"Of course." He waited until I was nearly to the door before he asked, "Do you really watch his food being prepared?"

"I did." I turned my head to look at him. "Every meal like a hawk,

Sir, until I began preparing it myself."

"Did you ever realize the ingredients could be poisoned before you came in?" There was a curious expression on his face, his eyes narrowed almost mischievously.

Discomfort beyond what already existed pushed itself within me. "I did eventually, Sir."

"So how can you ensure they're not poisoned?"

I cleared my throat and stared down at the floor to admit, "I taste everything before I give it to him now, Sir."

Many long seconds passed before he asked, "Have you told him that?"

Rather than tell our leader I had not informed the Reaper of that particular information either, I took a deep breath and wiped another tear from my face. "May I go, please?" I nearly begged.

"Of course," he repeated. That time, he did not stop me with any more questions.

I'd made it halfway down the hall when I heard a commotion behind me. I turned around and found the Guard who'd almost hit me on the floor, clutching his face, blood streaming through his fingers. Standing over him was our leader.

I was positive he was smiling.

Hurriedly, I left the unbelievable scene in search of Agatha.

I FOUND AGATHA WHERE SHE WAS every morning at the same time—cleaning the windows in the foyer. Dirty or not.

She noticed me immediately, of course, as she was on guard constantly.

When I got close . . .

"What are you doing here? Shouldn't you be working? Have you been crying? What's wrong?"

My head felt dizzy from my revelation, my conversation with our leader, the Guard on the floor, and Agatha's seemingly endless stream of questions.

"I spoke with our leader," I said, my voice much calmer than I felt. "You're to switch places with me today."

"*What*?"

"Yes, you can go speak with him if you don't believe me."

"Of course I believe your word." She balled up her right fist and rested it on her hip. "But why?"

"I don't wish to explain."

She frowned. "Aster, you cannot come to me with madness and then not explain to me what's going on."

I bit down hard on my bottom lip and stared away from her, guilt pressing on my heart.

"It's about that monster, isn't it? Aster—"

"I've had *enough* with you calling him that!"

Her jaw dropped, and I immediately stepped closer to her.

"I'm so sorry for shouting Aggie, I just . . ." I took a deep breath. "I'm sorry."

Her shock dissipated, and I believed her voice was as apathetic as she could manage when she asked, "What room is he in?"

"Four."

She began walking away the instant the number had come out of my mouth.

I rushed after her. "You have to watch his food being prepared."

She stopped and turned, disbelief all over her face. "What?"

"His food," I nearly whispered. "Please."

She shook her head, I believed *at* me, and turned again.

I rushed to catch up with her and tugged on her arm. "Can I trust you with this?"

"It seems I've given you reason to believe you can't trust me." Her eyes were filled with sorrow. Or perhaps something else. "I am very sorry for that."

"Please," I begged, tugging at her arm again.

Her expression softened and she touched my hair. She forced a tight smile at me before saying, "You can always trust me, my flower."

I nodded stiffly and watched her go.

I stood there, after she'd gone.

I'd not anticipated feeling the way I did. I'd expected to miss his company and to wonder if he noticed my absence. I'd not known I would feel a heavy pit in my stomach, warning me that if I did not ensure his safety myself in whatever ways I was able, I could not be sure of it at all.

I wondered if the shame inside me was worth it, so long as I could ensure he stayed alive while he was here.

Was it wrong to want him—a monster, a murderer—to live? Would I have to be evil like him in order to have fallen in love with him in the first place?

Was he truly evil? Was he a monster for breaking a man's wrist? Or was the man whose wrist he'd broken the true monster? All my time spent wondering about who he truly was, *what* he truly was, if *anything* was different from what I knew, and now . . .

I would not discover an answer.

For once in my life since coming to the Valdour House, I had asked for something and received it. Asking for things, I had learned, was pointless. I hadn't learned from having asked but knowing.

Nothing would be given.

The worst that could've happened, before, was asking and having reinforced that I could have nothing.

I never thought I would regret asking for something so immensely.

CHAPTER NINE

QUESTIONS AND ANSWERS

ALL DAY I DID AGATHA'S WORK, and all day I thought about the Reaper. I also thought about the things our leader had asked me to think over, though distantly at first. Try as I might, I could not initially put much thought into those other things.

Mostly I worried over the Reaper's food. Stupidly, I found myself wondering if he missed my silent company the way I was missing his. I wondered whether Agatha was treating him horribly on account of my feelings for him and if she was terribly angry with me for forcing her to be around a Reaper.

Halfway through the day, I forced myself to think on the subjects I had been given and absolutely nothing else. When I'd gotten through one of them, I went on to the next, until I believed I had found answers for them all that were satisfactory enough to placate our leader.

Agatha did not speak to me that night, and I cried myself to sleep. She did not comfort me as she normally would have, had I been crying over something more acceptable. It was all right that she didn't. I did not believe I would've comforted myself, had our roles been reversed.

I could've been wrong.

The next morning, I once more found myself standing outside our leader's office. The improper-yet-polite Guard from before was standing there, but the other had been replaced with another.

"I'll tell him you're here, Miss," the first Guard said.

"Thank you, Sir," I told him.

He gave me a stiff nod and stepped inside. He did not seem so easily amused and relaxed as he had the previous day.

When he emerged to inform me that our leader was waiting, I felt inclined to say, "I apologize for my words and actions yesterday, Sir."

"He had it coming." He nodded toward the door. "Go ahead." Even the small smile he offered me appeared to be somewhat stiff. Perhaps he was tired or having an unpleasant day, or perhaps he'd been reprimanded.

I did as he'd told and stepped inside without concerning myself over it further.

"Good morning, Sir," I said to our leader, quiet and somewhat stiff once I'd closed the door behind me. "I've come to answer the questions you gave me."

A sly grin appeared on his face. "Have you?"

"Yes, Sir."

I eyed him with confusion when he stepped around his desk and plopped down onto the floor, crossing his legs in front of him. He leaned forward and patted the rug.

"I don't understand, Sir."

"Have you called him by his name?"

"No, Sir." I had not even called the Reaper by his name inside my head, though I did remember it.

"Do you call him Sir?"

"Sometimes, Sir," I admitted, wary that saying as much would result in some form of trouble for me no matter any insistences.

He waved me forward, appearing unruffled, so I took several steps closer to him.

"For a few minutes right now, you're going to sit down on the floor across from me," he began. "You're not going to call me Sir. We're both going to ignore what we are, and we're going to speak as friends."

"*Friends*, Sir?" My eyebrows seemed to strain as my forehead scrunched due to my confusion.

"Friends," he repeated.

I shook my head slowly. "I'm sorry, Sir, but I learned a very long time ago there is no such thing."

"And what led you to that conclusion?" he asked inquisitively.

"It was my father's friend who gave me to the Reaver that brought me here, Sir." Agatha was the only person who knew as much. She was the only one who cared how I'd ended up here. I likely would not have answered her as freely now as I had when she'd asked the question.

He narrowed his eyes. "Was it?"

I nodded in response.

He patted the rug once more. "Please. Sit."

I cleared my throat as I stepped forward, sitting down several feet in front of him.

"For now, pretend there is such a thing as friendship."

"I don't understand the purpose of it, but if that's what you wish for me to do, Sir."

Our leader was so very strange.

"No *Sir*," he insisted. "The answers?" He leaned his back against the front of his desk and brought his legs up, wrapping his arms around them.

He appeared quite young when he sat that way, and I wondered if he was the youngest leader who'd ever been here. I thought he might've been. If he wasn't, then he was very close.

Perhaps that was one of the differences, but perhaps it was not.

"The first question was what makes a person worthy of love from another," I began after a moment spent contemplating the bizarreness of it all. "But I must tell you that, when thinking on the questions, I found my personal opinions were likely different from what everyone else would think. I felt multiple answers were the only way to reach any sort of appropriate conclusion with them."

He grinned. "I didn't ask for multiple answers."

"That may be true," I said slowly, momentarily holding a breath in an attempt to calm myself down over this strange interaction. "But I believe there is no easy answer to difficult questions in life. At least not often, if there is."

I paused to see if he had anything to say.

If he did, he didn't say it to me.

After a short stretch of silence, I got to it. "I would assume people believe outwardly things are what make a person worthy of love.

Status, beauty, petty acts of affection or endearment. . . . Things of that nature."

"And what would *you* believe makes a person worthy of it?"

"Heart," I almost whispered. "Easier to say, but infinitely more difficult to comprehend." I stared at my feet for a moment, shaking my head. "I'd never known that, sometimes, your heart can tell you things. I've come to understand that sometimes you cannot talk reason into it, no matter how hard you try to do so." I cleared my throat. "I would prefer to answer the third question next."

He grinned again. "That's fine."

"You wanted to know if I could discover the difference between good and evil." I chuckled a little as I wrapped my own arms around my legs near the knees. "I've always thought there was a black-and-white answer to it. Something was either good, or it was bad. There has never been an in-between with those two things for me. I'm wondering now if I've been mistaken." I wondered now if I'd been mistaken over a great many things.

"I didn't hear an answer there," he pointed out.

"Intent," I said. "It's the reasons people have for doing things, I think. More so, possibly, than the actions they take."

He narrowed his eyes the slightest bit. "Did intent matter to you when you were forced into this life?"

"I was too young to understand intent at the time, Si—" I cut myself off. After a moment of seeming frozen passed, I took a deep breath. "Oh my." I said that under my breath as realization dawned on me.

"What is it?"

"Perhaps there *is* such a thing as friendship," I said to the tops of my knees. "My father's friend was possibly a friend to him, but not to me."

"But would you not agree that any friend of your father's should be a friend to you?" he asked. "In the most basic of ways, at the very least."

"I'm not so sure it is such a simple thing," I replied thoughtfully.

"How do you mean?"

"He and his wife waited a month for my father to return," I said. "It may not have been fair to give me away when I was not his to give, but how was it fair for me to be a burden on them when life itself is burden enough on us all?"

"Still, was it not wrong?" He barely shrugged. "Was it not wrong for him to sentence you to a life of servitude when, by all means, you should not have been?"

"It was the hand I was dealt, Sir," I told him firmly. "Wondering why does not change what is."

"Maybe not, but do you believe he and his wife were haunted by their actions? And I don't want to hear *Sir* again while we're sitting on this floor together."

I frowned and thought on his question for quite some time to formulate a response. "I would like to think that anyone who does wrong to another would be haunted by it, but I'm only my person. I wouldn't presume to know the feelings of another."

He sat there for a moment, brought one of his hands up, and rubbed at his chin.

"I would imagine they were haunted by it," I added.

"If you've just told me you couldn't possibly know, what would make you say that?"

"He lied to the Reaver lady. He lied to her and told her I was his."

"Why would he do that?" he asked, his brow furrowing as though he had genuine interest. The events that merged my past life to my present had always been somewhat ambiguous, so I could partially understand his curiosity.

"I've never understood it," I admitted. "I always liked to think he did it for my father, but I cannot fathom why it would matter." I cleared my throat uncomfortably. "I would sincerely appreciate if you'd not ask me any more questions on that particular subject."

He studied me for a long while. "Does the same grey answer apply to death?"

"How do you mean?" I asked.

"You know what Reapers do," he said. "Is there a black-and-white answer for it?"

"I always thought there was." I barely said it then cleared my throat. "I don't know why they do the things they do. Possibly, if I did, I could answer your new question for you."

He leaned forward slightly, resting his elbows on the tops of his knees, and then cupped his chin with his hands. "If they were forced into it?"

My brow furrowed. "The Reapers?"

He nodded.

"I would have to ask myself why someone so powerful would let anyone force them into anything they did not want to do. I cannot see how they ever would."

He grinned at me for a moment over his hands before chuckling a bit under his breath, and then he leaned his back against his desk once more. "The last? About perspective? Have you been able to find it?"

"The second is paired with that one. You wanted to know whether I could find a way to continue duty when feelings became a hindrance to it." I looked at the floor. "I believe I have found the proper perspective."

"And how did you come to it?"

"I couldn't stop worrying about his food," I admitted with an uncomfortable laugh. "I would rather ignore my feelings than the alternative."

He leaned forward again, crossing his legs once more and pressing his elbows into his knees. He looked hard into my face to ask, "Who ever told you that you weren't allowed to feel?"

"Everyone for the last ten years, Si—" I stopped myself and attempted to force some sort of passably pleasant expression onto my face.

"How many times have you been told to stay out of the library?"

"More than I can put a number to." It was not so difficult to smile then. "I'm sure you could take a proper guess at it, if you attempted to count the scars on my back."

His face flinched.

I felt inclined to add, "I apologize. I know you've already seen them. I didn't mean for my words to sound as they did."

Several long seconds passed before he spoke next. "You've never listened to them when they told you to stay out of the library."

"I've listened," I told him. "I just never believed they were right."

His eyebrows rose. "So why would you believe they were right about everything else?"

I opened my mouth and then closed it again. I smiled uncomfortably and scratched my bottom lip with one of my fingernails as I stared down at the rug. "For a moment, sitting here with you in this way, it was easy to forget that you could never understand."

"What do you mean?"

"What is a body, if it does not belong to the person occupying it," I murmured.

"Excuse me?"

"It's just something one of the men in the Guard said before," I told him, hearing myself chuckle shortly. "You're asking why I would listen to people when they told me that I'm not permitted to feel, am I correct?"

He nodded.

"What is the point?"

He said nothing; he simply appeared bemused.

"What is the *point*?" I repeated in a much firmer tone. "What could be the purpose of feeling something when I am not my own person? What does it matter, when my time is not mine to give? What does it matter when my own *body* is not mine to give?" I chuckled shortly again, trying to hold onto the somewhat forced amusement. "You've given me questions, and I have given you answers. Can you give me an answer to *that*, Sir?"

He reached his hand out as if he were going to rest it on my knee. Halfway through, he seemed to think twice and simply left it suspended in the air.

His eyebrows were again up when he said, firm, "Because you are *alive*."

"I am *property*, Sir," I said through gritted teeth. "Property does not feel. Property does not have emotion. Property has nothing to offer. Property has a *function*." I shook my head at him contemptuously. "You may say I am alive, but at the end of the day I will still go to sleep knowing what I am and what I'm forced to be. Your words are nothing more than empty sentiment. Your words change nothing."

I stood and began walking toward the door without asking him permission to leave.

"Where are you going?" I heard at my back.

"To do my job, Sir," I answered as I walked.

"Aster," he said, making me stop myself.

Slowly, he stood and walked over to me. He waited until he was directly in front of me before he spoke again.

"He's gone."

"Gone . . . Sir?" It felt as though all the air had escaped from my lungs at once.

I hardly noticed him nod his head or rest his hand on my shoulder as I attempted to process the two words.

He's gone.

"Would it comfort you to know he shared your feelings?"

"No, Sir, it would *not*." I was surprised by the loudness of my voice as I pushed his hand away and stepped backward. I shook my head at him in disbelief. "Your lies are a poison in my head."

I did not give him the opportunity to say anything else. I rushed from the room and continued rushing until I made it to the familiar stone balcony. And then I fell to the floor, put my face in my hands, and I cried.

I was unsure how long it took me to remember that the room—and balcony—was compromised. I hadn't needed it in so long . . .

I'd forgotten.

I tried so hard to comprehend everything and how it made me feel—a churning in my stomach and some strange sort of pain in my chest. It felt both heavy and empty at once.

I did not stay on the balcony long, because I had to see for myself.

I walked fast through the House until I came to room number four. The door did not open, though I stood there for a long moment waiting for it to. Eventually, I turned the knob myself and stepped inside. The drapes were hanging but open, and nothing was out of place, apart from one thing.

A small piece of paper rested on the desk.

I realized there were no words written on it when I moved closer, but it was not blank. It was a picture of a heart—two curved lines, connected together.

I fought back the image of a small hand holding a stick, digging it into the dirt.

Look, Father, I drew this for you, a high-pitched voice sounded in my head.

I shook the memory away before it could progress any further.

I felt as though our leader had done this, that he'd come in after the Reaper had gone and left this here to further poison my mind.

But there was a blotting of ink on the edge of the page, like the ones he left on those letters he would write. When I looked up, there was a smudging on one of the windows in the precise place it had been the first time he'd done it. The desk was moved a couple inches to the left, like I would've done when he was out.

He was gone.

I cleared my throat and took one step forward.

I had never taken anything in the Valdour House. I had never taken the books from the library. I had never taken anything.

But I took the tiny piece of paper, and I tucked it inside my shirt. I'd never had anything that was mine before, not in such a long time.

The small piece of paper with a heart drawn on it . . .

That small piece of paper was mine. And the Reaper had given it to me.

CHAPTER TEN

PROPER PERSPECTIVE

I DID NOT WORK AT ALL THAT DAY, and it was the first time since coming here that I hadn't. I laid on the stiff bed I shared with Agatha, waiting for our leader to come and have me beaten for my insubordination. I waited, though I knew he would not do it.

I spent half the time crying over my wasted and pointless feelings, over the leader's lies, and simply because the Reaper was gone. The other half of the time I spent staring down at the tiny heart on the small piece of paper. Several times, I traced it with my finger, imagining him sitting there staring out the window with his pen resting on it. How long had he sat there?

Agatha found me that night and, unlike the night before, she did comfort me. She pulled me somewhat into her lap and ran her fingers through my hair. For a long time, she did not say anything.

"I couldn't bear to tell you he was leaving last night," she told me eventually.

I pulled away from her and stared disbelievingly into her face. "You knew?" I asked through my quivering jaw. Why hadn't anyone told me? I could've . . .

I could not have done anything.

She nodded and a tear fell from the corner of her eye. "Oh, my flower." She shook her head. "How can you love a monster?"

I glanced down at the paper in my hands.

"What is that?" she demanded.

I brought it up to my chest, holding onto it tightly, and I watched her take a deep breath.

"What is it?" she asked more calmly.

I held it out to show her but did not allow her to take it from me.

"Did he leave this for you?"

I nodded.

"Does he even have a heart to leave with you?"

"That was my next question." A small sob built up inside me.

"What?"

"I let myself say two sentences to him every day," I admitted. "I was going to ask him today if he had a heart."

"Why didn't you tell me any of this?" Both sorrow and shame were clear in her voice and expression.

"Because you would call him a monster and tell me not to let him in my head," I said. "I tried to keep him out, Aggie. I just . . . couldn't do it."

She grabbed hold of my hands, gripped them hard, and stared into my eyes to very slowly say, "He kills people, Aster. It is his occupation. It is his life. Do you understand that?"

I nodded my head in response.

"*How?*"

"He wasn't a monster to me," I told her, not bothering to hide the desperation in my voice.

"How he was with you doesn't change what he truly is." She spoke firmly. "All Reapers are monsters. It does not matter how they treat one person, with all the other things they do. You cannot get around the fact that they are evil."

I pulled my hands away and heard a quiet laugh escape from my mouth as I scratched at my bottom lip.

"What's funny?"

Too many things clicked together inside my head at once.

Would it be better, then, to have someone love me in private and scorn me in public as Camden would have?

No, I could not believe that it would. When it came to love, only the people involved should matter. I may not have known much about it, but I knew that. How could you love a person who had no respect for you, no genuine care? I would rather love someone the world believed was a monster, if that person treated me differently—better—than everyone else had.

I had seen so many monsters in my life.

The tears had stopped falling from my eyes when I looked to her to say, "Don't worry, Aggie. He's gone. You don't have to burden yourself with my feelings for him any longer. I finally have the proper perspective."

I did not cry again.

THE NEXT MORNING, I was halfway through changing out of my nightclothes and into my work clothes when there was a knock at the door.

"Who in the world could that be?" Agatha wondered aloud on her way to answer it.

Frustrated, I hastily pulled my shirt over my head and tugged it down so I wouldn't expose myself to whomever it was should she—in some absentmindedness due to the oddity—open it without checking my state.

"Sir?"

"My god," our leader said as I turned around. He was staring around our room in what appeared to be disbelief. "Is this how you all live?"

"No, Sir," I retorted. "We're simply standing in here for the spectacular view."

"*Aster!*" Agatha snapped shrilly. She turned back to him, completely ignoring his laughter at my rude words. "I apologize, Sir. She has been quite distraught since yesterday."

"Oh yes, I'm aware," he said. "I must admit a good deal of that is my own fault."

"Your fault, Sir?" Agatha asked, puzzled.

I realized he'd been staring at our bed for an extended amount of time when he looked at Agatha and asked, "Do you not even have pillows?"

"Pillows, Sir?" she asked.

I drew his attention to me with, "You're kidding, aren't you?"

"*Aster!*" Agatha turned on me, gaping. "Do you want him to beat you for not calling him Sir?"

"Are you going to beat me, Sir?" I taunted, grinning, knowing he wouldn't.

After a few seconds, he looked from me to Agatha. "It's difficult when love is ripped away, is it not? One should be granted a small amount of leeway in grievance of it. Wouldn't you agree?"

"You're asking my opinion, Sir?" She was clearly shocked.

"Yes. It is unfair when circumstances or people rip love away, don't you think? Hard on the soul to deal with the loss."

I watched her suck her top lip into her mouth as she stared at the floor. I barely heard her words when she spoke. "Yes, Sir. It is very hard on the soul."

He clasped his hands behind his back and, in a businesslike manner, said, "I would like a few minutes alone with her, if you wouldn't object."

Agatha's brow furrowed. "Alone, Sir?"

"Yes, I would imagine she has some very nasty things to say to me," he told her, clearly amused. "None of which you would approve, I'm sure."

"Why would she have nasty things to say to you, Sir?" When he didn't answer her, she added, "Will she be punished for it, Sir? Her behavior."

"I can assure you she will not."

"No matter what, Sir?"

He smiled at her and words spilled out of her mouth.

"I worry about her mental state, Sir. She's been surprising me so often lately that I feel as if I don't know her at all."

He glanced at me in time to catch my reaction to Agatha's words. I only allowed the feeling of being slapped in the face to remain in my expression for a moment, and I quickly forced my narrowed eyes to return to normal.

"She won't be punished," he reiterated.

"And you'll not harm her, Sir?" she pressed.

He looked disgusted and sounded the same when he said, "Of course not."

She spared one last glance at me before leaving as he'd asked.

As soon as the door closed behind her, I could not stop myself from speaking in a tone of false excitement.

"Is it a day where we're to sit on the floor and pretend to be friends, Sir? Or is it a day of lies? Or another of both, like yesterday?" I plopped down on the floor, smiling hugely at him. "You could sit down with me here and imagine you were me, being thrown on this very spot as a child. Would you like to pretend to be my equal, Sir?" I heard myself laughing heartily when I added, "I must admit that I would very much like to see it."

I watched him step forward, carefully, and sink onto the floor in front of me. His voice was small when he said, "I am truly sorry for what you've been given in life."

"Given?" I asked in bewilderment. "What exactly, Sir, have I been *given*?" I heard myself laugh again. "Oh no, I've forgotten I don't have to use a title while we're on the floor together, isn't that right, Sir?"

He said nothing. He simply stared at me.

Time passed of it, and the humor faded from me.

I asked him, "Did anyone see you come down here?"

He shook his head at me, not as an answer, but in confusion.

"Do you realize how it will look if you're caught down here? Do you know what that will cause for me?"

"Cause for you?" he said, still not understanding.

I leaned forward, my face scrunching up in disgust at him, at everyone. "Do you think I don't hear them, Sir? When I walk by?"

"Hear who saying what? What are you talking about?"

"All of them," I said. "The Guard, the ignorant servers. Even some of the other servants."

The expression on his face told me he hadn't the vaguest idea what I was speaking of.

"*There goes the Reaper's whore.*" I realized I was chuckling under my breath when I added, "I don't even know what the word means in their minds, but I can gather enough. Now, if they find out you've been down here alone with me, they can call me your whore as well. Though what loss of myself and what I'm paid in exchange . . . they seem to know far better than I."

He reached a hand out, likely in an attempt to comfort me.

Quickly I said, "Please do not touch me any more, Sir."

He brought his hand back to himself, and I fought against the tears threatening to well in my eyes.

I would be stronger than the tears now. I had to be. "Are we being friends, Sir? Is that what we're doing right now?"

"Yes," he said softly, his hands clasped in his lap.

"If we're being friends, I would like to confide in you."

He nodded his head and, for a moment, I felt as though I were on the verge of insanity.

"Agatha asked me last night how I could love a monster. And I cannot tell you how many times I've heard it over these past weeks. They say it quietly, but they *want* me to hear them." I nodded. "'Look at her smiling as she goes to see that monster.' 'Look at her testing his food for him.'" I paused and, very slowly, added, "What sort of person can love a monster?"

He said nothing.

"I have gained the proper perspective, Sir, and I would very much like to tell you why. I believe if I can just tell one person, I wouldn't feel as though I needed to scream in his defense to everyone. Our fictitious friendship seems the perfect opportunity, so please . . . Ask me the question."

I sat there and I waited for it. I waited quite some time for the inevitable query.

"How can you love a monster?"

I felt the corners of my mouth tugging up. "Ten years I've been here." I finally felt and sounded placid, having it asked by someone to my face who would actually listen to the answer. When it was finally a question and not a statement. "I've heard about all the horrors that can happen to women. I've heard about all the horrors of the Reapers. I've heard the secrets and the lies whispered by people in the crevices of this House. I've watched so many people in your position cycle through here and be murdered for another power-hungry monster to take up residence." I paused, and I stared at him. "They've got it all wrong, you see. They're all wrong."

"About what?"

"*Everything*," I breathed.

"And how could you know that?"

I stared at the floor for a moment, contemplating. Then, I took a breath and looked up at our leader's face to say, "Because being around him and knowing he was here . . . it's the only time I've ever felt safe in these ten years."

"You felt safe with a Reaper?" He appeared stunned.

"Very," I answered. He pursed his lips at me as I asked, "You said before that you know I'm more intelligent than I let on. How intelligent do you believe me to be?"

"Why are you asking?"

I felt a slow smile spreading across my face. Very deliberately, I leaned forward and whispered, "I know what you are."

He chuckled. "What are you talking about?"

"Are you going to break my neck, Sir?" I whispered in a tone of mock-innocence.

I watched as he narrowed his eyes and tilted his head slowly to one side.

"You shouldn't do that. It gives you away."

Immediately, he stood and stormed toward the door. As soon as he opened it, he snapped, "I've allowed you to attempt to eavesdrop this entire time. I'm going to have to insist you leave now."

"I sincerely apologize, Sir." Agatha's voice quavered.

"I need you to leave." He didn't want her apologies. He wanted her to go.

I saw her peek around his arm at me, and I couldn't stop myself from grinning at her.

"I won't hurt her. Go." When she didn't move right that instant, he said, "*Now.*"

She did.

He stormed back over to me after slamming the door, and I continued sitting serenely on the floor.

"What are a few secrets between friends, Sir?" I asked him, still using the innocent tone.

I had seen our leader joking, amused, and serious. For the first time, I could see a different person lurking beneath the surface. I could see the uncertainty in his eyes. *How did I know? Was I bluffing?*

"If you're not going to kill me, I'd prefer that you sat back down in our friend space."

He did in fact sit himself back down, his form much stiffer than I'd ever seen it. "Did he tell you?"

"No, he didn't. Do you believe me incapable of discerning something on my own?"

He looked into my eyes as if searching for something as he slowly shook his head. "No." All at once, almost all traces of the young man I'd come to know as our leader vanished. I supposed he found whatever he was searching for. "But you are far more perceptive than I would've given you credit for."

"Would you like to know how I figured it out?" I asked. "That way you're able to work on your form."

When he nodded, I got to it.

"First, you're still alive."

He smirked, though I was not joking.

"You pretend to care, when none of them have."

"And how would you deduce what I am from that?" he scoffed. "From caring?"

"It's out of character," I told him matter-of-factly.

He narrowed his eyes.

I carried on, with my attempt at assistance. "They don't care. None of them have. You ask me questions about why. They don't care about the why in anything." I paused to ensure my tone would be entirely serious when I said, "I don't know why you're here, but you were not given proper information about the way you should behave."

He sat there staring at me for a moment before he said, "Still, that is not enough."

"The questions you made me think about for you," I went on. "When I imagine the questions he would want answers for . . . they are very similar."

"How so?"

"That first night I met him, he thanked me for calling him a monster," I said. "I would imagine he would wonder what made a person worthy of being loved. At first, I believed you wanted me to answer those questions in an attempt to give me perspective in my own life. You were asking for yourself. Weren't you?"

He continued to narrow his eyes at me until, all at once, he stopped. He took a deep breath, smiled, and shook his head.

"The questions," I started again. "About the food."

"What about them?"

"You were stunned I would do it for him," I stated. "Anyone else would've been appalled. I've seen it enough to know. You weren't disgusted, only stunned."

I heard him let out a small breath, as if he were still stunned on the matter.

"I would imagine that, had I not divulged my feelings for him, you would've assumed I did it out of duty." I shook my head. "I would not do that out of duty for anyone in this world, I can assure you. And I would willingly take any punishment I'd receive for my refusal of such a thing."

He said nothing.

"Do you want to know when it really hit me?"

"I do," he admitted.

Quiet, I said, "When I caught you smiling for breaking that man's face."

He leaned back almost lazily on his hands, and I watched that same slow smile spreading on his face again. And I felt quite certain

. . .

That's him.

"Will you be done telling me lies now, Sir?"

"Ahren," he said. "You can call me Ahren."

I leaned forward and whispered, "Your secret is safe with me."

He must've believed me when I told him, because he did not kill me.

CHAPTER
ELEVEN

AHREN

THE FOLLOWING DAY, new beds—with pillows—were hauled down to the servants' quarters.

It was a large thing that had all the servants in as much of an uproar as they would get to, which was a hushed and rushed one. There was a great deal of hurrying to tell one another, which was how I learned of it. Someone had hurried into the room I was in, looked around it, realized it was only me, and left without a word. The strangeness drew me out, where I discovered those beds and such being hauled down.

Finding several others speaking quietly to one another with a sense of confusion, awe, and urgency before rushing themselves in directions they shouldn't have been going confirmed for me that they were in fact informing one another.

I went to Ahren's office to ask why he was wasting such things on us and why he would bother with it at all.

He'd looked up from the papers on his desk and said, "Because I don't care about any of that."

It made me wonder what, exactly, he was doing holding office and why, exactly, he was there.

I knew he worked, though I could not figure out what he actually worked on. I assumed whatever he was doing had nothing to do with being in control of the city and that he'd been placed here on some sort of mission. I had to assume that, if he did not care about this wretched city, he was more of a friend than I ever could've known. I despised this place and its repulsive people with every fiber of my being.

When I was finished with working that day, it wasn't long at all before he showed up at my room. I was alone there at the time, and I allowed him in.

We were only very shortly into a conversation when Agatha opened the door, halting herself at the sight of him standing in the middle of the room.

He told her with a smile, "We were just discussing the room. I hope you'll be satisfied." He then let himself out.

She looked to me with a baffled expression and question in her eyes.

I nodded. "We truly were just discussing the room."

I did not tell her that we'd mostly been discussing it as a meeting point, as the place least likely to be overheard.

You'll be seen, I'd told him.

He'd assured me of a plan for that, and time began passing.

Ahren told people he was speaking to me about improving the life of staff in our House. And he did talk to me about that, but we mostly discussed other things.

I gave him pointers on how he should be behaving—as supreme dictator—and he listened to me. He didn't usually follow advice, though I believed he appreciated my tips on things he should not do if he didn't want to be discovered as a Reaper. I'd always assumed they would've been better taught. It did cause me to wonder what else I might've been wrong about.

I told him secrets I'd overheard during the last ten years. I told him about dirty citizens and their atrocious affairs. I told him about a lot of things I had never once spoken of. I had never even told Agatha about those secrets, though I always listened intently when she would tell me information she'd overheard.

I still did my work of course, although Ahren went through the list of things that we were all required to do and made some adjustments.

We did not have to dust the same rooms every single day. We did not have to reclean things that were already clean.

There was one day in my room where he and I had a long discussion as to what point, precisely, something could be considered unclean. He laughed a great deal at what I had to say on the matter, and I felt . . .

It was a pleasant experience.

I still did not feel entirely safe, but I felt a contentedness—not only for myself but for the others in the House as well. They were pointlessly worked too hard.

I'd always wanted the leaders to go so I could return to the library.

I did not want Ahren to die. Truly, he was . . . a nice young man, despite what he was. I at some point began not to worry so much about when I could return to the library. Before, it had been the only positive thing to look forward to in my life. Since the Reaper had come, it did not seem so important.

I kept the paper the Reaper had given me inside my shirt while I was awake, and I slept with it beneath my pillow at night, clutched tightly in my hand. Sometimes, while walking with Ahren in the halls, I would catch him staring at the little lump of it near my collarbone. He never asked me what it was, and I did not tell him.

I didn't give myself a two-sentence allotment with Ahren because I did not worry about him invading my head. I enjoyed his company. After a month or so, I came to truly consider him a friend. There was something about him that made me feel at home, something comforting. We still sat together on the floor when we were alone in a room, but he did not treat me any differently when we were standing. He never made me call him Sir, and I did not accidentally use it in sentences when speaking to him.

Over that time, two different Reapers visited. I didn't ask Ahren if it would be him. Ahren would tell me that we'd be expecting a guest and then willingly offer me the information that it was not.

The other Reapers only stayed for a night or two before they would leave to go on their next mission. I did not go anywhere near either of them, nor was I expected to. My daily life almost in no way changed on the days of their arrival, past the two sentences or so that he would take to inform me that it wasn't him.

I asked Ahren once why he had stayed for so long when the others never did.

He'd said it was because of me. He always smiled at me in a sad sort of way when speaking of it.

Agatha believed me to be in love with Ahren. When I would tell her I was not, she would assure me that *love may blossom yet*. She did not know he was a Reaper, of course, or she would never have approved. Sometimes, I wanted to tell her he was, simply so she would shut her mouth on the matter. But I would take his secret to my grave. No matter how Agatha persisted, I could not see him in that way.

It was approximately two months after our first conversation in my quarters that I bluntly asked him why he was here. I'd been hoping he would tell me on his own.

He hadn't.

He ran his hand along the grey stone wall as we walked down the corridor. "Because I have to be."

"Do you have someone test your food?" I asked him, chuckling.

"Would you do it?"

"No, I most certainly would not." I fought the urge to allow my laughter to turn into hysterics.

He stopped walking.

I stopped with him and asked, "What's wrong?"

"I'm just wondering . . ." He looked down at me. "Do you regret not telling him how you feel?"

"I still am what I am. I could never truly have anything with a person." I paused and apologetically added, "And being what he is, I doubt he truly could either."

He nodded and resumed walking.

I followed and after a moment asked, "Have you ever been in love?"

"Yes." Had everyone? Was it unavoidable?

"And did you tell her how you felt?" I looked over at him as we walked together.

He didn't meet my gaze, nor did he make an effort to answer me for a while.

I kept watching him.

Eventually, he shrugged before saying, "She could never have seen past what I was."

"Did you give her the chance to?"

He suddenly stopped and stared hard at me. "Should a person have to try to make another see past what they are?" His brow furrowed. "I don't believe it should be that way. Do you?"

I reached out, having a strange urge to comfort him, but I pulled my hand back.

I said, quiet, "Sometimes eyes don't work as well as we'd like for them to. It takes a moment to adjust to the sun when you're not accustomed to it." I shook my head distractedly and said, "I should get back to work."

"So should I."

THE NEXT MORNING, Ahren opened the door to my quarters—without knocking—just as I was slipping the piece of paper into its proper place inside my shirt.

I gaped at him over my shoulder, in a way amused at him but mostly relieved he'd not caught me just shortly before. "Are you being exceptionally rude this morning?"

When he did not laugh like I expected him to, I turned to face him. I watched as he stepped into the room and sat down on my bed.

Agatha and I had our own separate beds now.

He never sat on mine.

"Apparently so," I added. I was somewhat confused, not knowing why there was a change in his behavior.

"Will you do me a favor?" he asked gravely.

"Of course," I told him without hesitation. "So long as your request involves nothing of food." When he remained grim, I frowned at him. "What in the world is wrong with you this morning? Are we not friends anymore?" Was falling out of friendship easier than falling into it?

"Of course we're friends." His eyes narrowed almost mischievously at me. "If I were to tell you we're to have a special guest, what would you do?"

I stood entirely still, not even breathing. I could not allow myself to hope it would be him. I forced myself to breathe before saying, "I wouldn't imagine I could do much of anything, Ahren." I frowned. "Is there to be another ridiculous party, then?"

"No party."

I cleared my throat and began tidying the already-tidy room to distract myself. I just couldn't stand still to ask, "Was it not a successful mission?"

"It was a successful mission. He just insisted there be no party."

I took a deep breath. "Is it him?" I asked, squeezing the clothes I'd picked up tightly.

I watched a slow smile spread across Ahren's face.

"Is it really?"

He nodded.

I still could not allow myself to hope. I would have to see him to believe it as truth.

Ahren finally removed himself from my bed and came to stand in front of me. I did not flinch when he removed the clothes I was holding, put them back where they had been, and took my hands in his. I was simply too stunned to take real note of it.

"Tell him how you feel," he urged. "Please."

A stiff laugh fell out of my mouth. "Why?"

Softly, he said, "Because I don't want you to make the same mistakes I've made."

I smiled at him and looked down at the floor to shake my head.

The smile immediately dropped away from my face. "Ahren, why is there blood on your hands?" I pulled my own hands away.

"Don't worry about it," he said quickly, hiding them behind his back as if that would make me forget what I'd seen.

"Who have you beaten?" I demanded.

"How do you know I haven't killed someone?" He sounded far more amused by it than he should've been.

"Because your own knuckles are bloody." I took a step closer to him. "Who have you beaten?"

I didn't flinch when he used one of his bloody hands to tuck a strand of hair behind my ear. I didn't always have to wear my hair up now, though I still did while I was working. Most of the time.

"Don't worry about it," he insisted when he'd replaced that same hand behind his back once more.

"Ahren, was it one of the servants?"

"*What*?" He gaped for a moment and seemed to be working through what I'd asked. "Of course not. It was one of the Guard."

"And what did he do?"

He looked away, shrugging his shoulders. "He made some re-marks."

"Remarks about what?" I asked, unrelenting.

He brought his gaze back down to my face. "Remarks about *you.*"

I fought against the urge to laugh. "Do you remember what I told you about words?" I asked him. "Words mean nothing. Don't let remarks about me jeopardize your mission, Ahren."

"You don't *know* my mission," he stated in a firm tone.

"You're right, I don't," I conceded. "But I'm hoping that at least part of it entails burning this wretched city to the ground."

A few seconds passed before he narrowed his eyes, somewhat playfully. "And what if it doesn't?"

I shouldered past him with a sigh. "Then I will simply have to do it myself."

He and I both laughed as we walked toward the door together, but all at once I stopped moving, feeling like I could go no farther until I was absolutely certain.

"Is it really him coming? Is it really?"

He smiled widely when he said, "I promise."

I couldn't convince Agatha that there was nothing between Ahren and me in the way she for some reason hoped. One day, she'd told me she was certain he was falling in love with me. Judging by the genuine smile on his face when he told me the Reaper was returning, I knew it was not possible. Ahren was a friend, more of a friend than I ever could've asked for. Though I never would've.

If only Agatha could've understood.

Ahren helped me comprehend so much more about giving time. I had wondered before if it was the same when it was given to any-one. I fully knew now that it was not. Time with Ahren was enjoy-able, but it was not the same as giving time to anyone else. I was glad to find there could be many different kinds of time given and that more than one of them could be a pleasant experience.

I did not let myself wonder why the only people I enjoyed spend-ing time with were those that others considered monsters, nor did I let myself dwell on what that said of my person.

I was beginning to believe everything was backwards—that the monsters were people, and the people monsters.

Was everyone wrong, or was I?

CHAPTER TWELVE

SAD STORIES AND HOPE

I MANAGED TO AVOID AGATHA for the first half of the day, but I was unsuccessful in my attempts at work. Every few minutes, I would lose myself in thought and realize I was staring off into the distance. I found myself pacing in the foyer several instances, each of them taking quite a while before I would stop and wonder how in the world I'd even ended up there.

Ahren found me on one such occasion and laughed boisterously at me. It did not make me angry, as it would have if he were anyone else, only slightly embarrassed.

"One of the Guard told me you'd been here on and off all morning," he said, a warmth in his eyes that was visible to me as he stepped closer. "Come take a walk with me. It will get your mind off the waiting. Walking is all you're doing right now anyway. You may as well have some company while you do it."

I sighed and followed him, sparing one glance over my shoulder at the main door of the House as we made our way away from it.

I hadn't really meant to glance a second time, but I realized he'd caught me when meeting gazes with him.

His eyebrows rose minutely. "Have you ever heard of playing hard to get?"

"No," I answered. "What would be the purpose of it?"

He chuckled, the laugh lines around his eyes crinkling. "To make things interesting."

"How do you play?" I asked, curious.

For some reason, my question made him laugh so hard that he had to stop walking. I peeked around the corner of the wall we'd stopped at to look at the main door again.

When he'd stopped laughing enough to speak somewhat properly—properly enough to be understood, at least—he said, "You keep a person at a distance to make them more interested in you."

"All the stars!" I exclaimed. "Is that why he has feelings for me? Because I've hardly spoken to him? Oh my, I didn't know things worked that way. How am I supposed to tell him the way I feel about him, then? Wouldn't that defeat the purpose of it?" I gaped at him, suddenly unsure of myself.

"*Oh.*" He covered his mouth to keep from chuckling again, or to keep it from being so obvious that he was or might, which in a great many ways defeated the purpose. "You are *so* very bad at this, aren't you?"

"You say I'm bad at this, yet you're the one giving me two entirely different explanations for what I should do." I scrunched my face at him in an affectionately teasing sort of way and began walking again.

Shortly after he began following me, I thought on something.

"Did you ever wonder if that girl you were in love with simply enjoyed playing that game you just mentioned?"

"Oh, I'm sure she didn't." His gaze was somewhat down at his feet as we strolled, his hands held loose at his sides.

"What does that mean?"

He snorted and glanced at me from the corner of his eye.

It took me a moment to gather what he'd alluded to. "Oh. You mean she was like the server girls here."

"No." He snorted again. "She wasn't like them at all. I believe she loved me very much for a time."

"But you said—"

"That she could never have gotten past what I was?"

When I nodded, he continued.

"Well, she ran screaming from the room when I told her, if that paints the picture for you."

I shook my head. "That's preposterous."

"Is it?"

He halted mid-step, and I with him. There was a moment of silence as he tilted his head, likely listening for footsteps or breathing that should not have been there. He did it quite often when we spoke.

"How did *you* react?" he finally asked. "You bawled didn't you, when I assigned you to him? You've trained yourself to show nothing for most of your life and you *still* couldn't hold yourself together. Would you have run screaming from the room if you hadn't been expected to hide your emotions?"

"I didn't love him at the time," I said softly, my eyes momentarily downcast as I thought hard on his situation. "How could she have reacted that way if she loved you? Did you give her the chance to think it over? Perhaps she came to her senses on the matter."

"She didn't have the time in life to think it over." The weight of his words sunk in the vast silence of the corridor.

"Oh." The word barely escaped from between my lips. "I'm very sorry. Would you like to tell me about her? Or would it make you too sad?"

He took a deep breath and continued walking. It was a long while before he spoke again.

I walked and waited.

"She had the most beautiful hair."

"*Hair?*" I hadn't known that males paid any attention to hair, unless they felt it their responsibility to ensure all things were just so. It was just something on a person's head, so I couldn't fathom why they would.

"Yes," he said. "It was the same color as my mother's hair, like straw. But it was so soft it felt like air when I touched it."

I began attempting to envision the girl Ahren had loved, which would've made me smile . . . if she weren't dead.

"I remember, when she would look at me, sometimes it was almost as if her brown eyes were glowing, like fire. She was beautiful."

I couldn't imagine seeing such a thing in or from someone. I also couldn't imagine what a person would have to feel or see, to be capable of seeing someone in such a way.

It took me a moment, but I asked him, quiet, "Was she a nice girl?"

"That would depend entirely upon your definition of the word." He gazed off into the distance, presumably reminiscing.

I felt my cheeks burn a little when I gathered what he was speaking about.

"She was sweet to me, which was far more than what I was accustomed to," he added.

"May I ask you . . ." We stopped again, and I looked up at him, the gravity of my question clear.

I didn't have to say the words.

He knew what I wanted to ask him, and he asked the question for me.

"How she died?"

I nodded, sure that I couldn't have actually said the words to him, but his back was partially to me. I wondered if he could hear my brain rattling around inside my head.

"Her entire family was assassinated."

"Ahren?" I said on a breath. "By whom?"

I watched his shoulders rise as he took in a deep breath. "By a Reaper."

I opened my mouth to speak, but nothing at all came out of it.

He turned around and I watched the struggle he was enduring to belittle the reality of the situation with some futile attempt at a comforting facial expression. "They're dead now."

I nodded my head again although I did not know if he was talking about her family, the Reaper, or . . . if he had done it himself and it had killed a part of him in the process. No matter how well I'd come to know Ahren, it was worrisome that I could not figure out which he meant. And I was too afraid to ask.

"Would you like to tell me about your mother?" I asked in an attempt to change the subject. If his lady had reminded him—even if only in one way—of his mother, perhaps it would be a more pleasant thing for him to speak of.

"One day," he told me, still struggling in the same way he had been. I realized then that a story of his mother would not be a happy memory, either.

I had never really spoken to very many people before, especially not to the extent where they would feel comfortable with telling me personal aspects of their past. I was more than slightly ashamed of myself for never realizing that everyone in the world—even the people you would never suspect—had their own sad stories to tell. I was not as alone as I'd always believed.

For the first time, I wondered if being locked away inside this House for most my life had spared me from having far worse experiences. Was that possible?

"Ahren? Did you know I would love him?" I asked. "When you assigned me to him."

He glanced at me for a second, then said, "I was simply hoping it would give you the proper perspective."

I KNEW AHREN could tell his story had shaken me because it was not very long after our talk when he stated that he had to return to his office and get some work in. It was possible the matter had rattled him as well, but I could not be entirely certain. Perhaps one day I would learn more about him—the amount of effort openness required and how long it took him to overcome obstructions in his mind. I sincerely hoped that, one day . . . I would discover how to read him.

He promised he would find me before the Reaper's arrival so I could continue my own work without peeking over my shoulder throughout the day. Work, he said, was its own form of time travel. And he was right about that.

I was fidgeting as I stood in front of a sink washing dishes, and it took me far too long to realize someone was watching me. I turned and found Agatha eyeing me suspiciously.

"Why are you so antsy today?" she asked.

I scratched my bottom lip guiltily then wiped away the suds that lingered there with the back of my arm. I opened and closed my mouth several times, attempting to formulate words that would not tell a lie but would also not inform her of precisely what was going on.

I could not think of anything.

Eventually, she said, "Our leader called me in to speak with him."

I was beyond thankful she'd decided to change the subject herself.

"Oh really?" I asked, faking nonchalance as I turned back to the dishes. "What did he have to say?"

"Do you love him?" She had asked me this before, and I always had the same answer. It was growing tiresome—her not understanding that no amount of asking could change the answer.

"Ahren?" I frowned, my brow furrowing as I glanced over my shoulder at her. "I'm unsure how many times I must tell you this, but no, I do not. At least not in the way you're inquiring."

"He allows you to call him by his name."

"As do you," I pointed out.

"In front of anyone," she added.

"As do you," I repeated.

"It is *not* the same thing," she said, her tone firm. "Your relationship with him is more than that. I've heard people saying they see the two of you walking the halls together when you should both be doing your respective work. I know he comes into our quarters to speak with you alone, more than the few times I've caught. It smells like him down there sometimes. He is with you quite a lot. Alone."

I turned around to face her, feeling no anger or frustration then, only weariness. When being given that list, I understood how people could've drawn the conclusion she had. If I were outside the situation, I likely would've assumed the same.

But I wasn't outside it.

"Have you ever had a friend, Aggie?" I asked. "Someone you could trust and confide in without fear of judgment or condemnation? Have you ever had a friend?"

"I don't believe the two of you—"

"It is what we are." I spoke in a firm tone, not unkindly. "I can understand if you wish for me to love him, but I do not. And I can assure you his feelings for me are the same as mine are for him."

"But maybe—"

"It would be like being in love with my own brother," I told her in the same tone.

"You do not have a brother to know." Her voice sounded condescending, as if she'd just told me something I wasn't aware of.

"No, I do not," I conceded. "But I can imagine it would be much the same."

She stared at me with a blank expression for quite some time before frowning. "I understand now, what he was getting at when we spoke earlier. It's that Reaper, isn't it? You're still in love with him."

I stared straight into her eyes when I admitted, "I am."

"But you said you had the proper perspective, Aster." She was clearly frustrated. "You said—"

"You misunderstood what I was saying at the time," I told her apologetically. "You heard only what you wanted to hear when listening to my words on the matter. All this time, you've never truly listened to me. You don't have to agree with the things I feel, but you must understand that they are my feelings to be felt. I ask you to respect that much, at least."

It took her a moment to recover from the shock of my words, at least enough to carry on. "And what are you going to do if he hears stories of you and our leader?" She threw up a hand, also shrugging in a small way. "What are you going to do if he truly has no heart to give you? What are you going to do if his feelings have changed? Have you thought of any of those things?"

"I've thought of them all," I told her. "They are my circumstances to deal with, if they come about. I must say I would be very glad to simply have the opportunity to deal with them."

She stepped over and took my sudsy hands in hers.

"My flower," she began, her voice much calmer than I could've expected. "You walk around here, forgetting what you are. Our leader has given you too much leeway. He and that Reaper have both distorted your mind. Make no mistake about it, our current leader will be overthrown eventually. Your Reaper will leave you again and not ever return from one of his missions. What are you doing to prepare yourself for that?"

"I'm hoping you're wrong," I told her, my voice quiet and my mouth hardly tugging up at the corners.

"Hope," she said on a breath.

"Yes, Aggie," I said. "*Hope.*"

Her expression was somber as she cupped her hand against my face.

"My flower . . ." She took a moment to look away and regain her composure. "When you've lived as long as I have, seen the things I've seen . . . you'll realize there is no point in wasting your energy on such a word. Some things in life are inevitable, and no amount of a useless word can change that."

I squeezed her hand tightly and whispered, "I'm hoping you're wrong."

CHAPTER THIRTEEN

RETURN OF THE REAPER

"ASTER," I HEARD AHREN SAY from the doorway.

I dropped Agatha's hand and hastily wiped my own still-sudsy hands on a nearby cloth. An overwhelming sinking feeling began in my stomach before I'd even fully turned toward the door.

Was it time?

What if he didn't want to see me?

What if my head had made this out to be so much more than it actually was, and what if Ahren had not been telling me the truth all this time?

But then . . . he stepped into the room.

I'd spent so much of my time wondering whether he had a heart. Looking at him standing there next to Ahren in the doorway . . . I did not need to wonder any longer.

He was smiling so hugely at me that it took me far too long to realize I was holding my breath.

He did have a heart. I would have to think of a new question to ask him next.

I'd never wanted to physically throw myself at a person before, but I found myself wanting to run across the room, just to be close to him. Was I moving forward?

When I felt Agatha nudge me, I discovered that I'd not been moving at all. I took one step, slowly, then another. I did not register the fact that he was moving too, and I did not register that both of us had stopped walking when we reached the middle of the room.

I only knew we got there.

Standing only a foot away from him, my entire body felt too light. It felt as though my head had floated away from its place above my neck. I heard myself breathe in, and then out. It sounded too loud in my ears, but I didn't hear him make any sound at all.

Agatha said, "All the stars."

Her statement was followed shortly thereafter by Ahren saying, "I told you."

Regardless of who he was talking to, he sounded smug.

The first thing I said was, "You kill people."

The smile slipped away from the Reaper's face, pulling down to a frown, but he nodded his head and said, "Yes."

I took another deep breath before asking, "*Why*?"

Quiet, he said, "Because I have to."

Agatha was saying something behind me, but I did not hear her.

"I understand now," I told him. "What you meant before when you said we weren't so different. I understand."

His gaze softened.

I cleared my throat. "You look as though you haven't eaten at all since you left." That was likely a rude thing for me to have said. "Would you like me to get you some food?"

He shook his head, and his nose crinkled a little. Watching it still made my stomach feel quite funny.

He said, "How about we go together . . . and get each other food?"

My face felt as though it was burning or crumbling apart, I couldn't tell which. "I would like that."

He stepped aside and waited for me move first before falling into step beside me. I didn't spare a single glance for Agatha or for Ahren. I wasn't able.

I didn't truly notice anyone we passed as we walked down hallways, but I did know that we passed people. They did not say any of the things they likely wanted to say about me. They would not do that while he was with me. I decided I wouldn't have cared if they had.

Shortly after we began walking, he spoke.

"Are we past the two?"

We had been not-so-discreetly stealing glances at one another. I didn't want to look away from him, but seeing him again was so distracting that I had doubts as to whether I could walk correctly if I did not focus enough of my attention on it.

I chuckled, somewhat stiffly. "I don't want any more twos."

"I'm very glad to hear that."

"Are you?" I asked curiously.

He nodded, which made me laugh again, though a bit stronger.

"I'm going to need to have a discussion with Ahren about that game he mentioned to me earlier."

"What game?"

"He called it 'hard to get,'" I said. "Apparently nobody informed you of the rules for it either. I'm inclined to believe he made it up himself."

He laughed so boisterously that the sound of it bounced off the walls in the hallway. I was happy he found me funny, and I did not let myself wonder if that was the most noise he'd ever made in his life.

Though, part of me had to admit that I would not have been displeased if it had been.

IT WAS THE EVENING and the entire kitchen staff was gone, apart from the two who stayed late in case Ahren should want something in the middle of the night. He kept strange hours and I was unsure as to whether he actually slept at all. When we opened the door, they took one look at us and nearly scuttled from the room.

They stood where we'd paused by the door for only an instant before one of them asked, "If you're to be in here, Sir, may we stand outside until you've gone?"

He did not smile at them as he nodded, but he stepped aside to let them pass comfortably. Or as comfortably as they could.

His cheerful expression returned when he walked farther into the room and they had closed the door behind them.

"Does it bother you?" I asked him. "Everyone fearing you that way."

"You get used to it," he stated nonchalantly. "Some of us enjoy it."

"I would imagine you all do, to an extent."

He had been peeking into the pantry, but my statement caused him to close the door and turn to me.

"I could see it being beneficial, given the things you have to do." I'd done a great deal of thinking on the matter, and being near Ahren had helped. "But I would imagine it hurts your heart at the same time."

His face fell for only the briefest moment before . . . "Do you want breakfast?"

"*Breakfast?*" I asked in both confusion and amusement. "Do you know what time it is?"

"I like breakfast in the evenings sometimes."

I couldn't believe that. "Do you really?"

He nodded in response.

"Why didn't you ever tell me? I could've brought you some in place of dinner."

"I was waiting for you to ask." He said that then bit down slightly on his bottom lip as he resumed rummaging through the pantry.

"If you like breakfast in the evenings?" I laughed. "Why would I ever think to ask that?"

He shrugged. "I was hoping we'd get to it eventually." A few seconds passed before he said, "I'm glad we did."

"So am I," I barely said, letting myself think briefly over how unbelievable this all was. Then, I cleared my throat. "What would you like?"

He seemed to ponder it for a moment before plunging his hand forward and pulling out a wrapping of meat, likely bacon. "What would you like?"

"Why?"

"Because I'm going to make it for you."

My eyes widened in disbelief, and I expected him to tell me he was joking.

He said, "Yes, I'm going to make it for you, whatever you want."

I stood there for what felt like an eternity as I went through my life. No one had ever asked me what I wanted or offered to give it to me freely. Not for such a long time. . . .

A different life.

"Griddlecakes," I blurted out. "I want griddlecakes."

I stared at him, more than a little dumbfounded, as he went around the kitchen in search of ingredients.

"Can you really cook?"

"Of course I can cook." He laughed. "Do you think we're treated the way you see us treated here all the time?"

"I just assumed. . . ."

He laughed again. "We're not."

He began placing things onto the counter in a neat little row, I realized in the order they would be used. He was very strange, but I found I liked that about him.

"We go on extremely long missions sometimes, so we have to know how to take care of ourselves. And when we're not on those missions, or here, we do have houses. Some of us do, at least."

"Houses," I mouthed. I could not picture him—or any Reaper, for that matter—with a house of his own. "What about servants? Do you typically have those in your . . . *houses*?"

He made a noise that was almost a chuckle but wasn't quite and stopped moving things around on the counter. Then he turned and gestured me forward.

When I got close to him, he pointed out the window.

"Past these walls . . ." He paused. "The world out there isn't like it is here. Not exactly." He finally looked down at me in a concerned sort of way before almost whispering, "Don't you remember what it was like being free?"

How did—

Ahren must've . . .

I could feel my eyes blinking at him as I slowly shook my head.

He smiled sadly at me and took a few steps away.

I watched him open the bacon, sniff it, then move onto the griddlecake ingredients.

Each thing, he sniffed; the dry ingredients he also touched, rubbing them between his fingers.

Most things he also dabbed onto his tongue.

I asked, "What are you doing?"

"Checking for poison," he answered simply.

"You would know if it was in there?" I asked in amazement, taking a step closer. "Just by what you're doing?"

He glanced at me. "Are you surprised?"

I supposed whatever he saw on my face was what made him smile.

Still, I shook my head and shrugged my shoulders at once. It was a strange response for me to have.

"Only two Reapers have visited since I left, correct?"

"To my knowledge, yes," I replied.

He nodded thoughtfully.

"Why do you ask?"

He laughed shortly. "Do you know how often we're required to take each other out?" He glanced over at me and the hint of amusement over his question was gone. I wouldn't have known it had been there at all, if not for the sound. One of his eyebrows rose. "Why do you think we never visit here together?"

"I've never really thought about it," I admitted.

I watched him check over the last ingredient and, for a moment, I felt guilty I'd asked for something that required so many of them. He didn't seem bothered, though.

I asked, "Do you have to do that every time you eat? Even in your own home?"

"I don't have a home, but yes." He turned to me and leaned his back against the counter.

"How in the world are you still alive, if you're all so intent on killing one another?"

He grinned. "I'd like to imagine it's by sheer force of will, but mostly . . . it's luck."

"Not skill?" I would've assumed that would be the only way any of them stayed alive and did the things they did.

"It's helpful, but no. Now." The grin dropped away from his face. "Is there something you'd like to tell me about food?"

I opened my mouth and then closed it again. His eyes became increasingly more narrowed in my direction before I said, "No."

"No?"

I shook my head.

He stepped closer and said, "Don't ever do that for me again. I'm serious."

"Would you have done it for me?"

He appeared distant for a moment, though I couldn't understand why—he would either do it, or he would not. Then, he smiled a little before asking, "Would you have wanted me to?"

"No." I gestured to the ingredients spread out across the counter. "We should probably cook this food or else it will spoil where it sits. Then we can accuse one another of intent to poison."

His smile widened before he turned to the fire.

While we were standing close together, cooking one another's food, I blurted out a series of questions. "How do you not have a problem? Doing things like this with me? Being seen with me, or being seen doing these things?"

He checked on the progress of my griddlecake and then looked down at me. "Are you ashamed of me?"

"No. I'm not ashamed of you, or of my feelings for you."

He seemed genuinely pleased at my words, but I turned back to the fire.

"Will you teach me?" I asked, glancing over from the corners of my eyes. "How to check for poison. Will you teach me?"

I caught him frowning when he said, "I think that would be a good idea."

A servant was not a person worthy of being noticed, though they should've been, given all the secrets I'd been able to tell Ahren. But a girl that a Reaper had strong feelings for? A girl like that could not stay invisible, no matter how badly she wanted to.

Something popped into my head then—two sentences from a night I tried very hard to forget for quite some time.

Ahren's voice saying . . . *This guest is very special to our city. Please ensure you keep that in mind.*

I knew now from being around Ahren and him never saying the same of any of the others, it wasn't something to be said for them.

I did not know what made the boy standing next to me so special to New Bethel. I only knew that whatever it was likely could not mean good things for me.

Chapter Fourteen

Taking Steps

I WAS FILLED WITH DELIGHT as we sat together at the wooden table in the kitchen, sharing our griddlecakes and bacon. The sharing had of course been his idea, as it would never have been mine. I found, though . . .

"This is my new favorite thing."

He smiled in a closed way while finishing chewing. After he had, he said, "Breakfast in the evening, sharing food, sitting together, or actually carrying on a conversation?"

"All of them," I admitted. I had never shared food with a person before. It was quite an interesting and enjoyable experience.

"What was your old favorite thing?"

A small, stiff laugh escaped from me. "Do you want me to be honest?"

He nodded.

"Waiting for a leader to die so I could have a few weeks of sneaking into the library."

The smile instantaneously dropped away from his face. There was a short stretch of silence before he quietly asked, "Why did you do that?"

"To look at the pictures in the books." It was my standard answer when asked that question.

"I'm not asking what you did while you were in there. I'm asking why. What made it worth the beatings?"

I was going to ask him how he knew about that and also whether Ahren had told him absolutely everything.

Before I could, he added, "Some of the scars come up past your collar."

As if he'd been able to read my mind.

I supposed anyone could've or would've been wondering the same.

I forced a smile down at my plate, thinking on answering his question. I admitted, "To be happy that people at some point in time could experience something good. And to imagine there could still be some good in the world now. Somewhere."

Someplace far away.

I looked up to him. "You don't have to tell me it's silly; I already know it is."

"I understand."

"Do you?" I couldn't keep from sounding sarcastic.

"Yes, I assumed that was why you did it," he said. "I've just always wanted to ask you and actually hear you tell me the answer."

Another uncomfortable chuckle fell out of my mouth. "I've never even explained it fully to Agatha." I couldn't explain it fully. "I just—"

His words repeated inside my head.

I thought hard on them for a moment before focusing back in on him. "You said you've *always* wanted to ask me. We only met a few months ago."

He grinned and stuck another forkful of griddlecake into his mouth.

"You're very strange," I told him. "Do you know that?"

I watched the slow smile spreading farther across his face as he chewed and then swallowed his food.

I shook my head at him, sighed, and then grabbed my plate. "It's getting late."

"So?"

I'd begun to stand, but I sat back down at the word. "What do you mean, *so*?"

"Are you ready to be done seeing me for the day?"

I opened my mouth and then closed it again.

"Will you be able to sleep?"

I shook my head.

"Then why are we going to go to our rooms so that we can both lay there not sleeping?"

I gaped for a moment before telling him the only answer there was. "Because we have to."

He cocked his head to the side. "Who says we have to?"

Again, I opened my mouth to speak and then closed it.

"Why?"

"Because it's not acceptable," I stated. "What would we do? Walk around the halls for hours?"

He leaned forward onto the table. "What do you want to do?"

I stared at him for a while, blinking hard as I let myself contemplate something I'd not ever allowed myself to think about. "If I could do anything right now?"

He nodded.

I told him, "I'd like to go into the garden."

"Then that's what we'll do." He stood and grabbed his plate.

He'd made it several steps away before I stammered, "I-I'm not . . . I'm not allowed outside."

Slowly, he turned to face me. "Not even if you stay on the property?"

I shook my head.

"Are you being serious?"

I nodded.

"You're telling me the balcony you go on is the only time you've been outside in ten years?"

I nodded again.

He looked away from me and quietly said, "Oh my god."

After a short moment of staring at the wall, he moved. Rather than take his plate to the sink, he returned to the table and placed it back precisely where it had been before.

He gestured for me to stand. "Come on."

I didn't move. I did nothing but sit there and continue staring at him.

"I'm taking you outside. Right now. Come on."

I felt as though I were in a daze when I rose from the seat. He'd taken a step toward the door and then stopped when I said, "But the Guard."

When he looked back at me and smiled that slow smile of his, it finally hit me.

So long as he was here . . . I could do whatever I wanted, within reason.

I had never really thought about wants before to know what they were, or what they might potentially be. I never let myself.

I stood from my seat and followed him out the door, hearing my heartbeat pounding in my ears.

I left my plate on the table. I knew it was added work for someone else. I just . . .

I was struggling to keep up with his pace down the hallway when he suddenly stopped.

"Should I go get Ahren or Agatha, so we can be supervised?"

I expected the word *yes* to come out of my mouth because that would've been the proper and acceptable response, but it did not.

"I don't want to be supervised with you." I had been alone in his room with him many times before, after all. I did not believe supervision was necessary, nor did I desire having it in the slightest.

He studied my face for several seconds. "Are you sure?"

I felt my head nodding. "I'm positive."

"If you change your mind . . . tell me."

"I won't," I said assuredly.

He pursed his lips together and began moving forward again. When following after him, I did not allow myself to wonder what he would do to the men in the Guard if they refused to allow me outside. For the first time in my life here . . .

I realized I shouldn't need another person's permission to step through a door. I resolved myself to be perfectly fine with whatever getting through that door entailed.

MY STOMACH BEGAN SINKING the closer we got to that door. It sank simply at the thought of going out, but it mostly sank due to one of the people standing in front of it. I didn't know of one of the men, but I recognized the Guard whose face Ahren had damaged on my behalf outside his office, ultimately assisting with my discovery of him as a Reaper.

Should I have been thankful for the man and his hostile ignorance?

Should I not have?

I did not know why I expected the Reaper to act as though he felt any apprehension at all toward dealing with the Guards. As I somewhat sank against the wall—partially attempting to act as if I were invisible and partially attempting to appear as if I had every right in the world to be doing what I was currently doing—I watched him calmly step up to them.

"May I ask what you're doing, Sir?" the unknown Guard asked, his voice polite.

"I'm going outside." He said that then turned slightly and pointed at me. "I'm taking her with me."

I cringed when the Guard Ahren had beaten spoke, though I was nearly positive my face remained expressionless. It was an internal cringe at the very least.

"She's not permitted clearance on the grounds, Sir."

I caught the briefest glimpse of a smile before the Reaper's back was to me again.

"Moore, is it?" he asked.

The man in the Guard nodded, but I could barely see the action.

"I've heard all about what your leader did to your face." I watched his shoulders rise as he took in a breath. Somehow, it sounded happy when he released it. Quietly, he asked, "Would you like to see what I could do to you?"

"No, Sir," Moore said blankly.

"Aster? Do you intend to run away?" The Reaper turned to me.

The unknown Guard watched my face for a reaction.

I stared into his eyes as I shook my head and almost whispered, "I just want to go outside." I wondered if I sounded as desperate as I felt.

The Guard blinked hard at me several times before placing his hand on the door. He opened it, and I stood there, staring out at the space beyond. I took one step forward and then stopped.

I watched the Reaper stare down Moore, who hadn't moved an inch. "I don't want to see your face when we come back through here." I couldn't understand the pensiveness in his voice. "You should be grateful she's with me now. You might not be so lucky the next time I catch you."

I took several steps closer to him and opened my mouth, but he answered the question I was going to ask without me having to voice it.

"I'm waiting to see if he glares at you when you pass."

"Why?" I asked quietly.

He did not answer that question. Instead, he said, "If you're tempted, you should leave now."

Moore slid two paces down the wall and began walking away. Somehow, he managed not to look at me at all.

"I don't suggest you turn around."

Moore stopped walking for an instant, and then he continued without looking back once.

I barely said, "Was that really necessary?"

The Reaper finally turned to face me, and he smiled somewhat sadly. "People should understand that everyone is entitled to their own dignity. No person should take away the dignity of another unless it's necessary." He glanced at the other Guard member. "Wouldn't you agree?"

"I do agree with that, Sir," the man replied. "I hope you have an enjoyable remainder of the evening with your lady. She's been missing you horribly these few months."

I felt my head tilting to the side as I stared at him.

He smiled at me. "I have eyes, Miss."

I could not help smiling back at the man. I wondered now if some of the Guard felt no different than me after all. It was so strange, when having thought I was invisible most my life to discover I may not have been.

I hesitated in the doorway when I reached it, looking down at the toes of my shoes at the edge of the threshold. I knew that taking one step forward would be a step I could never take back. I glanced over at the Guard, who had distinctly averted his gaze. Then I looked at the Reaper, now standing on the other side, waiting patiently for me.

"Come on," he said quietly, again holding his arm out for me to move forward. "I'll take care of you."

Not being able to go back would be all right, I realized. It would be so much better than never moving at all.

I took a deep breath, and I stepped through the door.

Chapter Fifteen

PROMISES AND GRIDDLECAKES

I DID NOT MAKE IT VERY FAR. I had both my feet on the grass—grass!—as I stood there in disbelief and amazement. I picked each of my feet up and put them back down again in turn, thoroughly enjoying the softness of the ground beneath me. It was not hard stone. It was the world.

I realized I was gaping to the point of ridiculousness when I looked over at the Reaper. I didn't have a chance, really, to truly look at him, as the door creaking behind me drew my attention.

Turning briefly, I caught a sad smile on the face of the Guard. I disregarded it and looked back to him.

"Do you know how wonderful this feels?" I asked him excitedly as I picked my feet up and set them back down several more times. I stared up at the sky for a moment, admiring the orange and pinkish colors swirling together, before closing my eyes and breathing in the cool air so deeply it hurt my chest. "I'd forgotten the feel of it."

Amazing, I thought, that air could feel differently when your feet were on the ground.

It took a moment for it to fully strike me what I was doing.

"I'm sorry." I chuckled, looking to him. "I'm sure I look properly absurd right now."

"You look happy."

"*Happy*?" I asked him as I laughed.

No, I was not laughing. It was something lighter than that.

"I believe I've never made that sound before. Isn't that strange?" I stopped making that noise—whatever it was—and I frowned at him. "Is this really happening right now, or am I dreaming?"

Giggling. I'd been giggling.

The corners of his mouth tugged up the slightest amount. "Do you have dreams about me?"

"Yes," I admitted shamelessly.

Before he could ask me what they were about, I darted forward a bit and then plopped my rear down onto the ground. I reached my hand out, touching a flower, finding myself somewhat glad for the length of his absence. It had given the world time to come back to life.

"It's alive," I told him as I gently rubbed its red petals between my fingers. I didn't want to harm it.

"There are live plants inside the House." I could hear a small smile in his voice.

"But they're not in the ground." I whispered, almost as if I were telling him a secret. I looked up at him. "Do you know how long it's been since I've touched something that was truly attached to the world?"

"Ten years." I ignored the clear sadness I heard in his voice.

"Do you realize what you've done for me?" I asked him in disbelief.

He blinked hard at me as I wiped a tear from my face.

Why was I crying if I was not sad? "Thank you."

The smile on his face confused me, but it was irrelevant.

I looked up at the sky; the light was fading but was not yet entirely gone. Warmer weather brought longer days with it, like the world was celebrating. It was not mocking me now as it had always done before.

Had it been mocking me or simply showing me all this time that it was waiting for me?

I closed my eyes and took another deep breath before asking, "How long can we stay out here?" I ran my hand across the blades of grass, enjoying the coolness against my fingers. It felt different than I remembered, sharper.

"As long as you want."

I looked over at him and asked, jokingly, "And what if I wanted to stay here all night?"

He shrugged. "Then that's what we'll do."

I narrowed my eyes at him. "And you'd stay with me?"

"Of course."

HE AND I WALKED around the garden together, and I looked at absolutely everything that I'd only ever seen through windows. I touched most things that I passed, and some textures—the feel of leaves or the bark of trees—naturally attempted to spark old memories from the recesses of my mind rather than create new ones. I almost felt guilty, as I was torn between looking at the colors of newly blooming flowers dotted along in neat, organized increments, and looking at him.

Everything appeared so different when examining it up close.

That it was even happening was unfathomable to me, and my lightheadedness did not help me believe it was real.

I stopped moving suddenly when I reached a part of the garden that could not be seen from the balcony. It was under a covered walkway that curved and wrapped around, leading back from a different angle.

I reached out and touched a statue of a man. I had never seen one before outside the drawings in books of the library. The man stood so straight and tall in his frozen state. I could not decide if his sculpted face appeared to be cold or warm. One hand rested on the top of a sword, the tip of which touching the foundation near his feet. At the base of his sword was the mark of our Branding. Words were carved into neat lines at the foundation.

"What's wrong?"

"I was just thinking about how different the world appears when you're looking at it from a different perspective." I looked up and gestured at the space around me. "I didn't even know this was here." I heard myself laugh humorlessly. "It's been right here this entire time . . . and I could never see it."

He took a step closer to me, but he said nothing.

"Is this life?" I asked, my voice firm. "Is this what life is like? Walking past invisible spaces until you're granted permission for your eyes to see them?" I shook my head. "Is this life? Endlessly random circumstances all leading to that permission being granted?"

He said nothing.

"Do you realize . . ." I took a moment to compose my thoughts. "Do you realize that, if you hadn't come along . . . I would never have seen this? I would've spent the entire remainder of my life stuck between the walls of that House." I shook my head at him again. "But is it worth having the ability to see something when you cannot have it?"

His brow furrowed. "Who says you can't have it?"

Frustration swelled inside me. "You and Ahren with your words." I shook my head at him. "Look around us and think about the reality of our situation. Ahren is going to be overthrown eventually. Given your occupation, you are going to die. It's only a matter of time. I don't mean to sound selfish, but where will that leave me? I will be stuck in that House again, dreaming of being out here in a world that simply does not exist to me."

He held his hands up in the air, looking all around us as if to prove some sort of point.

I had no idea what that point could be if not proving my own.

"Do you know what I see?" He did not wait for a response. "I see you, standing here with me. That is the world I'm standing on right now. It exists."

He reached a hand out and, on reflex, I cringed away from it.

His mouth dropped open, and I opened mine to speak, but nothing came out.

He closed his eyes and stared at the ground to say, "I am so sorry."

Without looking at me again, he turned on his heel and began walking away. My mouth was still open, and I tried to force something to come out of it, but . . .

Nothing came. There was barely enough light to see his retreating figure. Just before he passed the corner that would take him out of my sight, I called out.

"*Chase!*"

He stopped, and I stood there for a moment, staring at his back.

Then, I walked most of the way to where he was standing and said, "I am not afraid of you."

When he'd turned around to look at me, I shook my head as tears welled up and spilled from my eyes.

"Do you know what happens when men touch women here?" I almost whispered.

He stepped closer to me but stayed several feet away.

My face felt like it was breaking when I said, "They come in and they hurt them when they're alone. Sometimes, a woman's belly grows with a baby. Nine months she spends with it, feeling it growing inside her. And then they come and take it, and she never sees it again." I looked down at the ground and tried to calm myself, wiping desperately at the tears. "They take away the only good that comes from something evil, so all she's left with is the bad. Only bad and no hope at all for anything more. That's my reality. That is the world I live in."

His voice was calm when he said, "You're worried that's going to happen to you."

"It's *going* to happen!" I shouted at him. "Sometime when you're gone and Ahren is dead. Or perhaps it would happen with you, and they'd come to take it from me even then. They would do that, even if it was yours. They would still take it." I shook my head at him. "You cannot protect me from everything."

He stepped all the way up to me and leaned down close to my face. I did not move away from him. Instead, I analyzed him to calm myself. I watched his jaw clench, unclench, and then clench again. I watched wetness spreading in his eyes. I counted the freckles on his face that I'd not had the opportunity to count before—the one on his nose, the two on his forehead, five others on the left side of his face, and eight on the right.

Eventually, he said, so quietly that I almost couldn't hear the words . . .

"One day soon, I'm going to take you far away from this place." His brow furrowed. "Do you believe me?"

I shook my head slowly and said, "I'm not sure."

"I need you to trust me."

I did not know if I could believe him. If he was going to take me away, why couldn't it be now?

I didn't ask him why he wasn't doing it now. I looked at his face to see if he was lying.

I kept looking, waiting to see it. I kept waiting for just a hint of it on his face—some sort of deception. Instead, all I saw was absolute, unyielding conviction.

I nodded my head and watched him release a breath. He believed his words, at the very least.

He held his hand up close to my face, showing me what he was doing and giving me ample opportunity to move away if I wanted.

I clenched my jaw tightly and felt my nails digging into the palms of my hands, but I did not move. And he stood there waiting, with his hand held in front of my face, until my jaw had unclenched and my hands were not balled into fists.

I closed my eyes and . . .

He touched me.

My entire body was shaking as he ran his thumb along my cheekbone. His hands were softer than I would've expected them to be— far gentler than I ever could've imagined, given the strength I thought they would need to break people's bones. Though I had pictured this happening in my head, I'd not thought it would feel the way it did.

I startled, which made him pull his hand away, when I realized . . . "It doesn't hurt."

"I won't hurt you," he assured me.

My breathing was choppy and ragged, but I did not care.

"Do you believe me?"

I nodded quickly and he took one of my hands in both of his. I only had a moment to marvel at the way it felt before he placed my hand on his face and took his own away.

He watched my face while I touched his. I was distracted by the way it felt—the stubble growing just at the surface of the skin on the lower half of his face and prickling at my fingers, the feeling of his jaw clenching under my touch. It was strange, and it took me a long while to look back into his eyes.

It felt so different.

He waited until I was looking into his eyes to tell me, "There's not anything I would give to you that another person can take away. I won't let that happen." His breath felt like feathers brushing against my face. "Do you understand me?"

I nodded again and realized I'd been staring at his mouth when he'd started speaking. I looked back at his eyes, and then again at his mouth.

I hadn't noticed that my face had been moving forward without my own volition until I heard . . .

"Are you sure?"

I almost wondered what he was inquiring, but I did not ask him to clarify.

"I love you," slipped out of my mouth, and I immediately pursed my lips together, as if that could somehow take back what I'd just done.

His smile then was not slow; it was fast, and it seemed to reach all the way to his eyes. He said, "I love you, too."

And in an instant, somehow, my heart feel like it had shot up my throat.

Then it was not my face moving forward, but his.

He stopped advancing when his mouth was right next to mine, and he stood there waiting. For several breaths, I was entirely still, trying to figure out how to make my heart return to normalcy. When I realized I had no hope in the world to manage it . . . I pressed my lips against his.

I didn't have a clue what I was supposed to be doing. His mouth moved, and mine tried in vain to follow after it. I was just beginning to get past the strangeness of it and realize it was somehow more enjoyable than touching his face when he took in a sharp breath and stepped away.

"I . . ." I started and then stopped, feeling my eyebrows scrunching together. "I'm sorry if I was bad at that. I've never done it before." I had seen it done, several times.

"Neither have I," he said in clear discomfort. For some reason, he was rubbing at the back of his neck.

"How could you not have? I know you're older than I am. And I just assumed, with the server girls when you first got here . . ."

He looked at me, his eyebrows raising. "Do you think I've gone around touching every girl who threw herself at me?"

I opened my mouth, but I did not answer him.

"Do you think that was the first time I've ever been here and turned them away?" He shook his head slowly and then looked down at the ground. "Do you think I'd never seen you before?"

"I was invisi—"

"No you weren't," he interrupted. He stepped close to me again. "Do you want to hear about the first time I ever saw you?"

I nodded, despite the strange and unknown feeling welling in my stomach.

"I was twelve when they brought you in. They drugged you, didn't they? I remember standing outside my school, watching them drag you here by your tiny arms. I remember the bag over your head. I remember what you were *wearing*, for god's sake. A brown shirt and a dirty pair of trousers with a hole in the knee, like you'd fallen repeatedly."

It took me a moment to ask, "How could you have noticed that? How could you even *remember* it? I can hardly remember those things myself. How could you even know it was me?"

Firmly, he said, "I noticed because I've been trained to notice *everything*. And I can remember it because that day is *burned* into my memory."

I opened my mouth to speak.

Nothing came out.

He shook his head slowly at me again. "I followed behind them when they brought you to this House. I followed them inside. I remember the leader then taking the bag off your head and staring at you. That's how I knew Agatha's name. I heard him tell them to take you to her, and when I saw you with her later, I knew who she was." He paused for a moment. "He caught me." He nodded. "Right after they dragged you away, he saw me standing there." He blinked hard at me several times before asking, "Would you like to see what he did to me?"

Deliberately, I shook my head. I did not want to see.

He turned around, pulling up the back of his shirt. It was just light enough still for me to see several long scars running along the entirety of his back, and he only kept it up long enough for me to catch a glimpse and wonder how I could've *possibly* missed them the instance of seeing him without a shirt. Then, he was leaning down in my face once more.

"He tied me up," he began again, his face twitching in either anger or disgust. "He tied me up like an animal and beat me with a whip until I told him I'd followed you here. Do you want to know what he said to me?"

Again, I shook my head. I watched a tear fall from his eye as he stood there with his mouth hanging open. He did not listen to me.

"He said . . . *You wait until I get my hands on that little girl of yours.*" He laughed once—humorlessly—before adding, "I'm not going to tell you what I did to him when he untied me."

It felt very much like all of me had stopped.

"You see," he continued after a short pause, breathing in through his nose and wiping a tear away from my face. I did not flinch when he touched me, even after what he'd just said. "I've spent almost half my life concerning myself with you."

"I don't understand," I whispered. It was all . . . *unfathomable.*

"You're wondering why I didn't come to you sooner if that's true, am I right?"

I nodded.

He tilted his head for a moment, listening. When he was satisfied enough that no one else was near, he asked, "Do you know what happens to Reapers when they go rogue?"

I shook my head.

"We're hunted down like dogs. Relentlessly." He raised an eyebrow. "Do you understand what I'm saying?"

"I don't," I admitted. I didn't feel that I currently understood much of anything.

"I didn't come to you sooner because I had to make sure I would be in a position where I could keep myself alive to keep you safe when I took you away."

"And can you?" I asked, still whispering.

He said nothing, but that slow smile spreading on his face seemed to be answer enough.

"How did you know I would love you?"

"I didn't, but I came to hope you would." A few seconds passed. "I swear to you, nobody will ever hurt you again. And if they do . . . I'm going to kill them." He watched me for a moment before asking, "Are you afraid of me now?"

I stared into his face, thinking over everything he'd said to me.

"I'm not afraid of you," I heard myself say again before I pressed my lips against his.

I was not so concerned with the kissing then. I found myself pondering over the downright absurdity of his words . . . paired with the realization that he tasted of griddlecakes.

CHAPTER SIXTEEN

WATCHING EYES

IN THAT HIDDEN PLACE OF THE GARDEN that I'd never seen from the balcony or any windows, Chase and I sat down across from one another with our legs crossed in front of us. Rather than speak to him, I thought about all the things he had told me. When I become overwhelmed by that, I thought about the way our hands felt together, held between us on the ground.

I was touching the world, and I was touching him. It was strange for me to realize that touching them both somehow felt like the same thing to my heart in that moment. I wondered, in his gaze being fixed at our hands . . .

Was he feeling or thinking the same?

It was quite a while, though I was not entirely sure how long, before I heard a throat being cleared relatively close by. Chase did not look away from our hands at the sound, though I did, finding Ahren.

"I believe I should walk you back to your quarters now," Ahren said, presumably to me.

Chase finally brought his gaze to mine and offered me a small smile.

I was torn on the matter. Part of me did not want to leave, but the other—infinitely more sensible—part knew I had things to do tomorrow and that I should go at least *attempt* to sleep.

Chase brought his hand back to himself only for a moment before reaching out to my face.

I still did not flinch.

He said, "If you decide you don't want to see me tomorrow, I'll understand."

"Don't be ridiculous," I told him. "Of course I'll want to see you."

I stood to leave at that. Even through the darkness, I did not miss Ahren's extremely large grin as I walked toward him. Before I turned the corner that would return me to the main portion of the garden, I stopped and glanced over my shoulder.

Chase had been staring at the ground, still sitting in the same spot on the grass, but he looked up at me and smiled again. It was a very nice image to leave with—him smiling because of me.

I hesitated before I stepped back into the House shortly after. I stopped and turned, taking the sight of the garden while standing in it and thinking of how much stranger the world was than I'd ever realized.

When I went back inside, I stopped once more in the doorway. Moore hadn't returned and had since been replaced with another Guard. I did not pay any attention to the newcomer, looking only at the man who had opened the door to allow me outside.

I stared at him for such a long time that a confused—or possibly uncomfortable—expression took over his face.

"Did you enjoy your evening with him, Miss?"

I nodded and realized I was crying again, though I still was not unhappy. It was so peculiar. Why would a person cry if they were not sad? Perhaps someone in the world knew the answer to that question, but for the life of me . . . I could not discover it.

"I can understand if the only reason you did what you did was out of fear, Sir," I began. "But I want to sincerely thank you for showing me kindness. I'm afraid that, until recently, I did not truly know what the word meant."

His expression transformed from confused to wholly and genuinely warm before he said, "Why should a person fear another when they've done nothing wrong, Miss? Reapers are people too, if I'm not mistaken."

"I'm very glad someone else is able to see it." I was so glad that I could now.

The smile on his face transformed into more of a small grin. "I have eyes, Miss."

"Perhaps one day, everyone else will discover that they have them as well."

"I truly hope so," he said, his voice full of sincerity.

I offered him a small smile—not at all forced—before walking away.

Ahren and I had made it down several hallways before I halted and blurted out, "I kissed him."

He halted as well. "Did you really?"

I nodded my head quickly.

"I knew you'd kissed, given that your hand hasn't left your mouth since you walked away from that Guard. I'd just assumed he'd kissed you."

I shook my head as I stared at the wall.

He leaned down a little and asked, quietly, "How was it?"

I snorted. "Well, I must admit that I don't have a clue in the world how to do it properly, or what it's supposed to be like, or anything about it, really." I stopped speaking and paused, looking up at his face to admit, "To be wholly honest, I feel as though I don't have a clue in the world about anything at all in this moment."

He chuckled. "It's wonderful, isn't it? That feeling."

"It's strange. I feel as if I'm floating up to the ceiling right now. And I'm just so . . ." I paused, trying to find the appropriate word. When I discovered it, I wondered how such a simple word could be so complex. "*Happy*. I'm just so happy. And it's extremely ridiculous, but I'm having a nearly uncontrollable urge to hug you. Isn't that silly?"

He narrowed his eyes at me. "Are you really?"

"Yes, I can't quite explain it."

I was more than a little startled when he took a step back and opened his arms wide. And I was so far past more-than-a-little startled when I found myself very nearly jumping into them.

His arms wrapped around me, and mine wrapped around him. Again, I found myself thinking about how unbelievably strange the world was. But then . . . there was something else that was strange enough to draw me away from my pondering.

He laughed extremely loudly and stepped back. "Why are you sniffing me?"

"The last man I hugged was my father," I admitted in discomfort.

"That doesn't explain why you were just sniffing me."

"Well, you . . . you sort of smell like him, in a way." Underneath the distinct smell that I'd come to associate with Ahren, there was a faint, nearly undetectable hint of it. I realized . . . I'd forgotten, until just now. Did memories ever really leave you? I tilted my head up at him and asked, "Isn't that strange?"

"Perhaps your nose is simply confused along with your brain," he suggested.

"Don't patronize me," I told him, frowning for a moment. I needed to change the subject. "May I ask you a question?"

"Sure." It was odd, but I almost thought he sounded wary.

"Chase," I started.

He held his hand up for me to stop, and then he tilted his head to listen. When he was satisfied and nodded, I went on.

"Are you friends?"

He seemed stunned by my question, but he answered it. "He's one of my best friends. One of only two."

"Is he really?" I asked, incredulous.

He seemed to be quite uncomfortable for some reason, but I was unsure if that was due to my question or if he regretted answering it.

"Is that why you care about me?"

Several seconds passed as he seemed to be contemplating over what to say in response. He said nothing. He reached out a hand, putting it on top of my head, and began shuffling it around.

"What in the world are you doing?" I demanded, though I stood entirely still throughout the peculiar process.

He pulled his hand back to himself and laughed loudly, likely at the mess he'd made.

I pointed at it. "I insist that you fix this."

"I don't think so."

"Well, I can't see it to do it myself!" I started pulling my hand through my hair, attempting to get it to lay smooth again.

"Hold still," he said after a short moment of laughing at my feeble attempts. He was entirely focused as he fixed the mess he'd made on the top of my head.

Presumably fixed.

Flatly, I told him, "I'm quite unhappy with you right now."

He scrunched his face up at me in a teasing sort of way, and I returned the gesture. When he'd done a good enough job with my hair—or as good a job as he was going to do with it—he began walking again.

I followed after him. "You know . . . he didn't even look at my hair."

"He looked at your hair." He sounded both sure of what he'd said and amused.

"I'm nearly positive he didn't, and you weren't there to know," I pointed out. "At least . . . I think you weren't there."

"I wouldn't have to be there to know that he did. I doubt he's seen your hair down before. Besides, it's in our blood."

I stopped moving again. "How would looking at a girl's hair have anything at all to do with blood?"

"How did you know you wanted to kiss him?"

"I . . ." I started and then stopped, contemplating over it. "I just did."

He shrugged. "There's your answer."

"You speak very funny sometimes," I told him. "Did you know that?"

He and Chase both did, though I would not have said anything about it before now. For the first time, I believed, I saw Ahren open his mouth and then close it again. He nodded his head rather than answer me aloud.

"Still, that's not a satisfactory answer." I tried not to smile. "I believe I shall let you pass on this one occasion. I'm not entirely certain my brain could retain much more useful information tonight."

"Oh, you're going to *let* me pass?"

I couldn't help grinning. "I believe that's what I said."

He shook his head at me, but he laughed again before saying, "Come on. Let's get you down there so you can deal with Agatha and go to sleep."

I made some sort of grumbling noise that I had never once made in my life, but after a short time it transformed into to more laughing as I walked with Ahren.

I thoroughly enjoyed having a friend. I only hoped that I'd been wrong most my life in thinking there was no such thing.

THE LAUGHTER DIED away before I arrived at my door. Ahren waited at the end of the hallway, watching me as I walked down. I knew because I turned around to smile at him—which he returned—before stepping through and closing the door behind me.

Agatha sat up in bed, and I stayed planted precisely where I stood.

She and I stared at one another for an extremely long time before I could not stand the silence any longer.

"Aren't you going to ask me if I'm aware of what time it is?" I asked. "Or if he took advantage of me? Or if I had to watch him kill a person? You want to ask me those things, don't you?"

"No, my flower." Her voice was quiet as she shook her head. "I'm not going to ask you those things." Agatha always bombarded me with endless questions when she was concerned.

I could not fathom her stopping now. But if she was . . .

"May I ask you something, Aggie?"

"Of course you can," she said without hesitation.

I sat down at the edge of her bed and gently took her hands in mine. "Those men who hurt you—"

"Aster, don't ask me if I wish I'd had someone willing to stand up for me and stop it from happening. I didn't. So many of us haven't."

"No." I felt my face scrunching when I whispered, "Do you wish you'd been able to stop them yourself?"

She blinked hard at me as her own face scrunched up, and then she cleared her throat uncomfortably. "Are you asking me whether I wish I'd been physically strong enough to stop them myself? Or are you really asking me if I wish I'd been able to punish them for it?"

I supposed . . . "Both."

She took her hands away from me and wiped away a tear that was falling down her cheek. "I'm going to tell you something, though I don't know if I should. I've had four children; you already know that. You asked me before, if I'd ever been in love."

"You said you had once," I recalled. She had never volunteered the information—or even hinted toward it—before I'd asked her.

'All men have some sort of evil inside them, my flower. You may not see it, and they may not see it, but it's there.' That particular information had been given to me freely many times in ten years, reinforcing what I already knew.

Never anything about her having loved a man, until I'd asked.

"The fourth child I had was his," she said. "He was new in the Guard, and I wasn't yet twenty-four. I didn't know that such a thing as love existed before I met him. I didn't know there was such good left in the world. You asked me if he treated me like a servant or a person, and I told you both. I'm going to tell you now that he treated me like a person in front of everyone apart from the leader. He didn't care. They mocked him for it relentlessly, but still . . ." She shook her head. "He didn't care."

"But you said—"

"The reason I said both is because . . ." She trailed off for a moment. "Because when I had his child, he let them take it. It didn't matter that he didn't want to. He let them take it."

She stared at me, and her jaw quivered from the strain of the memory. For a moment, when looking in her eyes, it appeared the burden of it all was going to break her.

"I'm going to tell you what I did," she said deliberately. "Because I think you're to the point in your own life where you might possibly understand."

I opened my mouth to ask her what she'd done, but I quickly closed it again. I could not imagine Agatha ever having done something she had not been told or expected to do.

"I've beaten invisibility into your head since you were first thrown onto my floor. I'm going to explain to you now why I've done that all these years." She breathed in deeply, her lips briefly pursing. "Did you know my fourth child was the only one they didn't even let me see?"

I shook my head, though she was already aware that I did not know. Agatha had never spoken to me about any of her children past informing me of their existence in the world and the manner in which they had been conceived.

Her mouth hung open for a long time before she went on.

"I waited." She said that then paused, her eyes widening minutely as she must've been thinking on whatever had occurred.

I could see a warring within her, taking place behind those widened eyes, and I knew with unyielding certainty that whatever she felt the need to tell me . . . she'd never said aloud before.

"I waited until enough time had passed for them to forget all about me, but not long enough that the leader would be killed." She leaned forward and whispered, "They don't see us, Aster."

"You killed a leader," I said on a breath. I could see it written all over her face, though I could not believe what I was seeing.

"Yes, I did," she told me firmly and without the slightest hint of shame. "They didn't even think about me, but he knew I'd done it."

"But you're here," I said. If she'd been found for murdering a leader, she would've most certainly been killed for it. Immediately.

"He went and confessed he'd done it." Her gaze was down at her blanket, almost as if she were speaking to it and not me. "The damn fool."

"Why would he do that?" I asked the question so quietly that I barely heard it myself. "Why wouldn't he just play it off, since they didn't suspect you?"

She looked to me. "Don't you understand?" Her voice was full of desperation.

I shook my head. I was finding I did not understand anywhere near as much as I'd always thought I had.

"He did it to pay me back for what he'd allowed to happen. His best friend told me that." She stared off for a moment. "Do you want to know the last thing I ever said to him?" Her brow furrowed, and it appeared painful. "*I hate you.*" Again, her jaw quivered as tears fell freely down her face. "I didn't hate him."

I felt a tear falling down my face, almost mirroring hers, when she said, "I know you and that boy love each other, but you have to understand why I *cannot* be happy about it. He and Ahren have both taken your invisibility away from you. And now, when the time comes and you need to be unseen . . . everyone will be able to see you. Everyone will be watching. There's nothing you can do about that now."

I DID NOT SLEEP IN MY OWN BED that night. I curled up with Agatha on hers. For once, it was not me that needed the comfort. I ran my fingers through her greying hair while she cried silently to the stone walls, lost in her memories.

I did not bother her with any more questions. Instead, I laid there thinking about monsters.

I did not think of Agatha as a monster, though she had admitted to killing a man. I could not blame her for what she'd done. I did do a great deal of thinking on people viewing others as monsters for doing things they themselves had done, how and why that might be. While I knew I was only scratching the surface, the conclusions I came to saddened me tremendously.

I did also think of my next question for Chase as I laid there.

Only when I was positive that Agatha had fallen asleep did I allow my mind to rest.

Still . . . sleep did not come easy for me.

CHAPTER SEVENTEEN

CHOICES AND STABBING

I WOKE THE NEXT MORNING utterly confused as to what I should do. Now that Chase had returned, was I to tend to him as I had before, or was I to carry on with my regular habits and duties?

I was standing there staring sightlessly at the grey enclosing me when there was a knock at the door. Though I heard it, my head did not fully register the sound as I stared at my surroundings. It was so different from the world I'd been shown last night.

It wasn't until Agatha said, "Good morning, Sir," that I turned.

"Good morning." Ahren sighed then asked, "How many times do I have to ask you not to call me Sir?"

"It's bad form, Sir," she told him. I was sure *bad form* secretly meant she did not want to get into the habit of it and slip up with our next leader if—when—Ahren was killed. "I'll just be going now."

He forced a polite smile until Agatha vacated the room and closed the door behind herself. Then he turned to me with a serious expression on his face.

"What's going on?" I asked. "Has something happened?"

He narrowed his eyes at me and took in a deep breath, like he was steeling himself. Then he sat down at the edge of my bed, patting next to him. I went over and sat where he'd indicated without hesitation.

He said, "I need to speak with you about something."

"Is Chase all right?"

"What?" He shook his head like he was shaking himself of the question. "Yes, of course he is. He and I both agreed I should speak to you about this alone, so you don't feel pressured into anything."

Lost, I slowly said, "All right."

"You asked him a question last night." He was speaking so carefully, which was very unusual. "About poison."

"Do the two of you tell one another everything?"

"Close enough." He sounded quite apologetic.

I took in a deep breath and let it out as an extremely loud huff of air. I would certainly have to keep the knowledge in mind. He reached out and took my hands in his and I allowed it because I knew he would not hurt me.

He leaned close and whispered, "I know what he's planning to do with you."

I opened my mouth, but he held up one of his hands and I closed it again.

Still speaking quietly, he went on. "Do you realize the life you'd be getting into? A lot of the things he said to you last night were to make you really *think* about it. He told you we're hunted when we go rogue, didn't he? Have you thought about what you'll have to do?"

"What I'll have to . . ." I shook my head, still lost. "What do you mean?"

"Do you think poison is the only worry we have?" He was trying to speak quietly, but there was such passion in his voice that it was almost past the point of quietness. "It may be years before someone is able to track you down—or weeks, if even that." He paused and very slowly asked, "What are you going to do if he's gone when another Reaper comes?"

I didn't say anything, though he waited for it. At least for a time.

After a moment, he looked away from me. "He and I have so badly distorted your view on what we are. Do you realize how quickly he and I alone could dispose of nearly everyone in this House? Do you realize that?"

"There are so many in the Guard. . . ."

He leaned forward and clenched his jaw for an instant before speaking. "They wouldn't see us coming. They wouldn't hear us. All the Guard could be together in one room and they couldn't take us down. Improperly trained bodies, wasting space—that's all they are. Do you believe we would think twice about it?"

Though I felt certain he was simply making a point with what he said on *all of them in a room*, I said, "Yes."

"*No.*" He corrected me firmly. "If they stood in the way of a mission, we would *not* think twice about it. We're made to be this way. Can't you understand that?"

"Could you kill *me*?" I snapped.

"Yes," he said, entirely calm. "But I wouldn't. There's a very large difference."

I pulled my hands back to myself, placing them in my lap, and I stared unblinking at the wall.

"I'm trying to make you understand."

"You're trying to make me think you're a monster," I said assuredly. "Don't confuse the two."

He gently grabbed my face between both his hands, turning my head so I had to look at him. "They'll hunt him down, Aster. They will hunt him down because they'll be sent on a mission to do it. They won't care if you're standing in the way. They won't care that he's one of them. The Reapers in this city?" He shook his head. "They won't care."

"You were sent on a mission to kill that girl's family," I accused. "The one you loved."

Slowly, he nodded.

"And did you?"

I watched the tears spreading in his eyes when . . .

He shook his head. "Can't you hear what I'm trying to tell you?" His green eyes stood out vividly through the tears threatening to fall. "They didn't care about how I felt. We don't care when we're not involved. We *can't.*"

I wiped away my own tears and nodded in understanding. "You're trying to tell me to stay here."

He shook his head almost wildly then said, "You remember that day when I had you think about those questions for me?"

I nodded again, then in response.

"I'm going to give you questions to think about for you now."

I sniffled. "And what are they?"

"The first one is: What do you want?"

I opened my mouth to answer him, but he held up a hand to stop me.

"The second is: What are you willing to do to have what you want in your life? And the third is: What are the limits of your capabilities?"

I opened my mouth once more, but he spoke before I could.

"I'm asking you to *think*," he said, his voice unyielding. Then he stood from the bed and pulled me to my feet. Again, he reached out and held my face in his hands. "When have you *ever* had the chance to choose what your life would be? I'm asking you to choose. *This* . . ." He removed his hands from my face and pulled me close to a wall, grabbing one of my hands and running it down the cold stone.

"Or *that*." He pointed toward the single tiny window at the very top of the room, right near where ground level was, close to the ceiling. Not in any way large enough even for a body to get through. If it could be considered a window. It was more for air than anything.

It was our window.

He said, "Think about it."

He had made it to the door by the time I said, "Ahren."

He turned toward me, and I clenched my jaw. I felt as though my heavy breathing was taking up every inch of space inside the room.

Firmly, I pointed to the window.

"What are you willing to do?"

"Anything," I said on a breath.

"Can you kill a person?" His voice had gone entirely blank.

"If I had—"

"I didn't ask if you *had* to!" He nearly screamed at me.

The sudden change caught me off guard, and I involuntarily flinched.

He took a deep breath, and his voice was almost calm again when he asked, "Are you capable?"

He and I stared at one another for a long time in silence. Eventually, I watched him take another deep breath and shake his head at the floor. I looked down at the floor as well shortly after, thinking about evil.

I thought about those evil men who had hurt Agatha and the other women here. I thought of the people who had taken Agatha's children away from her. I thought about that drunken man, touching my body as if I were worth nothing more than the dirt on the ground beneath his feet as he walked freely in the world that I was not permitted entrance to. I thought of the Reaper who had killed the girl Ahren loved. I thought of the people who told me I was property, that I was not a person and could not feel. I thought of them squandering the life and feeling they declared themselves able to have. I thought of the Reapers who would come later.

"Yes," I heard myself say, full of conviction.

When I looked up, Ahren was out the door and in the process of closing it behind him. He paused and analyzed me before seeming to make some sort of decision. Then he said, "Come with me."

I went with him, and I did not ask where we were going.

AHREN WALKED WITH PURPOSE down the hallways of the Valdour House, and my shorter legs struggled to keep up with his long ones. When he came upon a door I had never once passed through, he stopped and stared at the two members of the Guard who were standing in front of it.

None of them said a word, but it was almost as though some silent message had passed between the three of them. When the two men began walking away, I could almost swear that one of them was for some unknown reason smiling.

I did not follow Ahren through the door. Instead, I stood there watching the two men's backs. They went to the end of the hallway where it branched off, and they stopped moving. They did not turn to look at me.

Ahren had made it halfway down the next hallway by the time I'd closed the door behind myself and began hurrying after him. Though he was still walking with purpose, I was able to catch up with him due to my own pace. I was stunned to find myself grabbing hold of his arm and jerking him to a halt. I was more stunned that he allowed me to do it.

"How many of you are in this House?" I demanded.

He smiled that slow, deliberate smile and then opened his mouth to speak.

Rather than allow him the chance to do so and distort what I knew as truth into something as far away as he could get from it, I added, "Guards do *not* block hallways in this House."

They patrolled. They guarded. They blocked *doors*, including and especially the one they'd stood at before stepping away.

He narrowed his eyes at me slightly. "What do you think I do when I'm working?"

"I wouldn't know," I replied shortly. "You know everything I do with my time, yet you've told me nothing about the way you spend your own when I'm not a part of it."

He stared at me for a long while, smiling, before he opened his mouth to speak. "I began the process of instating them slowly enough for no one to take notice as soon as I . . . *came into this position.*"

I spent as short a time thinking on that as I could before asking, "Why?"

"Do you believe the only thing we do is kill people?" He seemed to be trying not to laugh. "We do *much* more than that. We deserve more credit than you'd like to give us."

Trying to discern what could be occurring . . . "Are the Reapers of the city staging a coup?"

He blinked at me, and he said nothing.

"Why? What would be the point of it?"

He wouldn't answer me.

"No," I said thoughtfully. I stared at the floor for a moment, shaking my head and trying to work through this. I looked back up at him when I'd come up with something satisfactory enough. "I'm not asking about the point of it right now. How could you pull it off? Surely people in this city have seen you before and know what you are. How have you gone all this time with no one noticing? *How?*"

He leaned down close. "You're finally allowing yourself to ask the questions. It gives me hope for your survival." Then he straightened himself and looked down at me. "I suggest you pace yourself."

"Why?"

"If you're stabbed ten times at once, it's highly unlikely you'll survive the injuries." He said that then lowered his voice. "If you're stabbed ten times over the course of your entire life, you may survive each of them in turn. The mind is the same way. You understand?"

I thought on that, attempting to discover what he meant by his words. He watched me for a time, but eventually he began walking away again.

At his back, almost loudly, I said, "You didn't answer my question, Ahren."

He did not stop, and I felt an anger growing inside me the likes of which I had never felt before.

"Would any person survive the *first* stabbing from you?" I shouted, my voice bouncing off the walls between us.

He stopped then, peeking over his shoulder at me and smiling widely. "If I wanted them to." He was still smiling when he asked, "Are you coming with me, or are you going to stand in place for the remainder of your life?"

I did not respond to his question aloud, but I followed after him once he began walking again.

I assumed that was a sufficient answer.

CHAPTER EIGHTEEN

TRUTH AND LIES

I WAS NOT HAPPY as I followed Ahren down several more hallways, and I did not speak to him again. I was so unhappy with him that I'd forgotten all about Chase's existence in the world until we stepped into a room and I saw him. He was staring at the door from where he stood next to a window on the opposite side of the room.

Without a word, Ahren began walking away, back in the direction we'd just come from.

Before he'd taken even two steps, I stopped him with, "Where are you going?"

"I can be seen with you as much as I like," Ahren said. "I can't be seen with him more often than I should."

"Go, then," I said rudely when his back had turned once more. "I hope you manage not to stab anyone on your way through the House."

He did not look at me, but I gathered he was laughing by the movement of his shoulders as he walked away.

I glared at his back until he disappeared around a corner and then, because nothing remained of him to glare at, I looked to Chase. "I'm finding that I'm quite angry with him."

"I can see that," he said, appearing as though he were having a difficult time concealing his amusement. I attempted to prevent that from exacerbating my hostile feelings.

"So what was the purpose in all his questions?" I asked, wanting to distract myself from the negativity and discover some point in this. "He asked me a lot of things then delivered me to you. I've never been in this part of the House. We're not even permitted to *clean* here. Did you know that? It looks just like the rest of the House, so I can't understand why we're not allowed here. It makes absolutely no sense whatsoever."

We were silent for a long time after I managed to stop rambling, staring at one another as I waited for him to speak.

When he did not, I asked, "What am I doing?" I frowned and started again. "No. What are *you* doing? He asked me those questions and brought me here without telling me why he'd even asked them. I'm assuming you know the next part."

Chase's gaze was down at the floor for a moment before he slowly walked over to me. "Do you want to leave with me?"

"Of course I do." I tried very hard not to become frustrated once more. How many times did I need to answer the same questions, though? The both of them were exhausting me this morning.

"Did he tell you what that would mean?" he asked. "What you would have to do?"

"He asked me if I could kill a person, if that's what you're talking about," I snapped.

"I told him not to bring you here if you decided you couldn't."

I narrowed my eyes at him. "And what would you have done if I'd said that?"

He did not seem put off by my demeanor.

"The same thing I've done for the last ten years," he replied. "*Wait.*"

I nearly shouted, "So you would have deprived me of your time until I'd had enough and decided I would do anything for it?"

He shook his head quickly, saying the word *no* several times and holding his hands in the air. "I told him not to bring you here if you'd said no. I would've stayed in room number four like I did the last time I was here, and I would've continued seeing you in front of everyone." He gestured around himself. "This is the choice you made."

"I don't understand," I said, bemused.

"In four days . . ." he began, speaking very carefully as if I were inept, "I'm going to leave this House. A lot of people will see me go; we'll make sure of it. Then, later that night, I'm going to climb up the wall, back into this room."

"You're going to climb . . . the wall?" Was that what he'd just said? *Was* I inept?

"Yes." He said it as though it were such a simple concept.

I looked down at the floor and shook my head as I attempted to process it. Rather than ask him how he thought he could manage that, I said, "I'm failing to see the point of this. Are we to see one another in secret now?"

"Yes," he said again.

I gaped at him and fought against the urge to slap him in the face.

Had I ever wanted to slap a person before?

I did not believe I had.

"You're still not understanding." He looked away and took a deep breath. "Why do you think he brought you here?"

"I've already asked you that!" I exclaimed.

"No." He shook his head. "I'm asking why you think."

"I don't have a clue. He asked me if I could kill a person. I told him I could, and he sai—"

The corners of his mouth tugged upward. "And he said what?"

"'Come with me,'" I answered under my breath to the floor. Then—quickly—I looked up to his face. "Is that why he's brought me here? For you to teach me how to kill a person?"

"He brought you here so I could teach you how to survive." He took in then released a breath before adding, "With me."

He and I seemed to analyze one another for what felt like an eternity before I asked him the question I had thought of the night before. I did not know why all the questions I needed answers to were questions I always worried I wouldn't like answers to. But necessity overruled pleasure.

"Do you like it, Chase?"

He blinked hard, seeming lost.

I clarified with, "Killing people? Hurting them? You were happy to break that man's wrist before. You *do* enjoy it. Don't you?"

"Sometimes, yes." No longer lost, his voice was blank when answering. "Sometimes I do."

"How could you? How could you have a heart and—"

He stepped all the way up to me and leaned down. "Imagine you were being attacked. Imagine that you were being attacked like how you told me about last night. What would you want to do?"

"I wouldn't—"

Firm, he said, "I didn't ask what you *could* do."

I clenched my jaw at the frustration of both being interrupted during my last two attempts at speaking, and also at the similarity of what he'd just said to what Ahren had shouted at me in my room. It was infuriating. Didn't requirements and capabilities matter?

"Don't think about the answer; just say it. What would you want to do in that situation?"

"Stop them from hurting anyone else," came out of my mouth.

"And would you feel bad about it?"

Slowly, I shook my head.

He stood up straight and began walking back toward the window, like the conversation was somehow finished at that.

"Have you only ever killed bad people?"

He stopped, and his body appeared to go rigid. Then, all at once, it sort of slumped when he released a breath.

"I said I enjoy it sometimes." He walked the remainder of the distance to the window, and he stared outside.

Very slowly, I followed him, but I didn't look out when I was standing next to him. I watched the side of his face instead. It was a long time before he said anything else.

"We're ordered on our missions," he began. "When you're first sent on them, you ask questions. You ask what the person you're being sent to kill has done and why you're being sent there. And for a while . . . it's fine. They give you easy missions at first, ones you'll feel little remorse for carrying out, if any at all. And then . . . the missions start to change."

I said nothing as I watched his face creasing.

"It's so gradual you don't ever really think about it. One day you're taking out murderers and, then, before you know it . . . you're killing people who did nothing more than say something that somebody important believed they shouldn't have said." He finally looked over at me to say, "They make it gradual to numb you to it. They make it gradual so you get to the point where it's just another mission. One day . . ." He shook his head. "One day you wake up and really think about it. You think about the mission from the night before and wonder why. And you wonder how you could've done what you did. So, before every mission, you start asking more questions. You don't want to go anymore when you hear the answers, but what else can you do? You know they'll just kill you and send someone else if you refuse. So you go. You go so they don't send someone worse instead. At least you know you'd kill them quickly where the one they'd send in your place may not. And you pretend. . . . You pretend they've done something horrible."

I still said nothing, just watching his face. I was unsure if he expected me to speak.

He stared at me for a while, blinking wetness from his eyes. "And then you stop asking the questions." He clenched his jaw for a moment. "That's *my* reality. That's the world *I* live in." He turned away from me again and looked out the window. "Are you ashamed of me now?"

My brow furrowed in understanding, and I shook my head in disbelief of it. "Is that your reason for telling me what you just did?"

He brought his gaze back to mine. "How can you accept me if you don't understand? What would you do later, if I kept part of myself from you and you discovered it on your own? You need to understand what I am. If you don't . . .? How can you be positive you're making the right decision?"

He was right. I would rather know what he was upfront, as horrible a thing as it was to know. I needed to think on it later, though, not when there were so many other more-pressing things.

I asked, "Why are you pretending to leave in four days?"

"Because five days is all the time I was given off between my last mission and the next."

I didn't understand . . . "Then why are you pretending to leave?"

"I have one month to make you as prepared as I possibly can for this," he said, ignoring my question. "That's all we have."

"A month," I breathed. "How long did you train?"

"My entire life."

"You mean your entire life since you were brought in."

His brow furrowed as he shook his head. "Reaper women have their babies taken away from them too."

Astonished, I nearly shouted at him. "There are *women* in your occupation?"

He nodded.

I'd heard things, but . . . I had never seen a female Reaper. "All the stars! How do they manage to take a child from one?"

"It depends on the woman."

"I wouldn't think they'd be able to do it properly," I admitted.

He laughed a little, which made me frown at him.

"I don't see what's funny about this." *Women Reapers* . . .

"You should hope that you never meet a female Reaper." He grinned. "They're *exceptionally* unpleasant."

"How so?"

"I'll explain it to you someday," he told me, not bothering to conceal his amusement. "But you just might discover the answer for yourself along the way."

I did not know what he meant, but I felt as if I couldn't waste my time pondering over it. Though it seemed I *could* waste time staring at the floor and shaking my head. I simply couldn't stop myself from expending a few moments for that particular purpose. Then, I had to get back to it.

I had to ask him, "What is your plan?"

When I looked up again, I saw him smiling out the window.

He brought his gaze to mine. "Have you ever heard them talking about plays in the House? Where people go to watch other people pretend?"

"Yes, I've heard people speak of them. How is that relevant to what I just asked you?"

What was he thinking—that he was going to take me to one? That was a preposterous idea. I would not waste my time on such a thing, even if I had endless amounts of free time to waste.

A month. I had no time at all.

"Those people on the stage?" The corners of his mouth tugged upward the smallest amount. "They're glorified liars; that's all they are. They put on shows for other people to watch and be entertained. I'm going to teach you how to do that. At least help you figure out the basics."

"Why?" I felt my eyebrows moving downward, not understanding how his proposition could be useful against Reapers.

His smirk was gone when he said, "Because you and I won't survive if you can't. Anything else I could teach you wouldn't matter a bit if you can't lie."

"And do *you* lie?" I asked him before I could talk myself out of it.

"All the time," he answered slowly.

A muscle in my cheek twitched when I asked, "To me?"

There was only the briefest pause, where he seemed to be thinking over the appropriate response, before he said, "Not directly."

My voice sounded very small in my own ears when I asked, "What does that mean?"

"It means that if I open my mouth and tell you something, it's not a lie. That doesn't mean I've told you everything. Some people count omission as lies. That's not even including misdirection."

"If you've just told me that you lie all the time . . ." I struggled to get out the question as I fought against the urge to cry. "How could I possibly believe anything you say?"

"If I was trying to deceive you, would I have told you that? Wouldn't I have lied and told you I don't lie at all?"

"I don't know," I barely said. Everything was becoming far too confusing. I'd been so accustomed to thinking somewhat simply that my head was struggling immensely to catch up. "You could've said it with the sole intention of being able to use that precise point against me when I asked."

I realized as I was looking at him that I truly did not know him at all. Knowing where a person preferred their dirty laundry and that they would go against what they wanted for your benefit . . .

It didn't tell me as much as I'd thought it had.

Would I ever know him? Would I truly know anyone? Would anyone ever truly know me? Did it even matter?

He reached out, wiping a stray tear from my face, and smiled at me sadly. His hand lingered on my cheek. "Do you know how long I've been planning this, to take you away from here?"

I shook my head.

"Since the first day I saw you." His forehead scrunched a little as he stared down at me. "I've had to do a lot of lying to make this possible. That's what I meant."

"And would you lie to me? If I asked you something directly that you did not want to answer truthfully?"

He shook his head slowly and responded with, "I just wouldn't answer you."

"Do you promise?" I asked. "That you'll never directly tell me a lie? That you'll simply not answer my question? Can you promise me that?" I could get past this, I knew, if he told me that he would do so. Still, how could any person ever completely trust a liar? Could I trust anyone at all in this world?

"I promise you can believe every word that comes out of my mouth, as long as it's being said directly to you."

"And if it's being said to someone else in front of me?"

"It would be best if you didn't believe it." He did not smile at that, though it appeared as if he were tempted.

"Do you know why Ahren is here?"

"Yes."

"And will you tell me?"

He said nothing, but that slow, calculated smile began stretching across his face.

I cleared my throat and looked out the window. I shook my head where I stood, staring out at the garden and seeing the little walkway that I'd not ever seen until the night before.

My voice was not happy nor excited but sounded somewhat resigned when I asked, "When do we begin?"

CHAPTER NINETEEN

IT ISN'T ALL PRETEND

"**S**LAP ME AGAIN," Chase directed.

I did as he asked and slapped him across the face.

He sighed and wiped at his forehead with one of his hands for a moment, in a way that seemed to be absentminded. I could see the immense disappointment in his eyes where they were focused on a nearby wall and not at me. I tried as best I could to work through the thoughts and feelings it brought about inside me.

He did at some point seem to get over his dissatisfaction enough to begin dealing with me. "You're thinking too much into it. It's not believable."

"It's not believable because I don't want to slap you!"

He chuckled a little, which made me angry.

"You've not even explained the purpose of this."

"We have to put on a show," he stated.

I threw my hands up in exasperation.

He sighed again. "I have to give them a reason to believe I wouldn't come back for you and that, if I tried, you wouldn't have me. And that, even if I tried to *force* you to have me, I wouldn't be able to. There's a plan in place, but no plan is entirely foolproof. If they realize I've gone rogue instead, I don't want them to think of you until long after we've gone. Does that make sense to you?"

"Don't act as if I'm an imbecile, Chase."

"I'm not," he said quickly. "I'm asking if it makes sense to you, if you understand why now."

Calmly, I said, "I've never been in that sort of situation to know exactly how I would react to it. I'm not entirely sure that any amount of this sort of practice could tell us how I'd behave."

"You're saying you want me to assault you now, so you can understand how you would actually feel? Can't you *imagine* how you would feel? I'm sure you've spent a lot of time imagining it."

"Do you understand how I'm going to feel at the time?" I demanded. "You're going to assault me and then leave, am I correct?" I didn't wait for an answer. "Do you believe I want that to be stuck in my head until I see you next? What if you're so convincing that it—" I shook my head. "I don't know." I took a deep breath and attempted to explain it better. "I don't want to have a memory like that of you in my head."

"You're going to have a lot of bad memories of me in your head," he stated blankly. "At least with this one, you'll know it isn't real."

"But it *will* be real," I informed him.

He stepped closer and sighed again. Then he smiled in a sad sort of way. "No. It's all pretend." Slowly, a frown took over his face. "Do you need me to assault you?"

"*Could* you?" I challenged. "Right now? Could you just . . . *assault* me?"

He clenched his jaw for a moment. "I don't want to."

"I didn't ask if you wanted to!" I shouted at him. I felt startlingly smug, being able to treat him the way he and Ahren had both treated me today. "I asked if you could."

"I don't know."

"What does it matter?" I stepped close to him. "If it's only lies? If it's all just pretend? What does any of it even matter?"

I wondered why I was still not afraid of him as he stared me down while I continued speaking to him in such a way. I should've been afraid, I knew. No matter what had changed, I knew I still should have.

Why wasn't I?

"Do you want the first memory of me touching you to be that way?" He sounded entirely calm.

"You touched me last—"

"It's not the same," he said resolutely. "It is nowhere *near* the same thing."

I opened my mouth and then closed it again, pursing my lips together.

"Do you want it to be that way?"

I shook my head. Rather than tell him I did not want the memory of it at all, I heard myself ask, "Would you want to touch me that way?"

He looked away from me and rubbed at the back of his neck, almost laughing on an exhale of breath. Several seconds later, he nearly smirked and asked, "Would you let me if I told you I did?"

"I . . ." I began and then stopped, pursing my lips together again because I didn't know that I could—or should—answer his question. I felt my head nodding, though my brain had not given it permission to do so. "Do you want to?"

He smiled his slow smile at me, though it reached a bit farther on his face than it normally did. He raised an eyebrow and nodded his head. For nearly one instant, I had the time to ponder over the downright absurdity of a person wanting to do what he claimed he wanted to do. When I saw that he was moving closer to me, I realized . . . I'd just given him permission.

I started backing away regardless, watching him take back every step I attempted to place between us. I felt very much like some small animal being hunted in a calculated way by a predator. Then, my back was against a wall and I had absolutely nowhere else to go.

It was when the palms of my hands were flat against the wall behind me and he was directly in front of me with his hand reaching out for my face, his lips coming closer to mine, that I realized . . . he'd already caught me.

I wondered if I'd ever truly had a chance in any of this.

The kiss was not the same as it had been the night before. My lips did not struggle to follow after his; they simply had no say in the matter. I thought it was strange when he touched my tongue with his, and I nearly pushed him away to scream as much at him, but then I discovered there was something remarkably interesting about feeling his breathing in my mouth. It was almost as if we'd become one person somehow. It was quite . . .

Wonderful, in some inexplicable way.

It took me far too long to realize I'd gotten lost somewhere in his kiss, too long to realize that he had his body pressing mine against the wall and a hand gripping hard at my waist.

I pushed against his chest and slapped his face immediately after it had moved away from my own. Though I'd slapped him nearly ten times already, it was the first time the action left a red mark on his cheek. The rest of his face quickly turned red as well, which I'd never seen from him before.

"I am so sorry!" I rushed forward and reached out for his face.

He wouldn't look at me and he had his lips pursed together and off to one side. He was . . . embarrassed.

"It felt very . . . *strange* is all," I rambled, "and it was making me feel quite funny, and . . . I can't quite explain my reaction."

I stood there for several extended seconds as I took stock on everything. He still refused to look at me, but he was allowing me to touch his face after I'd just slapped him. I could not understand the way my body had reacted to him. But mostly, I wanted to know . . .

"Why in the world did you stick your tongue in my mouth?"

His eyes darted to mine then, but only briefly. He cleared his throat. "Ahren told me if I was going to kiss you, I should at least do it properly."

I shook my head over the preposterousness of it all. For one, that he and Ahren were discussing kisses. For another, that proper kissing was like . . . *that*. I could see now that it was, after having done it the two different ways, but . . . who in the world had ever realized as much? And how did one find out about it, if they were not told? Was there an endless string of people kissing other people and passing along the information? I supposed I must've missed seeing tongues the few instances I'd accidentally seen others doing it. Granted . . . I'd done my best not to truly *see* any part of it.

"Can we try it again?" I heard myself ask him.

He finally turned his face to mine. "Do you actually want to?"

"Yes, I'm quite certain I do." I answered distractedly.

"Are you going to slap me again?"

"I'm not sure," I admitted.

"How about this . . .? Given that kissing made you very confused and you're extremely uncomfortable about being touched, we can try the two separately."

"How do you propose we do that?"

He offered me a small—yet warm—smile and took both my hands in his. He pulled me closer to him and, in the process, wrapped my arms around his body until my hands were on his back. Then he released my hands from his and dropped them down at his sides.

I only fully realized that I'd removed my hands and held them extended in the air behind him when he quietly said, "It's okay."

I breathed in deeply, inhaling the scent of him when I did, and took the last step forward that had been separating the two of us. When I rested the side of my face against his chest, I noticed that my entire body was shaking horrendously. Still, he did not touch me with his hands. Though I had hugged Ahren the night before, this was not the same thing. It was nowhere near the same thing, just as Chase had said about the difference in the touching.

Very slowly, I returned my hands to where he'd put them at his back.

I did not squeeze him in excitement, as I had done with Ahren. For a time, I simply stood there, keeping my hands in place, but then . . . I moved them.

It was peculiar—feeling the way his muscles curved inward toward his spine. I could feel the scars from the beating he'd received ten years ago through his shirt. Though his body didn't tremble as mine did, occasionally one of his muscles twitched beneath my fingers.

At some point, he began touching my hair, running his fingers through it. Upon that discovery, I also noticed I had stopped shaking. It started again immediately when I thought of it, like my body was mocking me in an attempt to make me look as ridiculous as possible.

His entire body went rigid when his hand went past the end of my hair and onto my back. With the side of my face resting against his chest, I could hear the pace of his heart quicken because of it.

He did have a heart in there, no matter how it occasionally seemed or how questionable it sometimes was.

I could deal with my own trembling, though it was extremely embarrassing, but I would not be ashamed of the scars I had. In a sense, they told part of the story of my life—that I could find the strength within me to do something I believed to be important for myself, no matter the consequences. That was nothing to be ashamed of. I forced myself to remain calm and relaxed.

When he seemed to realize that I would not be ashamed of it, he pulled me so close to him it nearly made my neck ache. His breathing became ragged as he ran his hands down my back, feeling the rough lines of my beatings.

"It's okay." I whispered his words back to him.

It wasn't until I'd spoken that he finally released a larger, more natural breath. His head came down, resting on the top of my own, then he moved his fingers across my back, likely attempting to count the lines beneath them. It would not work; there were too many.

I realized, as he was doing it, that my hands were trying to physically comfort him in response to the sadness and anger I believed he felt over what had been done to me. It was strange. Was that a normal thing people did when they loved each other? I supposed . . . I supposed it was.

It had been such a very, very long time. . . .

It was then that I was struck by it. I likely could not count all the bad things Chase had done in his life. I could not count all the people he'd hurt, or killed, or all the lies he'd told. But . . . Did that make him unworthy of love? No more than being what I was—and spending the majority of my life doing things only because I was forced to do them—made me unworthy of the same. Was I really so different from him?

Was Chase guilty of the crimes he'd committed, or were those crimes at the fault of the people who had forced him into carrying them out?

They were not his crimes; I could see that now. Those things he had done were at the fault of a greater evil, an evil no one could escape from. But the fact of the matter was that . . . he was willing to do everything he could in an attempt to escape from it, despite the odds. And he was willing to do everything he could to take me with him when he did. Some people might've believed that was simply not enough or that it made up for nothing.

It was more than enough for me.

It was a long time before he took a step away from me, but he leaned down immediately, putting his face close to mine. He grasped my face gently between both his hands.

"I love you," he said, his voice firm. "Do you believe me?"

I analyzed his face, watching a tear fall from his eye and roll down his cheek. I watched his jaw clench and unclench several times. I saw his brow furrowed in sadness, or possibly confusion. Chase may have very well been a better liar than all those people who pretended on stages, but he was not lying to me.

"I believe you," I told him.

He nodded and removed one of his hands from my face to wipe at his own. I did not allow him to. I reached my hand out and did it for him.

Such a long, long time. . . .

"I understand now," I barely said, getting back to what needed to be done. Preparation. Pretending. "How to make this work."

Putting myself in a similar situation to discern how I would react in such a scenario was not what I needed to accomplish what Chase was asking of me. All I needed was to understand what was at stake and the things he was willing to do for me. I could pretend—if I needed to pretend—if he was capable of doing the same. I was more than capable.

When Chase and I got back to my lesson in playing pretend, I did not picture his face as I was slapping it. I made up an image of an imaginary man inside my head. I did not picture myself being attacked when I shoved at his chest.

I thought of Agatha and all the pain she'd endured throughout the years by the hands of evil. I slapped Chase and I cried silently, thinking of Agatha's children that had been taken from her. I thought of Reaper women who, though strong enough to kill a man, were not strong enough to stop men from taking their children from them.

Chase's face blurred in and out of my vision, being replaced with face after face of the leaders of New Bethel that I'd seen over the years. Faces of men who did evil. Faces of men who were not strong enough to fight against it or simply did not care to try. And I understood.

I understood why those people stood on stages and played pretend, and why people went to watch them. It was their only way of fighting back against something too powerful, something they were too weak, too afraid, or too uncaring to truly fight. I understood it, but all that understanding did was show me how worthless it truly was. Standing around doing nothing while the world fell to pieces.

I felt something inside myself as I stood there, allowing my eyes and my mind to distort the scene in front of me into what was really the truth. There was fury, deep inside my bones. Fury that no one would fight against anything in this world. I was too weak and un-knowledgeable to fight against it now, but there was a desire that one day . . . I wouldn't be.

I knew now that I could do more than I'd ever given myself room to think of. I also knew that I would not be ashamed of myself when I did any of it.

Had that always been there inside me, waiting patiently for the moment I would permit it freedom?

Yes.

I believed it had.

CHAPTER TWENTY

TRUST AND REAPER GUARDS

I T TOOK CHASE SEVERAL ATTEMPTS at saying my name before I snapped out of the imaginary scene inside my mind. When I properly came to, I realized he had both my arms in his hands, holding me at a distance away from him.

I quickly took several steps back. "I'm sorry."

"Don't be." He said that then sighed. When he spoke again, his voice took on a much lighter tone. "Can we take a break from this? My face is numb and I'm hungry."

"Don't be ridiculous." I chuckled. "Your face isn't numb."

He grinned. "It's not?" His nose crinkled a little. "Is it red?"

I pursed my lips to prevent myself from smiling.

"I'll take that as a yes."

"There's a mirror just there." I pointed toward the opposite end of the room. "You can have a look for yourself."

"I don't like looking at myself in mirrors."

"Why ever not?" I laughed, confused. "You're very nice to look at."

"You think so?" Though he was smiling, I was almost entirely positive he'd forced the expression.

I nodded and, slowly, the smile dropped away from his face.

"It just makes things easier," he said. "Do you look at yourself?"

"Not often, no," I replied. "We only recently acquired mirrors in our quarters and I'm simply so accustomed to not having one that I don't use it. To be honest, I've never really thought much into them. But what do you mean that it *makes things easier*?"

"It just does."

That was not a satisfactory answer.

I studied him for several seconds, watching his jaw clenching beneath another forced smile.

Quietly, I asked, "Are you afraid that, when you look at yourself, you'll see what everyone else sees?"

He intentionally dropped his forced smile, his expression so expeditiously turning apathetic, but he said nothing.

"Or are you afraid you'll look at yourself and begin to believe that what they see is what's actually there?"

I stared at him for an extended amount of time, waiting for some sort of response, but all I received was that blank look of his.

I took a step closer. "Do you know what *I* see when I look at you?"

He blinked hard at me twice, but again, that was all the response I received.

I took a deep breath and smiled sadly at him. "I see a person who is willing to show kindness to someone who has rarely seen it before in their life. I see a person who is willing to stand up and fight for something they want, no matter how hopeless it seems to be. I see a person who is willing to do whatever is necessary to have their own life, that has the courage to say *enough*."

I did not wait—or even check—for a response then. I took his hand and began leading him away to the other side of the room. Halfway across, he stopped, digging his feet into the floor in refusal to move farther forward.

"I'll pick you up and carry you, if you force it to come to that," I warned him. Though I was relatively certain that I could do as I'd threatened, I was not entirely positive. I'd worked hard for the majority of my life, and I had picked up a great many heavy things, but I had never once attempted to pick up a man.

He scowled at me, but after a little more tugging I was able to get him moving again.

I stopped when we were in front of the mirror, and he distinctly looked away from both the mirror and me. I patiently stared at the side of his face for what had to be several minutes before he gave in and brought his eyes to mine. I pointed at the mirror in front of us.

For the first time since meeting him, I believed that he was angry at me. His nose twitched—not crinkled—for an instant. Still, he looked forward and that was enough.

His eyes seemed to be darting frantically as he took in the image of himself.

I was silent for a long time, allowing him his moment of unhappiness at what he was seeing there before I quietly said, "It's only a reflection. It's as fake as me slapping you."

At that point, his eyes finally seemed to settle, looking only at their doubles in the mirror before us. "You *did* slap me."

I could feel my forehead and my eyebrows scrunching as I slowly shook my head at him. "I didn't slap you, even if your face and eyes would say differently." I watched him blink hard a few times before I almost whispered, "Do you understand?"

I watched as the hostility gradually drained away from his face and, very quietly, he laughed once.

"I understand," he told me with a small smile. I did not believe it to be forced.

"You have the right to decide what your own truth will be," I told him. "You've shown me we all have that right." I sighed. "Now, you've said that you're hungry. I'll go get us some food."

"My face won't be red in a few more minutes." He shrugged. "We can wait."

"No," I insisted, shaking my head. "If we're to make our scene believable, we have to set it up so it can be."

He tilted his head slightly to one side as he looked at me.

"Go on to number four and I'll be there shortly." I began walking away.

I'd made it a few steps when he asked, "Not here?"

I turned to look at him and shook my head again, quickly then. "It would be out of place were I not seen in the House periodically throughout the day and if I'm not going to the places I should be going. You're to go to the other room, and over the next four days I'll bring your meals to you there. When we're done, we can return here."

He grinned. "We're more likely to get caught if we're seen headed to this side of the House by making multiple trips."

I sighed again then said, deliberately, "I understand that this is what you do. . . . And I promise that on most things I will listen to you without objection. But you must understand that, for now, we're in my familiar territory. When it comes to what is noticed here and what is not, I would know far better than you. The simple solution for the problem you've voiced is . . . don't be caught coming here. I'm quite certain you can manage as much."

He allowed me to make it several more steps away from him before he asked, "Can you?"

Unhappy, I told him, "I'm sure I can manage to stay unseen by everyone apart from the Reapers in the House."

"Are you sure?" he pressed.

"Considering what you're expecting me to do when we leave here together, it would be quite nice if you had a little more faith in me. If I cannot manage to stay invisible to people who have no eyes, then . . . I'm afraid your plan truly will be hopeless after all."

He sounded believable when he said, "I have faith in you."

I turned and had made it two more steps before he opened his mouth again.

"How many Reapers are in this House?"

I turned back to face him and attempted to maintain my composure.

I watched him while he blinked at me, knowing it was an answer he already knew. I had the distinct impression that he was asking as a test; it wouldn't have been the first he'd given me. This was precisely like the knife he'd placed in plain view on his nightstand to see how I would react to it. Only now, it was not a reaction he was watching for.

I knew what the test was.

"Four that I know for certain, including yourself, and I have suspicions toward a few others." I frowned at him for a moment. "Ahren told me he began instating them slowly, immediately after coming into his position. I understand what you mean about lies. I believe that was a truth he told me, but not a complete one. I believe Reapers have been slowly infiltrating this House for some time now. I wouldn't be entirely surprised if every pair of two in the Guard was made up of at least one."

I watched that slow, calculated smile spreading on his face.

"I won't ask you why, though I'm sure you could tell me the answer," I said. "For now, I would rather spare myself of the knowledge that, though you may love me and expect me to trust you . . . you do not trust me."

The smile dropped quickly from his face and, although I loved seeing him smile, I was happy in that instance to see it gone.

"If I've successfully passed your latest test, may I go? I'm quite hungry myself."

I did not wait for any sort of answer. I walked out of the room.

THOUGH IT WAS STRANGE exiting a room and finding myself in a part of the House I'd only walked through one time, I did not get lost. It was laid out almost identically, but in reverse, to the other side of the House. I passed through the door that led to the outside hallway, finding the two Reaper Guards still standing at the point they'd blocked before I had stepped inside, and then I closed the door quietly behind me.

I took one step and stopped when I saw the hand of one shoot down at his side, palm out and down toward me.

Very slowly, I went and placed myself inside a nook near to the door, attempting to make my body as small as was humanly possible.

Nearly a full minute passed before I heard voices coming closer to where the Reaper Guards stood.

I heard the sound of one of the server girls laughing—they had very distinct laughs, for some inexplicable reason—accompanied shortly thereafter by a male laugh.

I fully expected for the sounds to pass by once they reached a certain point, but they did not.

"What are you doing?" a man asked.

I would've wondered who had asked, until I heard a voice I recognized speak next. It was Camden.

"Just taking a walk with my lady friend."

It was one of the Reaper Guards that had asked the question.

"It seems to me you've gotten lost while making your way," the second Reaper Guard stated.

"Come on, guys," Camden said, which was not only disrespectful in tone, but also incredibly frustrating—even for me. Was *guys* even a word?

"You know the rules," the first Reaper Guard said.

"I swear," Camden began, "you two are the only ones in the House that follow the rules."

"Which is why we're standing here, and you are not," the second said.

I put my hand over my mouth so I would not laugh and be discovered.

"Why are you blocking the hallway and not the door?" Camden asked, suspicion clearly evident in his voice.

"We wanted a change of scenery," the first replied. "Should we inform our leader you've decided to take a few minutes off to spend with your . . . *lady*?"

"Like he'd care." Camden laughed. "The only thing he's concerned about is that piece of trash. I wonder how he's handling her devil being back in the House."

It took absolutely every ounce of willpower I had inside me to remain hidden in my corner and not run out there and . . .

What would I do?

I did not know, but I discovered that I wanted to hit him. Very badly. Directly in the middle of his face.

"Why are you smelling me?"

"I should tell you," the first said, almost sounding apologetic. "I'm relatively certain your nose is not accurately informing your brain where the smell of trash is coming from."

My jaw dropped, I was certain, farther than it had ever dropped in all my life, and my eyes felt like they were ripping apart at the edges.

"What did you just say to me?" Camden demanded.

"I suggest you move along," the second said. "I've heard devils have remarkable hearing."

I sat there for several minutes, staring at the door from my place inside the nook in the wall. Out of my peripherals, one of the Reaper Guards appeared, clearing having backed down the hallway. He stopped when he came upon me. Not looking at me, he gestured with his fingers for me to come out. When I emerged, I saw that he'd been watching the other Reaper Guard.

Once I'd made it halfway down the hallway—staring at the hands of the stationary Reaper Guard as I moved forward—I stopped and looked for the other.

I could just barely see that he'd lain down on the floor inside the nook.

I frowned where I stood there staring at him, realizing that they must not ever leave their post. I took him to be the second Reaper Guard when he rolled over and shot me a glare, clearly telling me to move on.

I did.

I did not acknowledge the other Reaper Guard as I passed him, but I went the direction he told me to with one of his fingers behind his back, even though it was the opposite direction of the way I needed to go.

CHAPTER TWENTY-ONE

PRISON BARS

I TOOK THE LONG WAY to get to the kitchen, as instructed by the Reaper Guard. His pointed finger added nearly ten extra minutes of walking to my journey, but I was not complaining even inside my own head. I would have to do much more than walk ten extra minutes soon, and the time gave me a bit more uninterrupted time to think. Though I knew the direction had been about not being caught near that part of the House, I was extremely grateful to know it was the opposite of Camden.

Rather than think about things I likely should have thought about—perhaps first of all the fact that neither Chase nor Ahren trusted me—all I could find myself thinking over was that poor Reaper Guard curling up on the floor of a nook near a door he never left.

I had never truly wondered on it before, but . . .

Why was that side of the House off-limits? Was there something special about it, or was it simply because Ahren wished it to be so in order to maintain appearances? Why wouldn't anyone tell me anything? Was it good enough hoping all things would come to light eventually, or should I take a candle to them and shine the light myself? Would it make a difference to try such a thing if the candle would only be knocked out of your hand when you did?

No, I did not believe it would. Still, that didn't mean I would do nothing. I would simply have to think very hard and discover my options.

I wondered now if every interaction that had passed between myself and any of the Reapers in the Valdour House had been nothing more than tests. I felt as though I'd always had eyes that could see, but at the same time I had managed to overlook so many things that were directly in front of my face. I would have to pay more attention. I would have to be more like them. It was the only way to survive with them.

Though I'd always had eyes to see, I knew now that I'd also always kept my head down when I walked, and I'd only walked the halls I had. How many things had that caused me to overlook? How many seemingly insignificant details that could've told me such lengthy stories if I'd had the ears to listen to them?

I did not avert my gaze from the Guards I passed now as I usually did. I watched them instead.

When I looked at the Guards, some of them met my gaze and some did not. Some of them smiled small smiles at me. Some of those smiles were kind and others were knowing. I realized I was beginning to be able to tell the difference between them. Just because a smile was kind did not mean it was not a Reaper offering it. Just because they looked at me—or didn't—did not mean they were or were not Reapers. They were people, and they behaved as any one person would behave differently from another. I'd always been so focused on the similarities; I'd missed differences.

It was the blinking—of all the things in the world—that gave them away. It was something no one would notice, something they'd likely never been told not to do during their undercover operations. Because how could you erase basic human nature from a human?

Even if they did not look at me, they would know I was finally seeing them. An extra blink, just slightly different from the rest, was all it was. Almost as if you were gazing into the face of someone you'd not seen in a long while and it had taken them a moment to recognize you.

I returned all smiles offered to me, by Reaper or Guard. I did not let my eyes linger on any of them for too long. I did not count them. Once I had a better idea on how many of them were inside the House, I found I did not want to know the precise number.

But how—when Chase wanted to get the two of us away from them—could it be carried out with so many of them here? How in the world would it be possible to get past them?

We simply stood no chance; I could see that now.

Still, that did not mean it was not worth trying.

I DID NOT ALLOW anyone to make food for myself, or for Chase, when I arrived at the kitchen. I prepared it, though I could not check it for poison in any way he might do as much. I was not yet knowledgeable enough to survive in his world.

No. It was not his world. It was the same one I'd been living in all along. I simply hadn't ever thought I would need to know the things I so clearly needed to.

My hands shook while I stood at the fire, distractedly moving scrambled eggs around in a pan with a spoon while I thought of all the Reapers and the impossibility of my situation.

Though there were many people in the kitchen, none of them asked me if I was all right. None of them even looked at me to know that something was wrong, almost as if everything had gone back to the way it had been before. But it was just after the thought passed that a young girl stepped up beside me. I had never seen her before. I'd thought I knew the faces of all the servants here.

"Are you all right?" She sounded genuinely concerned, and her head tilted just ever so slightly to the side when she smiled at me.

"Yes," I said, forcing my voice to sound entirely calm and putting on a smile in response to hers. "Thank you for asking."

The expression on her face warmed for a moment, and then she walked away. I watched her as she went, seeing a large circle with a V that had bled through the back of her off-white shirt.

Though she had given herself away with the head tilting and her approach in general, she did not move like a Reaper. She hunched herself over as if she were made of dirt. She couldn't have been any older than fifteen, if even that. How could a child pretend so well that they were capable of fooling an entire House filled with adults? But more importantly . . .

Why was she here to do so?

I realized I was squeezing the handle of the spoon so hard my nails were digging into the bottom of my palm.

I wouldn't have noticed it at all if Francine had not come up and pulled me from my thoughts by saying, "That's Amber. She's only been here a short while, but our leader is so taken with her that he's already had her Branded."

I cleared my throat uncomfortably. "She seems very nice."

"Aster, you're burning your eggs," Francine said, frowning. She likely considered such a thing an atrocity. "Would you like me to make you more? You have to take some food to that Reaper, don't you?"

"He can have them the way they are." I didn't look at her face to see what sort of reaction she'd had to my words. I dumped the eggs onto a tray, covered it, and then vacated the room as quickly as I could possibly manage.

I needed to get away from the little Reaper girl.

"THEY'RE BURNT," I informed Chase immediately upon entering room number four, extending the tray toward him before he'd even closed the door behind me.

There was a grin on his face as he took it from my hands. "Did you do it on purpose?"

"No, but I didn't prepare you more," I said. "I suppose that's close enough to the same thing, isn't it?"

"Are you all right?" he asked seriously. "If this is about—"

"Oh yes, Chase, this is *all* about the fact that you don't trust me!" I nearly screamed my interruption. Then I shook my head and, with as much sarcasm as I could muster, added, "What in the world else could ever possibly bother me?"

"I think we should talk about this." His voice was calm, though wary.

"*Talk* about it?" I demanded. "Do you really think so?"

His eyes widened in shock at me for a moment before he quietly asked, "Don't you?"

I realized then that it was not only shock held in his eyes but also hurt.

I resigned myself not to care about it as I tested him for the first time.

"No," I said. "What I would *like* to do is go to my quarters and think on a way to broach the subject of a little girl in the kitchen who has been Branded to our leader. No." I shook my head. "That's not what I would *like* to do. It is what I am *going* to do."

He narrowed his eyes at me and said nothing.

I'd turned and was reaching for the door handle when he asked, "Have you eaten?"

"Not a bite," I told him flatly. "I believe I've lost my appetite." I left the room and closed the door behind me.

I attempted not to smile as I walked alone down the hallway. Regardless of whether he passed my test, I was discovering it was not so difficult to play pretend. All you had to do was find the appropriate emotion you needed from something else. That was the trick to it.

Not only had I discovered the trick, I also discovered that . . . I found it quite fun. Invigorating. But it only took me a moment to realize . . .

I still was not me. Whether the feelings existed or not . . .

NEARLY AN HOUR PASSED before there was a knock at my door.

I'd spent the entire time sitting on my bed, staring at the cold, grey stone walls that surrounded me. I could see the stone for what it was now—the bars of a prison cell, intended to keep people contained in the ground. People were not meant to be in the ground. Not until they were dead. I wondered now why I had allowed myself to be imprisoned all these long years. I wondered why anyone allowed it. It . . . disgusted me. It was the only thing I'd been able to think about as I waited.

Containment.

"Were you playing pretend?" Chase asked from the doorway.

I looked over and found both he and Ahren standing there together, almost appearing as though they were leery of entering my domain.

"I see that you received my message." I did not need to pretend at all to make my voice blank. Then, I looked to the wall again to add, "I suppose you truly are as intelligent as you all believe yourselves to be."

Ahren cleared his throat and closed the door loudly enough for me to hear it.

My eyes darted to his. "Don't pretend not to be what you are in front of me any longer."

"What?" Ahren asked in a confused sort of way. "What are you talking about? You know what I—"

I stood up quickly from the bed and stomped over to him.

"Would you like to see how I close doors?" I asked with a humorless laugh. I stepped between the two of them, opened the door, and then closed it again with a noticeable sound, the same as I always did. I looked up at Ahren's face. "How hard do you have to think to intentionally make a sound?"

His brow furrowed and he shook his head at me as if he still could not understand.

I opened the door widely then looked to him again. Calmly, I said, "Close the door."

"Aster, I don't see what—"

My hands were tightly balled into fists and shaking at my sides as my nails dug into my palms again. I took one step closer to him and, through gritted teeth, repeated, "*Close the door.*"

Ahren clenched his jaw, but he stepped past me and closed the door without making a sound. I shook my head as I watched him.

For me to not make a sound, I would have to think so very hard about it. I would've closed the door so slowly, trying to be silent, and I likely would have been even louder than I normally was in my attempt. He closed it as effortlessly as anyone would close a door, only there was no sound at all.

No sound at all with a door that always made sound when swinging.

I stepped closer and touched my toe onto a spot six or so inches into where the door swung inward.

"It squeaks," I said. "Right here." I tapped my toe several times onto the floor. "Every time, it squeaks right here." I stared down at the floor and laughed under my breath.

It hadn't squeaked at all when Ahren had closed it.

"What's your point?" Ahren asked impassively. "It's a door."

"My *point*?" I laughed again. "My point is I could never sneak past people such as you. What is the point of what Chase and I are planning to do when there are so many of you in this House?"

"I don't know what you're talking about."

"I am not *ignorant*!" I shouted at him. "Stop treating me as if I am!" Hadn't I always preferred people thinking it of me?

Perhaps there was a difference, when people looked directly at you and still couldn't see you.

Quietly from behind me, Chase said, "Give her something, Ahren."

I rounded on him. "You stay out of this. I am extremely unhappy with you right now."

"I'm trying to help you here," Chase said slowly. "Did you not hear what I said to him?"

"Do you believe the only reason I want anything productive to happen in my life is because you caused it to be so?"

His eyes widened in shock.

"If I haven't earned Ahren's trust in the time I've spent with him . . ." I shook my head. "I'll be damned if I'll have you force it on him or coerce him into it."

Ahren cleared his throat and sounded calm when said, "We should sit down."

"I will not sit on the floor with you anymore, Ahren!" I exclaimed. "I will not continue to degrade myself and act as though a person needs to be on the ground to be equal to me!"

Ahren shook his head deliberately as he stepped closer to me. "I didn't sit on the ground so I could be equal to you," he whispered. "I did it so I could feel, for just a moment, like you were equal to me."

CHAPTER TWENTY-TWO

THE ALLOWANCE OF LEADERS

I STILL REFUSED TO SIT ON THE FLOOR with Ahren. He, Chase, and I all sat at the edge of my bed instead. I only allowed worrying on Agatha's potential reaction—were she to enter the room and catch sight of it—to occupy my thoughts for a moment.

I sat between the two of them, putting my back to Chase and focusing all my attention on Ahren. I did not exactly know all the reasons I was currently unhappy with Chase, only that there were a great many of them and that I was.

For a long time, Ahren said nothing; he simply sat there and stared at my face. I could feel Chase's gaze burning into my back, but I still did not acknowledge him.

"I will tell you something," Ahren began, seeming to be thinking very carefully on what he was saying to me. "But only if you promise me that you won't ask me any more questions for a time. Can you do that?"

"Can you tell me why you would insist that of me first?" I attempted to keep my voice steady and calm. I could pretend as though I were feeling entirely reasonable now—despite the fact that I was not—if it would help with my cause.

"For the same reason I mentioned to you earlier."

"About stabbing," I stated.

The mind can only handle so much at once. That had been the point he'd tried to make earlier, I was sure.

He nodded. "Will you promise me that?"

"Will you promise to tell me more later?"

"Yes." He said that, but I watched his jaw clench in displeasure for an instant.

"And you don't mean you say one sentence and no more just now, that we're not even to speak on this?"

"Correct."

"Then yes, I promise I will ask you no more questions on the matter for now," I said. "So long as you tell me something satisfactory enough to make the promise worthwhile."

It felt very strange speaking to a person in that way, no matter how often I'd found myself doing it over the last several months. I couldn't decide whether I was joyous or angry that Chase and Ahren had awoken this new, incredibly unpleasant side of me. Or perhaps I'd always been so unpleasant and simply never realized as much.

Ahren looked away and shook his head at the stone walls surrounding us. Then, he huffed out a breath of air and quickly looked back at my face. "We're not from this city." Those few words spilled out in a torrent.

"What?" I laughed in a stunned disbelief, thinking I surely mustn't have heard him correctly.

"We are not from this city," Ahren repeated, slower then so there could be no mistaking it.

I looked down at the blanket beneath me and pulled part of it into my lap to hold onto as I thought over the implications and attempted to work it all out inside my mind.

I brought my attention back to his face for a moment and very carefully said, "You're from a different city."

He nodded.

"The Reapers of this city don't know you're here."

Slowly, but widely, he shook his head.

For the first time since sitting down, I glanced over my shoulder at Chase. He sat there, still as the stone surrounding us, doing nothing more than blinking.

"Chase is from this city," I said to Ahren as I brought my gaze back to him.

Again, he nodded.

"How is it then that the two of you are best friends?"

His eyes were not on me then, but behind me, looking to Chase. I wondered, possibly, if he were silently asking permission for something.

What an absurd thought and thing.

After a moment, Ahren looked back to me. "He told you a story, didn't he? About a little boy who followed a girl?"

My jaw clenched as I nodded. I should not have been surprised that Ahren knew of the story, though I had to admit I was startlingly unhappy that someone else was aware of a portion of my own life story I myself had been unaware of.

Ahren's voice was quiet when he asked, "Did he tell you what happened *after*?"

My gaze shot behind me to Chase once again, who still sat there like a blinking statue. I'd not asked him what happened after the portion of it he'd told, assuming it had involved copious amounts of blood, but . . .

Would he have told me if I had asked?

I looked again to Ahren and shook my head.

"I ran away," Chase said from behind me.

Slowly, I turned my attention back to him, angling my body in his direction.

"I ran away as soon as I had the opportunity—to test this city's limits and those of our Reapers, to see if it could be done and find a place where I would go later." He blinked hard at me for a moment before adding, "I met a man."

I asked, "What kind of man?"

"Another Reaper." Chase said that then smiled and laughed softly, glancing down at the blanket I was still holding in my hands. "We sat around a fire and exchanged sad stories." He brought his eyes back to mine, and the amused look slowly drained away from his face. "He told me he was planning a revolt, that he was in contact with a great many Reapers who were not happy in a nearby city, and that they were planning to overthrow the one in control there. So he sent me back here to spy on this city for him while I bided my time. You should never put all your eggs in one basket."

It took me a moment to realize what he was saying.

"There is a Reaper in control of every city?" I asked on a breath, his words sinking like stones in my gut. "How is that possible?"

"They sit in pockets," Ahren replied. "Reapers sit in the leaders' pockets in cities like yours. Most cities are controlled openly by one Reaper. I can assure you that, under most circumstances, a good deal of us don't care who we kill . . . as long as we're allowed to do it." He paused for an instant. "Cities such as this are the most vulnerable. There aren't many of them. It's why the leaders here are always killed so quickly and easily. It is not so simple in most others. Usually."

I cleared my throat as I sat there, thinking over all this new information. I didn't want to believe any of it.

Eventually, taking the easier route, I said, "That still does not explain how the two of you are friends."

"Can't you see?" Ahren grinned. "The Reaper in control of my city is the man Chase found. Or . . . the man who found him, I suppose you could say."

"And he's sent the rest of you here to take over this one," I stated in disbelief. It took me a moment to regain my composure as I struggled with the gravity of this situation, but when I came close enough to managing it, my eyes shot to Ahren's. "Is he a good man?"

He blinked hard at me a few times and then looked away. "As good as any of us can be."

I nodded, though I was not entirely sure how much his answer was worth. Then I realized . . . "You still have not told me how the two of you are friends."

Ahren chuckled a little. "I handled all communications between Chase and the man he met. Eventually Chase came to trust me enough that he told me his story. It was after I'd lost Evelyn, so you could say I felt as though I needed to take care of him."

"You knew who I was," I accused, my jaw dropping. "You knew who I was when you came here, and you still had me beaten."

"You could get away with it now, given our relationship. But what was I to do when one of the Guards informed me they'd seen you go in there? It would've been out of place, wouldn't it, for me to have shown preferential treatment to a person I'd never spoken to?"

"Still—"

"Given you understood that you and Chase could not discuss the Reapers in this House while in room number four, I believe you should understand. If you haven't learned by now that sometimes you're required to do things you desperately do not want to do in order for something important to happen later . . . you quickly will. I suggest you come to terms with that sooner, rather than later."

I stared at him as I shook my head in utter disbelief.

"Life is a series of choices," Ahren continued. "You have to be smart in the choices you make because every step you take leads you away from a different direction you could've gone. You have to think things through so that, when you're at the end and you find yourself looking back on it all . . . you can know you went the right way."

"You're not going to ask me if I understand what you're saying to me?" I shot at him after an extended moment of silence.

"No," he said simply.

I felt as though I sat there shaking my head at absolutely nothing—and yet everything—for an entire hour, but it was likely only seconds.

"So there's no cause to worry about the Reapers in the House?" I asked him. "They clearly wouldn't have any reason to care about me and what I did. Given that Chase knows your leader, I would imagine all the Reapers here are already aware of our plan to leave."

Ahren smiled. "There's no cause for you to worry about the Reapers in the House."

I couldn't explain why, but his statement did not offer me any comfort. I felt as though it were another of those partial truths where I was told only one side of something honest.

Suddenly, he and Chase both stood from the bed.

"I'm going back to the room we were in earlier," Chase said as he turned to leave. "See if you can get there without being noticed."

They'd both made it to the door when I called out to Ahren.

Chase did not stay; he exited the room and closed the door behind him without a single backward glance for me. I ignored the action, along with his apparent hostility despite it making no sense to me.

"Why is Amber here?" I asked Ahren. "She is so young."

"She wanted to be here."

"She is a child," I quietly clarified for him. Apparently he didn't realize as much.

"Some would consider that of you," Ahren said, his voice flat. "Should the opinions of others dictate what a person does with their own life?"

"Your leader . . ." I began after a moment and then paused to clear my throat. "He allows people to make their own choices?"

"Occasionally," Ahren answered. "But he's quite fond of Amber. She's like a daughter to him, in a way."

"Why would he allow this to happen to her, then?" I shook my head frantically, not wanting to believe a person would willingly send someone they cared for into such a situation. "Why would he allow her to come here and be Branded? Why would he put her at risk with the men if he cared for her?"

"Because she went to him and asked him to have faith in her capabilities," Ahren said. "One person does not allow things to happen to another. They simply . . . happen."

He had turned again to go, but I said, "Give me permission to clean the other side of the House."

He was grinning when he looked back at me over his shoulder. "I might. If you can manage to get there unnoticed first."

"It's the middle of the day," I stated quietly. "It's when the Guards are most active."

"You should've thought of that sooner." He said that without apology then exited the room.

I was left sitting alone on my bed, staring blankly at the door.

ANOTHER HOUR PASSED while I sat alone on my bed, mapping out the House inside my mind, carefully recalling spots where I knew Guards would be waiting.

They were not in front of every door, nor were they patrolling in every hallway.

This House was a labyrinth, but it was one I had walked through so many times that I knew it as I knew the back of my own hand. None of the Guards changed out their posts at the same time. Their schedules were as complicated as the House itself. I was not anywhere near as familiar with it, given that I'd never deemed it something worthy enough to pay proper attention to.

Every so often while I sat there planning, I would feel guilty for Chase, who was likely already waiting in that other room for me. It would appear as though I was not capable of this, that I couldn't even move around effectively in my own familiar territory without being discovered. It was distracting. I did not want to appear incapable to him, no matter my current unhappiness.

I had just stood from the bed to attempt it when there was another knock at the door. I frowned as I stepped over, assuming it was Chase coming to fetch me.

When I opened the door, it was Amber standing there with a covered tray in her hands. I was more than a little stunned as I stared at her, wondering what in the world she was doing.

"I know you didn't eat." She was speaking very carefully, as though she were wary. "I've brought you some food."

"Did Ahren tell you to?"

She shook her head. "No. I assumed you didn't eat because of me."

Rather than admit my lack of appetite had been on account of her, which it partially had, I said, "It's not normal to bring a servant food."

She smiled that slow smile I had seen so many times on the faces of other people, other Reapers. "Nobody saw me."

I heard myself breathe out loudly before I asked, "Would you like to come in?"

CHAPTER TWENTY-THREE

THE MEASURE OF A PERSON

AMBER STOOD IN THE DOORWAY, frowning slightly at the space between us. I almost had the urge to laugh at her. She was behaving as though she were afraid of me, which was simply ludicrous.

I told her, "You don't have to come in, if you don't wish to do so."

She brought her eyes to mine and asked, "Were you ever given a choice in things you wanted to do?"

I smiled at her with as much warmth as I could manage and responded with, "Not until very recently, no."

She nodded her head as if my answer had settled some unknown thing inside her and began to step past me into the room.

"Here, I'll take that from you," I offered as I reached out for the tray in her hands.

She frowned at me again, in a way, but she allowed me to take it from her.

Once I sat down at the edge of my bed to eat the food she'd brought me, I glanced over at her. She was standing with her back to the wall, her arms crossed over her chest as she watched me. The dark-blond bun pulled tightly at the back of her head appeared to be draining whatever vibrancy she could've had from her face.

I chuckled. "You're staring at me as though you've poisoned the food and are waiting for me to eat it and fall over dead."

She gaped. "I would never."

"I was kidding," I informed her. "You can sit down if you'd like. Clearly, I couldn't hurt you. There's no cause for you to be defensive."

I sighed as she sat down in the precise place where she'd stood against the wall. It hadn't necessarily been what I'd had in mind, but it was better than nothing. She looked so small, sitting there.

I was taking my first bite of food when she asked, "How did you know what I am?"

"You tilted your head slightly when you smiled at me," I told her between bites. I wondered if any of them realized how often they did that.

"Ahren said you were observant." She narrowed her eyes. "He said you'd figured him out by seeing things he hadn't intentionally shown you."

I chuckled again. "I believe nearly everything I saw from him was intentionally shown."

"It wasn't." She sounded sure and insistent.

I forced a small smile at her and, wanting to change the subject, I asked, "Do you like him?" I did not like the feeling of being interrogated. "Ahren?"

"He's like a brother to me."

"I feel much the same way," I admitted.

She narrowed her eyes once more. "Do you?"

I nodded quickly and did not have to force the next smile at her. "I get incredibly unhappy with him sometimes, as I would imagine siblings do. We argue quite often but get on very well otherwise. I never had a sibling to know, but I could picture it being as such."

"Do you wish you'd had a sibling?" The narrowing in her eyes began to fade.

"They would've ended up here, same as me," I told her, shaking my head. "Or they might've been taken to another place entirely. I'm not sure I could've handled seeing a family member be subjected to this life, especially not while being powerless to protect them from it."

A thoughtful expression overtook her face. "But what if they would've been the one worried about protecting you?"

"But they couldn't have." I offered her another short smile before saying, "It's not the way things are. There's not much point in concerning myself with it." I took in a deep breath then released it slowly. "Do you have any siblings?"

She shook her head.

"Do you wish you had?"

She nodded then.

"See though, you could protect them, with the training you've had." I paused for an instant. "That's the difference."

She said nothing to that.

I was halfway through my meal when she finally spoke again.

"Why aren't you afraid of me? Is it because I'm a girl?"

I laughed beneath a breath. "No. I'm not afraid of you for the same reason I'm not afraid of Chase or Ahren."

"But you know them," she pointed out.

"Yes, but if you think of Ahren the same way as I do, and he of you, why should I be afraid? And I'm sure I've not done anything to make you hate me. We just met and all."

"You laughed about the poison," she stated. "What if I *had* poisoned your food?"

"Have you?" I asked her as I took another bite. I tried very hard not to smile when I swallowed it.

She frowned and shook her head. "Still, it's not intelligent to take food from us. There could be more than you know going on in front of you."

"There will always be more than any one person knows going on in front of them," I told her. "That is not reason to be untrusting of another person, or unkind to them, as it would have been if I hadn't taken the food you offered me." The time with them had taught me a great deal on the matter.

"What if I were in love with Chase?"

"Are you?" I asked her curiously.

"No," she answered. "But what if I was?"

I tried not to laugh. "Then I would say he's much too old for you."

She smiled at me for a moment but quickly pursed her lips together. After a short moment sitting in that way . . . "Do you love him?"

"I do."

"Why?" she asked quickly. "Is it because he wants to take you from this place?"

I shook my head. "I would still love him if he didn't." It seemed *everyone* knew more than they had any business knowing.

"Why? Don't you know what he's done in his life? How could a person like you love a person like that?" I was unsure how my face responded to the last of her questions, but she quickly threw her hands into the air and added, "I didn't mean that how it sounded."

"I'm quite sure you did," I stated shortly. "The reason I love him is because he's never once acted as if I were one thing and he were another. That's why."

"But you're a good person," she barely said.

Carefully, I said, "I'm not certain of the things Ahren has told you about me, but I can assure you that you don't know me to make such an assessment."

She seemed to ignore what I'd just told her and, still in a hushed tone, said, "Aren't you afraid he'll ruin you?"

I inhaled a deep breath and let it out as a sigh while I stared down at the floor separating the two of us. "Do you know what I'm more afraid of?"

She shook her head.

I wiped a little at my eyes, willing them not to begin watering, though I could tell they were tempted to do so. "I'm more afraid of what my life would be like without him, or perhaps more so what it would've been."

"What do you mean?"

"Did they tell you what life is like for women such as myself before you came here?" I asked. "Or did they spare you of the knowledge in the hope that, while Ahren was here, you would never have to see it?"

"I've heard a little about it," she admitted in a small voice.

"It's not something you've ever had to worry about, is it?"

She did not respond to me in any way.

"Chase told me that your women have their children taken away from them, but I would imagine most those children are conceived out of love. It isn't that way here. Perhaps you know a little about feeling powerless, given your defensiveness about being a woman, but I can assure you that you cannot fathom life as I've known it to be for most of mine. Even if you've felt powerless, you still know you have the capability of defending yourself and that, if you were required to do so, you would not be punished for it."

She sat there for a long while, appearing to be thinking over my words.

The conclusion she must've come to was, "So you love Chase because you feel like he can protect you."

I heard myself sigh again. "No, but I will admit that was part of it at first."

She seemed to be trying, but she eventually shook her head. "I just can't understand."

"Someday . . ." I began, choosing my words carefully. "Someday a person will come into your life and, no matter what you do or how desperately you try to fight against it, they will change your entire perspective. They'll remind you that you have eyes and show you parts of the world you've never seen before. I may love him for not treating me as if I'm something different from himself. I may love him for showing me all the things he has. But mostly . . . I love him because he made me realize that I have the right to all those things, that I'm worthy of them, just as he does and is. Can you understand that?"

She didn't even take a moment to think on it. "How do you know he loves you back? That he's not just pretending?"

I spent a long while thinking over her question. I did not doubt that Chase was capable of deceiving me if he wished to do so. Still, it was not the point.

"Because I have eyes," I told her.

She stared down at the floor and quietly said, "He *does* love you." Then she looked up at me. "I overheard him speaking to our leader about it."

"Did you?" I asked, both curious and wary.

It was strange. Reapers always listened before speaking of important matters, to ensure no one else was near, and I could not imagine Chase speaking freely of such things.

"I'm very quiet," she said, almost as if she could read my mind.

"What did you hear?"

"He said something very similar to what you've just told me," she said. "If I hadn't seen your face when you said it, I would've believed the two of you had rehearsed your stories together."

"When did you hear this?"

"Not a week before I left to come here," she answered. "He'd stopped to speak to our leader while he was away on his last mission for this city."

It was strange, but there a jolt of what felt like sparks running through my body at her words. *His last mission for this city.*

"Could you be happy with him?"

"I would imagine so," I said with an uncomfortable laugh.

"You wouldn't survive. The two of you alone would never survive for very long. It would be suicide to try. You know that, don't you? You *have* to know that."

"I do know," I told her with a tight, forced smile. "But we would be happy while we could. That's more than enough, and it's far better than the alternative. It's more than I ever thought I would have in my life." I sighed and, determined to change the subject once more, I asked, "Do you have someone taking care of you here?"

My diversion worked because her forehead creased in response. "Taking care . . ." She shook her head, confused. "There's Ahren."

"No, I meant a woman," I clarified. "Francine, possibly?"

She shook her head again in the same way. "What could another woman do?"

I realized I was frowning at her and quickly forced another smile onto my face. "Do you have someone to clean off the Branding on your back?"

She shook her head once more, in response this time.

"If you don't clean it properly, it will become infected. Surely you know as much, but . . . Have you ever had an infection like that?"

"No. We're always given medicine when we're injured."

"Well, you can become very ill," I told her. "It can become quite bad. Occasionally it happens even with cleaning. I would imagine you're not allowed medicine for it, so you can properly play your part." If she healed too quickly from that, it would draw suspicions. The Branding itself drew too much attention, and people would be watching her for a while. "Would you like me to clean it for you?"

She blinked very hard at me and asked, "Would you do that?"

"Of course." I smiled. "Just allow me to gather the appropriate things. It will only take me a moment."

I knew all the things that I needed for the job; I had seen Agatha gather those items so many times when she'd have to work on my own back. They were all things that were permitted in our room, so truly, it did only take a moment.

I pointed toward the far wall. "If you'd like, you can put your front toward this wall here, in case someone enters the room. That way no one will see you at all with me blocking you." Anyone but Agatha would've never been much of a concern before, but after Ahren had entered without knocking . . .

She stood from her spot by the door and slowly walked across the room. Very hesitantly, she turned her back to me and pulled off her shirt. I tried not to make a sound as I sucked in a breath, seeing the fresh Branding. The middle of the circle rested over her spine, the edges of it touching each of her shoulder blades. That was not what provoked my reaction to it.

"I don't like the look of this," I said. "How long has it been since this was done to you?"

"A few days," she barely said.

"This is going to hurt quite badly," I warned her. "But it's only water and a cloth. Don't be angry with me for the pain. It will be better for it in the end, even if it doesn't feel that way now."

I watched her nod her head quickly.

"If you'd like, you can talk to me to distract yourself," I suggested. "It's what Agatha used to do for me." It was what she'd always done for me until I had no longer needed her to.

I wetted the cloth and held it out behind her back, waiting patiently for her to speak.

"Why are you doing this?" she asked. "Taking care of me."

"When I was very little . . ." I began before starting the process of cleaning at her back. I wiped away some of the ooze escaping from the sore. "My father always told me that every person needs someone to watch their back."

"Why would he say that?"

I tried to ignore the way she twitched in response to the cloth, and I also tried to disregard my own reaction to it. How many times had I subjected Agatha to this very thing?

"Well, we lived far away from any city," I told her. "There are many things to worry about in the wilderness, but they are not the same worries as you would find in a place such as this. Our biggest concerns were predators. And every time he would leave for more food, he would tell me to stay in the house so the Reavers couldn't find me."

"Reavers?"

"Yes, they're the people who take little children from their parents," I explained. It was all they did now. "Perhaps they call them something different where you're from."

"Is that how you ended up here?"

"Yes," I said. "His friend lived not too far from us, and I knew the way because I'd gone with him a few times. My father didn't come home for a very long time, and I ran out of food in his absence. So, I went to his friend, and he and his wife took care of me for as long as they could. When it was apparent my father was not ever coming back, he gave me to the Reaver who brought me here."

"What do you think happened to your father?"

"I'm quite certain he's dead," I told her, unruffled.

"How could you know?"

"Because he would never have stayed away so long," I said. "He would've never allowed this to happen to me, if he were alive."

"But what if he'd just been caught up?" she pried.

I heard myself sigh again as I attempted not to be frustrated. I believed I finally understood how Agatha had felt with any badgering I'd done to her over the years, persistently asking her to relive unpleasant aspects of her life. I'd kept it at a minimum, I felt, but . . .

Even just a little time of it was quite horrendous.

"He wouldn't have been," I stated. "He was gone a very long time." I secured a fresh bandage over her wound. "There, I'm done."

She hastily began putting her shirt back on.

While she was in the process of that and getting it tugged into place, I told her, "I want you to come back here tonight so I can clean it, and then again in the morning. I'm certain if our paths hadn't crossed today, you would've been very ill in a few days' time."

By that point she was properly clothed and had turned around to face me. She stood there staring at me in a very strange way for what felt like an eternity before she said, "May I ask you a question?"

"Of course you may." I laughed. "You've asked me quite a lot of them since you've come in here."

"Do you hold a grudge against your father's friend for giving you away? Do you blame him for the life you've been forced to lead?"

I shook my head at her, forcing an uncomfortable—and very stiff—smile onto my face.

She pressed on. "Are you so good that you can't even point blame where blame is rightfully deserved? Are you so good you can't even be angry about it?"

The smile felt so tight on my face when I stared down at the floor. I had to tell myself she was only a curious child, a curious Reaper child at that. It was not her fault that it was in her nature to question things she did not understand.

"Again, I believe you are mistaken about the measure of my person," I told her when I looked back at her face. "I've always blamed my father."

CHAPTER TWENTY-FOUR

MASTERING AN ART

I WANTED TO BE AWAY FROM AMBER and her unintentionally hurtful questions so badly that I did not worry about being caught in my attempt to get to the other side of the House. I simply walked as I normally walked—as though I had some sort of a purpose that put me in the direction I was headed—and not a single person stopped me to ask where I was going or what I was planning on doing when I arrived there.

It was only when I found myself two hallways over from where the Reaper Guards would be standing that I stopped and listened. I felt as though my ears could not work properly, that they could never be as effective as a Reapers'. Still, I listened and heard nothing, so I walked on.

When both Reaper Guards came into view, I watched their hands. Every so often, I would glance at their faces—which were unsurprisingly blank—in case I might see something that needed to be seen there. They made no hand movements or facial expressions, and they let me pass beside them without so much as a blink.

When I'd made it to the door, I stopped for an instant to look at them again. Their backs were straight where they stood, and they did not turn to look back at me. They'd simply pretended as though I were invisible.

I was frowning all the way to the room that Chase had been in earlier.

And then I frowned even more deeply when I found him sitting at a desk, eating an absolutely *heaping* plate of food.

"Where did you get that?" I asked him with narrowed eyes.

"Kitchen." He spoke over his shoulder with a small grin.

"You've been in the kitchen?"

He pointed toward a wall, and I frowned at it, knowing with certainty the kitchen was not in that direction. It was not even anywhere near this side of the House.

I stepped back into the hallway, opening the next door in the direction he'd pointed. The room looked identical to the one I had just exited.

So, I went down the hall, opening every door in turn until I found . . .

Another kitchen. Smaller, but it was what it was no matter the size. It was empty of people but not of kitchenly things.

I stomped back down toward the room where Chase was and, inside my head while I went, I attempted to work out the point of him not telling me that particular piece of information. Earlier. Before the eggs.

I nearly slammed the door behind me after I entered and had him back in my sight. "Is every word you do or don't say to be a test?"

"Half of them," he replied, unperturbed. Though he did not turn his face to me again, I was certain he was smiling.

I contemplated slapping him. I could play it off as more pretending, after all. Possibly. Instead, I stepped back into the hallway and began walking toward the door that would return me to the normal half of the House.

I was not expecting for him to come after me, nor was I expecting that, if he did, I would not hear him come up behind me. I nearly screamed when I felt a hand grab hold of mine.

When I jumped in my startle and found him there, I saw that he was smiling hugely at me, almost as though he were pretending in his mind that I was not angry with him. It was quite possible he was not pretending anything and was simply amused by the entire situation.

He said, "Let's go back."

I gave him a tight, forced smile. "No thank you." I was giving out a great deal of those today, it seemed.

His nose crinkled a little as he brushed back a bit of my hair from my face. "I'll make you griddlecakes."

"I don't want any of your griddlecakes."

His smile widened. "No?"

"No."

"Why not?"

"Because I've already eaten," I stated.

"If you hadn't, and I made you some, would that be enough to get you to come back even though you're angry with me?" I could tell he was trying very hard not to laugh at me.

"If you're going to teach me something productive in there, you could simply say as much," I told him unhappily. "I don't currently have the mental energy to participate in more of your mind games."

He chuckled. "Come on, then." He then began walking back in the direction we'd come from.

I began following. "What are we going to do?"

"If you're asking me to stop playing . . ." he started slowly. "I'm going to poison you."

I stopped moving. "What did you just say?"

He nearly smirked over his shoulder when looking at me. "I said I'm going to poison you."

I replayed his words in my mind, ensuring I'd heard him correctly. Then, I repeated the process.

"Come on."

For the life of me, I could not understand why my feet began moving again.

I WATCHED CHASE in silence as he made eggs. When they were very nearly done, he walked away toward a bag that was lying on top of a nearby counter.

Wary, I asked, "What is that?"

"A bag of toys."

I could just barely see the hint of a smile on his partially turned face. I did not want to see inside Chase's bag of toys, so I remained precisely where I stood.

He procured a smaller bag from within the other, leaving the large and returning with the small. He poured a minuscule amount of its contents—dried green flakes—into the eggs and then scooped some of them onto a plate, setting it in front of me. I assumed that would be it, but he then proceeded to dump quite a large amount into the rest of the pan before putting them onto another plate. I noted, inside my head, that he had not burned the eggs as I had done earlier.

He had not burned them, no—only poisoned them.

He placed a fork in my hand and curled my fingers around the unwanted instrument in silence.

He did nothing more than blink at me while I stared into his face.

"Am I going to become ill?" I asked him quietly.

As a response, he tapped his finger on the rim of the plate that was less poisoned.

I wanted to slap myself when I stepped forward, gathering up a tiny amount of eggs with the fork. I was only partially surprised when he took the fork from my hand and scooped it full of them then handed it back to me.

My eyes were focused on two tiny little pieces of green in the eggs as my hand moved toward my mouth.

What in the world was I doing? I mentally screamed at my hand to stop moving.

It did not.

I chewed it briefly, tasted nothing, and swallowed.

He took the fork from my hand again, gathering eggs from the other plate. Before he handed it back to me, he firmly said, "Do not swallow this."

He held the fork extended in the air in front of my body, and I frowned at it. Then I frowned at him. Again, he grabbed my hand and curled it around the fork. It took me nearly a minute to do what he expected me to.

My teeth bit down, releasing the taste into my mouth.

Then I ran to the nearby receptacle.

I spat it out, and my stomach heaved out all the food Amber had brought me. It was not the expected effects of the poison that were making me ill; it was the taste alone. It tasted of dead earth, and it was the absolute vilest thing I had ever tasted in all my life.

I scowled at him when he handed me a damp cloth once my stomach had mostly settled, though I did take it from him. Before using it to wipe at my face, I grabbed a glass filled with water sitting nearby and swished it around inside my mouth, spitting it out in the receptacle as well. I repeated that process several times, but I still could not quite get the taste of it off my tongue.

While I was drinking the last of the water . . .

"How do you know I didn't put something else in the water when you weren't looking?"

I held the small amount of it in my mouth and contemplated spitting it in his face rather than swallowing it.

"I didn't. I'm just asking."

I wanted to be angry at him for what all had just occurred as well as all the other things, but I simply couldn't be. He'd told me what he was going to do and had given me ample opportunity to refuse. More importantly, I'd asked him to show me how to do this. I could not be angry at him for what that entailed. Besides, I didn't need yet another reason to be upset with him.

I asked, "Am I going to be ill later from that first bite?"

"You won't feel a thing." He shook his head. "In order to survive something, you need to understand it."

"So, what is it you want me to understand about that?"

"Methods."

When I felt my forehead scrunching, he went on.

"Firstly, not all Reapers use poison. Some of us consider it a waste of valuable time. Secondly, those that do don't always use lethal amounts flat out. Sometimes they do, sometimes they don't. Occasionally, when a Reaper is deep undercover, they'll poison over an extended amount of time. Or, occasionally they'll do it that way just to be sadistic because they want to watch their mark die slowly. Most of the time we're granted quite a bit of leeway. Unless instructed otherwise, the ones who issue orders don't care how a mark dies, as long as they die."

"I see," I heard myself say in a very small voice.

"Do you?" He barely raised a dark eyebrow. "Do you know how long we train with poisons?"

I shook my head.

"It's not just learning to detect them for ourselves. We spend enough time to learn what foods mask which of them. How much to use in what without it being detected. Where to find them in the wild. How to store them properly. What method to use to dispense them most effectively. How to handle them without exposing ourselves to them. And that's strictly poisons, not including venom." He frowned when he added, "It takes quite a bit more time than a month."

It took me quite a while to get out, "I understand."

His frown deepened. "If you understand, tell me the point of what I just said to you."

"You asked me earlier how many Reapers were in the House so I would look for them and see just how many there actually are, not because you expected me to already have an answer for the question. Am I correct?"

"Yes." His eyes narrowed. "What does that have to do with what I just asked you?"

"In my quarters, I asked Ahren if there was cause to worry about them being here," I said. "He told me there was no cause to worry."

He stepped very close to me and—bending down in my face—whispered, "There is *always* cause to worry."

I forced my voice to be even and my head up. "Yes, and you told me what you did just now to remind me how utterly hopeless our situation is."

I watched him blink hard several times before his expression softened. He shook his head and said, "It's not hopeless."

"You have one month to drop knowledge into my head that you've spent your entire life learning," I pointed out. "One month to teach me how to defend myself against people who have spent their entire lives learning how to kill." I nodded. "You're right, it's not entirely hopeless. There's just very little hope to be found."

He reached his hand out, cupping it over my cheek. He smiled sadly at me while saying, "There's as much hope as we make. It's only a little hope if you allow it to be only a little. We're going to make this work. Okay?"

I stared up at his face, saying nothing.

He sighed and repeated, "Okay?"

He smiled genuinely when I gave him a stiff nod.

"Would you mind if I wanted to be alone for the remainder of the day?" I asked him as I stared down at the floor. "I . . . I have some things I need to think over."

"You never need to ask my permission for anything." He bent over and kissed the top of my head. "Can I ask you what you're going to think about?"

As I looked up into his eyes, I wondered which version of Chase was more real. Was he more Reaper, or was he just a boy standing with a girl, looking incredibly worried that the things she would be thinking over pertained to him in some negative sort of way? I also wondered which me was more real. Was I more servant, or was I just a girl, willing to do anything to fight for her own life?

Or was I something else entirely?

I smiled at him as I quietly said, "I've had my sight pointed in many different directions in a very short time span. I believe I need to straighten things out in my head so I'm sure I'll be seeing them all from the proper perspective. I want to ensure I'm going into this correctly so that my view doesn't become distorted."

He nodded his head as if he were pleased, and I began to walk away. I had almost made it to the door when I felt a nagging feeling, as if I'd been dishonest with him about something. I couldn't quite explain it.

"I spoke to Amber." I turned back around to face him. "She brought me food before I came here. I'm still not sure what you meant about women Reapers."

He seemed to ignore my last sentence, though I'd meant it as something of a joke. His entire body stiffened. "What did she say?"

I breathed out deeply and said, "She told me she overheard a conversation between yourself and the Reaper in charge of them that took place before she came here. She said that you love me."

"Is that all?" he asked quickly.

I nodded and responded with, "Generally, yes."

He strode across the room so fast that it caught me off guard. "Did she mention us leaving?" His eyes began widening.

"Yes," I said, hesitant. "She said we wouldn't survive, leaving alone together."

"*No.*" He shook his head frantically. "Did she mention *when* we're leaving?"

"No."

He firmly grabbed hold of my arms. "Don't tell anyone when we're leaving, Aster. Not *anyone.*" He spoke with such desperation and intensity that it took me a moment to respond.

"But, why? Surely—"

"*Please* trust me," he begged. "Please."

Amber had asked me how I knew that Chase was not pretending to love me, and I'd told her it was because I had eyes. He'd asked me if I trusted him before, but never this way. I did not care if someone was a master at playing pretend. A person could not fake the level of fear I saw in his eyes.

I assured him, "I won't tell anyone."

It was only when he released a deep breath he must've been holding as he waited for a response from me that I realized his hands were shaking where they held onto my arms.

Chase had shown me a lot of things. He'd offered up parts of himself to me that I hadn't known existed within people. Amber could tell me that Chase and I would not survive for long, but it was something I had already come to terms with. I wondered if something was wrong with me that I was not so afraid of it. If Chase, who had trained his entire life to kill, was afraid . . . I likely should've been too.

But perhaps . . .

Perhaps this was what I could do for him, when he offered so much to me. Perhaps I could be the voice of hope for him. He seemed to be in need of it.

"Don't worry." I stood up on my tiptoes and kissed him lightly on the lips. I remained there, as close as I could get to eyelevel with him to say, "We're going to be all right."

When he smiled genuinely at me and nodded his head, I realized I did not need any more lessons in playing pretend.

I finished walking to the door and had my hand on the knob when he spoke again.

"Aster."

I turned around again to look at him, finding him standing almost awkwardly where I'd left him.

"Try to get everything worked out in your head today." He looked away to add, "We don't have very much time."

I nodded and finally left the room.

CHAPTER
TWENTY-FIVE

CONSCIENCE

I HAD NOT BEEN PRETENDING when I'd told Chase what I wanted to think about.

I spent the remainder of my day taking turns sitting at the edge of my bed and pacing around my quarters. I did not stare at the stone walls surrounding me. I went over all the things I'd learned, the conversations that likely held so much more inside them than I had yet discovered, and all the things to come. I did not focus on what would happen when Chase and I left the Valdour House, the people who would be coming or what would be waiting for us out in the big, wide world. I thought about the imminent future, of the things I knew would happen with certainty.

I would spend the next month learning. He would teach me everything he could in that time. I tried not to think about why I needed to know how to kill or to use or discern poisons. Focusing too hard on the necessity of the future could distract from the necessity of the present, I thought. For now, it was only knowledge and not application. I resigned myself not to wonder about when that may change or how many times he had used the tactics he would be teaching me. Those things were not pertinent.

It took me the entire day to get everything properly straightened out inside my head, but it got straightened.

I would not allow myself to become distracted from my goal. I would not allow unhappiness with Chase or anyone else to get in the way of it. If that happened, I would not learn. If I did not learn, I would not survive.

When I heard a knock at the door, I glanced at the tiny window near the ceiling that was almost precisely level with the ground above me. It was very nearly dark outside.

When I made my way over and opened the door, I was not entirely surprised to find Amber standing there with another covered tray in her hands. I smiled at her and stepped aside so she could enter, but she did not. She stood there for a moment with her mouth hanging slightly open before she spoke.

"Chase came to the kitchen and made himself some food earlier."

I did not know what I was supposed to say in response to that, so I offered her an awkward smile.

"He said you were distracted and likely hadn't eaten. He made you this and was going to bring it down to you himself, but I told him you'd wanted me to come back."

"Well, thank you," I told her sincerely.

I tried not to sigh when she still did not come inside.

"I'm sorry," she said quickly. "If questioning you about your father and what happened to you upset you. And I'm sorry for the way I acted about you and Chase. It was wrong of me to assume things about the two of you, but . . . I've never been in love to know what it's like. I guess I just can't understand."

"It's quite all right," I told her with a small laugh. I was in love and still didn't understand it. "You can come on inside and I'll get that bandage of yours replaced."

She finally stepped inside then, but while I was gathering the appropriate things she asked, "Don't you want to eat first?"

"No, it's fine."

"But it'll get cold."

"I've eaten quite a lot of cold meals." Another small laugh escaped from me. "One more won't hurt anything."

She seemed hesitant, but she walked over to where she'd stood earlier, putting her front to the wall and removing her shirt.

Again, as I had done earlier, I waited until she spoke to begin cleaning off the Branding.

"Why are you so nice?"

I made a noise that was somewhat similar to a snort before saying, "I'm not so sure I am."

Quietly she asked, "Do you think that, after you've been around him for longer, you won't be anymore?"

"This is assuming I truly am a nice person." I took a moment to think on what to say. "I believe every person who enters another person's life has the capability to change things for them. But at the end of the day, you still are who you are. Someone can change your perspective without your permission, but they cannot change your person unless you allow them to do so."

"Would you want to marry him?"

I laughed quite loudly. "*What*?"

When she said nothing in response, I laughed again, quieter then.

I told her, "I'm more concerned about surviving. I haven't thought of that sort of thing at all."

"I didn't ask the right thing." It mostly seemed as though she were saying that to herself. "I meant to ask whether you think he's the only person you'll ever love. If you think there's no one else out there for you, or if there's only one person made to fit with another."

"There are a great many people in the world," I said. "What a question such as that all comes down to is what you can offer a specific person and what they can offer you in return. When looking at it that way, I don't think there's another person who could give me what he's given me, though I will admit that could change in the future. What I can assure you will not change is that I have absolutely no desire to go looking." I paused. "May I ask you something?"

She barely said, "Yes."

"Why do you ask me such strange questions? Normally someone would have to be very close with a person to feel comfortable asking them such deep things *and* to expect a truthful answer in response to them. I'm beginning to feel as though you're interrogating me."

"I've never had someone to ask these kinds of questions," she answered in a very small voice. "I'm sorry."

For an instant, it felt as if my heart broke into tiny pieces. I cleared my throat. "It's quite all right. You can ask me anything you'd like. I was simply curious." I secured a new bandage over her back. "I'm finished."

She replaced her shirt and turned around to face me. "Can I ask you one more thing tonight?" Her forehead scrunched in something that seemed to be sadness or worry.

"Of course," I said without hesitation.

I wouldn't have thought it possible, but her forehead scrunched even tighter before she whispered, "You said earlier that you know the two of you wouldn't survive alone together. Are you afraid to die?"

I realized this was probably her first mission. I sincerely doubted she'd ever killed anything in her life but was aware that she would be required to do so eventually. She would probably be too ashamed to ask that same question to another Reaper.

I shook my head sadly and told her, "I'm afraid of not living."

Amber looked at the door an instant before it opened.

"*Oh*," Agatha said, startled. "I didn't know we'd be having company tonight."

"I was just leaving," Amber said to the floor and then moved with haste to make an exit.

I told her, "Don't forget to stop by again in the morning."

She stopped and smiled warmly at me over her shoulder for just a moment before leaving.

Agatha focused in on me once the door had closed. "What's wrong, my flower? You look as if you've seen a ghost."

"Amber asks me very difficult questions," I said in a distracted sort of way. Though I was staring at the wall, I felt as if I weren't even seeing it.

Agatha chuckled a little. "And now you know how it feels."

"Yes, I believe I do." I frowned a little when I admitted, "I'm happy to answer them for her. I hope my words are able to help her in some way."

Agatha stopped in the process of turning down her bed to smile at me and warmly repeat, "And now you know how it feels." It sounded so different the second time she'd said it.

I realized I was smiling where I stood.

I eventually carried on, though.

It was a very long time before Agatha spoke again. I had already finished eating the slightly cold griddlecake Amber had brought down for me.

"I had a conversation with Francine earlier today."

"What about?" I asked. I expected a question about why I had been so distracted this morning.

"She was telling me about your new friend," Agatha said. "She said you were the only thing that girl talked about today."

"*What*?" I laughed. "You must've taken her words out of context."

"I didn't!" she exclaimed with another small chuckle. "Francine said she went on and on about how kind and beautiful you were. Said she talked about you like you were the most fantastic thing in the world."

I shook my head in disbelief. "I simply cannot understand her distorted view of me."

"Distorted?" Agatha snorted. "I wonder sometimes whether you have the vaguest clue about who you are."

That gave me a great deal to think on.

I folded my hands in front of me and watched Agatha as she prepared herself for bed. Then I went and fluffed my pillow.

When I made my way to blow out candles in our room—which was my job because Agatha was frightened of the dark—I paused in front of our new mirror. I analyzed the girl who was standing in front of me, imagining I was someone else looking at her rather than myself. I wondered while doing so when the last time I'd properly looked at my own reflection actually was.

Had I ever?

My hair was lighter than I'd realized, as if age had changed its color somehow. Or perhaps it simply appeared lighter when it was not held in a tight bun. I didn't think I had caught a full-on image of it down in years without looking away, and I'd been so focused on the colors on my face the night I'd met Chase, that had held most my attention. My eyes were the same color as they'd always been, though they were held open wider than I could ever recall them having been before. The planes of my face had changed. I assumed that, at least, truly did have something to do with age.

I almost laughed in stunned disbelief when I discovered . . .

I did not look like a child anymore.

I blew out the candles, apart from one, and found my way into bed.

I TOSSED AND TURNED RELENTLESSLY in an attempt to get comfortable, but I could not sleep. I was certain my lack of comfort was mental and not physical. There were two things circling around inside my mind, taking my ability to sleep from me.

I eventually sighed and opened my eyes. I could barely make out the shapes in the room, but I knew precisely where everything was.

If I was going to be making changes in my life . . . I should make changes.

I decided to deal with the worries in my head, rather than lying in my bed awake thinking about them the entire night. I should take care of them and allow myself some peace. I could do that. I *needed* to do that, given what Chase and I would be doing for the next month. If I was tired, I would not retain information.

Carefully, I removed my blankets and lay there for a moment listening to Agatha's muffled snoring. She was so afraid of the dark that she slept with her blanket over her head every night, as if it could protect her somehow. It had given me much to think on over the years.

I slipped out of bed and tiptoed around the room, changing out of my nightclothes and back into my normal clothing. I grabbed two things from beneath my bed and went to the door.

Agatha would wake if the door creaked, as she always did at the slightest sound. She would ask me where I was going, and I did not want to tell her. I would tell her anyway and then she would make me stay. I did not want to stay and lie awake. In some ways and for some reasons, I *couldn't*. I wondered . . .

I grabbed the doorknob, turning it gently and pulling it one inch or so toward myself. Then, I put pressure upward, wondering if the door only creaked because it was not at the appropriate level. I held my breath and tugged it toward myself.

It did not creak.

I struggled to control the excited and pleased feelings as they did unpleasant things to my stomach.

I had to remind myself to pull upward as I closed it again. I almost forgot to do so in my excitement. Once I was safely in the corridor, I took a deep breath and began walking through the House.

For a long while, none of the Guards asked me where I was going. They would watch me pass, glancing at the items in my hands. Some of them snorted, some of them grinned, some of them narrowed their eyes, and others didn't react in any way whatsoever. Every time I received any sort of reaction, heat would rush to my face. I would remind myself that I had absolutely nothing to be embarrassed about.

Eventually, I did get stopped.

"What are you doing walking around the House after hours?" one Guard asked.

Quietly, I said, "Walking, Sir."

The next question was, "Why do you have those things in your hands?"

The other Guard, who I assumed was a Reaper, smacked his arm. "Oh. Carry on."

Again, heat rushed to my cheeks and I proceeded to go somewhere different than where they all clearly assumed I was going.

I walked down the hallways that would take me to the other side of the House. I found one of the Reaper Guards who blocked the entrance to that special hallway standing there in the same place I had seen him earlier. It was the first one—the nicer one—who was standing there alone.

He looked down at me and the items in my hands, his brow furrowed. After a moment, he gestured with his head for me to proceed, though he seemed very confused.

When I found the grumpy Reaper Guard curled up once again in the little nook, I frowned. He nearly jumped out of his skin when he rolled over to face me at the sound of my approach, and I tried very hard to ignore the hand that briefly darted not to the sword at his side but somewhere else that he didn't make it to before stopping. Assessing.

"I don't want those things," he grumbled at me in a volume that was something relatively close to a whisper.

I knelt next to him and was nearly not whispering when I said, "I don't care if you slash them into ribbons once I've gone, but I had to make myself look rightfully awful to bring you these, so you *will* use them to placate me. If you don't, I will sit here and torment you until you do."

His frown deepened, but it did not seem like he was going to attack me, so I moved forward a little, bending over and sticking a pillow where his head would be once he laid back down.

While I was in the process of covering him up with a blanket he asked, "Why are you doing this?"

"I couldn't sleep, thinking about the two of you sleeping on the floor with nothing."

He laid his head down on the pillow, cleared his throat, and whispered, "Thank you." The two words sounded like they'd been a great strain for him.

I smiled happily and patted the blanket over his arm, ignoring the way he flinched at the contact as if he were afraid for me to touch him. Sincerely, I said, "You're very welcome. Please sleep well."

When I stood up, I barely heard him say, "You as well."

I offered him another smile and began walking away. Though the hallways were very dim, I still watched the other Reaper Guard's hands on the off chance someone else would be walking them at night.

He made no gestures of any kind.

I glanced at his face as I passed, and he smiled at me a little. I wanted to thank him for earlier, about how he had stood up in my honor to Camden, but I didn't do it. Perhaps one day soon I would have the chance to.

I did not head back to my quarters, and I ignored the chuckling Guards I passed. Did what people thought of you matter if you knew in your heart that they were wrong?

Though I told myself it didn't matter and I had done nothing wrong, I still felt the sting of embarrassment and shame. I knew how my actions would be construed, so I should not have been surprised. I just hadn't known how it would make me feel.

I stopped moving when I reached room number four.

CHAPTER TWENTY-SIX

LITTLE TALKS

CHASE OPENED THE DOOR QUICKLY, faster than I could've anticipated or prepared myself for, but he did not look at me. He nearly shouldered past me as he stepped out into the hallway, hastily glancing in both directions. He did not ask for my permission when he grabbed hold of me and pulled me back into his room with him, though I doubted I could've found it within me to protest against it in how stunned I was at his behavior.

"Are you okay?" he asked once he'd closed the door, urgency in his tone. "What's wrong?"

Despite having seen him with his shirt off before, I had not prepared myself for the possibility of seeing it again. It took me far too long to realize I was gaping at him as I'd done the first time, but there was something incredibly fascinating about the way the muscles on his chest and abdomen appeared in the dim lighting of his room.

He nearly shook my arms when he repeated, "Are you *okay*?"

"*What*?" I looked up at his face. Once my mind fully registered what he'd asked me, I said, "Oh, yes. I'm fine."

"What are you doing here right now?" He sounded shocked, or possibly something that went beyond it.

I had to admit I was more than a little shocked at my actions myself.

I told him, "I have a question."

"A question?" He gaped. "Couldn't it have waited until morning?"

I realized I had become distracted by his body again as I shook my head in response to his question. It could not have waited until morning.

I brought my eyes back to his and quietly asked, "Do you think I'm beautiful?"

"*What*?" he asked, bemused. After several seconds, which seemed to be expended working something out in his head, he laughed. "You spent half the day thinking about everything we're going to have to do and *that's* the question that made you come to my room in the middle of the night for all the Guards to see?"

I couldn't quite explain the stinging feeling that ran throughout my entire body at his words.

I forced a smile at him. "You're right. This was wildly inappropriate. I'm so sorry."

I'd taken one step toward the door when he grabbed hold of my hand. He laced his fingers through mine, and I was taken aback at how pleasant my hand felt while touching the warmness of his. I hadn't even noticed I was cold until then.

He pushed back some of my hair with his free hand. "I've always thought you were beautiful."

The stinging feeling was replaced with something that felt lighter than air, yet heavier at the same time. I didn't know what it was exactly, but it was very strange and made me somewhat lightheaded.

"Now, will you tell me why you couldn't wait to ask me that question?"

I cleared my throat and responded with, "I couldn't sleep."

He grinned. "You couldn't sleep because you wanted to know whether or not I thought you were beautiful."

"Well, partially," I admitted. "And I also couldn't sleep thinking about those Guards with no blankets or pillows."

He laughed. "*What*?"

"Yes, I took them a blanket and pillow before I came here."

He kept laughing. "Did you really?"

"Yes," I said quietly. "I was mocked by the Guards the whole way there and then here."

"Did you realize what they'd be thinking when you left your room?" he asked, almost apologetically.

I nodded.

"And you came anyway."

I nodded again.

"You know this causes problems for—"

"Yes, I thought about that too," I interrupted. I knew this would make our pretending seem unbelievable. "I'll just have to leave quickly."

He narrowed his eyes and grinned. "You could stay."

Disbelieving, I asked, "And do what?"

"Whatever you want." He shrugged. "Sleep?"

"I should go." I spoke so fast that my own ears almost couldn't make out the words. I could hardly make anything out inside my own head. I had to leave because—for some inexplicable reason—I was more than a little tempted to stay, after he'd suggested it. It was irrational and . . .

Well, it was just completely ridiculous.

He said, "The offer's on the table, if you change your mind."

I cleared my throat. "I'll keep it in mind." I needed to get away from him and his attractive grin. There was something about the lighting in the room; I felt as though it were taking all coherent thought right out of my head. I wondered why that was. . . .

I had made it two steps away when he asked, "Did you wake Agatha up leaving the room?"

I shook my head and decided not to point out that I clearly wouldn't have been here if I had. "The door didn't squeak."

"How did you manage that?"

"I pulled up."

He smiled, and I could tell he was extremely pleased with me. That did not help with my body telling me to stay and my head telling me to leave.

I realized I was staring at him with my hand on the doorknob when he said, "Aren't you going?" His head tilted a little as the smile transformed into another grin. "Or are you staying?"

"Would you want me to stay?" I asked him, curious though I shouldn't have been. I should've already been gone.

I probably should not have come at all.

He chuckled and put his hands over his face, rubbing at it for a moment in a state of clear discomfort. "I'm contemplating breaking the door."

"What does that mean?"

"It means I want you to stay badly enough that I'm contemplating breaking the door so you can't leave."

"I see," I said, my voice quiet. I cleared my throat again. "Could you do that?"

He laughed. "Yes."

I realized that I'd been staring at his bed across the room for an extended amount of time when he said, "Please make up your mind."

"Do you wish I was more like the server girls?" I asked.

"What?" He sounded confused, and it was only then that I realized my question likely seemed to come from nowhere.

"Do you wish I didn't have to think so hard about whether or not I wanted to stay," I clarified. "That I could stay without thinking twice about it, simply because it would make you happy."

"*What*?" He almost sounded angry. He took a step closer and firmly said, "Don't ever stay or not stay because you think it's what I want. If you want to stay, I want you to. If you don't want to, then I don't want you to."

"You said you wanted to break the door," I pointed out.

He laughed and covered his face with his hands again. That time when he did it, I was struck by the way his muscles moved, which likely had something to do with the proximity. It was simply fascinating.

"I love you," he said. "I'm not going to break the door to keep you here if you want to go." He paused to laugh again. "I'm not going to lie and tell you I'm not tempted to, but I wouldn't actually do that."

"Part of me wants to stay," I admitted in a small voice. Part of me did, but absolutely none of me could understand why. I needed to sleep. As did he, surely.

"When that changes to all of you wanting to stay, you're more than welcome to come back."

"And if I only wanted to sleep next to you?"

"Then we would sleep," he said believably.

221

I cleared my throat once more and admitted, "I believe I would very much like to try that sometime."

He laughed again and said, "So would I."

I felt my cheeks flush at his words, then I whispered, "I'll think about it."

He laughed quite loudly then and rubbed the back of his neck with his hand. "So will I."

Again, I found myself distracted by his body.

I believed a substantial amount of time had passed—even if only substantial seconds—when he said, "Goodnight."

My face nearly felt as if it were burning off. Why was it so difficult to leave? "Goodnight."

"Don't forget to pull up on the door," he reminded me when I'd opened his.

I stood there for a moment, wondering what in the world he was talking about.

A grin stretched on his face. "To your room."

"Oh, yes," I said as he stepped closer. "I had every intention of doing just that."

He nodded his head and grinned wider, clearly telling me that he did not believe my lie.

Well, it had not technically been a lie. I was nearly positive I would've remembered at some point before I got back.

I watched him as he leaned against the doorframe.

"Goodnight," he told me again.

I offered him a sheepish look. "Goodnight." I finally pulled myself away.

I glanced over my shoulder halfway down the hallway and found him still leaning against the doorframe, watching me leave. Even with the dim lighting, I saw him smile. I quickly brought my gaze forward as I walked.

I was unhappy to admit even to myself that I was not certain precisely how many times I looked over my shoulder to glance at him before I found myself in the next hallway.

One thing was certain. I had a new line of questioning for Agatha.

I PULLED UP on the door to my quarters.

Unfortunately, my effort to remain silent was in vain. I knew as much the instant the door was partially open because more than one candle was lit. I found Agatha sitting up on her bed in a way that appeared to be serene, though I knew that was not possible.

Her eyebrows rose. "Did you have a nice walk?"

"I, um . . ." I started and then stopped. I closed the door behind myself and tried again. "Yes, I did."

"Do you want to try again?"

"Try . . ." I started and then found no more words to say.

"Try again to tell me what you were doing," she clarified.

Carefully, I said, "I did walk."

"Aster," she said, clearly unhappy with me.

My words began spilling out. "Well, I took a pillow and blanket to a pair of Guards who never leave their post. I couldn't sleep, thinking about them being there with nothing."

"And?"

"And I went to Chase's room," I said, bracing myself for the inevitable blow that would follow.

"*Aster*," she repeated in the indignant tone, only it was slightly more high-pitched.

"You asked me!"

Only a moment passed of her lips pursing before she took in a deep breath. "Were you intimate with him?"

"*What*?" I gaped. "*No*! I went to ask him if he thought I was beautiful."

She laughed. "That's all?"

"Yes." I frowned.

Why was that such a funny thing to everyone? I understood it was more than slightly ridiculous, but I did not think it was funny.

She sighed loudly and patted her bed. "Come over here and sit down. I believe you and I need to have a very important talk."

THOUGH I HAD PLANNED ON ASKING AGATHA about the things she wanted to discuss with me, I could not have anticipated the things she would actually say.

My eyes were so wide it felt as though they were ripping apart at the corners when I found myself lying in my own bed later, staring through the darkness at the stone wall in front of me.

I was glad I was so stunned over the surge of utterly insane information because a part of me was still tempted to return to Chase's room. Truly, it was an even larger part of me after the talk because I was ridiculously curious as to whether things were as Agatha said they were. It was simply so unbelievable.

Being so stunned kept me from moving even an inch.

The talk had been incredibly awkward, but I felt as though I were more prepared now for things that may possibly happen later. I was quite certain that, had I not been warned, I likely would've done more than slap him. I was nearly positive I actually would've run from the room.

A small part of me was angry that she'd never told me the information before, when we'd had talks about things relatively close in nature. I was sure that, if she had told me any of this before I'd fallen in love, I would have never allowed myself to do so.

It was most unfortunate that we'd had our little talk before bed, because I still could not sleep. My curiosity warred with my disgust and left my mind exhausted. At least I finally understood all the startling and confusing ways my body had been reacting to Chase. That was something positive.

Well, the feelings were not positive, but at least I understood them.

At least I believed I did.

Perhaps I was only lying to myself on the matter.

All of it just sounded so . . .

Disgusting.

CHAPTER TWENTY-SEVEN

PROGRESSION

WOKE TO A KNOCKING at the door, which I promptly ignored.

The knocking persisted.

I grumbled unintelligibly in the direction of the source. I sat up quickly when the door squeaked though, finding Ahren standing there frowning at me.

"Good morning." His tone did not quite match his expression. "Do you know what time it is?" One sounded somewhat cheerful. The other appeared the opposite.

"No." I rubbed at my eyes, trying to ensure I wasn't mistaken.

"It's nearly ten in the morning."

That was like a jolt.

I jumped out of bed—ignoring the fact that Ahren was in my room while I was wearing my nightclothes—and began gathering my normal clothing.

He said, "Chase and I have been running interference all morning for your little escapade to his room last night."

"Huh?" The noise escaped from my mouth unwittingly. "Interference?"

"Yes, attempting to get the ideas out of everyone's heads about what happened between the two of you."

225

I frowned. "Nothing happened."

He frowned right back at me, only far more so.

I reiterated, "Nothing happened."

"Then why in god's name were you still asleep just now?" he asked unhappily.

"Does that happen?" I stopped in the middle of the process of grabbing a shirt. "Do you sleep for a long time?"

He snorted. "Now I believe you."

"I'm offended you didn't take me at my word," I shot at him. "And I was still sleeping because I couldn't fall asleep last night."

"He said that was why you came to his room. Because you had a question and couldn't sleep until he answered it for you."

"Yes, and he answered my question."

"And you still couldn't sleep?"

My voice sounded far more high-pitched than normal when I said, "No, because I had an extremely disturbing conversation with Agatha when I came back down here."

"About what?" Concern was clearly evident in his tone.

"About the way the world works."

"You mean . . ." He stopped to laugh loudly. He did not stop laughing when he said, "I'm sorry. I'm not making fun of you."

"It seems like it," I said under my breath. Then I sighed loudly. "If your only purpose in coming here was to wake me up, then your mission is accomplished and you have my permission to promptly vacate the premises. I need to find Amber and patch up her back."

"Agatha's already done that," he told me. "She didn't wake you when Amber came in. She's already taken Chase his breakfast as well."

"Oh," I said quietly. I wondered how I had slept through that. I wondered how I had slept so late at all no matter how little sleep I'd gotten. "What am I supposed to do now?"

"Pretend as if you're cleaning the other side of the House," Ahren replied. "If anyone says anything to you on the way, send them to me."

"They won't." I was sure they wouldn't.

"No. You learned a very valuable piece of information yesterday."

"And what was that?" I asked, curious. I had learned a great deal of valuable information yesterday, but I did not know which bit he was speaking to me about.

He grinned. "That sometimes the most efficient way to remain unseen is to walk directly in front of a person's face."

Unhappy, I informed him, "You could've spared me an hour of preparation yesterday if you'd simply told me as much."

"Yes, but you wouldn't have learned it for yourself, would you have?" he asked. "Being told something is good, yes. But learning something for yourself is more gratifying by far."

"I don't currently have the time to worry about gratification," I reminded him. It was not something I had ever concerned myself with, and now would be a horrendous time to start.

"Then you'd better hurry up," he told me with a small laugh.

He left my room then, without the door squeak, and I hurriedly prepared myself for the rest of the day as best I could manage.

I GRABBED SEVERAL CLEANING SUPPLIES before heading toward the opposite end of the House. Nobody said a word to me as I walked, but the nice Reaper Guard near the door smiled at me. The grumpy one distinctly looked away, but when I passed by the little nook, the blanket and pillow were not shredded into ribbons. The blanket was neatly folded in a corner with the pillow resting on top. I smiled to myself the rest of the way to the designated room.

I found Chase staring out the window, which was not unusual for him.

He turned in my direction, though.

"Sorry for your busy morning," I told him. I sat all the cleaning supplies down near the door and stared at him after closing it.

I saw that he was very unhappy when I got a good look at his expression.

"What's wrong? Are you angry with me?"

"No," he said, his voice quiet. "I've just had to say a lot of things I didn't want to say this morning."

"Such as?"

"Things to set up what we have to do in a few days." Though he was turned toward me, he gazed out the window when he spoke rather than at me. "Word travels remarkably fast here, and Agatha came to give me a . . . very stern talking to."

Quiet, I asked, "You were saying nasty things about me, weren't you?"

He clenched his jaw for a moment. "Yes." I heard him sniff a little and he said, "I told Agatha about us leaving."

"You did *what*?"

"She won't tell anyone." He sounded sure, but . . .

"Why would you do that?" I asked in disbelief.

"It was the only way she'd believe I was lying to everyone else and not the two of you," he explained. "She's like a mother to you. I don't want her to hate me."

"Chase—"

"Anyway, it's a good thing you were sleeping. Ahren and I have already pretended to get in one argument about you." He laughed humorlessly before adding, "I can't tell you how much I hate this."

"It's all right," I told him.

"You didn't hear the things I said."

"Did you mean any of them?"

He finally looked at my face again and quickly said, "Of course not."

"Then I don't care what you said. I know why you did it and I understand. Soon, none of that will matter. And I don't care what anyone in this House thinks of me, apart from a very small handful of people." I sighed. "We should get to it. I wasted nearly the entire morning sleeping."

"You're right." He stepped away from the window.

I followed him as he began to leave the room. I ignored the bag he grabbed along the way.

I STOOD NEXT TO CHASE at the fire in the second kitchen as he cooked more food to poison for me. We were silent for a long while, but he eventually broke that silence.

"Why are you looking at me like that?"

"Huh?" I found myself saying for the second time in a morning. "I don't know what you're talking about."

"You're looking at me differently."

"Well, you're not looking at me to know how I'm looking at you," I shot at him.

He brought his eyes to mine, presumably to watch my face as he frowned at me. I believed he was trying to prove some sort of point with it, but I was unsure what it could be.

"I'm not looking at you any differently."

"You're looking at me like my head is on backwards."

"I'm not." My voice was quiet as I moved my gaze to a wall.

"What's wrong?" he asked seriously. "Were you just telling me you weren't mad about the things I said this morning to make me feel better about it?"

"What?" I shook my head. "No, it's not that."

He had completely taken his attention away from the food and brought it to me—which was making me quite uncomfortable—to ask, "Then what is it?"

I scratched my bottom lip with one of my fingernails and told him, "I had a talk with Agatha, when I went back last night."

He grinned. "Did you forget to pull up?"

"No, she was already awake."

"What kind of a talk could you have with her to make you look at—" He stopped speaking immediately.

I watched him look up near the ceiling and tilt his head slightly.

It was several seconds later when he said, "Oh. It was *that* kind of talk."

I cleared my throat and pretended to be particularly interested in something on the counter in an attempt to hide my discomfort. I picked up the object without thinking properly and unfortunately realized too late that it was an empty wooden bowl. I set it back down on the counter, although the awkwardness of it all probably only made things even worse than they already were.

"Did you really not know anything about it?" He sounded curious and seemed to be overlooking my discomfort, for which I was grateful. "I figured you did, given how afraid you were about something happening to you."

I contemplated picking the bowl back up, thinking—for some incomprehensible reason—I'd feel more comfortable with something in my hands. I was staring down at the floor when I said, "I was given a great deal of information I'd never heard before."

"Like what?"

Without my volition, my gaze darted from the floor to his body. When my eyes finally found his face, he was smiling hugely at me.

"I believe I have basic understanding of the mechanics of it now." I sounded meek as I stood there wringing my hands and eyeing the counter. Damn that bowl for not being something more useful to me. And damn my voice for sounding so ridiculous.

"No wonder you couldn't sleep." He laughed. "Do you feel better about it now that you've had some time to think on it?"

"Well, I thought on it for quite a long time," I admitted, then instantly wanted to smack myself in the face.

He was still smiling when I looked at him.

I hurriedly said, "Not like how it—" My face scrunched. "I'm going to stop speaking now before I make things worse for myself."

"You don't need to be embarrassed with me."

"I'm not embarrassed."

He grinned. "How many times have you thought about picking up that bowl again?"

Carefully, I admitted, "A few."

He laughed again. "Clearly you don't feel any better about it."

"I do, actually," I said, my voice quiet.

He raised an eyebrow at me, which I found to be particularly pleasant for some inexplicable reason.

"Well, Agatha told me . . ." I took in a deep breath. "She told me it could be quite a beautiful thing, when it's your choice and you love a person."

"But you're still afraid."

I nodded my head, and he turned back to the food.

"I'm sorry to say," he began as he stirred the ingredients, "but you might not want to let yourself get any further with it for now. In three days, I'll be setting back every bit of progress you've been able to make."

CHAPTER TWENTY-EIGHT

ALL THE WORLD'S A STAGE

THREE DAYS PASSED too quickly.

I learned all sorts of things in the time, some that I'd not expected to learn. Mostly, Chase and I dealt with poisons. He had forced me to look inside his bag of toys.

I'd had a few toys as a child, and I knew with unyielding certainty there were absolutely no toys inside that bag.

The poisons I paid absolute attention to, taking in everything and committing it to memory. The other things, I did not. Those other things, I paid only as much attention as I both could and was able.

He didn't teach me anything about defending myself.

When I asked him about it, he said, "I'm not showing you anything like that until after I pretend to leave. If I do, you'll likely do it on instinct when we're putting on our show. It would be too suspicious."

When asking him the point of a single lesson in playing pretend with that scenario, he said, "I needed to see if you could manage it. That's all."

So he was leaving me to my own devices to fend him off. The excessive slapping had been nothing more than a valuable lesson on the importance of pretending and, apparently, a test in my capabilities.

Though I did wonder once or twice how things would've differed had he reached some disparate conclusion from whatever he had on my capabilities, I tried to remind myself that was not what was important. And I could not blame him for the lack of defensive knowledge. It made perfect sense and I agreed with him on the matter completely.

Agreeing with and liking were not the same thing.

We did not kiss again, nor did we touch at all.

When inquiring about that, he gave me a similar answer to that of physical defense.

"I don't want you to get too comfortable with it until after."

As the days were winding down, I realized I would not have to do as much pretending as I'd initially believed. At least not with that particular thing. He was going to attack me and I was going to be afraid. One of my worst nightmares would come to life. And I was agreeing to make it real.

Real and not-real blurred together quite often in my thoughts. Sometimes I compared it to good and evil, unsure if there was such a distinct line between the two as I'd always believed.

Chase and I had walked around the House a little together over those three days, for show. He'd been exceptionally cold to me during those times, but he always made up for it later in some way or another. I ate quite a lot of griddlecakes over the course of those three days. They were never poisoned.

I did not like the times when the both of us were pretending, but I understood how important it all was. In that respect, I was very glad we did not have much time. Soon we would be gone from this place and we would never have to pretend again. Anytime I was unhappy about it, I reminded myself of that fact. He reminded himself of it as well, I was sure.

Before I knew it, the three days were up and I found myself walking through the hallways with Chase sometime late in the evening. I knew precisely where he was taking me. He'd told me where it would happen—two hallways over from the foyer. There were no Guards in that hallway, but they were near enough to hear me when I began to struggle.

And he would get me to the point where I would have no choice but to struggle. I knew it was the only way. Believability was the key to a lie.

The most believable lies came when standing on a very hazy line, with fact on one side and fiction on the other.

I forced a smile onto my face as I intentionally stole glances at him as we walked together.

He did not smile at me, but he *did* smile. I'd never seen that particular one on his face before, and I did not like it at all. Only when we found ourselves in the appropriate hallway did that horrible expression drop away from his face.

Once we'd gone halfway down it and stopped, he whispered, "I don't want to do this."

"You have to," I told him.

Necessity and desire rarely seemed to coalesce.

He put his hands over his face and rubbed at it for a moment before looking at me and shaking his head. "I'm sorry." The two words seemed to fall from his mouth into the space between us.

I backed myself against a wall, and he did not waste any time in pursuing and pressing his lips against mine. The beginning of the kissing was sweet, almost as if he were using a few moments of it to physically show me that he was sorry for what he was about to do.

I kissed him back, though my stomach was sinking.

I was still returning his kisses when they began to change. Slowly, they transformed into something similar to what they had been a few days previously, just before I'd slapped him.

I was still tempted.

He pulled his face away from mine and rested it for a very short moment close to my ear.

"I'm so sorry," he whispered again right before he bit down on my neck.

That was the beginning of my struggle.

I pushed against his chest, not because I had been told to but because I couldn't stop myself from doing it.

I wasn't strong enough to budge him an inch.

His mouth went back to mine, but it was not pleasant in the way it had been before. It was too rough and unfeeling.

I felt his hands roving all over my body, but even when I managed to push one of them away, it came right back.

I heard myself gasping for air as I struggled to keep his mouth away from mine and his hands from places where I should not have been touched. But all of that was not the worst of it.

I screamed when he removed my body from the wall and put me on the floor, pressing his weight against me. I was not pretending.

He covered my mouth as another shrill scream escaped me, and I sobbed.

I sobbed, and I screamed, and I ignored his mouth and his hand that was not masking my sound. I shut my eyes and waited, remembering what he'd said to me, repeating it over and over in my mind.

Don't look at my face when I'm pretending. Even if it seems like I'm going to, I won't actually hurt you. Just close your eyes and wait.

Suddenly his weight was lifted away, and I heard the sound of a fist hitting flesh. I kept my eyes closed tightly where I was on the floor sobbing.

I heard Ahren cursing and shouting, along with Chase's mocking laughter.

Their interaction did not sound pretend in the slightest.

Someone picked me up, and I struggled against it.

"It's okay," Ahren said, his voice soothing. "I've got you. He's gone. It's okay."

I could tell he was moving with me in his arms, though I did not open my eyes to see where he was taking me.

Just close your eyes and wait.

"Should I get Agatha?" someone asked from close by.

I thought I recognized the voice, but it sounded somewhat different, and I couldn't recall from when.

I didn't care. I did not care who it was.

"No, I've got her," Ahren replied, shifting my weight in his arms.

My own hysterical cries drowned out the sound of his shoes hitting the floor as he walked. Distantly, I wondered how much effort it was taking him to make the noise.

I knew that he stopped moving at that pace at some point because I no longer felt the air brushing against my face. He sat down and curled me up into his lap like a child, holding me close to him and running his fingers through my hair.

"It's okay," he repeated over and over. "It was all pretend. It's okay. You're okay."

I did not think about myself as I cried. I thought about all the women who had suffered real attacks, women who did not have anyone to save them. I cried for them and the pain they had to go through. It was not right for anyone to have to endure such things.

Worse things.

"All those women," I croaked, my words a jumbled mess mixed with sobs.

I was certain I said Agatha's name more times than I could count, feeling I'd seen something much like the hidden place in the garden.

Ahren did not tell me it was okay any more after that, but he kept me in his lap.

I WAS UNSURE HOW LONG I SPENT curled up in Ahren's lap, for some reason finding comfort in the touch of a man when it was the touch of a man that had me so hysterical. It felt like an eternity. But by the time Ahren's body stiffened, I had calmed down enough to notice the change.

I looked up at his face, but his attention was not on me. He was staring at something inside the room.

When I turned my head, I saw Chase standing there. I felt my jaw quivering as I took in what I could of his appearance through my blurry vision.

His bottom lip was split open on one side, and he looked disheveled. But none of that really mattered. It was his expression that mattered as he stood there not blinking at all.

Shame marred his face, and his eyes were bloodshot.

I couldn't exactly explain it, but I crawled out of Ahren's lap and ran across the room, throwing myself into his arms. I went into hysterics all over again as I cried against his chest.

"I'm so sorry." He repeated the words so many times.

He did not return my embrace, but he let me touch him. I knew his hands were hanging in tight fists at his sides because I could feel the rigidity in his form.

"How much time do you need?" Ahren asked from behind me.

I ignored him.

"I don't know." Chase sounded distant, as if he wasn't even sure where he was.

"I'll be back in an hour." I did not hear Ahren's footsteps as he walked to the door, but I heard him slam it behind him and felt Chase flinch slightly when he did it.

Several extremely long minutes passed before Chase said, "That was the worst thing I've ever had to do."

"You've done a lot of bad things," I managed to get out somehow, though it was muffled by his chest.

"Not like that." His words were a whisper in what he said next. "Can you forgive me for this?"

"It wasn't real."

"You've been crying for hours."

"So have you," I pointed out.

"Aster . . ."

I pulled away from him and reached for his hand. He jerked it away. I took a deep breath and resolved myself to be calm.

It had only been pretend. I was all right. I had not been hurt, not really.

Why did it feel like I had?

I asked, "Are we going to be safer?"

He nodded slowly, but he was not looking at me.

"Will this give us a better chance at being successful?"

"That's not the point."

"Then what *is* the point?" I demanded.

He put his hand over his mouth as he stared at the wall. Then he seemed to realize what he was doing and nearly jumped out of his own skin. He stared down at the floor and shook his head.

"If those aren't the points to what happened, then what is?" I could find no other point.

I reached for his hand again and he let me take it then, though I could tell he was hesitant. When I brought his hand to my face, he quickly stepped away, putting his back to me.

"I need you to touch me," I told him.

I watched him shake his head.

"Chase," I said, my voice firm.

He turned to look at me and clenched his jaw.

"I need the memory of that out of my head. I *need* you to touch me."

He was clearly hesitant as he took a few steps closer to me and held his hand out. It almost felt as though he thought we were starting over, that he had to wait for me not to be afraid of him.

I was not starting over. I simply needed to be reminded that it didn't hurt when he touched me and was not pretending.

He looked away from me again, and I watched a tear fall from his eye. I moved my face forward to where his hand was waiting. He bit his lip hard where it wasn't split and looked even farther away. But very slowly, his thumb began moving along my cheekbone. I closed my eyes.

It did not hurt.

I was not afraid.

He was not hurting me.

He would not hurt me again.

I had seen him cry, but I'd not ever heard him cry. I could hear him then, if only just.

It was not long before he pulled his hand back to himself and sat down hard on the floor, putting his face on his knees.

I looked down at him for a moment as I worked it all out inside my mind. It would not help matters to make him feel guilty over something we'd planned on doing, no matter how bad of an experience it had been. We would likely endure worse things. Or I could hope that we would. It would mean we were alive to endure them. It would not help matters any to cry anymore over it myself. We had planned it, and I had agreed to it.

I sat down next to him and rested my head against his arm, feeling it moving as he cried quietly.

Eventually, I whispered, "We're going to be all right."

I almost thought he laughed once at that.

There was too much to do, and neither of us had the time to dwell on this.

"Come on," I said as I stood up.

I tugged on his arm, and he stood up willingly, allowing me to lead him wherever I wanted to. I walked over to the bed that Ahren had been sitting on with me for what was likely hours. Chase stopped there and shook his head.

"You're going to get on that bed," I told him.

"No, I'm not." His voice was as unyielding as his stance.

"Listen," I said as I poked my finger against his chest. "You're going to get on that bed with me. We're going to lay there together and you're not going to hurt me. We're going to lay there and work all this out inside our heads. I'm going to leave, and then we're both going to sleep. And when we wake up, we must be done with this because we don't have the time for it. I want to survive long enough to get far away from this place with you, and I can't do that if you're not focused. Do you understand me?"

He blinked and nodded his head.

"Then get on the damn bed."

He did what I told him to without further objection. I kicked off my shoes, but he had not done so. He laid there on his back, staring up at the ceiling, and I was surprised that I did not hesitate when climbing into bed with him.

I scooted close to him and, though the contact was strange, I was quickly able to find the perfect place to rest my head—inside the crook between his arm and his chest. Slowly, I reached my hand out, placing it on his abdomen.

I looked up at his face, but he continued to blink at the ceiling, almost as though he were attempting to convince himself that I was not even there with him. His hand that was not resting on the bed behind my back went over his face.

"Do you want to know the only thing I could think about that entire time?" he asked through his hand.

"Yes," I said.

I wondered now when my answer to that question had changed. I'd always said *no* when being asked if I wanted to hear unpleasant things.

How had I changed so much so quickly?

Had I changed, really, or did I simply understand now that I would be told the unpleasant things without agreeing to hear them?

I would rather it be my choice.

He finally looked at me to say, "All I could think about was how, if that was really happening to you, you wouldn't be able to stop it. God, the Guards would be bad enough, but another Reaper?" He looked away, his expression appearing pained, and he shook his head.

I desperately felt as though I needed to get his mind on something different. And him asking me that question made me think . . . "Chase?"

He brought his eyes back to mine.

"That man who beat you when I first came here."

He blinked hard at me and said nothing.

"Was he the first person you ever killed?"

His gaze went back to the ceiling as he said, "I didn't kill him."

"But you said—"

"I said I wasn't going to tell you what I did to him," he clarified as he took in a deep breath and clenched his jaw. He laughed humorlessly once, though it sounded more like exhaling a breath. "The man I met? He came back here with me, and he killed him. He called it . . . a show of good faith." Then he laughed several more times.

"What did you do to him?" I barely managed to get the words out.

He sniffed in through his nose and said, "He told me to wait until he got his hands on you." I felt as though he were testing me again when he turned his face back to me, doing nothing more than blinking. "So I cut off his hands."

My gaze instantly shot away from his face, down to his torso. I heard my throat clear.

"Are you ashamed of me now?"

I forced my breathing to be even as I reached for his hand that was resting on the other side of his body. I took it in mine and quietly said, "No."

Only then did he touch me with the hand that had been resting on the other side of me. It came up on my arm, rubbing gently up and down. It was so strange and terrifying that hands which were capable of inflicting such pain as his were could also be capable of something so far from it. But weren't all hands capable of inflicting pain?

Hands were only hands. It was knowledge and drive that directed their actions.

Was Chase a monster?

I didn't know. He was not a monster to me. Agatha had said before that it did not matter; it was what a person was to everyone else that mattered. I still believed Agatha was wrong.

Was Agatha wrong?

Agatha had to be wrong because I'd never felt safer than I felt with Chase's arm around me. Not in such a long time. . . .

"How many of the leaders here have you killed for them beating me?" I asked him, still speaking quietly.

"More than I want to tell you."

I glanced up at his face. He had tears falling from his eyes, but he wasn't making a sound. I wouldn't have known he was crying again if I hadn't looked.

"I love you," I whispered.

He didn't say it back, but he leaned down and kissed the top of my head.

I hoped that one day I would not need Chase's protection. But for now, I simply was not knowledgeable enough to protect myself. Still, I would not complain about having him here. So long as I was next to him, so long as I was touching him or could see him, nobody could hurt me.

I hoped that, one day, I could return the favor and protect him.

But mostly? I hoped that one day . . . I could protect myself. I hoped that one day I would not feel so weak.

CHAPTER TWENTY-NINE

HEART AND SOUL

I FELL ASLEEP faster than I believed I ever had in my life, at least in my life since coming to the Valdour House.

I stirred, but I did not wake entirely when I felt my body moving. I was simply too exhausted from the events of the day to fully wake up. I could feel someone's arms beneath me, and I inhaled a scent I recognized immediately.

Ahren. Harsh with subtle undertones of sweetness and comfort from another life. I was not upset that he was taking me away from Chase. I felt safe with Ahren, too.

I dozed on and off as he walked with me in his arms as he had earlier, cradling me to his chest like a child. I felt air on my face and thought of my father, lying awake at night as he held me close to him.

Go to sleep now, Flower, he would say. *I've got your back. I love you. You're safe.* He'd whispered that to me every single night.

I had always felt so unbelievably safe when wrapped in my father's massive arms. I'd always felt so safe, feeling him close and knowing he was there. Then he died and took every bit of my safety with him.

But I'd found it again, though I had not even allowed myself to hope for it. I appreciated it more now that I fully understood all the things in the world there were to be afraid of.

"I believe she's all right now," Ahren barely said. "I gave them some time together. I'm sure that helped her more than anything else could have."

I heard Agatha's muffled crying as Ahren placed me on my bed and covered me up.

"I gave her the knowledge, but I've been trying to spare her from the pain of the experience," Agatha whispered and then sniffled. "I can't believe she volunteered herself for that. You know how she feels about men."

"She loves him."

Distantly, I realized he almost sounded as if he were crying too. I wanted to fully wake up and comfort the both of them, but I simply did not have the energy to do so.

"I believe she'd do just about anything to escape from this life with him," he continued. "I only wish I'd had the spirit to do it myself."

"Do they stand a chance?"

"I'm trying," Ahren said almost desperately. "There's only so much I can do."

"Does she know?"

"I should go," Ahren said, his voice urgent despite the softness of it.

I heard nothing else apart from Agatha scooting into bed with me. When I felt her arm around me, I felt myself drifting back to oblivion.

I JUMPED WHEN I FELT a hand on my face.

Shooting up in bed, I found Ahren sitting there at the edge of it, watching me. Light was filtering in through the small window near the ceiling, and I rubbed at my eyes.

"How are you feeling?" he asked.

"I'm fine," I answered. "How are you?"

"Fine." It was clearly a lie.

"You look as though you haven't slept at all."

"I haven't." He rubbed at his red-rimmed eyes. "I had a discussion with Chase and then did some work."

"You didn't hit him again, did you?" I asked and then yawned. I found I wouldn't have minded so terribly much if he had.

"No," he said shortly and laughed. "But he and I both agreed you should start physical training today."

"What does that mean?" I asked. "Learning how to kill people?"

"Something like that." He frowned. "I've brought you a bag of things you'll need. Clothing and whatnot."

"Clothing?" I asked, lost. "I'll have to wear something different?"

"Yes, so it doesn't get in the way." He opened the bag and pulled out a small mess of black fabric.

"What is that?"

He unfolded them and showed them to me.

"Those won't get in the way of anything!"

I had never seen such small clothing before; they would hardly get in the way of my womanly parts. They appeared as though they were made from similar material to that of the ridiculous black dress that I'd had to wear the first night I'd ever seen Chase. If I'd thought that dress was wildly inappropriate due to its lack of coverage, the clothing was indefinably worse by far.

Ahren almost smiled, but it seemed as if he couldn't quite manage it.

"I should warn you," he started seriously. "He's going to have to get very physical with you today. If you're uncomfortable with that due to yesterday, or even because of the clothing, I can have another Reaper assist with this."

"I don't want another man's hands on me," I said in quick response. I did not know how or why he believed that would be helpful.

He nodded. "Let him know if you change your mind. He'll understand."

Ahren stood from the bed, and I grabbed the clothes he'd dropped.

I had to know . . . "How in the world am I supposed to fit into this?"

"You'll fit," he said with a small laugh. "Make sure you don't wear those anywhere apart from the other side of the House. It's standard Reaper issue for training."

I did not realize that I was smiling down at the clothing in my hands until I heard the door squeak.

Then I frowned at it again when I realized I would certainly have to waste time shaving my legs. That was quite unfortunate.

ONCE I WAS PROPERLY CLEANED and shaved, I found myself walking down the hallways, clutching the bag tightly in my arms. I could feel the Guards watching me as I passed. They did not snort nor chuckle at me now, as they'd done before. When I glanced at a few of them, they promptly looked away, even the Reaper Guards who likely knew our scene yesterday had been planned. I was glad I'd not seen it from the outside.

I almost thought, when looking into the eyes of some of the Reaper Guards, that they were angry. Perhaps some men were better than I had ever given them credit for, if such a thing could affect them so. Or perhaps not.

I was not walking for very long when a Guard stopped me.

"Would you like an escort, Miss?" He sounded concerned.

"No thank you, Sir," I said quietly to the floor as I stepped past him.

I found that I was angry over his question, like a woman was only worthy of an escort *after* she'd been attacked. If they were so concerned with it, why did they not insist that all women were escorted from one place to another at all times?

I did not know if it was irrational for me to be angry about someone trying to be nice, but I did not believe it was irrational to be angry that only women would need an escort for such a reason and never men.

Whatever it was that Chase would be teaching me . . . I very much hoped it would make me laugh hysterically when a person asked me if I needed an escort.

It was the grumpy Reaper Guard who was awake and on his own as I walked past.

He glanced at me, and I offered him a very small smile. He did not return it even slightly before looking away and nearly turning his body the same.

The nice Reaper Guard was asleep in the little nook, but he woke up as I passed and quickly fell into step beside me as I walked through the door.

"I'm very sorry for your experience yesterday." Indeed, he did sound very sorry.

"You know what it was, I'm sure," I told him.

"Still."

I glanced over at him and saw that his jaw was clenched.

"It was very difficult to see you after."

I supposed that meant Ahren had carried me to this side of the House afterwards and I had simply been too incoherent both times to discern as much. I was not surprised by either thing. This side of the House was safer in its seclusion, and I'd been quite incoherent.

I nearly laughed. "You don't know me."

"That doesn't matter." After saying as much, he chuckled a little and added, "I had to talk Stanley out of going back there to at the very least punch him himself five different times last night."

"Who?"

"My partner."

"The grumpy Guard." I nodded.

"Yes, I can see where you'd get that," he said, chuckling again. "I'm Stewart, by the way."

"Stanley and Stewart," I said, mostly to myself.

I glanced over at Stewart, finally getting a proper look at him. He was younger than I had realized, younger than Stanley by around ten years it appeared, likely in his mid-twenties. Disheveled blond hair, and warm, brown eyes.

I shook my head and laughed a little. "I don't know why you'd lie about him wanting to punch Chase."

"I'm not lying," he said indignantly. "You remind Stanley of his daughter."

"He has a daughter?" I asked, curious.

He didn't seem the fatherly sort.

"Well, she was taken from him, of course." He frowned. "But he told me he wants to believe she would've been like you."

"Neither of you know me at all," I reminded him.

"You're right," he conceded. "But I don't know very many people who wouldn't be able to sleep thinking about us not having a blanket and pillow. A normal Guard possibly, but not what we are. Especially not here."

"Well, I don't know very many people who would stand up for a servant's honor when they don't know them at all." I cleared my throat knowing that now was my opportunity to say, "Thank you for that."

"Do you know how many people I've killed?" he asked me curiously from out of nowhere.

When I glanced over at him again, he was watching me as he walked.

"I couldn't possibly," I stated. "Do *you* know?"

"One hundred and twenty-seven," he replied immediately, like he'd known I would ask.

I felt my eyes widen, my gaze shooting to the floor as I attempted to make them return to normal. Unfortunately, he stopped moving which made me feel inclined to stop moving along with him.

"Do you think Reapers have souls?" He sounded quite curious again.

I had never asked myself whether or not they had souls, only hearts. Still, I supposed it boiled down to the same thing, so I felt confident responding with, "I do."

"Do you know how many times I've cried in my adult life?"

I shook my head.

"One hundred and twenty-seven. No more and no less." He looked at the floor and shook his own head. "It's so funny."

Quiet, I asked, "How is that funny?"

"I would never pretend as if I were a good person. But I know I have a soul in here somewhere." He narrowed his eyes and asked, "Do you know what it's like? Killing someone."

"I couldn't possibly," I repeated, though it barely came out.

He leaned closer and held his mouth open for an instant as if he were thinking twice about speaking. Still, he spoke, as quietly as I had.

"When you're looking into a person's eyes as they die . . . you wouldn't believe the things you can see there. Eventually you can look in almost any person's eyes and see who they really are. That boy, the one who said that about you? He's dead behind the eyes. I didn't say what I said to defend your honor. I said it because it was true from where I stood."

"That doesn't take away my appreciation for it," I said. "Though I'm sure you told me that just now, hoping it would."

He grinned. "Why would I do that?"

I ensured my voice was impassive to say, "Because all of you like to present yourselves in the worst light possible."

The grin slowly began dropping away from his face and I found myself quite glad to see it go.

"All of you want to make people think as badly about you as you think of yourselves. And you test everyone who gets even remotely close to see if they'll run away screaming." I shrugged. "I'm sorry to tell you that your efforts are wasted on me."

"Why?" he asked, his curious tone returning.

"Because while you do those things, you all crave that one person who won't think of you that way," I said. "You wouldn't have told me how many times you've cried if that wasn't true. I would be more than happy to not think of you as a monster, despite the bad you've done in your life."

He leaned closer and whispered, "Do you know how quickly I could kill you right now?"

"I would imagine you could snap my neck before I turned to run." I smiled to add, "But you won't."

"You're too credulous," he told me firmly as he shook his head.

"And all of you are too skeptical. Perhaps one day we shall all find a happy medium."

He laughed a little.

I added, "It was very nice to be formally introduced to you, Stewart. I'm quite certain I can find my destination alone now."

I had started to walk away—pleased that he heard me silently telling him that I wanted to be left alone, clear in him remaining where he'd stopped—when he said, "Don't ask Chase how many people he's killed."

I turned around to look at him with narrowed eyes.

"I can see it on your face that you want to." He shook his head before firmly adding, "*Don't.*"

"Why not?"

"I saw your reaction to my number, even though you hid it relatively well," he said. "Our city has many more Reapers than this one, and Chase is their favorite here. Put two and two together."

"He's their favorite?"

He raised an eyebrow and nodded.

"Why?" I barely heard the word slip out of my mouth.

He smiled a little as he looked down at the floor. "You'd probably be surprised to find that the best Reapers are the ones with hearts. But the most efficient ones don't have them at all. But you see . . . he's always kept his heart hidden with you. He has one; it just never gets in his way." He laughed a little—and though the sound was small, it was full of amusement—before he added, "I'm curious to see how good he can be when his heart is dangled in front of his face."

CHAPTER THIRTY

SCENARIOS

I WAS SOMEWHAT DISTURBED even still, when I walked into the room and found Chase, not staring out a window as he usually did but sitting in a chair and staring at a wall.

I truly wished all the damn Reapers would stop acting like Stewart had. I was certain they all said things with the sole intent of disturbing me. I understood the desire to both pull closer and push away, but was it necessary to do it *purposely*?

Startlingly, it was not the thought of Chase's . . . *number* that had me so troubled. It was the last thing Stewart had said, how he'd implied that me being close to Chase would somehow make him weak.

When he looked from the wall to me, I asked, "Do you believe I'm a weakness to you?"

He frowned. "You've been talking to Stewart."

"Well, yes, he followed me most the way here and we stopped and had a small discussion." I knew . . . "You changed the subject."

His frown deepened. "In a way."

"I see," I said on a breath, my gaze moving from him to the wall.

I heard him sigh as he stood up and began walking over to me. He stopped before he got to the window he'd have to cross and, when I looked at his face, he gestured for me to come closer.

"You have to understand," he said when I got close to him. "I always know what to do in any given situation. Always. I keep putting together these scenarios in my head involving you, and I don't know what I would do. I go back and forth with everything."

"How do you mean?"

"Three Reapers." He held his hands in the air like he was presenting the scenario to me. "One of them is getting ready to snap your neck, and I've got two on me. Do I take the risk that I could kill the two before the one could kill you? If I took out the one holding you, the other two would take me down and kill you once I was dead anyway." He paused for an instant. "Where's the solution?"

"Could you kill the three by yourself if I was not in the picture?"

"It would depend on how good they were." He shrugged uncomfortably.

"Could you?" I pressed.

He frowned again. "Under most circumstances, yes."

"Then the simple solution is to teach me how to take care of myself," I told him. "Even though we may not have very much time here, we'll still have time when we leave."

"I know you think you're capable of it, but you don't know what it's like," he said, his voice firm. "Until I've seen you kill and seen how you react to it . . . I'd still be worried about you in that scenario."

"Well then you'd better teach me well," I told him blankly. "Or else I'll get killed before I get the chance to show you I can." I sighed. "I need to change into those ridiculous clothes."

"When you're done changing, leave the room, keep going down the hallway, make a right and go six doors down." He began to walk away and then stopped. "Can you remember that?"

I glared hard at him. "Yes, I'm quite certain I can manage, Chase."

"Are you sure you're not going to have any issues with me touching you?"

"Please shut your mouth and leave the room," I told him. "I really don't feel like being angry with you today."

He smirked a little, but he shut his mouth and left the room as I had told him to.

I WAS GLAD that I'd not tried the clothing on while I was still in my quarters. If I had, I likely would've accidentally left them on my bed.

I felt entirely naked with my exposed arms and legs, the black material of the bottoms reaching just above my knees. I felt something far worse than naked with the tight-fitting fabric sucking in my body and clinging to it like a second skin that somehow seemed to be tighter than my first. I sat down and put the boots on my feet. They were not as heavy and clunky as they appeared they would be. Those, at least, were quite comfortable.

I moved over to a mirror in the room and immediately wished I hadn't. My eyes went so wide as I took in my appearance. I quickly looked away from the mirror and down at my chest and realized . . .

I actually had a chest.

"All the stars," fell out of my mouth as I shook my head.

I turned my body around several times, analyzing it.

I'd had no idea it looked this way. When in the world had it happened?

"All the *stars*," I said again, only then I did not barely say it.

I hastily removed myself from the vicinity of the mirror and vacated the room. If I'd remained staring at myself, I most assuredly would've changed back into my other clothing. I would see this one time if the horrible clothing was necessary. If it was not, I would never wear it again.

I realized that Chase asking me if I could remember the directions was not such a preposterous thing for him to have done, given my confused and shocked state over my body. I turned left, rather than right, at the next hallway. Then, I was certain I walked past six doors and had to start over. When I finally found the appropriate room, I opened the door as though I were not feeling any of the things that I was feeling.

Truly, all I felt once I caught a glance at the room was confusion. It nullified the shock and horror I was experiencing due to the sight of my own body—along with the embarrassment of the difficulty locating the room—though likely only temporarily.

Chase was waiting for me inside the empty room. There were no windows or furniture at all in the rather large space. When I saw him, all the other feelings I'd been attempting to repress came back to me.

I held one of my arms with the opposite hand, draping an arm over my chest to hide my chest as I walked. Though I was clothed, I didn't feel it was covered. Or perhaps the other way around. When I stepped close to him and he cleared his throat and looked away, my gaze went down and I saw that I was only making my chest worse with my effort.

What could you do to hide such a thing?

He had changed his own clothing into something that was made from the same material as what I was wearing. It didn't fit him in the same way, but there was something undeniably spectacular about it.

"How are you supposed to teach me anything if you can't even look at me?" I asked. "Is it that awful?"

"What?" His tone almost implied he'd forgotten I were even there with him. He shook his head quickly and said, "No."

"I look ridiculous," I stated humorlessly.

He laughed. "I wouldn't say that."

I couldn't escape from . . . "You're going to have to touch me again, aren't you?"

He looked at the wall. "Quite a lot."

"Then I believe you and I should become better acquainted with one another's bodies."

He balked.

"We must be businesslike about this, because we don't have any time to waste with distractions. If you can't even look at me, I'm quite certain we have a very serious issue."

A few seconds passed before he said, "You're right."

I felt very naked again as his gaze roved over my body. I tried extremely hard not to fidget because of it. But I also discovered that I . . . somewhat enjoyed it—him looking at me. Part of me despised it, but a part of me did not.

How strange.

He cleared his throat once more and walked away toward the center of the room. I followed after him without hesitation, presuming he'd gotten acquainted enough.

"You need to understand something very important before we begin," he said. "We're taught how to poison, but we rarely do it unless the situation calls for it, as I said before. You have to understand that when a Reaper comes for you, they *come* for you. We're taught to throw knives, but we generally only do that if we need to take someone down quickly. When they come for us, they'll likely take me out that way and then come for you."

"Why?"

"Because you're not a threat and we like to get our hands dirty." His voice was impassive. "My first priority is teaching you how to fend people off. It can buy you the time to save your life. If we have time for the other things while we're here, we may get to it. We may not. We may not ever."

I looked down at the floor and heard myself say, "It's funny."

When I looked up at him again, he was frowning at me.

"You want to teach me how to save my life when you all know how to take them."

"The first thing we're taught as children is self-defense," he said. "They teach us that so we're able to get people off us quickly and then kill them. If you can't defend yourself, you're going to get killed."

I fought against the urge to blurt out that we were going to get killed anyway.

"Start teaching," was what I said instead.

He narrowed his eyes. "Don't you want more information?"

"I want teaching," I told him.

He grinned at me. I would almost have been ashamed to admit that a very large part of me was excited about what we were to be doing, especially after the day before. I would rather learn how to defend myself than kill. There was nothing to be worried about while learning something like this. I didn't believe there was anything questionable about it.

"Okay." He chuckled. "Teaching it is."

He moved behind me and I turned around to look at him. He moved behind me again, and I turned around.

He chuckled once more before saying, "Stand still."

I remained still when he moved that time.

"You know how quiet we are."

I fought against the urge to move. Knowing he was behind me and not knowing what he was planning made me uneasy.

"We will *always* try to sneak up on a person first," he explained. "That's why we're always listening. No matter how quiet a person is, they still make some sort of sound. A breath, a footstep, clothing rubbing against clothing, *something*. So you listen for it all the time."

"That sounds like a miserable way to live."

"It is," he confirmed. "But it's necessary." He sighed. "I'm going to have to touch you, but I won't hurt you."

I cleared my throat. "All right."

He was closer when he said, "Don't react, but think about how you would react."

I expected for him to move slowly, but he didn't. His arm shot around my neck and pulled me backward against him, faster than I ever could've anticipated.

How could a person move so quickly?

He held me tightly for a moment then loosened his hold. "Reaction?"

"Shock."

I heard him laugh quietly once before he said, "No. What did you want to do?"

"I meant that I was shocked and couldn't think of anything to do," I clarified.

"Thinking quickly could mean life or death," he said, his tone serious. "And there are always options."

"And what are my options?"

"You literally have a second to take in your opponent, even if you can't see them," he began. "You feel my presence here. You know I'm bigger than you are, physically stronger. The key to everything is shock. You react quickly and they don't expect it. They would never expect you to know how to fend them off. Just know that shock is their intention for you as well." He paused. "What do you think your options are?"

I was suddenly very conscious of his body, after him talking about sensing his presence. It took me a moment to say, "I don't know."

"Think about it," he insisted.

"This is quite distracting," I told him apologetically, fidgeting.

I heard him laugh quietly again, but he did not move away. "Say you and I are in that situation I told you about earlier. They'll take me out and come for you. They'd likely hold you this way and force you to watch me die. Reactions?"

My face immediately went hot with fury. "Would they really do that?"

"They would likely do worse," he said, his voice impassive again. "You can't always depend on it, but one of the biggest flaws in Reapers is that a lot of them can't help teaching people lessons before they kill them."

"Like what you did to that man." I cleared my throat again.

"Yes," he admitted without hesitation.

"What will they do when they catch us?" I almost whispered, looking down at his arm still across me above my chest.

"They'll either do what I told you about," he answered. "Or they'll throw a knife and wound me enough to take me down but not kill me. Then they'd make me watch as they tortured and killed you before they killed me. Or they'd just kill us. It would depend entirely on the Reapers that were sent."

I tried to come to terms with what he'd said, but . . . "They'd send more than one at a time?"

"For us?" He laughed. "Definitely."

I shook my head for a moment before what he'd said registered. "You said for us."

I felt his entire body stiffen behind me.

"Not for you. Why would you say that?"

"You're with me."

I shook my head again, knowing with certainty that it was another of those times where I was not getting the full truth.

"We're off subject. If you're being held this way, you have several options. It would be different if you had a knife to your throat or something similar. But for now, we're just going to focus on this."

"What are my options?" I asked him again, resigned.

"If a person was shorter than I am, you could throw your head back into their face," he said. "Breaking a person's nose is a definite way to catch them off guard. Keep in mind that getting a tooth in your skull is not a pleasant experience if you miss."

"You sound as though you've had that happen to you."

"Second option," he went on quickly. "Elbows." He grabbed my arm gently with his free hand. His other arm was still just below my neck, with that hand resting on my shoulder. "You have specific places to aim. Here—" He tapped my elbow against his body. "Ribs. Here—" He moved my arm down and aimed my elbow. "Stomach." He moved it farther up and said, "Chest.

"Your third option," he continued. "Throw every bit of your weight back. Only do that if you're positive, and I mean *absolutely positive* it will catch them off guard. They're going to take you down with them, but if you surprise them, they may release you for long enough to get out of their grip. If they're very skilled, they won't let you go. If they're very much larger than you, it likely wouldn't work anyway." He paused for a moment. "Clearly the third option isn't the best one. It's advisable to take the pain you'll inflict on yourself with the others. You'd stand a better chance."

Curious, I asked, "How many options do *you* have in this exact same situation?"

"More than I can count." He chuckled. "We may get to others eventually." He finally released me, and I heard him take a few steps back. "Okay, I'm going to come at you again. I want you to react this time. Don't think about it now, just do it. Don't worry about hurting me."

I was going to say that I likely *couldn't* hurt him, but I didn't have the time to say that or anything else before he grabbed me. He was too tall for me to bust him in the face with the back of my head, and he would be expecting me to throw my weight against him because it was the easiest option. I shoved my elbow back, but he moved his body away and I wasn't able to touch him at all.

He said, "You spent too long thinking about it."

Without warning, I threw my weight against him and tumbled backward.

Even as I fell, his arm was still around my neck. I landed on top of him, and he released me when we hit the floor. I rolled over to frown at him. His smile did not stop my frown.

"You let me do that," I accused.

"No." He laughed. "I was just getting ready to say something else, and I didn't tell you to continue trying to take me down. I wasn't expecting it." The hand that was attached to the arm he'd had around my neck had moved to rest lightly on my hip.

My face felt very hot when I looked down at his. His eyes were very pretty when he smiled, I realized. I knew they were blue, but I'd not realized they were so bright.

"You have very pretty eyes," I told him without thinking.

He chuckled a little and said, "So do you."

I felt like I spent an entire lifetime staring down at his mouth. "Will you kiss me?" I asked, again without thinking.

He grinned. "Do you think that's a good idea?"

"No," I admitted. "Will you do it anyway?"

He leaned forward slightly, reaching for my face with the hand that was not already touching me. He pressed his lips against mine, and I realized I was smiling as I kissed him.

They were the nice kisses—sweet, and caring—and I believed I was finally figuring out how to do it at least *somewhat* properly. I didn't concern myself so much with the *how* then. Perhaps the lessons with him would be something like kissing and you simply had to do it enough times that you figured it out somewhere along the way.

He squeezed my hip for an instant before he pulled his face away from mine. Then he narrowed his eyes and said, "You should probably get off me."

"What?" I asked, then looked down and realized I was basically lying on top of him. "Oh." I jumped up as fast as I could. "I'm sorry."

He smiled a little, staring down at the floor after he'd stood. "I'm not."

I smiled a little myself when I said, "I lied. I'm not sorry either."

CHAPTER THIRTY-ONE

STAYING ALIVE

"NEXT LESSON," Chase said after he cleared his throat. "Frontward attack."

I frowned. "But shouldn't we work on the other more first?"

"Not yet. I want you to get the ideas for both in your head. We'll work on getting them down after you have the information. This one is important, given . . . yesterday." He moved over in front of me and put each of his hands on either of my shoulders. "You have a lot of options when you're attacked this way, but it's a lot scarier having to face an opponent head-on."

"Are you ever afraid?" I asked him. "I mean . . ." I tried to think of a better way to put it. "Have you ever killed a person who was as skilled as you were?"

"Yes." He pursed his lips briefly. "Fear is nothing to be ashamed of. It's good for us to have just enough of it. When you start to think you're invincible, someone comes along and shows you that you're not. Arrogance is worse than fear."

"You seem quite arrogant sometimes," I told him apologetically.

He chuckled a bit at that, though I didn't see how it was humorous. "I pretend a lot."

"Why would you feel the need to pretend with something such as that?"

"It's better to present ourselves in the way we're expected to be," he replied. "You're straying off subject again."

"Sorry."

"As I said, we're going over the absolute basics for now, nothing too difficult."

I interrupted wherever he might be going, to say, "When someone is in your face wanting to hurt or kill you, everything about it would be difficult."

"That's not what I meant. I should've said, 'nothing too complex.'" He patted my shoulders. "Okay, we're going to pretend for now that you still have use of your hands." He took one of my hands in his. "If you can get to their face, the easiest is palm to nose."

"Huh?" I asked. "That wouldn't break it, would it?"

"Maybe not, but you can kill a person like that."

"You're not serious!" I exclaimed. Surely it could not possibly be so physically simple. Despite knowing how many leaders of this city had died, I'd not ever realized the human body was so . . . fragile.

Were we all naturally weak?

He laughed a little. "I'm serious. You'll more than likely just give them a bloody nose if you don't know what you're doing. But yes, it can be done." He put my hand over his nose and said, "Don't do it now, but what you do is try to hit them here and push up really hard at once. Unless you've trained for an extremely long time, you won't ever get your hands anywhere near a Reaper's face to do it."

"Then why are you bothering to tell me about it?"

"Because there are more people than Reapers in the world and this would work on a lot of them," he said. "Next is the eyes."

Wary, I asked, "What about eyes?"

"You gouge them out," he stated, nonchalant.

I pulled my hands back to myself and said, "That's disgusting."

"Yes, but it might save your life." He shrugged. "Disgusting doesn't matter so much if it keeps you alive. As I said with the last, this one is pointless to try on a Reaper unless they're entirely distracted by something else."

"Please tell me the next," I said, frowning due to my disgust and trying to get the mental image of gouged eyeballs out of my head.

"If you can manage it, a punch to the throat works pretty well."

I told him, "I've never punched anything in my life."

He sighed and, with a frown, said, "We'll have to fix that." After a moment, he smiled a little. "Say your hands are restrained. A surefire way to give you at least a few seconds is your knee."

"My knee?"

He grinned and nodded.

"And what would I do with it?"

"What do you think?" he asked, clearly amused.

I shrugged.

He laughed. "You knee the person and hope to god that if they manage to get away, you at least took their ability to have children from them."

"Oh," I said. "You mean . . . manly parts."

He laughed loudly and said, "Yes, I mean manly parts."

Heat rushed to my face then for some reason.

We were talking about taking people's ability to have children from them, after all, and it was not anything to find myself embarrassed about.

He added, "Hurts like hell for females as well, or so I've heard."

I cleared my throat and said, "I see."

"If all else fails . . . bite them."

"Bite them?" I asked in disbelief. "Where's the honor in biting a person?"

He raised an eyebrow. "Where's the honor in killing a person?" He shook his head a little. "Honor is like disgust. It doesn't matter so much in the grand scheme of things."

"What does matter, then?"

"Staying alive," he answered as though I should've known.

"How can you say that when your occupation prevents people from doing just that?"

He blinked hard at me for a moment before turning his head away. "I'm going to make you a promise." He brought his eyes back to mine. "I promise you that I will not kill another person unless they're a threat to either one of us."

"That's not saying much," I informed him quietly.

He smiled at me and asked, "It's not?"

I shook my head slowly and the smile dropped away from his face. I realized then that it had been forced.

"Do you know how many people I've killed that were *not* a direct threat to either of us?"

Again, I shook my head, just as slowly.

"It's saying a lot."

He walked away then, and it took me several seconds to work out everything inside my head and begin to rush after him.

"I'm sorry," I said once I'd caught up. "I just meant that you're probably going to have to kill quite a bit more."

He stopped suddenly and turned around to face me. "Yes, I will. Does that bother you?"

"No," I told him quietly.

"You just made it sound like it did. You've always known what I am. Maybe you've been thinking about the wrong things all this time."

"I just . . ."

I stopped speaking for so long that he turned away again.

He had made it a few more steps when I heard myself desperately say, "I just wish you didn't have to do everything!"

He turned to me slowly then with his head tilted to the side.

"All these things you've done for me," I said. "All the bad things you've had to do in your life. I need to do something. I don't want you to stand there and show me my list of two or three options. When we leave, I don't want you to be the only one looking over our shoulders. I need to protect you."

He walked the steps that he had taken away back to me.

"Protect me?" He said it carefully, as if he'd misheard my words.

"If you have my back, then I need to have yours," I told him. Then, quieter, "You've spent almost half of your life worrying about me, haven't you? I think it should be my turn now."

He smiled and took a deep breath before reaching his hand out to my face. "Not yet." He barely said it, shaking his head.

"Then teach me so I *can*," I told him, my voice sounding desperate again.

He brought his hand back to himself and raised his eyebrow. "Is that what you want?"

"What do you think I'm doing here?" I demanded.

"Remember that you asked for it." He grinned then pointed to a wall and said, "Run around the perimeter of the room until I tell you to stop."

"What?" I asked in disbelief. I heard myself laugh once.

What did running around a room have anything to do with what I'd said to him?

He bent over and leaned down in my face. His voice was very deliberate when he repeated, "Run around the room until I tell you to stop."

I frowned, but I began walking toward the wall he'd pointed out.

"I said *run!*" he shouted.

I turned and gaped at him for just an instant before he began stomping toward me.

Then, I ran.

CHASE DID NOT TELL ME TO STOP running, but he also didn't seem to care so much about my pace so long as I was moving. Once, I stopped to ask him if I could have some water, but he began screaming at me before I could get a single word out of my mouth. I didn't have a clue what it was that he was actually saying. It took me quite a few more laps around the room before I found the courage to ask him in passing.

"Water?" I gasped. It had sounded like *waa*.

All he said in response was a very firm, "*No,*"

I had done endless amounts of walking in my time at the Valdour House, but I'd not run for long since I was a child. I was not allowed to do so here. Running was not civilized, and servants were property to be told what they could and could not do. I had thought I was in decent physical condition from carrying heavy things up and down stairs and being on my feet for days on end.

I discovered that I had been so very wrong in my self-assessment.

I wasn't entirely sure how long I ran, but I began counting how many times I passed by the door to the room.

By pass thirty-four I was beyond lightheaded and it became quite difficult to count. But it was on pass fifty-seven, I believed, that I slumped down on all fours and vomited on the floor.

"I didn't tell you to stop," Chase snapped.

"Just . . . thrown up . . . everywhere," I said through heaving breaths.

When I brought my eyes to his, he shook his head and slowly—but firmly—said, "I don't care."

I stood up and began running again. I stopped attempting to count the passes. I also did not count how many times I became ill, but I knew it was more than once.

Chase did not tell me to stop.

AT SOME POINT I realized I was not running anymore, though I could not recall him ever having told me that I was allowed to stop.

I found the top half of my body in Chase's lap, where I was coughing up water. I did not know how I'd gotten there. The muscles in my legs twitched as if they still believed they were moving.

"Drink slow," he advised.

"Were you trying to kill her?" Ahren asked from somewhere nearby. I could hear the unhappiness in his voice.

"I'm trying to get her in good enough shape that she can stay alive," Chase replied. "Ask her if she's angry with me for it."

"Aster," Ahren said, but I was still trying to find my breath and couldn't look at him. When he seemed to realize I was not going to turn to him he, in a somewhat joking tone, asked, "Are you angry with Chase for running you until you passed out?"

"I . . . passed . . . out? How long . . . did I?"

Chase said, "Nearly two hours."

I realized I was smiling up at him and that he was smiling down at me. I had run for nearly two hours straight—at a rather slow pace, sure, but I'd still done it. I hadn't known I was capable of it, but I knew that I was now. I also knew that running for nearly two hours straight unfortunately caused me to pass out.

Apparently Ahren saw my face and took it as an answer for his question because he said, "You're going to ruin her."

"No," Chase said as he brushed a bit of my hair back from my face. He was still smiling down at me. "I'm going to keep her alive."

CHAPTER THIRTY-TWO

REFLECTION

AHREN STOOD A GOOD DISTANCE AWAY with his arms crossed as Chase helped me over to a wall. I sat down on the floor, putting my back to it. Very slowly, as instructed, I drank water.

Chase was down on a knee in front of me, quite close to my face when he said, "Your body is going to be very unhappy with you."

"It already is," I informed him. I had mostly caught my breath by that point, but it still was not what it should've been. My chest burned like it was on fire.

He smiled a little, but he did not laugh at me. I was quite grateful that he didn't.

"Everything in the world has to adapt to change," he said softly. "Your body is no different. It will get mad at you and protest, but you have to fight against it and know that you're stronger."

I frowned. "How can you be stronger than your own body?"

"Because it's your head that matters most," he replied. "You keep telling yourself that you'll do whatever it takes, that you're not going to listen to anything, not even your own body until you've reached your goal. You push past the pain and fatigue, and eventually . . . you'll find yourself pushing less and less."

I nodded my head slowly in understanding.

 264

"Ahren and I had a discussion while you were running."

"About what?" I did not want to admit that I was not observant enough to have noticed Ahren in the room at the time. It did not give me very much hope for my potential.

"About the purpose of this."

"The purpose of this was to make me believe I was learning and allow you to continue to look after me."

He grinned a little when he said, "Something similar, yes." His grin transformed into an apologetic smile. "If you're truly serious about this, if you know what you want . . . I'm going to help you, and I don't care what anybody has to say about it."

"Ahren didn't want me to learn anything," I said. "Did he?"

"He didn't want you to *have* to learn."

"So he would rather I become the reason we both end up dead." I glanced past Chase to Ahren.

I found him very nearly glaring at me. He was far enough away that I doubted his ability to hear what we were saying, but I assumed he had a general idea.

"No," Chase said. "But a month . . .? It's not very much time. I'm going to have to push you extremely hard. You're going to get angry with me, but you're going to need to get it straight in your mind that you'll do what I say, no matter how unhappy you are."

"I just ran until I passed out," I told him with another frown. "I'm relatively certain that alone should tell you I'll do as you say."

"It'll be worse than that." He grinned again. "Just keep reminding yourself it will all be worth it in the end."

"I don't have to remind myself of that," I told him. "It's all I've been thinking about."

"You're going to go walk around with Ahren once you've caught your breath and make yourself some lunch in the normal kitchen," he said. "While you're gone, I'll write up a schedule for the rest of the day. You'll read it and then burn it. I'll have one made up every morning for you from now on."

I blinked hard at him, and he smiled.

"What?" He laughed. "I know you can read."

I fought against a smile. Nobody knew that I could read. Not even Agatha had discerned as much, but Chase knew.

My legs were wobbly when I started to stand. He reached out to help me, but I shook my head at him.

I could stand for myself.

I almost walked past him, but I stopped myself. "Why did you leave me the heart if you know I can read?" I asked him, thinking of the drawing I'd found. "Why not a letter?"

He smiled sweetly. "I thought it said enough."

It took me a few seconds of standing there happily before I realized I should not be wasting seconds. I walked to the door and looked at Ahren. Loudly, I asked, "Aren't you coming?"

"Aren't you changing your clothes?" Ahren asked back, at the same volume.

Rather than admit I'd forgotten all about the outfit, I retorted, "Of course I am."

He finally smiled, for what felt like the first time in ages. "I think I'll stay here while you're doing that."

I made a face at him, which he promptly returned in his own way, before exiting the room and heading back to the one that contained my normal clothing.

I was slightly unhappy to admit even to myself that the longer I wore the clothes, the fonder of them I became. They weren't rough, or heavy, or chafing. But of course I caught another glimpse of myself in the mirror and cringed.

For a moment.

No. There was nothing wrong with these clothes, I realized upon closer examination. There was nothing wrong with my body. Apart from the way it felt after running, of course.

I had felt naked in the clothes before, but looking at myself?

I did not exactly feel that way anymore. Still exposed, yes, but there was something else about it. I couldn't quite figure out what it was.

I stood there for too long attempting to discover the word for it. I should not have been wasting seconds, but I felt as though it were something important enough to spend the time on. It took me such a long time to discover that the word I couldn't initially locate inside my head was . . .

Free.

And it was not just the clothing. It was this side of the Valdour House. The other side was my cage, but this was my freedom. Even if Chase told me to do a million things I may not particularly want to do, it was all in an effort to be free—free to wear what I wanted, to kiss him if I wanted, to run, to step through doors and place my feet on soft grass.

Free to live my life and make my own choices.

As I dressed, I felt as though I were stepping back into a prison. And it was so strange, but I couldn't wait to return to this side of the House. I couldn't wait to be done walking around with Ahren and eating, so I could come back here to expand my brain and further exhaust my body.

I was smiling as I stepped out into the hallway and found Ahren standing there frowning.

"What in the world took you so long?"

I admitted, "I was looking at myself in the mirror."

He laughed. "Were you really?"

I nodded.

"What had you so perplexed about your own reflection?"

I said, "I believe it was the first time I've ever truly seen myself."

He just barely narrowed his eyes. "Did you like what you saw there?"

"More than I could've expected." I realized that my voice sounded somewhat astounded. "I'm glad I've never really looked before. I'm not sure my answer would've been the same if I had."

He wrapped his arm around me, and we walked together, past the door that returned us to my prison. Past Stanley and Stewart. Down hallways I despised with every fiber of my being. Past Guards who were oblivious to the world. Past Reapers who pretended to be something they were not.

I laughed once beneath my breath before Ahren gently elbowed me in the ribs. I was not supposed to be laughing. I was supposed to be shaken and broken, due to the events of the day before.

But I couldn't help laughing at the realization that I was now pretending to be something I was not, along with the Reapers. Somewhere along the way, I had stopped being a servant. I didn't know what I was anymore, but I did not care.

No.

I knew exactly what I was.

I was finally Aster, and absolutely nothing else.

AHREN WAS NEARLY DEAD ON HIS FEET by the time I sat down at the table in the kitchen to eat.

"Go to sleep," I told him.

When he shook his head, which I found humorous, I insisted.

"I'll be fine, I promise. Go to sleep."

He sighed and stood to leave without further objection. Shortly after, Amber came and sat down beside me. I was not even slightly surprised that she did.

"How are you feeling?" she asked.

"Fine, thank you," I said. "How is your back?"

"Agatha said it's healing well. She's been taking care of it."

I smiled. "Yes, she told me that she has." I noticed she was nearly fidgeting out of her seat, so I sighed and asked, "What is it?"

She looked over her shoulder for a moment before whispering, "Do you still love him?"

"Amber . . ." I used the tone that Agatha used while saying my own name when she was telling me to leave a matter be. I would never have expected that tone to come from me. I supposed sometimes it simply had to.

"I'm sorry," she said quickly. "It's just—"

"Can we please not do this just now?" I asked her, realizing I was completely exhausted and that I sounded as much.

She looked away guiltily and nodded her head.

"We can talk in my quarters later, if you'd like." I felt guilty for being so short with her, but I simply did not have the energy for it.

She smiled for an instant, but it faded away. "What if you're sleeping?"

"Then you're more than welcome to wake me up, even if Agatha tells you not to."

"Really?"

I nodded and she stood to leave. She didn't leave, though. She leaned down and whispered in my ear.

"I don't know what he's had you doing, but you look exhausted. It'll pass today because of what happened to you yesterday, but you're going to have to pretend through the exhaustion."

I looked up and smiled at her again; she returned it and seemed quite pleased that she'd been able to offer me some advice for a change. Still, as usual, I wanted to get away from her as quickly as possible.

I hurriedly ate the remainder of my food and fought against the urge to go running from the room. I was glad my body would not have allowed me to run right then no matter how badly I could've wanted to. It would've been quite suspicious, I thought.

CHAPTER THIRTY-THREE

DEALING WITH EXERTION

THOUGH I COULD READ, I was not good at it. It took me a long time looking over Chase's scrawling handwriting to figure out precisely what it was that I would be doing for the remainder of the day. The instructions were easy enough, though detailed. It reinforced my belief that he was very particular about things. The schedule pinpointed down to the hour.

I was glad Chase left the room while I was reading. I did not want him to see me struggling so much with something he would likely consider to be a remarkably easy task. He'd started a fire while I'd been away eating and, once I was done reading, I burned the page.

After changing my clothes, I grew worried as I went down the next hallway and opened the sixth door, finding a man standing there with Chase. Warily, I walked over to where they were standing in the middle of the space.

"Hello," I said, my voice quiet.

The man said nothing; he simply turned his face away from me as if I wasn't there at all.

"What are you doing?" Chase asked me when the man began walking away.

I only knew he was asking me and not the man because I'd been watching him go.

I whispered, "Who is that?"

"What are you doing?" he repeated, ignoring my question.

I frowned. "One hour of observation."

He smiled at me a little and finally said, "That's Chandler. He's going to be assisting with your learning experience."

"What do you mean? That he's . . ." I didn't know what else to say.

"He's going to ensure you and I don't become distracted by one another," Chase explained. "And also ensure I don't go too easy on you."

I opened my mouth and then closed it again. "What does that mean?"

Chase laughed. "It means you're not going to like Chandler very much."

I looked over at the man—Chandler—where he stood near one side of the room with his arms crossed. He was not trying to hide the fact that he was glaring at us. Even though Ahren had been unhappy where he'd stood in nearly the same spot earlier, this man was not the same. He gave off an air of . . . extreme unhappiness covered in indifference, and I realized . . . I already did not like Chandler.

I followed Chase as he walked toward Chandler, and I found myself wishing I could hide behind him. I'd met many Reapers over the past few months, but I had always considered them people since spending time with some and realizing that they were. As I peeked past Chase's arm to get a better look, I could think of Chandler as nothing more or less than a Reaper. It was quite difficult to think of him as a person.

Perhaps a wall.

Chase pointed. "Go ahead and sit down over there."

Once I was properly on the floor where indicated, he went on.

"Chandler and I are going to show you what the things you and I went over earlier actually look like, where to aim and what each move does. We're going to do it slowly, and we're not going to really hurt each other. This is just for you to have a visual so you can better understand."

Chandler had turned sideways, and Chase stood several paces behind him. Without warning Chase threw himself forward and slightly up, grasping Chandler's neck in—what I assumed was—the same way he'd held me earlier. Before I could properly get a grasp on what was happening, I heard all the air whoosh out of Chase's body as he was thrown backward.

I stood without thinking, my hand outstretched as if I could do something about what had happened. I only even knew I'd stood because Chandler stomped toward me.

Harshly, he said, "Close your mouth. Sit down. And open your eyes."

"Yes, Sir," came out of my mouth as I hurriedly plopped myself back down. I stared at the floor, my eyes wide, looking at his boots in front of me and desperately wishing they would step away.

Chandler suddenly took hold of my face, wrenching my head upward as he stared down at me. "If you can't watch him take a blow to the gut, you should go back down to your little stone walls." He barely said the words. "You harden yourself or you'll both be dead, and I'll have wasted my time for nothing. Are you hearing what I'm saying to you?"

"Yes, Sir." My voice shook.

"Don't cry," he said firmly as he released my face from his hands.

I looked down at the floor again, and still, he did not walk away. I forced myself to look at his face rather than his boots when he crouched down in front of me. My jaw clenched as I fought against the urge to keep crying.

"You keep your eyes open and your head forward or I'll have someone come in here and hold them that way." He smiled before he asked, "Would you like that?"

It took me a moment to say, "No, Sir." My voice still shook.

He leaned close to my face. "Don't call me Sir again."

I bit my bottom lip and nodded my head. Only then did he step away from me. I looked at Chase as Chandler was walking back toward him, but he distinctly looked away.

I kept my eyes open and my head forward as they showed me things. I did not move an inch, I kept my mouth firmly shut, and I tried incredibly hard not to blink. It did not become easier to see Chase knocked around, though I had to admit I was slightly pleased when the roles were reversed and it was Chandler who was on the receiving end, though I couldn't imagine what strength was or would be required to move him. Even when having seen it.

Despite having told me they would not really hurt each other, it did not seem that way to me. I watched them as they repeatedly showed me all the things Chase had explained to me earlier, and each of them looked as if they hurt quite badly. And despite having told me they would move slowly, they did not. It was difficult for me to take in their movements.

I believed I finally understood, after having seen Chandler, why Reapers acted the way they did. Not only was he imposing in his demeanor, but Chandler was the most frightening man I had ever seen before. Chase was quite tall and muscular, but Chandler was a stone wall. I fought against the urge to cringe every time one of his massive biceps wrapped around Chase's neck.

Almost as if on cue, both of them stopped. I assumed that meant my hour of observation was complete.

"What are you doing?" Chase asked as he stepped over to me. I did not know how he was walking—or even breathing for that matter—after what I'd just witnessed.

"Physical training," I answered in a very small voice.

"Get up," Chase ordered.

I stood and did not tell him that my body currently felt as though it could not do any more physical *anything*.

I watched him for a short time as he showed me movements that would supposedly strengthen my body. And then I was expected to do them. Anytime I was not doing them in a satisfactory way or as quickly as Chandler wanted them done, he would lean down in my face and shout at me.

I had never been shouted at in such a way, nor had I ever heard half the words that came out of his mouth. It repeatedly brought the prickling sensation of tears to my eyes. He laughed at me when I cried and when I became ill. Both those things happened more than once.

Time became a hazy blur where the only things I saw were my sickness on the floor and Chandler's face in front of mine. I did not see Chase at all in my blurry vision.

"Run," Chandler said after what felt like an eternity spent doing those movements.

I stood from the floor and started running slowly. Chandler yelled at me to run faster, but I could not do it when I tried. My breathing was ragged, and every time one of my boots clunked against the floor, I sniffled unwittingly.

It did not help when Chandler fell into step beside me.

"I told you to run, not to cry."

"I'm doing both," I told him through gritted teeth and gasping breaths.

"I didn't tell you to do both."

"I don't care." I forced myself to speed up in an attempt to get away from him, no matter how my body protested, hoping he would leave me be if I did.

He did not.

He ran beside me and shouted in my ear. The only things I could do were keep moving and tune him out. I did not listen when he laughed at me. I did not listen when he shouted at me.

I kept moving forward.

WHEN I CAME TO, I was not on Chase's lap again but sprawled out across the floor. My hand weakly shot to my head, which was pounding as though I'd been hit over the top of it with a heavy pan.

I saw Chase sitting down close to me, holding a glass of water. Chandler was behind him, standing there with his arms crossed.

I did not take the water. "Am I done?"

Chase said, "For today."

I nodded and pushed my body up; it was such a struggle. I had made it only a few steps when my legs gave out from under me. Chase grabbed my arm, and I did not fall.

"Let me go," I said through gritted teeth.

He frowned at me, said nothing, and kept his hand on my arm.

"I'd rather fall to the floor than have him see you keep me up. Let. Me. *Go.*"

He released me and he held his hand extended in the air, almost in precaution. I looked away from him and slowly walked forward.

"Do you think she'll come back in the morning?" I heard Chandler ask in an amused manner.

I did as I had done most of the day. I ignored him and kept moving forward.

I wanted to collapse onto the floor again when I'd closed the door behind me, but I would not do it. I leaned my weight against a wall as I walked; it was the only thing that allowed my body to go on.

I had to lie on the floor to replace my clothing in the other room and, though I wanted to, I did not remain lying there when I was done. I rolled over and pushed my body up with my hands and knees. I grabbed hold of a nearby chair to pull myself up the rest of the way.

I walked against walls until I found myself standing in front of the door that would take me to Stanley and Stewart. I knew I could not walk on any walls the remainder of the way to my quarters. Fifteen minutes. I could move for fifteen more minutes. I could do it because I had to.

I realized I was crying, leaning against the wall, when Stanley opened the door and frowned at me. He stepped over and grabbed hold of my arm, and I weakly jerked it away from him.

He pursed his lips together tightly when I said, "I can do it myself."

He took several steps back and allowed me to pass. I did not look at Stewart's hands as I walked toward where he stood. I was permitted to be on this side of the House now. But I thought of Amber's words and repeated them in my head.

Pretend through the exhaustion.

I told my legs they could stop moving soon, but not yet. I could not move as slowly as I wanted, but I could still cry. Crying would be understandable. So I allowed myself to cry rather than walk at the pace my body was begging me to.

Somehow—someway—I found myself in my quarters. I felt outside myself as my body collapsed onto my bed. My muscles twitched as I lay there, but thankfully . . . I slipped away quickly.

"ASTER," SOMEONE SAID.

I felt my body shaking, but was sure I was imagining it, that it was only my muscles complaining further.

More firmly, and more recognizably, "Aster."

I rolled over and looked up into Ahren's face.

He extended a glass in front of me. "You need to drink this."

I shook my head on my pillow and closed my eyes again.

"Aster."

I opened them and frowned at him.

"It will make you feel better. Drink it."

"Will you let me sleep if I do?" I murmured.

"After you eat as well."

"I'll become ill if I eat." I closed my eyes again.

He shook me. "You'll get sicker if you don't."

I heard him move and put the glass down somewhere. He picked me up easily, placing my rear on my pillow and my back against the wall. He held me up as Agatha scooted onto my bed in front of me with the glass in her hands.

"Drink all of it before you eat," she urged.

"What is it?" I asked.

Neither of them answered me, and Agatha put the glass in my hand. I realized I was extremely thirsty and began moving it closer to my mouth.

"Slowly," Ahren warned.

I struggled to heed his advice as I drank. It was not water, although it almost appeared as if it were, but I did not know what it was. It tasted quite bad, but it was still liquid and I did not throw it up. When I'd finished that, Agatha put a tray of food in my lap. I began eating, not knowing or caring what it was. I fell asleep at some point and was shaken awake again.

I realized Ahren was talking, though I was relatively certain he had said other things before I began catching his words.

"It will help your body deal with the exertion."

I shook my head. "What?"

"The drink," he said. "You understand that we spend our entire lives training. You're going to have to work harder. Unless, of course, you've changed your mind."

I wondered how I could possibly work any harder than I already had.

"Is that why you sent Chandler?" I demanded. "To get me to change my mind?"

"Chase insisted on Chandler," he informed me. "Have you changed your mind?"

"Leave me alone," I said weakly. "I just want to sleep."

He didn't say anything more, but at some point I felt my body moving again. I assumed Ahren did not think it would be a good idea to allow me to sleep while sitting up and had lain me back down.

I was gone before my face hit the pillow, and I was not woken again.

CHAPTER THIRTY-FOUR

BLOODY HANDS

THE NEXT SEVERAL DAYS passed by in a painful and exhausting blur.

I'd gone to the other side of the House the morning after the first day of it and found strange equipment that would supposedly assist me in getting stronger taking up some of the space inside the once-empty room. I did not know how they'd managed to get it inside or move it about the House without being discovered, but it was there nonetheless.

I cried more than I cared to admit over the several days, but it usually wouldn't happen until later in the day, when my body felt as though it were going to fail and I was required to keep going so far past that point. But I'd cried almost immediately upon my arrival that next morning. They'd made me bite off my fingernails, as far down as I could manage to get them.

"Go ahead and cut your palms up or rip them off," Chandler had said with a cold, uncaring laugh. "But don't come crying to me when that happens."

I could not quite explain my reaction as I bit them off and spat them on the floor, not so discreetly in Chandler's direction. But it almost felt as though I were stripping myself of something womanly just after discovering I was a woman.

So I'd cried silently as I chewed and spit like a disgusting man.

Then, it was time to move on.

They continued to run me until I passed out. They forced me do those movements until I became ill. And they made me punch some contraption until my knuckles were bloody and I could not feel my arms. They did not give me water and I did not ask for it, but several times throughout the day they would make me stop in the middle of doing something and drink more of the liquid Ahren had brought to me in my quarters. It did not ever make me feel better like Ahren said it would, and I never got to choose when I would drink and when I would not.

By the end of five days or so, I was beyond certain I would recognize Chandler's awful laughter in a room full of laughing people. He knew I ignored him, but he still laughed anyway, and he still shouted. I wondered how the entire House—or even all of New Bethel as a whole, a few instances—did not hear him shouting at me. It was possible the sixth room was somehow soundproof. That was the only somewhat logical explanation I could find, though it was still not anywhere near entirely logical.

I did not talk to Chase and he did not try to talk to me, at least not in a conversational sort of way. He talked to me about information, about movements and training. Sometimes I would catch a glimpse of him doing his own training on the other side of the room, but I was never allowed to pay any attention to it, or to him—not while Chandler was near. And he was always near.

Chandler was my personal ghost. He haunted my steps while I was in his presence, and he haunted my thoughts constantly. Several times I found myself jolting upright in the middle of the night, believing I was still inside the sixth room with him.

Sometimes my muscles would twitch so hard in my sleep that I would wake anyway. It almost felt like punishment for committing some unknown yet atrocious crime. My mind and body would not allow me to rest, even while I was asleep, no matter how exhausted both were.

Chase had been correct, though. I did not like Chandler at all.

The days seemed to grow longer, and despite Chase's assurances that bodies eventually adapted to change . . . mine had not yet done so. I almost thought I could feel it becoming stronger somewhere underneath, but all that covered the surface was weakness.

Every muscle I had was so exhausted I could barely function. I persisted and made them do what they were required to while I was inside that room, but as soon as I was gone from it, I could hardly force myself to stand.

It was late in the evening on the sixth day when I found myself slowly walking back to my quarters in a now-familiar daze. They'd told me it had something to do with my brain after strenuous physical activity—that haziness.

I had passed by Stanley and Stewart as I always did, on my way. I was finally able to watch their hands through my daze, regardless of not technically needing to. I figured it would be good form to try to pay as much attention as I could to as many things as I could. Watching Reapers for silent signals would be good practice, I thought.

It was in the second hallway over from where the two of them were that I bumped into someone. Being in the haze and filled with exhaustion, it had taken too long to realize anyone was there until it was too late. Hardly anyone walked so close to the private side of the House, so I was not accustomed to watching out for people despite knowing some passed on very rare occasion.

They grabbed hold of my arms and steadied me.

"I'm sorry, Sir," I said quickly, my eyes shooting upward.

When I saw Camden, I hastily took two steps back. I had not seen him at all since his interactions with Stanley and Stewart. I discovered the urge to punch him was still there inside me, despite the fact that Stewart had already done far better than. At least in my opinion.

"How are you feeling, Miss?" he asked in a startlingly convincing tone. "I've been quite concerned about you, after the incident you recently had to endure."

I laughed; I couldn't help myself. "Have you really?"

He narrowed his eyes at me. "Where's the Sir?"

"I'm not calling you Sir," I informed him.

He raised an eyebrow. "No?"

I smiled as a response—as he was not worth anything more than that—and stepped past him.

I'd made it quite a few steps before he grabbed hold of my arm and yanked me to a halt.

I jerked away from him and glared up at his face. I'd nearly forgotten that, by rule, he could punish me for my insubordination. I did not believe he would enjoy the punishment he received in turn for it, though. I knew Ahren would not stand for it. And here in this House, Ahren's word was law.

"Yes?" I asked him harshly.

His eyes were still narrowed at me, and he said nothing.

"I assume you have an important question to ask, for you to have put your hands on me in such a way."

He leaned down a bit and slowly asked, "What are you doing behind that door?"

"Cleaning." I was surprised by how convincing I sounded, but I knew by his expression that he wouldn't have believed me, even if I had been telling the truth.

"You're not."

"Ask Ahren if you don't believe me. Now, if you'll excuse me—"

I turned, and he grabbed my arm again. That time, he did not let go of it.

He leaned down close to my face, with his eyes still narrowed. And for just a moment, he did nothing more than look at me, but then he began shaking his head.

"What is it about you?" he asked quietly.

"I don't know what it is that you're asking."

"You fall in love with a Reaper and then he leaves you. Then you somehow manage to get our leader—Ahren, is it? You somehow manage to get *Ahren* wrapped around your finger. You get him to ignore his duties and make your life easier. You're not particularly exceptional looking, nor are you particularly pleasant, and yet you have our leader wrapped so tightly around your finger that he would attack a Reaper in your honor. And I've heard stories about that Reaper."

I almost laughed at his words, hearing *I find you quite beautiful, Miss* playing at the edges of my memory.

He paused and leaned so very close to my face to whisper, "*How?*"

I smiled at him and, just as quietly as he had spoken, whispered, "Do you believe this is an intelligent thing for you to be doing, then?"

"Are you threatening me?"

"You're the one who has hold of me," I stated through gritted teeth. "I highly suggest you let me go."

Still, he did not let me go.

"Do you hear yourself?" He laughed. "Do you think the lies of one person change what you are? I don't know how our leader has managed to stay alive as long as he has, but eventually, he's going to be killed. And where will that leave you? You'll go back to your hole in the ground and be required to do as you've always done. What are you going to do when there's no one left to take care of you?"

"I suggest you let me go," I repeated.

"I don't think so." He grinned, shaking his head. "You've had a person diluting your mind. I believe I should remind you of what you are."

"And what is that?"

"Property." He said it as though it were such an obvious answer. "Nothing more than an object to be used for a purpose."

It took me far too long to realize what he was saying.

I tried to jerk my arm away from him and run back in the direction of Stanley and Stewart once I had, but he pulled me close to him and then slammed my back hard against a wall. The back of my head hit on the contact, and I shook it trying to reorient myself.

He leaned down in my face again to smile and say, "It's for your own good."

He had just pressed his body against mine and put his face on my neck when I bent my face over and bit down hard on the crook of his neck. I ignored the taste of blood in my mouth as he jerked back, and I pushed hard against his chest.

I only made it one step before a hand closed around my ankle and pulled me to the floor. I landed hard on my left wrist, but I did not care. My wrist was irrelevant.

"You *bitch*," he said as he rolled me over and backhanded me across the face.

I felt my bottom lip burst open and warmth running into my mouth and down my chin. I struggled for an instant as his weight pushed down on me, and I screamed once before his hand shot over my mouth.

It was not even twenty seconds of him grasping at my body and me struggling against it in whatever ways I could before I heard a very wet-sounding *thunk*.

They had been such long seconds.

He quickly jumped up and took me with him, holding me from behind and facing the direction of some unknown thing.

I found Chase standing at the end of the hallway, almost serenely, with a small knife in his hand.

"What are you doing here?" Camden demanded.

Chase smiled a little and flipped the knife once in the air. It landed perfectly again in his hand, though he was not looking away from Camden.

Low at my ear, almost like a hiss . . . "What is he doing here?"

I felt startlingly calm for some reason, possibly from exhaustion, or possibly because I knew Chase would not allow anything more to happen to me.

I did not answer the question.

"I see what this is." Camden laughed. "It was all an act, wasn't it?"

Chase simply stood there, tossing his knife into the air and catching it perfectly in his hand.

"So," Camden went on. "Have you come to kill me, or to join me?"

I could see Chase's smile widen where he stood at the end of the hallway.

Camden's breathing became heavier and he nearly grunted. "I don't know why you're trying to intimidate me with that knife. You missed on your last throw."

Still Chase said nothing. He stood there smiling, and he tilted his head slightly. I did not only think that Chase was trying to teach him a lesson. It was almost as though he were . . . *playing with him*. I did not believe Chase had missed in his throw. It had made contact somewhere on Camden's body and had likely been precisely where Chase had intended. The expression on his face was validation of that.

In the strain of contact, I could almost feel Camden intending to move when Chase said, "I wouldn't do that."

He kept hold of me, reaching with his other hand above his opposite shoulder. I heard something dart just past my face and another *thunk* before Camden shouted and released me.

As soon as he had, I took off running toward Chase. I did not see a knife in his hand anymore.

When I got to him, he wrapped his arms around me tightly. I managed to turn, and I saw that knife through the middle of Camden's hand. Stanley was holding onto him from behind, but I did not know how he'd managed to come from that direction.

I was entirely stunned when Chase turned us around to leave, but then Camden laughed, and I stopped as Chase tried to urge me onward.

"Go on and take your worthless bitch with you," Camden said. "But you'll leave, and even if you kill me, this will happen to her eventually. You should've known before you got involved. It's no more than she deserves, being what she is."

I did not realize I was stomping back down the hallway until Chase grabbed hold of my middle from behind. It took a moment of struggling forward, mindlessly attempting to attack Camden, for me to register what I was attempting to do.

Chase turned me around to face him. I felt breath huffing out of my nose and blood running down my neck from my lip. My entire body was shaking—not out of fear, but pure rage at that disgusting man who thought I was nothing. He had wanted to remind me that I was nothing. I wanted to show him precisely what he was.

Chase had bent down and was looking into my eyes when he quietly asked, "Is that what you want?"

I didn't say anything. I only clenched my jaw in response. I wanted to hurt him, like he'd tried to hurt me. That was what I wanted, but I would not tell Chase as much.

He shook his head slowly and whispered, "Not yet."

Chase did not turn me around to leave again. He left me alone where I was standing and walked down the hallway toward the two of them. He stood there, staring at Camden, and I watched his back. Then, for no explainable reason whatsoever . . .

Stanley released his hold.

I did not see how Chase got Camden on the floor, but he was over his chest with his fist pounding into his face. The first two sounds were almost normal, but they became increasingly . . . *wetter* as time progressed forward. I heard one break in the otherwise silent space of the hall, followed by another, and then another before more arms were around me, trying to turn my body away.

"*Stop*," I demanded, not caring who was trying to prevent me from seeing what was occurring, only knowing I had to see it.

Whoever it was did not let me go, but they did not try to turn me away again and that was good enough. I noticed somewhat distantly that the hand of the arm that was not restraining me was gently tugging my clothes back into their proper place. Was it Ahren? No. The smell was not right. Perhaps today was different.

I watched as Chase calmly stood up—almost as though he had discovered it was time for another activity to begin—and turned around then came walking back toward us. I looked to the floor down the way, at Camden's form, which was not moving at all. I could not see anything of his face. It was entirely covered in blood and even from a distance . . .

It did not look right.

"Is he dead?" I heard myself whisper.

"He's not done with him yet," I heard low in my ear.

I startled when I realized it was Chandler who had hold of me.

When Chase came closer, I could see blood dripping from his fingers. Whether it was his own, or Camden's, or both, I did not know. When he was close enough for me to properly see his face, I saw no emotion there. No anger over what had happened, no shame, simply . . .

Nothing.

And I realized, as Chandler stood there with his arms wrapped around me and Chase walked toward us with only blankness on his face after nearly beating a person to death . . .

Everyone had good and evil inside them. It was only a matter of which they chose to allow other people to see.

Chase extended his non-bloody hand toward me, but I did not take it. I grabbed the other and hurriedly left the scene with him.

CHAPTER THIRTY-FIVE

A GOOD FRIEND TO HAVE

I FELT AN OVERWHELMING SENSE OF NUMBNESS where I sat, curled up on Chase's lap on the floor inside his room. I knew what had almost happened to me. I understood precisely what would've happened had I been farther away from Stanley and Stewart.

I would've expected myself to have been hysterical. I had been hysterical only a week ago after we'd pretended, and this had been so very real, even if it did not quite feel like it.

For a long time I sat there, not blinking as I stared at a wall. As I sat, I thought over reactions. I wondered now whether my reaction a week ago had been inaccurate, or if the current one was wrong. Perhaps they were both right and wrong in their own respect. Or perhaps there simply was no cut-in-stone reaction to such a situation. Perhaps I'd changed more than I realized.

I did not know the answers for any of those things.

I did not know much of anything.

Chase rubbed my back and held me close to him, but eventually I pulled away and looked at his face. He reached a hand out and touched my split lip, which made me flinch.

I barely said, "I thought you were going to kill him."

He had told me he would kill anyone who hurt me, hadn't he?

"Do you want me to?" he asked blankly.

I shook my head then said, "You're going to hurt him again."

He blinked hard at me for a moment before saying, "Unless you tell me not to."

I looked away and said nothing more on the matter. What I said was, "I have to go."

His arms came away from me and I stood, walking out of his room and not once glancing back at him. I did not head in the direction of my quarters again. I went into the room that held my training clothing and put them back on. Then I walked down the hallway, turned right, and opened the sixth door when I came to it.

I stepped over to the punching contraption and stared at it. I had spent a week destroying my body. I had gone a week with almost no human interaction, apart from shouting, and then this happened. And I had been so utterly useless when it mattered.

Only when I began punching the large bag did I begin to feel the tears finally falling from my eyes like they should've done all along.

I pictured Camden's face in front of me as the scabs over my knuckles ripped back open and began bleeding. I pictured him smiling at me in that disgusting way, and then I pictured me on top of him as he lay on the floor. I pictured me destroying his face as Chase had done.

It should've been *me* doing that. It was *my* right to teach him the lesson Chase was teaching him. *I* should be the one who went and continued to hurt him for what he'd tried to do to me. It was my right.

I was so sick of feeling weak.

At some point, strong arms began pulling me backward.

It took me a moment to realize I was screeching in absolute fury. I had no idea what was coming out of my mouth, but I recognized several words escape from it that I had never heard until they'd been shouted in my ear this past week.

"It's okay," I heard in my ear from a voice I was not expecting.

My body stiffened and I stopped struggling immediately. The arms turned me around but remained on mine once they had me in place. I hurriedly looked away and wiped the tears off my face.

Chandler leaned down close and repeated, "It's okay."

It was not okay.

None of this was okay.

Crying was not okay.

He'd mocked me enough for it already for me to know what he thought of it.

I had almost begun to walk away, but his arms wrapped around me again and pulled me close to him. I thought at first that he was restraining me and for an instant I struggled against, but then I realized . . .

He was hugging me.

That realization was the break. I'd been able to stop myself from hysterically crying over what had happened until the utter shock of Chandler hugging me took away my ability to prevent it from happening. I knew I was sobbing uncontrollably against his massive chest and that I was speaking, although I still did not know what I was saying.

"Would it make you feel better to hit me?"

"What?" I asked, taking one step back.

"Would it make you feel better?" he repeated, his voice impassive.

I opened my mouth, wanting to tell him that no, it would not. But although he'd unbelievably been comforting me, I could not forget all the shouting. So I would not lie and tell him it wouldn't make me feel better because I believed it possibly may, even if only a minuscule amount.

He almost smiled when he took a step back and patted his cheek. Almost.

"Are you going to hurt me?" I asked quietly, my breathing coming in and out in ragged bursts that distorted my simple question as it escaped from my mouth.

"I won't hurt you," he said believably then patted his cheek again. He even bent over to give me a better angle, because he was so tall.

I waited, expecting a catch. Chandler would not just allow me to punch him in the face. He would not let me—

"All the stars, I'm so sorry!" I had punched him in the face.

"That wasn't too bad," he said, almost sounding appreciative. Some of the blood from my knuckles had smeared across his cheek. "Was that exactly where you were aiming?"

"I don't really know where I was aiming," I said quickly. "I didn't even realize I was doing it until—" I had punched him in the face. "I'm so sorry."

He laughed a little. "Don't be sorry. I've dealt with much worse."

Chandler could laugh without harshness? Then he sighed and looked down at me. "Now. Why didn't you do anything we've been showing you?"

I felt my jaw quivering. "My body just feels so weak. I can barely make it back to my quarters in the evenings. How am I supposed to fend off a man?" Very quietly I added, "I *did* bite him."

Chandler laughed. "*Did* you?"

I nodded.

"Tomorrow, you'll start practicing on me."

"What's the point?" A humorless laugh nearly escaped from me. "That's two times I've been in a situation like that, and I'm utterly useless."

He grabbed hold of my shoulders and leaned down near to my face again to say, "You're not. Your body is worn down and it's wearing on your mind. Add what happened tonight on top of that and it's a horrible combination. You just have to fight harder."

"I can't fight harder!" I nearly screamed at him. "I've done everything you've told me to! What else can I *do*?"

I expected him to be angry about me screaming up at his face, but all he did was sigh again and say, calmly, "Don't you realize what you've just said? You've done everything I've told you to."

"What does that have to do with anything?" I demanded.

He barely said, "Did you ever truly think you could?"

I opened my mouth, and he stuck his hand under my chin to close it. I realized I was staring into his eyes and slowly shaking my head.

He smiled warmly at me, which was so far past shocking. "Keep doing what I tell you to, and I promise things will get better."

He left me standing there in a stunned daze, attempting to discover why he was acting as though he cared for me, but he stopped after taking only a few steps.

"I'll be harder on you tomorrow."

He was grinning when I brought my eyes back to his face.

I nodded my head, and he began walking again.

It was while I was watching the back of his dark hair walking away and picturing his blue eyes in front of my face when I made the connection.

"All the stars," I heard myself say under my breath.

Chandler was Chase's older brother.

They hardly looked alike. Chandler was a good deal older and was built completely differently, but there was something about the eyes.

I did not think about the implications as to what that meant for Ahren and his plans here. I thought about the real implications for the things Chandler had been doing to me for the past week instead. Truly, he was not trying to destroy my body. He was trying to make me strong enough to survive for his brother.

I stared back at the punching contraption for a moment and then turned away from it. I would not waste my energy in the night. I would go rest and come in tomorrow with a stronger mind. Now I did not only need to prove to myself that I could become strong enough. . . . I needed to show Chandler. I did not want him to be convinced within the month that I could survive. I wanted him to be convinced that I could ensure his brother survive as well.

I would fight harder. I could fight harder. And then I realized . . .

"Chandler, wait," I said loudly.

He was all the way at the door by that point, but he turned to look at me and did not seem frustrated by me keeping him from going.

"I pushed him down. Camden. I pushed him when I bit him."

He tilted his head. "Did he hit the ground?"

I nodded quickly, knowing that could've been the only explanation for Camden grabbing my ankle as I was trying to get away. He'd been on the floor.

He smiled, almost proudly—which made my heart feel for an instant as though it were soaring through the sky—and said, "Good girl."

Then he was gone, taking that bit of pride with him, and I was alone again, with those two words hanging in the air.

ONCE I WAS PROPERLY CHANGED into my normal clothing, I found myself stopped in front of Chase's room. I blinked at his door for a moment then walked past it. I made it all the way to the door that would take me back to Stanley and Stewart and, again, I stopped.

I was unsure as to how much time I spent standing there, but eventually Stanley came through the door and stared at me.

"Are you all right?" he asked quietly.

I could not quite explain it, but I found myself throwing my body toward him and grasping my arms around his back.

"Thank you," I whispered, feeling a new wave of tears spilling from my eyes.

He cleared his throat. "For what?"

"For receiving my message and listening to it."

"Your scream?"

I nodded.

Again, he cleared his throat, then said, "We'd already heard the two of you struggling before that."

"I'm very glad that, if it had to happen, it was near enough to the two of you," I told him. "I fear that if I'd been somewhere else, events would not have played out in the way they did."

Only then did his hand come up and pat me awkwardly on the back. "Would you like an escort back to your quarters? I don't ask it to insult you, only to be cautious. It's why you were standing at the door, wasn't it? Because you're afraid to go the entire way there alone?"

I nodded shortly and whispered, "I don't want to be afraid anymore."

He stepped back enough to smile down at me. "Fear is a good friend to have. It can keep you sensible enough to stay alive. Be glad that you feel it. The day you wake up and don't find it there any longer, you will discover yourself living the first day in the ending of your life."

I blinked hard and said nothing, finding no words inside my head that would form a satisfactory response to such a statement.

He reached his hand out and wiped a tear away from my face. "Always look around yourself and find something important. You find something important enough to hold onto and you'll always have something to fear. Losing that thing is the worst fate imaginable, and the fear of it gives you something to fight for." He smiled again. "I pray you always have reason to be afraid in your life."

I reached out and took hold of the hand he'd touched my face with, squeezing it tightly. I barely said, "And I pray you find something in life to bring yours back."

He straightened himself up and looked away from me. "Would you like an escort?" It clearly told me our current line of speaking was unquestionably done.

"No thank you," I said. "I understand what you mean about fear, but too much of it cannot be a good thing. If there's too much, it can keep a person from being afraid of the proper things. I believe I'm going to conquer one of mine now, to assist me with getting things into their proper order."

CHAPTER
THIRTY-SIX

CONQUERING FEARS

FOUND MYSELF standing outside the door to Chase's room again, staring at it. Only this time, I did not move away. I turned the doorknob.

He was standing there, directly on the other side of the door, staring at me in a very confused sort of way. I was certain he'd been standing there expecting me to pass by again and was stunned that I'd not done so. I ignored the sight of him lacking a shirt and found myself somehow able to manage as much.

Quiet, I asked, "Can I stay with you?"

He didn't say anything, but he stepped aside, which I took to be answer enough. Very slowly, I walked into his room and he closed the door behind me.

I did not know what I was expecting, but he took my hand and led me over to a chair. Him doing so made me realize that, whatever I'd been expecting . . . a chair certainly was not it. Still, I sat down on it, and he walked away.

When he returned, he had a wet cloth in his hands. "I'm going to clean that blood off you."

"What bl—" I started to ask and then remembered that I'd had my lip split open. I nodded my head.

He bent down in front of me and reached out.

His face flinched a little when I cringed at the pain of it. It was almost funny that it did not hurt enough for me to be aware of it until it was being poked at.

I heard Agatha's voice inside my head from a time that felt so long ago. *Sharks in the water, Reapers.*

Chase did not look like a shark circling some bloody thing in the water. I'd read in a book that they did as much and had told Agatha about it when I was younger. I had not known what a shark was until I'd read about them, and she had not known until I'd told her. I believed Agatha secretly liked my excursions to the library, though she would never admit as much and I would never ask her.

I also believed that Agatha simply assumed I had an overactive imagination, fabricating words and information.

When Chase had moved away from my mouth and was wiping at the dried blood under my chin, I felt the need to clarify my intentions.

"Only to sleep."

He smiled in an amused yet warm way and said, "Okay." Then, slowly, the smile faded. "Are you staying because you're afraid to walk back?"

"Stanley offered to escort me back," I told him. "I'm staying because I'm afraid to stay."

He stopped what he was doing for an instant and his brow furrowed. It took a moment, but he began cleaning again. "How does that work?"

"Because I believe I've been afraid of the wrong things," I said. "Or perhaps not necessarily of the wrong things, but of too many things. It won't hurt me to stay."

He chuckled. "I'll be happy to help you conquer your fears, then."

"And now there won't be any reason not to progress with them."

He brought his eyes to mine for just a second.

"Because now we won't have anything setting them back, like before you pretended to leave. There's no reason not to move forward now." I paused. "That's correct, isn't it?"

"Yes, it is." He smiled. "Are there any other fears you want me to help you with?"

"May I have something to sleep in?" I asked him.

He raised an eyebrow at me but nodded. "You know there's

clothing in all of the drawers in the rooms." A few seconds passed. "I'm done with this. Do you want me to find you something?"

I looked away. "Yes, please."

As soon as he'd stood, I looked at him again, watching the muscles in his back as he walked. The scars from his beating stood out in stark contrast from the rest of him and I found myself suddenly staring at the floor between us instead.

He did not open more than one drawer. I should not have been surprised that he'd gone through everything inside the room he was staying in.

"Here you go." He was holding some sort of fabric in his hands.

I was pleasantly surprised that there appeared to be much more of it than what I'd expected.

I walked over and forced a smile at him as I took the fabric from him.

I began to walk one way—toward the door—and he began to walk another. Then, I stopped and took in a deep breath, steeling myself.

I was halfway through removing my shirt when he quickly asked, "What are you doing?"

I finished the process—covering the front of me with the fabric—and listened, no longer hearing his footsteps moving in either direction.

Quiet, I admitted, "I'm afraid for you to look at my back."

"What?"

I realized then that he still had his back turned toward me. He sounded very far away, though I knew he was not.

"You asked if there was another fear you could help me with," I stated. "I'm not ashamed of my life, but I'm afraid of your potential reaction to it."

"You want me to look at you?" He almost sounded as though he were extremely confused. It was not such a confusing thing in my mind.

"At my back," I clarified.

"I will if you tell me why first."

I wiped at my stupid eyes that never seemed to stop spilling liquid from them. "I realized something earlier. That people only see what we allow them to. You allowed me to see several sides of you tonight that you didn't want to show me."

"And what sides are those?" Impassiveness had taken over his voice.

I took a deep breath and turned around, walking until I was directly behind him. "That loving me doesn't change who you are. You didn't miss throwing that knife. You were playing with him. But you showed me you're willing to walk away from something you don't want to walk away from, if you believe it's in my best interest. You showed me you're willing to do something horrible and allow me to see it just because I want it done."

"So what side are you showing me?"

I put my back to him again. "That I can move forward, even when I'm afraid to."

I heard him turn around then.

I glanced over my shoulder in just enough time to catch the reaction on his face—his eyes widening and then narrowing as he clenched his jaw. Then I put my face forward and I stood there.

It felt like an entire lifetime before his hand reached out and ran gently from the top of my back to the bottom. I closed my eyes.

I did not know what I'd expected for his reaction to be and why I feared it so greatly. I worried he would be angry. I worried he would be disgusted. But when I peeked back over my shoulder again and saw wetness in his eyes, I discovered he was sad. Only sad and . . .

"You feel guilty."

He brought his gaze to mine.

"Don't you?"

"If I'd come for you sooner . . ." He shook his head. "So many things would be different than they are."

"But you came," I pointed out as I turned around, making sure I had the shirt firmly covering me. "And you're here now. I don't care about things being different than what they are. They're not and there's no point to it."

"Aster, I ne—"

"I don't care," I told him firmly.

He pursed his lips together.

I smiled. "Nothing in the past matters."

He looked away. "We should go to sleep."

I nodded and he began walking away, but he stopped and faced me again.

He said, "Please be properly clothed when I turn back around."

I felt my smile widen. "If that's what you want."

He opened his mouth for a moment as if he were thinking of something to say, then he closed it and frowned.

I watched his eyes as they began to go down my body, but they shot back to mine when I asked, "Is that what you want?"

"Are you . . ." he started and then stopped. Quickly, he asked, "Are you teasing me?"

"I don't know," I admitted with a small laugh. "Is it working?"

"Please stop talking or I'm going to come over there and put those clothes on for you."

"Would you like to do that?"

At that, he covered his ears and began walking away. I realized I was standing there laughing at him when he put his face on the wall opposite me. I stared at his back for a moment, and I shook my head.

I had no explanation for why the words had come out of my mouth, or his reaction to them. Still, I found it quite funny, despite how inexplicable it was to me. I put the nightclothes on and folded my others into a neat pile, placing them on top of a nearby desk.

Very slowly, I walked over to him, reaching a hand out toward his back. I was not expecting for him to jump when my fingers touched his skin. He jumped, and then I jumped, and then we both laughed.

We just laughed.

It faded, though.

Once it had, I asked, "Are you angry with me?"

"Oh yes, because you were being so hurtful."

"Was I?" I asked. "I didn't mean to be."

"I was just joking." He shook his head. "Like you were joking a few minutes ago."

I smiled. "I wasn't joking."

He frowned. "I'm beginning to think this is a very bad idea."

"Why?" I asked. "You don't want me to stay?"

He narrowed his eyes. "To sleep."

"You don't want me to stay if we're going to sleep?" I asked. "What else would we do?"

"You know what?" Words seemed to spill out of his mouth. "I'm not listening to anything else you say tonight."

I felt my mouth drop open, not understanding what I'd done to make him say such a thing.

He moved away and got into bed, ignoring my reaction.

The blankets had already been pulled down, likely because he'd been lying there before I'd intruded.

I watched him there, looking at me, with the blanket covering the bottom half of him.

I wasn't entirely sure how long I was standing there before he asked, "Have you changed your mind?"

When I looked at his face, he was smiling again.

I had accidentally fallen asleep with him a week before, but I'd not planned on doing so, and he had been entirely clothed at the time. Having the intention of sleeping made for quite a different feeling inside me.

He said, "I can have Chandler escort you back to your quarters."

I shook my head quickly.

"Are you going to sleep standing up like a horse?"

I frowned at him which made his smile widen. I took a step forward, halted, and then took two steps back.

He jumped out of bed and started to walk past me, saying, "I'll go get Chandler."

My hand shot out, and I grabbed hold of his arm.

He stopped and then came to stand in front of me. Very quietly he asked, "Why are you so afraid of staying with me? Are you afraid I'll hurt you?"

"I'm afraid . . ." My face scrunched.

He frowned and nodded his head in what appeared to be understanding.

When he started to walk away again, I heard myself blurt out, "I'm afraid I won't want to sleep."

He turned, tilting his head at me. His eyes were narrowed again when he slowly asked, "Really?"

I nodded.

He took a deep breath, looking away. "We're going to sleep. Do you believe me?"

"That's not what I said," I told him quietly.

He laughed a little. "I'm sorry, but I can't help you overcome things you're afraid of wanting or not wanting. But I can promise you we'll sleep. Is that enough for now?"

"I . . ." I thought hard on it. "Yes."

He stepped close to me and leaned down, reaching a hand out for my face. "Do you want to know when I fell in love with you?"

"Haven't you always been?"

He shook his head. "I wanted to protect you. For a long time that was all it was. I couldn't explain it; I just knew I had to do it. Do you know when it turned into something else for me?"

I shook my head.

He smiled. "The first time you stepped past me into my room and didn't cringe. I realized then that you weren't afraid of me anymore, even though you knew what I was. Do you remember what day that was—when you stopped being afraid?"

With so much apology, I told him, "I don't."

"The first day I smudged the window." His nose crinkled slightly.

I could not prevent the smile from forming on my face; it felt as though I had absolutely no control over it whatsoever.

Him smiling back at me in that infectious way he had did not help. "Do you trust me?"

"I've already told you I do," I replied.

Without warning, his leg moved forward and knocked mine out from under me. He grabbed hold of me at the same time. I heard sounds escaping from my mouth, but my brain was stunned to the point where I couldn't distinguish them. He got onto the bed and, when he got there, dropped me four or so inches down onto it.

It was when my back hit the mattress that I realized I was not screaming, as I'd expected myself to be. I was . . .

Laughing.

He plopped himself down ungracefully onto his side next to me. When I looked over at him, I was laughing so hard I was crying, but he was just lying there smiling.

I rolled over and pushed at him. Though my hysterics, I asked, "Did I pass your test?"

His smile widened, he nodded, then he laughed and said, "Look, you're on the bed and nothing is happening."

"And now you've reminded me of it!" I pushed at him again, but rather than pulling my hand back to me, I kept it on his chest.

I only realized my face was moving closer to him when he turned his into his pillow and said, "We're sleeping."

"But we haven't kissed in such a long time. I'll have forgotten how to do it."

I heard him laugh before he removed his face from the pillow, but when he looked at me, he was frowning.

I was nearly positive he was only pretending to be unhappy with me when he said, "If you want me to keep my promise, you shouldn't make it more difficult than it already is to keep."

"Is it difficult?"

He grinned and, again, covered his ears with his hands. Unfortunately, that gave me too good a view of him shirtless. I supposed I was not being as discreet as I likely should've been because he grabbed the blankets and brought them firmly up to his chin. He laughed quite loudly when I frowned at him, but I was not pretending to be unhappy as he'd done before.

I realized I was still scowling when I rolled over and put my back to him. Only a few seconds passed before he scooted closer and covered me up with the blankets. His hand slowly came to rest on my hip, but he only left it there for a moment. I closed my eyes as it went from my hip to my abdomen, and I kept them closed when he scooted his body up behind mine.

I knew I was breathing too heavily, but I also knew there was nothing to be afraid of. It was all right—what we were doing. He gently pulled on my shoulder with the hand that had been on my abdomen, and I felt as rigid as a board when I flopped over onto my back.

His body ran along the length of mine, and he had his head propped up with one of his hands. He used the other to push some of my hair back.

Quiet, he said, "I think you're confused."

"What?"

"I think you're confused over what happened to you earlier," he clarified. "It's understandable."

"I don't know what you mean," I told him.

"You're not entirely acting like yourself," he said, almost apologetically.

"I'm not sure I know who I am to act a certain way anymore," I whispered, my voice distant.

"I know who you are." He sighed. "You remember when you came to my room and I told you that after you'd thought about it, you could stay when all of you wanted to?"

I nodded.

"You made a conscious decision tonight about staying and the reasons you had for doing so. When you're not afraid of wanting to not sleep, we won't sleep. But that will only happen after you've thought about it and made the decision. Okay?"

I barely said, "Okay."

He leaned down and kissed me softly, which did not help with what he was saying, but it was only for an instant and only on my top lip. Then he kissed my forehead and said, "I love you. Now go to sleep."

I smiled and rolled over, feeling his body coming behind mine again. Then, his hand did not linger anywhere; it wrapped around the front of me and he held tightly onto my shoulder from the front.

I closed my eyes and said, "I love you too."

I felt him kiss the back of my head before he settled in and, even though he was settled, it did not feel like he was. The tension in his body said he would be awake at a moment's notice, if need be, that he would take care of me.

What a miserable existence.

I put my hand over the one that was resting on my shoulder, hoping it would alleviate some of his tension, but it did not. I did hear him breathe in and out once in a way that sounded content.

It was all I was going to get from him. And it was enough.

It had to be enough.

CHAPTER THIRTY-SEVEN

BABY BROTHER

I WOKE TO SHOUTING near the general vicinity of my head.

At first, I was certain it was another of those unpleasant dreams where I found myself inside the sixth room with Chandler. Then I realized I was no longer lying down and was actually, in fact, standing up and moving. Clearly, I was not dreaming. My head was fuzzy as I tried to take in what he was saying to me.

Something about *one second* and *change your clothes*.

Had I slept at all? I wasn't entirely certain that I had.

I was reaching out for my clothing that was resting on the desk when Chandler got in my face.

"Not *those* clothes," he said in an angry way that I knew was not forced. "Do you know how many times another Reaper could've killed you in the time it took me to drag your ass out of bed?"

"Once," I replied groggily.

"Shut up and put your clothes on," he said, but I thought he had almost laughed.

I was so out of sorts that I didn't even realize what I was doing until he shouted again.

"Not in here!"

I looked around myself for an instant—realizing distantly that I'd nearly begun changing my clothing in front of Chandler—before I stepped out into the hallway.

Where was I? This was not the hallway outside my quarters.

I felt arms moving me in some direction before a door opened and I was gently shoved inside the room. The door closed behind me, and I was alone. My training clothes were piled neatly where I'd left them the night before. It hadn't taken very long to get where I was. It always took a long time.

It was only while I was in the process of changing and doing what little I could to get ready that I remembered I'd stayed with Chase despite him not having been in the room when I woke. I was only slightly more awake because of that when I made my way through the sixth door. And I was only slightly surprised when Chandler got back in my face.

"Why are you smiling?"

I sucked in my top lip. I hadn't realized I had been.

His voice was quieter, but was still taunting when he asked, "Are you smiling because you slept with my brother last night?"

"*Chandler!*" Chase shouted from somewhere relatively close by.

"She already knows," he said dismissively to Chase. Then, he looked back at me. "You figured it out last night while we were talking, didn't you?"

"The answer to both is yes," I told him.

"Then you finally know why I'm doing this." Chandler nodded his head, pointed toward a wall, and said, "*Run.*"

I was already moving before he'd told me to because I already knew what he wanted. I did not stop when I heard Chandler's yelling, but I nearly did when I realized it was not directed at me for once.

I glanced over my shoulder and saw him still pointing at the wall. I almost snorted when Chase began running the perimeter as well, but I kept silent, not wanting Chandler to focus his attention back on me.

My effort to remain silent was wasted. Chandler was entirely focused on Chase and I doubted any snorting on my part would've changed that fact. When they lapped me, I overheard only a small snippet of his shouting in Chase's ear.

"Can you keep her alive, baby brother?" He laughed. "I'm not so sure you can. You couldn't even keep that scum's hands off her last night. Doesn't look well for your odds, does it?"

I only heard that much because I did what I did best—tuned Chandler out. I did not want to hear him yelling at Chase. I wanted to hear that even less than I wanted to hear him yelling at me.

And then I realized . . . I did not want his attention away from me and on someone else, especially not Chase. I would not have to listen to it if I could redirect it. I increased my speed to catch back up with them.

It took some time, given their pace and the fact that they were half the perimeter of the room ahead of me when I was struck by realization, but I eventually caught them.

"Oh, you want to keep up with him, do you?" Chandler laughed as he fell into step beside me. Almost quietly he said, "Don't let me see you fall behind."

I glanced over at him out of the corner of my eye and saw that he was looking at the back of Chase's head.

"Increase your speed, baby brother."

Chase took off, and I felt my jaw drop. I had never seen anyone move so quickly in all my life.

"Close—" was all Chandler got out of his mouth before I closed mine like I knew he wanted and took off after Chase.

I was not anywhere near as fast as he was, but I tried as best I could.

As soon as I felt my speed decreasing drastically, I heard Chandler's voice in my ear.

"Push through it."

It took me a moment to realize that he was not shouting at me.

He was encouraging me.

I did as he said and pushed through it until a cramp in my leg sent me flying through the air. I was jerked backward and up by Chandler before I came close to hitting the floor.

He released me immediately and said, "Run at your normal pace for a minute."

My chest already burned like it was on fire, but I did as he said just as I always did. He left me to my own means and went to shout in Chase's ear again, but only—literally—for what I believed was one minute. Then he headed back to me.

"Speed up."

He stayed by me as I ran fast, and he went to Chase when I ran slowly.

On and on it went that way. Fast and then slow, fast and then slow. He did not allow Chase to run slow at all and, every time they lapped me while I was not running fast, I heard bits and pieces of an extended, one-sided conversation.

What would you have done if you'd been two minutes later? What are you going to do when they catch you? You know they're going to catch you, baby brother. You know they will. What are you going to do when he finds out? You know he won't listen. He won't care. You're trying to save her from this life, but at least one of you is going to end up dead for this. And it's going to be your fault.

Chase did not stop running until after he'd punched Chandler in the face. I'd not been near enough to hear what sentence had caused it, but perhaps it was the combined weight of them all. I was sure that Chandler would've seen it coming, but he still ended up on the floor anyhow, clutching his hand to his cheek.

Chase stood over him with his hands clenched into fists at his sides, but he didn't move a muscle apart from breathing, and even that was not as much movement as it likely should've been after all the exertion.

Even after having been genuinely physically attacked . . .

Chandler was in no way brought to anger, in no way hostile. He was in no way *up in the air*, and I wondered . . .

Had it all been forced with me at first?

Was *that* him?

He *was* a wall.

Chandler just sat there, shaking his head at his brother. "You didn't even break anything." His voice went quiet. "How do you think you're going to do this? What are you going to do when she's standing there and it's him instead of me?"

I barely caught a glimpse of Chase's face when he turned to me, and he only looked at me for an instant. He had tears falling down his face. Then he stormed from the room. I stared after him for a moment, contemplating following after and telling him that everything was going to be all right. It seemed as if he needed a bit of hope.

I jogged over to Chandler instead. He was looking at the wall across from the door and he also had tears on his face.

"Do you want to hit me too?" He didn't look at me.

I extended my hand in front of his face. "I want you to scream at me."

When his eyes met mine, I could see that, while Chase may not have broken Chandler's face, he had done some damage. I suspected it would leave quite the mark for some time—for a few hours, at the very least.

When he made no effort to move, I loudly said, "Get up and scream at me so I can keep your brother alive."

He blinked hard for a moment, took my hand, and pulled himself up from the floor by it. There was a second of his weight feeling like it would pull me the other way, but it all got righted and he was up.

He felt the equivalent weight of a wall.

We carried on.

Chase was gone for quite a while, but not for nearly as long as I suspected he would've been. I tried as best as I could to keep him out of my head while he was away, but I'd worried about him. When he entered the room and fell into step beside Chandler and myself, neither brother apologized to the other.

I suspected neither of them were sorry. I did not believe that either of their actions or words warranted an apology. But later, while I was doing my movements, I saw the two of them hugging one another tightly.

Hugs were better than apologies, I thought, as actions spoke so much louder than words.

TRUE TO HIS WORD, Chandler insisted I begin attempting to fend him off. He assured me that I would not hurt him, but it was all I could think about. Ahren came into the room at some point near midday. I wanted the three of them to have faith in me, but I was so unbelievably bad at it.

And I cried. Not the silent tears I'd become accustomed to while inside the sixth room, but loud, frustrated sounds because my body and mind would not allow me to do what needed to be done.

Chandler shouted at Ahren instead of me and made him leave because he was *making things worse*.

Ahren did not go far. He was waiting for me just past the door when I went through it after an utterly wasted hour of my life. I walked with him to the main kitchen and we did not speak to one another at all, though we walked arm in arm. The entire time we were eating at that wooden table in the kitchen, he frowned at me from across it. I did not need to look at him directly to know he was doing it. I stared down at my plate of food in something I realized was shame.

Had I ever felt such shame before?

I did not believe I had, not on the same level.

Amber didn't bother me, though in my peripherals I saw Ahren shake his head minutely once at something behind me. I assumed she wanted to ask me whether or not I was all right after what happened to me the night before and Ahren assumed that I did not want to be bothered. If that were the case, he was correct in his assessment.

While Ahren and I were walking back to the other side of the House, I asked, "Does everyone know what happened with Camden?"

"Not everyone, no," he answered. "Hardly anyone does, actually. Agatha said you never came back last night. Would you like for me to send her to you? She's been quite worried about you."

"No, I'll be going back this evening and I'll see her then," I said to the floor. I did not need nor want Agatha to watch me inside that room. I was unsure which would be worse—for her to see me failing in such a way or for her to see me succeeding with it.

"I had a discussion with Chandler last night," Ahren began, which made me look up at him. "Since I am technically leader here, his new . . . *occupation* will be your protection. He'll be following you everywhere."

"He already does," I said with a short laugh.

"No, I mean, unless you're with him or myself, Chandler will be with you at all times," he clarified. I took *him* to mean *Chase*, given that it was not entirely safe to say his name aloud in the halls. "Agatha's already agreed that he could stay on the floor in your quarters."

I stopped moving. "What about my agreement on the matter?"

Ahren frowned. "Do you object to it?"

I opened my mouth, but nothing came out.

Before I could say anything even had I known what to, he added, "Last night only proves you need someone watching your back constantly."

My mouth remained open, and I heard a small laugh escape from it. I nodded my head in understanding and quickly proceeded forward.

Ahren tugged on my arm. "I didn't mean that the way you took it."

"How did you mean it then, Ahren?" I demanded. "Because I'm quite certain you meant it precisely how it sounded and that I took it in the appropriate way."

He allowed me to walk away then, but I knew he was still following behind me, despite the fact that I could not hear him. It was only when I found myself past the door Stanley and Stewart guarded that I rounded on him.

"Do you have something else to say? Would you enjoy further pressing how utterly worthless I am? Don't think it's not going through my mind constantly in that room." I shook my head. "Chandler's right. You're only making things worse. I want you to stay away from me while I'm in there. I don't need you watching over my shoulder and making a list of my failings."

I'd started walking away again when he ran up behind me.

"Aster," he said quietly.

I stopped and nearly shouted, "*What*?"

He looked at a wall and said, "The next time you're doing combative training . . ." He took a deep breath and brought his eyes to mine for an instant before looking at the floor. "Don't imagine Chandler. Imagine Camden instead."

"Is that what you do when you're training—imagine it's someone else?"

He nodded.

"Who?" Perhaps, if he told me something of that nature, I would be inclined to get past my current unhappiness with him.

"I used to imagine someone different than I do now," he said to the floor. He looked up at me and forced a smile. He opened his mouth as though he were going to perhaps say who it was, but then the smile quickly dropped away from his face. All he said before he walked away was, "You're not worthless."

I was very confused when I went through the sixth door, as I could not understand why he wouldn't answer such a simple question for me. Did he truly trust me so little with his confidences?

Apparently so, though I'd never imagined it was as small an amount of trust as it so clearly was.

I was even more confused when I found Chase and Chandler standing around. Chase had a small bit of fabric in one of his hands. It was odd, but mostly it took my mind off my unhappiness with Ahren.

"You didn't make me a schedule today," I said. "What is it that I'm doing now?"

Chase, too, forced a smile at me before he answered with, "Sensory training."

"What does that mean?"

SENSORY TRAINING WAS . . . INTERESTING. It involved me standing in the middle of the room with that fabric from Chase's hands covering my eyes. Either Chase or Chandler—I did not know which—circled around me and, if I heard any sort of movement at all, I was required to point in the direction I'd heard it.

If I was correct, I heard nothing. If I was incorrect, even by a hair, I received a noise in response from the one of them who was not trying to sneak. Sometimes it was a whistle, and sometimes it was a tongue click. I heard a great deal of intentional noise.

It was when I felt a hand on my back—after hearing absolutely no unintentional noise whatsoever behind me—that I shrieked a little and jumped into the air, pulling the fabric away from my face. Again, the stupid tears of shame welled in my eyes as I looked into Chase's face once my feet were firmly replaced on the floor.

"I can't even do *this*," I said desperately to him.

"All you're doing is thinking about how bad you are at everything," he said. "Stop thinking and listen. That's all you have to do." He didn't give me a chance to respond. He leaned forward and pulled the fabric back over my eyes.

I sat down on the floor and, for an instant, waited to be shouted at by Chandler for sitting when he'd not told me to sit.

He did not shout at me.

I rested my elbows on the sides of my knees, put my face in my hands, and listened.

The room was utterly silent. I could not hear any sounds from the House. I could not hear any breathing from anyone, apart from myself. I'd never realized how unbelievably silent this House was. Quiet, yes. Not silent.

No. It was not silent even here. My stupid breathing took up the entire space of my ears.

I breathed in deeply, held the air in my lungs, and waited. Then I kept waiting, released the breath, and held another. I kept waiting. For a very long time.

And there it was. A nearly silent placing of a boot directly to my left.

Rather than point, I lunged. I expected to hit air and then floor, but the side of my face made contact with a leg. At least I assumed it was a leg. Maybe a wall had been moved to the middle of the room.

I heard a body hit the floor and pulled the fabric away again.

Chandler was laughing quite boisterously where he was sprawled out next to me, and Chase was chuckling from the other side of the room. So they had been taking turns being the sound and the watcher.

Chandler said, "I didn't tell you to attack."

"You didn't tell me not to," I pointed out.

He leaned forward. "For now, listen." He replaced the fabric. "Don't attack."

I nodded and returned to the same position I'd been in before. I sat there holding my breath for as long as I could, releasing it, and then holding it again. I was tempted to count the seconds as I did, but I resisted the urge knowing that counting would distract me from doing what I was supposed to.

I did not think—not about anything—and I listened. I did not allow myself to become frustrated when I heard a whistle or a click. But I discovered it was Chase who whistled and Chandler who clicked. And, as the hour passed with my rear on the floor, the intentional sounds came less and less often.

AFTER SENSORY TRAINING, I did more movements. I punched the contraption. I used the other contraptions in the room. And I ran—fast and then slow, over and over. I drank the unpleasant, clear drink.

And, at the end of the evening, Chandler said, "You did well today."

I forced a smile at his lie. Lie or not, it was nice of him and him being nice was a nice change. So long as I knew that it was not a truth, I would not become complacent from hearing it.

I stopped by Chase's room before heading back to my quarters.

He analyzed my face only for a second or two before saying, "You're not staying."

I shook my head and, though his tone had sounded sad, he was smiling when I looked directly at him.

I gave him a short kiss and said, "I love you."

"I love you too."

Although Chandler came up behind me at some point during the exchange—I knew it was him without looking, as his presence had a certain feel to it—Chase still watched me go. I checked several times over my shoulder.

I eventually glanced up at Chandler as we walked, and i nearly jumped out of my skin. I'd expected for him to be wearing the typical Guard attire, but he was not. His clothing was entirely black and he was strapped to the teeth with knives, like Chase had been when I'd first seen him and never since.

He smiled as we walked together. "They all know what I am here. There's no point in pretending. I'm your new visible shadow. It would be best if, out there, you didn't act like we speak to one another."

I looked at the floor and said, "I was always used to people acting that way towards me, until Chase."

He stopped moving suddenly when we rounded a corner, and I stopped as well. I stared up into his face, but he was not looking at me.

Then, all of a sudden his eyes darted to mine and words spilled out of his mouth. "Do you truly love my brother?"

"I do," I answered without hesitation. "If you're asking me whether the only reason I do is because he wants to take me away, you should already know the answer. It would be easier, wouldn't it, to simply stay here and live out our lives as they are? I would still love him if we did. I would still love him if he was forced to continue doing his job. But I love your brother enough to go with him and know what will be waiting when we do."

"Then why do you want to go, if you know what will happen?"

"Because it shouldn't be the way it is," I told him desperately. "This world is an evil place. I would rather be free to have my happiness in the way I should be allowed it than be stuck here inside this cage, never fighting for anything. There are some things that are worth fighting for in life."

"Even if it's pointless?"

"Fighting for something you believe in is never pointless." I laughed, then I shook my head and breathed out loudly. "No matter how it sometimes feels." I took in a deep breath, looking at his face. "I understand if it means very little to you, but I will do anything I can to fight for you brother the way he fights for me. It's all I can do to repay him for what he's given me."

"What's he *given* you?" he asked, bemused.

"*Life*," I answered firmly. "And I don't intend on losing it quickly now that I've found it."

Chandler nodded his head and the conversation was over.

I did not think about Chandler on the floor in front of the door while I lay in bed with Agatha shortly thereafter. I did not think about the argument that Agatha and I'd had with him where we'd insisted that he sleep on my bed. I wanted to be close to Agatha anyhow, so I left my own bed vacant in case he changed his mind.

I knew that he would not.

I spent a long time staring through the darkness at the stone wall in front of my face, listening to Agatha's breathing close to my head. I waited a long time, long enough that I hoped Chandler would be asleep.

Agatha was not. I knew her breathing as well as I knew my own.

"Aggie?" I whispered to the wall.

"Yes, my flower?" She spoke as quietly as I had, hoping—I was sure—our conversation would be private.

I felt a tear slip out of my eye when I asked, "Is it easier, because I'm not your real daughter?"

"Is what easier?"

"Knowing I'm going to die," I whispered and then sniffled.

I felt her tuck my hair behind my ear and then kiss me lightly on the side of my head. "You're the only daughter I have."

I grabbed hold of her hand where it rested in front of me, and I held onto it tightly until I fell asleep.

EPILOGUE

THE OTHER SIDE

MY TIME SPENT inside the room through the sixth door began to change with the days. I still ran and did my movements, but along with combative and sensory training came a new activity—stealth training. It was the exact opposite of sensory training. Chase stood in the center of the room with the fabric covering his eyes and I was required to be silent as I made circles around him.

I'd been given a very quick lesson beforehand—how to place your feet so they made less sound, how to walk so the fabric of your clothing did not rub together.

It was not testing for Chase. That much was clear to me, as he never pointed in any direction I was not standing. It took me two days of that activity to finally get the bent-over crouching down. I was not good at it, but I understood the mechanics.

But still, sometimes Chase would know where I was simply from a breath that I hadn't paid the proper attention to. So I began paying attention to my breathing at all times. After the third day of stealth training, I began paying attention to my breathing even while I was doing other activities. I could not always control it, of course, especially not while doing physically strenuous things, but I was conscious of it and the sound it made.

I was still hopeless at the combative training, but I found myself satisfied with my progress where it concerned that piece of fabric. I'd started off circling Chase around the edge of the room. I realized, after five days of doing it, that I'd been able to get halfway between where he stood and the wall before he detected me. And every day that passed, the unintentional noises I heard from him were from farther distances than they had been the day before.

I moved closer, and he moved away.

My back ached from the strange walking and my legs were still weak from exertion, but it was on the seventh day of stealth training that I found myself standing not a foot away from Chase's back, holding my breath.

I peeked around his arm to glance at Chandler where he stood on the other side of the room and Chase immediately turned to face me. I would've thought he'd allowed me to get so close if I'd not watched his eyes widen in shock for a moment when he removed the fabric from over them.

I had always thought I was invisible, but now I was learning how to be. Succeeding with something, even if only occasionally, gave me enough of a burst to keep moving forward in the other things.

So I tried harder in everything I did and, as the days progressed, I began realizing I could run for longer before my breathing became too heavy. I could punch the contraption for longer before my arms turned into horrible wobbly things. I did not become ill or lose consciousness as often as I had initially.

But despite my small achievements, I still could not defend myself properly, not even while trying to picture Camden. And that was what everything boiled down to.

IT WAS ONE WEEK AND A HALF after I'd been attacked by Camden that I found myself walking back to the sixth door after lunch. Ahren had not gone with me, which was not new. I'd been avoiding him since discovering that his trust with me ran to such a shallow depth. He'd attempted speaking with me on several occasions of course, but every time he did I would ask him the same question.

Who do you picture while you're training?

And every time, he would walk away.

I rounded the corner that would take me to the hallway that held the sixth door and stopped when I heard raised voices nearby.

The door was standing open.

I sucked in an incredibly large breath and very slowly began making my way down the hallway.

I almost lost my resolve—and my breath—when I heard what sounded like a fist hitting flesh, but I did not. Only when I was just before the door did I stop moving.

I heard Ahren's voice, though I could not hear what he was saying.

I felt my eyes narrowing when I heard Chandler firmly say, "You need to tell her."

"What does it matter?" Ahren nearly shouted back at him.

"What does it *matter*?" Chandler demanded. "It matters because she has the right to know and make her own decision."

"And are you willing to take the risk that she'll choose wrong?" Ahren laughed. "If you're so willing to take that risk, why don't *you* tell her?"

There was a shuffling—one of them grabbing hold of another?

I barely heard Chase say, "Because it's not my right to tell her you're her brother."

"That's not true," I heard myself say, realizing I was standing in the doorway.

I distantly took in the scene—Chase releasing Ahren's shirt and staring at me in some way that bordered on terrified.

But it was Ahren I was focused on. Ahren, standing there with wide eyes, staring back at me.

"That's not *true*," I repeated.

"Aster, let me—" Ahren started, but I didn't let him finish whatever he was going to say.

"I do not have a brother," I said firmly as I strode across the room toward him. "I do not have any family. My father would've told me if I'd had a brother, especially if he'd been abducted as a child."

When Ahren held his hands up in the air, I saw that they were shaking. Slowly, he said, "I wasn't abducted as a child. I was taken at birth." He took a deep breath and added, "Just like Chase and Chandler were taken from their mother."

It was the implications of what he was saying that took all sensible thought from my head.

I lunged at him.

I could not appreciate the fact that I got him down.

I could not appreciate the blood that poured from his nose after my fist made contact with it.

Strong arms wrapped around my body and pulled me off Ahren.

I was screaming, I realized. Screaming at who had me and screaming at Ahren for his lies.

Ahren stood up from the floor, plugging his nose between his thumb and pointer finger, and he leaned down in front of me.

I tried to hit him again, but whoever had hold of me had my arms restrained behind my back to the point where I could not move them at all.

Ahren released his nose from his fingers and shook his head at me.

A tear fell from his eye when he barely said, "Look at my face."

I continued screaming unknown things at him, but he simply stood where he was, biting down on his bottom lip and staring at me.

I looked at his eyes when another tear fell out of one. His eyes that were the same color, precisely, as mine. His eyes that were the same color as my father's.

I looked at his hair that was the same color as mine. I thought of his love, Evelyn.

She had the most beautiful hair. It was the same color as my mother's hair, like straw. But it was so soft it felt like air when I touched it.

I'd seen straw when I was a child, when I was still with my father. A memory blurred in my head, a hazy image of my father staring off at it.

Why are you looking at that dead grass, Father?

He'd looked away from it and smiled at me. Had he been crying?

I shook my head of the memory, the same as I did with all the other memories that I had of him.

I shook my head of it and him, and I focused on what was in front of me.

"*No,*" I said firmly. "My mother wasn't a Reaper. My father would've told me. He would've told me I had a brother."

Ahren looked away and put his hand over his mouth. He stood there, staring at nothing and shaking his head at presumably everything.

I heard a sob escape from my mouth when I said, "He would've *told* me."

Ahren had blood all down the front of him when he looked back at me. It was on his hand where he'd covered his mouth. But remarkably, he had already stopped bleeding.

He shook his head at me again. "Just because he didn't tell you doesn't mean it's not true." He pursed his lips briefly. "It's what we do."

Then I was shaking my head frantically. "My father was *not* a Reaper!" I screamed. "I would've *known*! I would've *seen it* before he died!"

"Our father *is* a Reaper," Ahren said firmly. Then, quietly, "And he is *not* dead."

I felt as though I'd been punched in the gut.

"He left me here?" I whispered. "He allowed me to be taken and he wasn't dead? Why didn't he come back for me if he was alive? He would've come back. He *always* came back." Apart from the one time that he did not.

"Where did he go when he was gone?"

"*What*?" I shook my head. "To get food."

Very slowly, he repeated his question because I presumably had not answered it properly enough to suit him. "Where did he *go*?"

"You're saying he was still working." I laughed. "I would've known if he was going off and killing people." I shook my head again. "You're lying. You're lying about *everything*." I jerked my arm and told whoever was behind me, "Let me go."

I caught a glimpse of Chase standing a few feet away when Chandler released me, and I turned to leave.

Ahren spoke as I was walking.

"Do you know how old I was the first time I saw my father in person?"

I heard myself exhale unhappily as I turned back to him, clenching my jaw tight.

"I was fourteen when he found me. He told me about what had happened with him and my mother. They'd taken me from them when I was born like we're always taken, and when they tried to get me back, and failed, they left. They . . ." Ahren looked off for a moment and chuckled before saying, "*Ran away*." He took in a deep breath. "They were caught shortly thereafter by a team of Reapers from a different city. They agreed to go with them and work for the leader of that city in exchange for their lives." He paused and another tear fell from his eye. "They didn't mean to have you. That's why I'm five years older than you."

I said nothing.

"Do you want to know what happened next?"

I stood there, feeling my nostrils flaring, but I did not answer him one way or another, knowing he would tell me anyway.

"As soon as they found out they were pregnant, they ran again. And they killed every Reaper that came for them from either city until our mother was too far along to fight properly anymore. They stayed in the wilderness and thought they'd gotten away because the Reapers stopped coming for them." Ahren shook his head again where he stood there, not blinking, telling me this unbelievable story. "They hadn't stopped. They were simply biding their time. No use in wasting good Reaper blood. They could at least take you once she had you, and then kill them."

I gritted my teeth harder.

"So they waited." Ahren laughed. "They waited until you were born. Our mother kept them occupied long enough for Father to slip away. She couldn't run with him, after just giving birth. He could go faster without her lagging behind. He could get away. So she stayed behind to let them kill her while he escaped with you. And for eight years he managed to stay alive and keep you hidden."

Ahren looked away and laughed again.

"How is that funny?" I asked.

"Oh, that's not the funny part," Ahren said assuredly. "The funny part is the rest of the story. Have you put it all together?"

I followed Ahren's gaze to Chase and saw that he was not looking at me.

Chase was staring at a wall.

"You've heard this story before," I accused.

Chase's voice rang in my head then. One sentence, as clear as day.

We sat around a fire and exchanged sad stories.

He brought his eyes to mine for an instant but then looked at the floor.

"That man you met . . ." This couldn't be. "That was . . . That was *my father*?"

Chase nodded his head.

"If that's true, why didn't he come for me?"

Ahren drew my attention back to him with, "Do you want to know how long it took Chase to confide your name to anyone?" His eyebrows rose. "*Ten years.*" Ahren nearly sobbed. "He confided your name to me, and I made the mistake of telling our father."

"Mistake?" I said on a breath.

Then it was Chase laughing. But when I looked, he was not laughing. He was crying.

"He made me a *promise*," Chase said loudly. "When I found him, I told him I'd seen a girl who was in a very bad position and I wanted to get her away from it. He told me I was too young, which I was of course. So I came back here to bide my time. I spent ten years of my life spying on my own city for him. He promised me the day I found him that, once I was old enough—strong enough—I could take you away from this horrible place. You see . . ." He stepped in front of me and shook his head. "We never tell people more than we should. I never knew you were his daughter. Not until I told Ahren your name. And then imagine my surprise the next time I come back from a mission and find Ahren here. He told me what was going on. The next mission I was sent on, I went and saw your father. Do you want to know what he said to me?"

I stared up into Chase's face, watching his jaw quivering.

And though he was crying, I did not feel as if he'd broken until he said, "'You can't have my daughter.'"

I said, "He can't say that."

"Oh, but he *did* say it," Chase insisted. "I didn't want to take you away from this House so that you could just end up in a different city. I wanted to take you away from this *life*. So I argued with him. My god, I said everything I could to try and convince him we loved each other, but he didn't care."

"That conversation Amber overheard," I said on a breath.

He nodded.

"All the stars," I said as things began clicking into place inside my head. I looked at Ahren. "You're here for me."

"Partially," Ahren answered. "But when you said . . . what was it? That you hoped my mission involved *burning this wretched city to the ground*? Well . . . plans change. So now, I'm partially here for you and partially here to have my way with New Bethel. It's not like we need a third."

"He has control over Reapers in *two cities*?"

Ahren nodded.

I looked at Chase, hearing myself sob. "You're planning on taking me anyway. Aren't you?"

Chase nodded.

"So we would have Reapers from three cities after us." I felt my legs give out from under me, and my rear hit hard on the floor. "That's why you told me not to tell anyone when we were leaving." I said it mostly to myself. "The Reapers in the House know you're here, but they don't—" I shook my head and repeated, "All the stars." Quickly, I looked up at Chase. "What will happen if they find out?"

"They'll kill me before I can take you," he answered immediately. "But I won't take you if this changes your mind."

"Changes my . . ." I started and then stopped. "What?"

"Your father," he said. "If you want to go with—"

"My father is *dead*," I told him firmly.

He shook his head in confusion as though I hadn't heard anything that had been said in this entire conversation. I'd heard every word of it.

"My father died ten years ago and left me to this life. This man you're speaking of? He may claim to be my father and have his face, but he is not the man I knew and loved. I will not go with that man. I will not allow a person to tell me what I'm allowed to have in my life. He is *not* my father."

"Aster," Chase whispered as he knelt in front of me. "You understand now that when they catch us, they're going to kill me and take you to him. You understand that, don't you?"

I did not know why, but words appeared in my head—words carved in stone, at the foundation of a statue.

We will not stand and do nothing while the world falls to pieces. We stand together to ensure no one is bereft. You reap what you sow.

We will reap the world.

I leaned forward close to Chase's face and, through gritted teeth and all my fury, said, "Then stop trying to teach me how to defend myself. You have to teach me how to kill."

DEAR READER,

First and foremost, I would like to thank you for picking up this book, however you came across it. I'd also like to thank you for making it this far.

I'm a firm believer in the power of words—their ability to help or harm, comfort or torment. I know better than I know most anything in life that a book can in ways be something more than a collection and combination of words, meant to do nothing but entertain. And yet I know that, sometimes, what we need most *is* something to 'entertain'. Sometimes what we need is to curl up under a warm blanket with a close friend (or one we're just getting to know) and let them tell us their story. Sometimes, we need a good laugh. Or a good escape.

Sometimes, we need to know we're not alone in difficulty, that there's hope somewhere even in the most hopeless of situations.

Sometimes we do just need that laugh, though.

I hope so much that the words in these pages brought you something good. If they did, I would greatly appreciate you leaving a review or telling a friend or family member. A story can be good on its own, but they're much better when shared. (I'll spare you me creating an internal debate about that in this letter.)

I've introduced you to some of my friends. Now, I hope they're yours as well.

<3 C

WHERE YOU CAN FIND ME

WWW.CMILLERAUTHOR.COM

Email: contactcmillerauthor@gmail.com

Amazon: www.amazon.com/author/millerc

GoodReads: www.goodreads.com/CMillerAuthor

Facebook: www.facebook.com/CMillerAuthor

WordPress: www.cnmill.wordpress.com

Instagram: @dolly_llama

Twitter: @cn_mill

My website is where any and all information is and will be available. Any news, any updates, information about books and where to find them. If you're looking for any of that, it'll be there!

If you want to stay up to date on new releases, please consider subscribing to my newsletter. It's strictly for relevant information (NEW BOOKS!) and perhaps an occasional letter.

I am quite 'shy' and tend to shy away from social media as a whole. I do have accounts and would be happy to connect with you there, but if you're looking to get in contact with me, messaging me through my site or email would be the best way.

Questions, comments, or just wanting to say hi? I'd love to hear from you!

CONTINUE ASTER'S JOURNEY IN ...

ELUDE

ESCAPING IS HARD.

SURVIVING IS HARDER.

Aster has lived a life of servitude for ten years, but now she is determined to be free. Countless Reapers stand between her and the gate to New Bethel, and more await just past the walls. She's spent her life being invisible, but in a world full of assassins, becoming close to any of them only makes you a target for the rest. Every step she takes puts her in more danger, closer to Reapers with unknown intentions. Unexpected friendships develop, but can she really trust any Reaper when they've all been trained to deceive? Aster knows what awaits her outside the city, but can she get past it?

In Aster's journey for freedom, she learns there are some things in life you can't ever truly escape from and that some steps can't ever be taken back.

Made in United States
Troutdale, OR
03/14/2025

29742881R10194